ALL THAT ENDS WELL

Book Three

PETER A. MOSCOVITA

All That Ends Well
Copyright 2025 @ Peter A. Moscovita

Library of Congress Control Number: 2025916718
ISBN: 978-1-968069-71-1 (Paperback)
        978-1-968069-89-6 (Hardback)
        978-1-968069-72-8 (Ebook)

The views expressed in this book are solely those of the author and do not necessarily reflect the views of the publisher, and the publisher hereby disclaims any responsibility of them.

Olympus Story House

CONTENTS

DEDICATION

To all the men and women who serviced
during the Second World War

- The British Intelligence Services.
- The American Office of Strategic Services.
- The French Bureau Central de Renseignements et d'Action.

Your sacrifice for freedom will always be remembered.

INTRODUCTION

The sudden and deliberate attack by the forces of the Empire of Japan December 7th, 1941, on the American Pacific Naval fleet moored in Pearl Harbor. This tragic attack forced President Franklin D. Roosevelt to declare a state of war with Japan in doing so, he also declared war against Germany.

The invasion of Poland, September 1st, 1939, by the armed forces of Germany forced England and France to enact the nonaggression pact signed with Poland. Britain's Prime Minister Nevil Chamberland had warned Chancellor Adolf Hitler if the German military attacked Poland a state of war would exist between them.

For the English people struggling to hold off the superior German military, America's declaration of war with Germany came as a blessing in disguise as their ability to continue holding off German forces was close to the breaking point. The United States with its enormous industrial capabilities could now openly proceed with adding the besieged people of England.

The American Army Corp commenced ferrying thousands of aircraft to England, followed by thousands of troops making the long journey across the Atlantic arriving daily. Now the Island fortress had a fighting chance of turning this war around but that would take another four years.

Major Karl Vita returning home after many months in Canada could not wait to be with his new wife, Claire. They had wed only to say goodbye ten days later when Karl along with other BIS personnel flew to Canada to instruct the newly formed American O.S.S in intelligence and field tactics perfected and honed by the English before and during the first two years of WWII. At that time, the life expectancy of a British intelligence officer was less than six months, new recruits were constantly in training, however seasoned veterans like Karl were always at the forefront of the real dangerous spy missions. Again, and again these officers and agents would penetrate the German defenses with intent to disrupt, destroy and kill as needed!

As the war progressed Karl's ability, as a former maritime officer would be called upon again to volunteer along with fellow officer Major Gunther Fisher and special units of the S.A.S, their high-risk mission to steal the merchant ship that would secretly transport the heavy equipment to an unknown destination in Norway. That top-secret cargo was to be used in the production of the world's most-deadly weapon, the Atomic Bomb. This mission would be so dangerous that returning from it would be highly unlikely, yet those that volunteered stepped forward with the conviction to stop that weapon from ever being produced. If they were unsuccessful the end of WWII would be eminent.

CHAPTER 1

RETURNING HOME

Major Karl Vita and his Intelligence team were heading home to England. The American OSS team they had been training would remain at the Shanganagh training camp in Ireland for another two months before relocating to their new base in England. The intense training between these new allies had started in the final days of 1941, taking over four months to reach the level of competence the High Command was striving to achieve. This first mission turned out to be a huge success, establishing a protocol for future trainees to follow.

The English BIS (British Intelligence Service) had an advantage: their skills had been honed over more than four years of espionage. Certain members of that team had faced the dangers, receiving severe wounds at the hands of the Gestapo and SS.

The commanding officer of the BIS camp in Slough, Major William Lowes, was on hand to welcome them back, anxious to find out more in the debriefing.

The intense meeting proved beyond all doubt that this new alliance did not have a substantial plan to counter the brutality of the Gestapo and SS interrogation methods. Major Lowes adjourned the debriefing, realizing many team members were anxious to return home to their loved ones. In high spirits, the team dispersed for that well deserved ten-day leave.

Karl, along with a few of his team members arriving at the Paddington Train Station, bid farewell to each other at the gate. They were happy soldiers, heading to their homes in different parts of the country. Karl made his way to the underground station to catch the tube to Kings Cross Station. He stood in front of the carriage door on the platform, not quite ready to climb aboard yet. He looked at the flowers and box of chocolates he had just purchased and thought, is this enough? Maybe I should have bought a romantic card as well? Too late for that now, as the public address system announced the train departure on platform #3 for Cambridge with stops in Welwyn Garden City, Stevenage, Hitchin, Letchworth, Baldock, and Ashwell was ready for departure. Karl climbed up into the compartment; finding a seat by the window, he took some reading material from his briefcase and settled in for the ride that would return him home to his wife Claire and his family.

He had made this trip so many times before, so he knew that Hitchin would be a mere fifteen minutes or so away when the train departed Welwyn Garden City. Reaching for his case, he put on his trench coat, then waited for the iron beast to slow, banging its bumpers in protest. As the train entered the station, Karl stood, staring into the smoke streaming past the open window, straining to get the first glimpse of his fiancée, Claire McGivern. He knew she would be there waiting on the platform for her man to return home. Through that smoke and steam, he caught the first glimpse of a striking English rose; it was, of course, Claire, waving madly at Karl, who was now doing the same. The train's bumpers began banging, signaling it was coming to a complete stop. Karl grabbed his case, bidding farewell to the other passengers smiling at this returning soldier. Karl opened the carriage door just as the train came to a stop; jumping down onto the platform, he was met by Claire, rushing into his open arms. "Darling, you're home! I have missed you so; kiss me, my lovable man!"

Karl dropped his case on the platform, throwing his arms around her and kissing her passionately. The physical contact flooded his senses with the warmth of her lips against his. "Claire, I have dreamed of this moment through all those long weeks in Ireland," said Karl as they walked back to the tunnel, his left arm firmly around her waist.

Claire, in her excitement, was trying to tell him all the news she had stored away for this first meeting, making Karl laugh at how fast she could talk. Karl turned his head, smirking a remark, "Lady Solicitor, I hope you don't talk like this in a court of law, or do you?"

Claire realized she was over excited; in an instant, she regained her composure, smiling at Karl. She gave him a rib bruising hug. "Sorry, Major, I forgot I was talking to an Intelligence officer. You blokes are not known to let loose, are you? Karl, hearing her sarcasm, stopped in the middle of the tunnel, spinning her toward him and giving her a kiss that could melt icebergs.

Passengers passing by were whistling; one yelled out a remark that made them both laugh, "The weather tonight will be warm and close with a little sun later."

Karl, hearing this, looked at Claire's face, saying, "Does he know something we don't know?"

Claire, smiling back, replied, "Interesting question, why don't you ask me that tomorrow morning, Lover Boy?"

Back in the car, Claire asked Karl if he was in a hurry to return home or if he would prefer to have a late lunch at the Fox Inn in William. "That's a wonderful idea; let's do that. It's close by, so we will still be able to grab a nice plowman's lunch."

Entering the familiar lounge, Karl and Claire decided to sit at the bar. Harry, the bartender and owner, smiled at seeing familiar faces. "Miss McGivern and Major Vita, so nice to have you back; it's been a while. I haven't seen you two since before Christmas won't ask why. I'm just pleased to see those smiling faces again. What's your pleasure? And put your money away; the first round is on me." Harry was a veteran of WWI, having served as an infantryman during the battle known as the Somme Offensive starting July 1 and ending November 18, 1916. The lounge walls were decorated with many military pictures and famous leaders like the Duke of Wellington and a big one over the fireplace of King George V with Queen Mary. Karl was starting to enjoy the warm and relaxing feeling of being with his future wife in this very same inn that Claire had taken him to for lunch when he was buying her MG-PB sports car. The magic had happened while they were sitting outside that day; within a couple of hours, they had fallen in love. Many months later, that love had become so much stronger. On weekends, they were inseparable, and during those special times when Karl was given an extended leave from his base in Slough. Karl's mother and family living in Baldock, a farming town near Cambridge, took to Claire immediately. They were relieved that Karl had met his future wife, and with her love and strength, she could dispatch those black clouds that had hung over him for too long after the tragic loss of his fiancée Kitty Johnson. She was killed while on a mission for the BIS in 1937, almost two years before the outbreak of WW2.

Karl had ordered a second round of drinks after polishing off the delicious lunch. "Claire, in these next ten days, we must take care of the things you need my input on for the wedding and such, you know any loose ends that you need me to be here for."

Claire reached over and took his hand; lifting it, she kissed the back of it. Smiling, she said softly, "Darling, everything has been arranged. While you were away in Ireland, Freida, Julie, Dorothy, and your friends Clive and Bill stuck our heads together and planned everything. The wedding, of course, with your approval, will be held at my parish church of St. Mary's here in Hitchin. The reception we felt could be held at the Letchworth Hall Hotel. Ronny has pulled some strings to have a military honor guard perform the Saber Sword Arch as we exit the church.

"Freida and I went to Cambridge a few weeks back, and, darling, we found a beautiful pale cream wedding dress. Karl, I would marry you just to wear that dress! By the way, Clive has requested, again with your approval, that all attending military personnel wears formal dress uniforms. He mentioned that yours needs updating, so I have arranged to have Dad's tailor measure you this week for a new one displaying your rank of major.

Darling, don't get mad at me, but this will be my wedding gift to you." Karl did not respond too quickly, which made Claire nervous because the look on his face meant he was processing all this news being thrown at him in a rapid-fire manner.

"Claire, it would appear all of you have organized our future, so what is left for me to do?" Karl was somewhat perturbed at hearing that the wedding plans were all but completed. Looking at Claire's nervous face, he finally embraced how she was enjoying planning their future together. Who could get upset with that?

"Well, Major Vita, am I in the doghouse? Or do I get a kiss for a job well done?"

Claire sat very still, waiting for Karl to respond. After listening to her rapid-fire update, Karl rolled his head, then started laughing, finally saying, "Come here, you sexy female; whatever you want will be fine with me. However, let me contribute in some way, will you, please?"

Claire, hearing this, took both his hands, kissing the back of them. Then, with a pointed smile, she answered by saying, "Karl, you are my wedding gift. I must be doing something right to be such a lucky lady. I get so excited, knowing I will soon be your wife. I was never that good at being single, but you have already found that out about me, haven't you? Now, why don't you take me home and ravage me? Call it a pre wedding test drive."

Karl again shook his head with that smile he had when Claire would lead him to do something, thinking, this woman has a way of getting me to do anything she wants, including the wedding arrangements. It must be love, I guess. "Harry, we are heading out. Can I get the bill? And again, thank you for the first round."

Harry looked at them over his glasses, then replied, "Bill? What bill are you talking about, gov? You have just returned home. I think Lady Claire needs some private time about now, so be off with ya. See you both tomorrow if you feel like stopping in that is."

Claire stood up, leaned across the bar, and gave Harry a big hug and kiss on the cheek, whispering in his ear, "Harry, you dear man, we are so fortunate to have you and thank you for making Karl's return home a memorable one. I'm taking your advice by taking this bloke of mine home; with any luck, I can work him over for the rest of the day."

Harry took Claire's hand, replying while her face was still against his, "I may be an old bugger now, but I will always have that picture in my mind of my wife Maude meeting me at the train on my return from those trenches in France. That first kiss was like nectar on my lips. Now, enough of this sentimental gibberish; go have fun. That bloke is one of the many who will keep us safe."

Claire, still smiling, moved back from the bar, giving a silent smile that thanked Harry for what he had just said. Karl shook

Harry's hand firmly in a silent gesture, one comrade to another. Karl was having a euphoric feeling as Claire turned the Wolsey into the driveway, "Claire, you have no idea how it feels being home again like this. I'm starting to feel this is truly our home; it has a certain strength to it each time I enter the driveway."

Hearing him talk like that, Claire stopped right there, halfway in the driveway, pulled up the handbrake, and then threw her arms around his neck. With tears in her eyes, she answered him, saying softly, "Karl, my dear man, how I have longed to hear you say that. Yes, my darling, this house is our home." Arm in arm, they opened the door, and there in the hall, Karl saw a banner that read:

Welcome Home, My Darling

Claire beamed as Karl stood, staring at the banner. "Claire, coming home to you makes all my headaches disappear; how I love you."

Claire held his arm with both of hers, squeezing him with all her might. She could not have wished for a new life that was better than this one. "Karl, do you feel like relaxing with a glass of wine in the living room? Why don't you call your mother while I get the wine? I told her you would call when you arrived home."

Karl took off his tunic and tie, then sat at the desk and waited a few minutes before dialing Baldock 3607. The phone at the other end rang about five times, and Karl was almost ready to hang up when Mama answered and, with her strong broken English, answered, "Hello, who is calling please?"

Karl answered her in German, saying, "Mama, it's me, Karl; I'm home. How are you doing, and how are Freida, Ronny, and Franchot? It's been too long since I saw or talked to you all." Karl, as always, was very careful what he said on an unsecured phone line.

"Karl, it's so wonderful to hear your voice again. Son, it's been a long time; are you coming to Baldock tomorrow? Claire told me earlier this morning that she would make sure you called when you got to the house. Karl, are you alright? No injuries like the times before? You always worry me."

Karl felt good telling his mother it was all classroom stuff with no danger of being injured other than a pencil point jab.

"Mama, I'm sure you and Claire have already mapped out my agenda while I'm home; is that correct?" Karl was kidding his mother, knowing that Mama, Freida, and Claire were thick as thieves, and that warmed his heart immensely.

"Karl, we have been teaching Claire how to speak German; she is such a fast learner. And in return, she has been helping me with my English. Do I sound any better? Be honest, son. By the way, when you come tomorrow afternoon, we will have the strudel she made with me yesterday; she is so intent on making you the perfect wife. Karl, she works at it nonstop, and I love her so much. If you so much as put one foot out of line, well, let's say I'll give you a smack with that wooden spoon. You're not too old for your mother to do that! Did you hear me say intent? That was one of my new words she taught me this week; this old lady is getting good at this English language."

Karl adored his mother; hearing her talk like this on the phone was music to his ears, and it was all due to his future wife. Karl jumped when a pair of arms encircled his shoulders, along with the familiar fragrance of Claire's perfume. "Claire, you've forgotten never to creep up on me like that. My reactions may get you hurt one of these days; blame it on the BIS training if you need to."

Claire had, in fact, forgotten how jumpy he could get at sudden movements behind him. "Everything all right at the bungalow, darling?" Claire's legal mind was constantly testing the waters before proceeding.

"Mama told me about your English classes and cooking lessons. When on earth do you get time to do all these things?"

Claire looked at him as he stroked the back of her thighs and pushed the swivel chair back so she sat on his lap, kissing his cheek, saying, "Darling, I can't remember being this happy.

Having you in my life is one thing but gaining the love of a new family makes my life complete. I'm that happy. What I would like at this point is your help with my German grammar. If we start conversing in German, you could correct my pronunciation and help me with new words and sentence construction that sort of stuff. That's the only way I'll learn to become proficient; it's not like I can go to night school here in Hitchin to learn German, is it? I'm marrying into a bilingual family, and I want to talk to you all like a Wiener madchen (Viennese Lady)!"

Karl smiled and kissed the back of her hand, agreeing it would be well worth the effort, continuing by saying, "Hell, you aced everything when you were in law school; this should be a piece of cake for you, my brainy egghead." Karl always loved her enthusiasm for new challenges, and this one would be no different.

"Claire, obtaining German textbooks could be challenging right now in the middle of a war with Germany. However, we have plenty of them in our library in Slough, and I don't think Bill will mind loaning you a few to get you started. I'll call Sally in the morning to put them in the post; this way, you won't have to wait to get started until my next leave.

"Now, you gorgeous thing, let's see how you would answer in German to the feel of an Austrian touch on your upper thigh?" Looking up at her, he started kissing her neck, knowing that would arouse those feelings within her. It had been a while since they last made love, after all.

Claire, answering in German, said nervously, "If that's what you want, that's what we will do, (das ist Sehr, Sehr gut)." Karl's right arm was around her waist, and with his left hand, he softly and slowly slid his hand up her skirt. This sensation stopped her talking, giving in to his touch. Her breathing quickened, becoming shallow, and her hand on his arm momentarily stopped his movement up her thigh. Finally, she spoke her words, having a nervous quiver to them, "Karl, you are not being very fair. I never know when you're going to start something. Wouldn't you rather go upstairs? It would be so much more comfortable in our bed." Karl gave her that look, his eyes focusing on hers, making her unsure of his actions.

Finally, Karl spoke, kissing her cheek. "My adorable Claire, I have missed this so much. Don't you know spontaneous actions like my hand on your thigh are the spice that makes you respond that much quicker? Now, close your eyes and embrace that sensation."

Karl, with deliberate action, took her hand off his arm, placing it on the side of his neck, then continued to softly slide up her thigh, stopping at her stocking top.

Claire, breathing heavily, anticipated his next move, which did not happen. Instead, he moved his finger pressure like playing a piano to continue the sensation. "Karl, you are teasing me unfairly; don't stop now. You're driving me crazy; stop playing with me?"

Karl smiled, knowing he had aroused his sweet Claire. She was now more than ready to make love to him, but not yet. Karl continued to kiss her neck with his tongue; the response from Claire was building, and her legs were twitching with each new sensation. Lifting her in his strong arms, Karl carried her to the couch. Laying her down, he lifted her skirt and removed her precious American nylons, then her underwear. Claire was flushed, her face giving her away. She wanted Karl so badly; waiting all this time, she could not get enough of his lovemaking. "Darling, you have no idea how I've dreamed about being here with you like this; sweetheart, don't make me wait any longer. It's been much too long."

Karl removed his trousers and shirt; instead of lying next to her, he put his head between her thighs, driving her to an orgasm that left her crying out in ecstasy. Karl moved up the couch; lifting her head, he cradled her until she stopped quivering.

Claire turned in toward Karl, kissing him with a look of total happiness. "My Lover Boy, don't think you can ever get away from me; you're mine, and that's all there is to it."

Karl just smiled, kissing her again. He loved Claire so much. "Claire, we are as good as married, and that suits me just fine." Karl was reassuring her that, in his mind, they were, in fact, married. "Darling, that was quite a torque you went through just now; I'll have to do that more often." Karl loved to tease her like this, making her do things she obviously had not really done before because the way she responded to his lovemaking convinced him she was beyond enjoying his techniques.

"Karl, darling, let me take care of you, or do you have another surprise up your sleeve?" Claire always prepared herself for those next moves he was capable of springing on her. *Was today another one of those days?*

"Claire, I'm getting older, and I'm going to wait until we're in our comfortable bed upstairs. Making love on the couch can be murder on my back, so lady, once we're upstairs, you can show me how much you missed me."

Karl had that look on his face. Did he still have something up his sleeve, or could it be he really needed that long overdue uninterrupted night's sleep? Claire thought as she sat with her arms around him. "Karl, why don't you go upstairs and have a nice hot bath? And I'll bring you up a nice cup of cocoa once I've cleaned up the kitchen."

Karl kissed her forehead, agreeing that was a wonderful idea. Claire, standing up, bent over him to kiss him back. In the light from the table lamp, she could see the stress and exhaustion in his face, thinking, these poor chaps; what they endure to keep us all safe. "Up you get, you old warrior; make me happy by having that hot bath. Use some of my bath crystals to relax your muscles; they will also help you sleep better tonight."

Claire pulled him up off the couch, gently pushing him in the direction of the stairs before returning to the kitchen to clean up and make that hot drink. Climbing the stairs about thirty minutes later, she entered the bathroom with a mug of steaming cocoa in her hand. Karl had already had his bath and gone to bed. Stealthily, she opened the door to find the bedside lamp still throwing a beam of light across the image of Karl, propped up with his head to one side, fast asleep.

Claire, standing by the side of the bed drinking his cocoa, started to think, what keeps these blokes going like this? Most of us will never understand that type of commitment. Returning to the bathroom, she washed up, then changed into her nightgown before returning to the bedroom. With her arm around Karl's neck, she removed the extra pillow before laying him back down and covering him up. Quietly, she climbed into her side of the bed, then, very carefully, so as not to disturb him, she put her arm over his chest. Lying there in the dark, a tear rolled down her cheek as she continued to think of all the men that willingly go into harm's way, some never to return.

Karl's time at home was the medicine he so desperately needed. Each morning, after he saw Claire off to her office, he would call the office, using the secure phone to obtain the latest statistics from his assistant in Slough. On one such morning, Bill Lowes called him before 0930 hours, the time he would usually make his call to the office. "Bill, if you're calling me, it can only mean we have a problem; is that correct?" asked Karl, reaching for a pad and pencil.

"Karl, before you left the other day, remember the meeting we had on how thin our defenses were in the Pacific? Well, we've just received a bombshell of a report from Singapore. I'll read it to you right now." Karl listened intently as Bill started to read the report.

"February 15th, The British Garrison in Singapore surrendered to the ruthless aggression of the Imperial Japanese Forces. Lieutenant General Arthur Percival and his army were almost out of food, artillery ammunition, and other essential military supplies desperately needed to halt the advances of the Japanese forces. With no possibility of reinforcements, General Percival made the painful decision to save as many lives as possible by surrendering; continued resistance would only result in the total annihilation of the city's civilian population and its military garrison. According to Prime Minister Winston Churchill, this capture would become the worst disaster and largest capitulation in British Military History. In all, more than 100,000 English, Australian, and Indian soldiers, as well as civilians, were taken prisoner, adding to the more than 50,000 taken in the Malayan Campaign.

Hearing this report, Karl's reaction to Bill was, "We can't keep this up; even with the addition of American involvement, we are losing too many assets! We need a new strategy. Our troops can no longer hold back the Japanese forces in the Pacific, and neither can the Americans. I repeat, our combined resources are stretched too thin. What's the take from General Jack's staff?

Have you heard from Clive about this disaster? Bill, I think I should plan on an early return to the camp." Karl had always put his responsibilities to the BIS first until Claire came along.

"No, Karl, stay where you are with Claire while you still can. Who knows what it will be like if this continues?" It seemed that Bill's confidence was fading regarding their ability to defend the British Colonies, which was not like him at all. But then again, this latest news would demoralize anyone.

"See you in ten days; keep your confidence up, Bill. This is no time to get depressed," concluded Karl.

This latest news didn't help make Karl's time at home very enjoyable; there was nothing to feel good about other than Claire and his family. With the telephone receiver still in his hand, he sat at the desk, thinking, right now, I need to get out of this house to clear my head. Going for a drive in his little MG with the canvas roof off could be the answer. He loved the exhilarating feeling it gave him each time he took it out, even though it was a cold, drafty winter's day. Today was not the sort of day for driving an open sports car, but right now, Karl needed to feel that cold air flowing over his head as he drove his MG on the winding backroads towards Baldock.

He was willing to overlook the icy air that was cutting against his skin like a knife; he really didn't care too much. It was nothing compared to the injuries he had endured so far in this war. The feel of the MG was the medicine he needed to move that dark cloud to one side, even though it would be short lived. In the open air, he focused on all that was good, allowing the MG to guide his movements. Before he knew it, he was pulling into the driveway at the bungalow. Spending a few hours with his mother and sister and playing with Franchot would stop him from thinking about the months and maybe years of war that lay ahead.

This brief escape was wonderful. His mother, on the other hand, saw through that weak smile. From the kitchen, she poured two cups of hot coffee; crossing over to the couch, she sat next to her son, saying, "Son, something is weighing heavily on your mind. I know you can't tell me, but everything is alright with you and Claire, am I correct?" Mama always challenged her son just to reassure herself all was still on track with Claire; she was that special to her and Freida.

"Mama, Freida, you know I can't tell you too much other than things are not going well for the Allies right now. On the radio today, you will hear about Singapore surrendering to the Japanese in Southeast Asia. Over 150,000 people are now prisoners and will likely be forced into slavery, building roads and bridges for the Japanese. Yes, I have a lot on my mind, so please forgive me for being such poor company."

As Karl was talking, the phone rang; Freida got up from the couch, walked over to the hall, and answered the phone. "Baldock 3607, who's calling, please? Claire, I should have known it would be you calling; we all need some cheering up about now. I'm assuming you've heard the news about the tragic surrender of Singapore in the Pacific." Over the next few minutes, Freida gave her the news Karl had given them earlier.

From the living room, Karl yelled, "Freida, tell her I'm leaving in five minutes."

Returning home, Karl came in through the back door; removing his raincoat, scarf, and gloves, he approached Claire as she was getting up from the table, a look of total fear on her face. "Karl, this is terrible news; are we going to be alright? I have been listening to the news, and selfishly, all I could think about was you having to go overseas; darling, forgive me, I'm so scared." Claire, sitting there alone, had been thinking about the times she had sent Patrick off to fly his Hurricane into harm's way, reliving that fateful day when he would never again return home.

"Claire, come sit down next to me, and darling, I need you to pay attention to what I'm about to say next. For some time, all of us in the BIS have been bracing for catastrophic disaster in the Far East. Our forces are stretched too thin to defend themselves or the line, and we are assuming there will be more losses in the months ahead. Now, how does that affect my position? As of right now, not much at all other than being overloaded with new responsibilities and blasted paperwork and not enough time in which to get them completed.

"Claire, I'm trying to prepare you for long lapses in between my weekends at home. When I was promoted to commanding officer of my new division, I was fully aware it would come with additional sacrifices. That time has arrived; in a few days, I will return to Slough, only then will I know more of what to expect moving forward. One of the first tasks I face is training additional volunteers to go behind enemy lines almost immediately. Under different circumstances, I would rather have gone myself.

"Don't worry, darling; for the foreseeable future, I'll be remaining in Slough, a curse of being the boss." Sitting, holding her hands, he was racking his brain to make her feel less threatened by these tragic events and those yet to come.

"Claire, try not to upset yourself. Doing so will have a negative effect on your health; I worry about you constantly, so will you help me in that department? We have only a few days left before I must leave again. Who knows what demands will be waiting for me back in Slough?

"In these last few days, there is nothing we can do to stop what is happening abroad. The only control we have over our limited time is to thoroughly enjoy being together, making wonderful memories that will fortify us through the times of separation. What do you say, you good looking woman?" Karl could feel the tension in her as he held her close, thinking, I'm being selfish. She desperately wants a baby. I'm not being fair to her; my fear of being killed is clouding that dream. I guess it's up to me to think differently about making that happen.

"Claire, this may not be the right time to say this, but then again, because of this war, we are all saying and doing things without any real planning. Under peacetime conditions, things could be different. Some time back, you told me you would like to conceive a baby. Do you still feel the same?" asked Karl, wiping the tears away from her cheek.

Claire, hearing this, wrapped her arms around his neck, her expression turning to a thankful smile. "Karl, my sweet, thoughtful man, you always know what's on my mind, don't you? Damn Intelligence blokes are all the same, always having the answer to whatever someone is thinking. So, Major Vita, I'm assuming you already know what I was going to suggest for supper tonight, am I right?"

Karl chuckled as she said that and simply replied, "Cornish meat pie and a pint of mild and bitter?"

"You bugger!" replied Claire, feeling a little less nervous about their future and what lay ahead.

"Come on; get your raincoat, and let's head to the Copper Kettle. That will cheer us both up; we can't let those negative clouds mess up our evening, can we?" concluded Karl, pulling her to her feet.

Claire and Karl were facing the fact that their times together would be less frequent; in the weeks ahead, their time together would become more infrequent, and their only contact would be limited to phone calls and long letters. Claire would strike off the days, counting down to when that smoking monster of a train would bring Karl home again for a few more precious days, such was the life so many lived in because of maniacs like Hitler.

On those weekends, Claire would share with him what new arrangements had been made for their upcoming wedding in her usual excitable way. Still, her real focus would always be to spend those precious days with Karl, making love, her expectations of becoming a mother high on her list. On those rare Fridays that Karl would return home, she would always be there waiting patiently at the Hitchin Train Station, making sure she had a happy welcome home look to her.

During the entire month of April and the early days in May, Karl only managed to get away for one short weekend at home with Claire. On that special Friday when he did come home, Claire had dressed up in her favorite burgundy fitted suit, her fair hair down around her shoulders, and her high heels making her legs so much shapelier than her everyday shoes. Claire, as the perfectionist, applied her makeup to finish the look she needed for that first image Karl would have of her as he got off the train. Waiting there on the platform, she was noticed by two Navy chaps that made sure she heard their remarks as they stopped nearby. "There's a lucky bloke on that train who will have her later tonight; she is an absolute smasher."

Claire, hearing this, turned toward them, laughing. She answered, saying, "See me here on the platform Monday morning, and I'll tell you if this outfit and make-up paid off for me. Have a wonderful weekend and thank you for that compliment."

Her excitement was building as she caught sight of the smoke trailing from the engine as it slowed to enter the station. The constant fear she carried would be stored away once again until Monday morning rolled around, and Karl would once again return to Slough. For Claire, it would be another week of more fear and apprehension. With his arm waving vigorously, Karl could see her through the open carriage window. Claire started walking faster, closing the distance; Karl waved and opened the carriage door simultaneously as the train slowed. The familiar banging of the bumpers and grinding of the brakes brought the train to a complete stop.

Claire, running toward Karl, and he, doing the same, made for quite the spectacle as they rushed into each other's arms, oblivious to others around them. With all his strength, his strong arm encircled her and swirled her off her feet, her skirt sliding up her thighs, giving those sailors a wonderful view of her stocking tops. "Karl, let me down; you've lifted my skirt, and those two sailors are twitching their knees over the picture I'm giving them." Claire was laughing out loud, enjoying the moment. Karl let her down, kissing her soft lips and really messing up her lipstick.

One of the sailors yelled to Karl, "You lucky blighter, I probably won't sleep tonight because of your lady friend there. It looks like it's been a while since you saw each other; don't wear it out, Major. Keep some for another day."

Karl turned toward them, his rank making them a little nervous. Karl, seeing the looks on their faces, put his right arm out, shaking both of their hands and replying, "Thanks, chaps, it's good to be home. Is Hitchin home to you as well?" said Karl with a genuine smile on his face.

"Waiting for my girlfriend, and Fred here is waiting for his wife and two kids coming from Buntingford in his father-in-law's van. We arrived about an hour ago on the train that stops at every bloody station before arriving in Cambridge. Nice talking with you, Sir, and to you, Miss. Take special care of him; by the look of those ribbons, he's one of those special blokes." Laughing out loud, the two sailors headed for the tunnel under the platform.

Karl turned to Claire, saying, "What nice chaps, were you flirting with them before I arrived?"

Claire, with a devilish grin on her face, quietly answered, "I'll never tell. Sailors will be sailors, isn't that, right? You're an old time sailor, are you not?"

Karl, with a big smile on his face, hugged her again, kissing her with all the love he could muster, then remarked, "This sailor is going to show you what he's capable of doing after being away so long from his woman."

Claire put her arm around his waist as they headed toward the tunnel, and answering him, she quietly said, "Why are you wasting all this time then? You will have to prove to me, kind sir, just how much you missed me. You've been gone so long that my bank is empty; I think you will need to make a few new deposits once we arrive back home enough to keep it full for at least nine months?" Karl let out a belly laugh, knowing exactly what she was suggesting.

Claire stopped the bantering and suggestive teasing and asked, "Darling, I thought we could stay home tonight, then have a night out on Saturday; how does that sound to you? It's up to you; whatever you feel like doing is fine with me."

Karl thought for a minute, then responded, "Well, Claire, seeing as you are all made up, why don't we go to the Fox tonight, then Saturday we can go to the Copper Kettle? Let's make Sunday our special day. We won't go anywhere. How wonderful it will be to have my fiancée all to myself. And Claire, I want all I can get from my future wife. Tonight, though, I need to show you off, and by the way, you can think about the dessert I intend to serve you when we arrive home."

Claire, thrilled at his last line of double talk, continued squeezing him as they walked on through the tunnel. They could not be happier; she always enjoyed his witty way of putting things. Over dinner, they talked about the wedding and what was happening at her office. Harry, behind the bar, always enjoyed serving them each time they came into the inn. Tonight, he looked at Claire's face as she was beaming and so in love with her beau. "Major, how long are you in for this time? I hope I get to see you more than once."

Karl, constantly aware of those around him, answered, "Well, we'll try to make it a point of seeing you again before I leave."

Returning home, Karl went to open the garage door, and, to his surprise, there was his little MG with a big red bow on its radiator. "Karl, I brought it over earlier today, so I could clean it for you. Tomorrow, I would like to go shopping in Luton for a change, are you alright with that? I think you'll enjoy driving the MG there." Claire was always thinking about pleasing him.

"Great idea, Claire. We haven't been to Luton in quite a while."

Once inside the house, Claire guided him into the living room for another surprise. Hanging on the door at the other end of the room was a long brown bag, and Claire pulled him toward it. "Well, open it, darling; it's your new uniform. I can't wait to see you in it. You know, when I see you wearing it, it's going to get my juices going? So, move faster, will you!"

Karl opened the bag. Feeling the material, he knew this was nonstandard issue, and he wondered where the new shiny insignias came from. Taking his tunic and trousers off, he carefully put the new uniform on, then his Sam belt. "So, how do I look, Claire? Good enough for you? Now, tell me about these insignias. How did you come by them? Wait, I should know the answer to that question already; Clive sent them, correct?"

Claire, smiling at him and rolling her head, answered, "You bloody spy. I thought I would keep you guessing. Come here, you crazy Austrian, and show me how much you missed me."

Upstairs, they had a bath together. Claire made the excuse that they needed to conserve hot water, and Karl laughed aloud at her lame excuse. Their lovemaking afterward felt different to Karl; it felt calmer, softer, and more meaningful. They were making love, with time growing shorter until their wedding day. Claire would do everything she could to make sure Karl gave her what she desperately needed to become pregnant. Over the next two days, they stayed busy, shopping in Luton and spending time with the family in Baldock. Over dinner on Saturday evening, Claire took him by surprise when she gingerly asked him if he would go to church with her at St. Mary's Sunday morning.

At first, he felt like a hypocrite by saying yes. Then, he thought more about what he had been through and thought, someone or something saved me on both occasions. "If that's what you want, Claire, then that's what we will do. Maybe after mass, we could talk to the priest about taking our vows. That would be a great idea, don't you agree?"

Claire was close to tears. Until now, she had refrained from asking him to join her at church, knowing everything that had happened to him since 1936. Another hurdle had just been eliminated! Sunday morning, Karl dressed in his older dress uniform, waiting for Claire in the kitchen, who was still getting herself ready upstairs. Karl, standing by the table, looked up as Claire entered the kitchen. Stopping in the doorway, she asked, "Do I look alright, darling?" She was still feeling somewhat self-conscious about asking Karl to accompany her to mass.

The church was close by only a few minutes' walk from the house. The sun was out, and the fresh air felt sweet as they walked hand in hand into St. Mary's. Finding an empty bench toward the front, she squeezed Karl's arm, saying in a hushed tone, "Karl, can you imagine that in June we will be walking down this very aisle to make our wedding vows?"

Taking her arm, he replied, "Claire, darling, it will be the best day of my life." Karl had not been near a church in over seven years; his faith had failed him to the point that he could not think about religion. Today, he was reconfirming that higher power.

Monday came early for Karl. Getting up at 0430 hours, he went downstairs to make coffee before getting dressed and ready to return to his command in Slough. Claire, half asleep, joined him in the living room around 5:10 a.m. "Morning, darling, I can see you're all ready and in your military frame of mind; is that correct?"

"Yes, dear, but today, I leave, knowing the time will fly by until I take your hand in marriage," replied Karl with a smile.

"Karl, you are so right. I agree that the time will go by very quickly for me also. I plan on spending a couple of days each week transferring cases to others in the office. Next Thursday and Friday, Julie is going to be here. Remember, she's coming Wednesday evening to help me with the final preparation for the wedding; it will be so nice having her stay with me at the house. Remember, darling; Clive is dropping her off on his way to Cambridge for some high-level meetings he will be attending for the next few weeks. Julie mentioned that if all goes well, Clive will arrange his schedule to coincide with your arrival at the Letchworth Hall Hotel that Friday before the wedding.

"Bill has already told me he and Dorothy will be picking you up on that Friday. I hope you remember to put that in your diary. I know it's still a way off, but if I start reminding you early, you won't arrange anything else other than coming home to me. Karl, I hate to badger you like this, but we have so much going on. I don't want to lose track of where we are on our wedding plans. Can you put your military frame of mind to one side for a while? You have a habit of not really focusing on the small stuff. For example, you're so used to buying a return ticket for the train; I'm willing to bet that on that last Friday, your mind will be so engrossed in some planning and forget to buy only a one-way ticket to Slough." Claire was exhibiting her sarcastic side.

Karl gave her a stern look and threw it back at her by saying, "So, I should ask for a single to Glasgow; does that sound about right?" Karl, standing in front of her, looked down at her, saying nothing else. This made her very nervous, and she considered that she had said too much, and silence would be a better option.

Karl could not keep a straight face; he needed to laugh at Claire looking so nervous. That did it, and they both started laughing, leaving the house arm in arm.

At the station, their goodbyes were upbeat with hopes that the weeks would fly by for them both. "Claire reached up to kiss him as he turned to board the train. Looking back at her, he said loudly, "Just think, by June, people can refer to you as Mrs. Vita, love you, darling." With that, he climbed into the empty compartment doing his usual wave through the open window.

Back in his office, Karl had decided he would put long hours in to review and write directives. The Allies were hitting back with around the clock day and night aerial bombardment of the German industrial areas. Unfortunately, there was a high price to pay for each success replacement aircraft and seasoned aircrews were the biggest problems. The High Command recognized these raids were having reasonable success, disrupting the ability of the German manufacturers to produce war materials. However, this bombing could not go on indefinitely losing aircraft by the hundreds, month after month, stretched the replacement of aircraft and new crews almost to the breaking point.

Aerial bombardment from English airfields was the only way to deliver the war to the Germans until the Allied forces could reestablish bases on the European Continent. This growing problem was vital in planning a strategic battle plan to return Allied forces to the beaches of France. For this future operation, the combined forces of the Allies would be under the overall command of American General Dwight D. Eisenhower, with the second in command General Bernard Montgomery. Eisenhower would be recalled to England from North Africa for this monumental invasion. These two generals had one objective to organize the biggest sea and land invasion sooner rather than later.

On another front, the U-Boat force had received orders from Admiral Karl Donitz to commence attacks on unsuspecting ships off the east coast of America, referred to by U-Boat commanders as, The Happy Times. Literally, hundreds of ships were sunk or badly damaged by these underwater sharks. Another report Karl needed to update was one he initiated the year before and would be successfully executed on March 28th1942. A high priority secret mission had been organized to immobilize access to the U-Boat base in Saint Nazaire, France. In Karl's report from the year before, he had stressed that the Achilles heel of that submarine base was the Lock Gates into the lagoon.

Direct bombing had been tried to no avail; the only way still open would be to ram a ship full of high explosive charges into those lock gates, assuming the ship made it that far. The plan would be to trigger time delay charges after the crew and commandos had successfully evacuated the ship. *Operation Chariot* was that daring plan; the ship, an old American Lend-Lease destroyer, was sacrificed to make this dangerous mission happen. The bow of *HMS Campbeltown* was packed with 4.5 tons of high explosives. The old four-piper had been modified by removing two of her funnels to resemble a German Naval Gun Boat.

Under cover of darkness, Lieutenant Stephen Halden Beattie would steer the *Campbeltown* toward the lock gates before the German shore batteries opened fire on them. The overall commander on that raid was Lieutenant Robert Ryder, leading a detachment of commandos ashore, destroying as many service areas as possible before being extracted from the beaches. When the *Campbeltown* finally exploded, the lock gates and everything around them were destroyed, the damage so severe they would remain inoperable for years to come. The report went on to say the raid was a complete success.

However, the price the British paid in dead sailors and soldiers and those that surrendered to the Germans would represent two thirds of the total complement. The English press made a big deal of it. The people of England needed a win to raise their spirits, and *Operation Chariot* did just that; hearing and reading about the success of this dangerous mission regained the confidence to soldier. It was Karl's report, when viewed by the High Command, that would become the guide to plan that raid.

In the Pacific, the American armed forces received a similar fate to that of the garrison in Singapore. General Douglas McArthur was forced to escape to Australia by sea, leaving over 75,000 American and Filipino troops behind to defend Manila. Against mounting opposition, General Edward King, running out of ammunition and food supplies, surrendered his army to the Japanese on April 9th, 1942.

Merciless Japanese guards forced the remnant of that army to march 65 miles from the Bataan Peninsula to POW camps; some were herded like cattle into boxcars waiting to take them to labor camps. Under appalling conditions, this forced march would forever be referred to as the Bataan Death March.

Daily, this depressing news would flood into the BIS, only to be filed for review; what else could be done at this point? Karl's team continued to train, regardless of the war updates. The day would come when their expertise would play a big part in the return of the Allies to the European Continent. Other reports referred to the horrific picture of brutality and terror for countless thousands of Jewish civilians being herded into concentration camps to be worked to death, their only crime being their religious beliefs. Others were luckier, finding refuge with sympathizers willing to put their own lives at risk by hiding them in creative hiding places. Sadly, however, the vast majority would be discovered, their fate sealed, and the vision of finding a way toward freedom lost forever.

CHAPTER 2

A WEDDING TO REMEMBER

Spring had arrived in Hitchin, and the daffodils were slowly blooming in the garden, bringing cheer to Claire, who had not seen Karl for a long month. The letters arrived almost daily, and the icing on this separation was the telephone calls every other day from Karl. On one such Sunday afternoon, Claire was reading a book, enjoying the warm sun in the garden, when that familiar tone from the secure phone meant one thing: Karl was calling her. Jumping out of the deck chair, she rushed to pick up the phone, trying to sound cheerful as she answered, "Hitchin 5015, who's calling please?"

"Claire, it's me, Karl; are you ready for some good news?" Claire's heart skipped a beat waiting for Karl to give her his news. "I'll be visiting Bedford again this Tuesday; there are some Italians I need to talk to, so expect me home Monday evening. I will be driving myself in a car from the motor pool."

Karl could feel the excitement in Claire's voice as she answered him. "Karl, you have made my day! Darling, it's been a month since I saw you last. How long will you be at the Bedford location?"

Karl was always sensitive to what was said by phone, even though it was a secure line. "Darling, I'll be commuting daily until the weekend, then I'll be home with you till Sunday afternoon. How does that sound to you?"

"That, my darling, is music to my ears. I know you don't care to hear this, but if you're going to be here over the weekend, we must really make time to meet with the priest and visit the Letchworth Hall Hotel. We need to go over the final seating arrangements and menu. I feel guilty asking you about these things, knowing all of you in the military are fighting to save us from German domination; sorry, darling."

Karl, listening to her, was thinking the very same thing, but he also knew how important this was to his fiancée. "My sweet Claire, no need for apologies; we both have priorities. Mine, however, are slightly more dangerous than yours."

Claire, hearing this, started laughing, then replied, "Karl, your warped Austrian sense of humor is coming through again. By the way, the daffodils you planted are coming up nicely; some city boy you're turning out to be. See you Monday evening. I must make a hair appointment for Monday; I need to look my best for a certain Major Vita. Bye, darling, think of me until we can hold each other again."

Karl replying, "I think I'll be thinking of something more than a hug, and I'm sure that hairdo will need to be redone after Monday evening. Bye for now, love ya, honey."

The five Italian officers Karl met with secretly at the detention center decided to surrender to British forces in a war they no longer could be part of. It was viewed by the British Commander as an act of mercy by saving their troops, preferring to live in captivity than die for a lost cause.

Karl and Claire tried to achieve as much as they could while he was home. Finalizing the arrangements, they headed to the King George IV for a pint of mild and bitter beer. Saturday, they took the family to the George and Dragon for lunch; food supplies were getting extremely hard to obtain, so lunch was somewhat Spartan but being together was the dessert they all needed. Sunday afternoon came too quickly, and Karl needed to leave. It was always difficult to say goodbye to Claire. Taking her in his arms, he kissed her tenderly, squeezing her backside as he kissed her.

"Karl Vita, why didn't you do that earlier today? Now, you'll have to fantasize about what could have happened as a parting gift. Hurry home to me, darling," yelled Claire. She watched him open the car door, then blow her a kiss as he started the engine before backing the car out into Hemming's Way. He made one last wave to Claire, looking very lost at Karl leaving. Driving back to Slough, he had that quiet time to reflect on the monumental task that lay ahead of the Allies. The logistics of planning an enormous invasion force, made up of thousands of troops and mountains of equipment, would present many challenges, including many languages and communication issues. Karl's new division would more than likely become the hub for this responsibility. Another glaring concern would be maintaining total secrecy, keeping it under wraps for what could be several years during the planning stages, and the actual framework for the return invasion of Europe. The High Command had started planning this right after the Dunkirk evacuation; it was hard to believe that was only a few years back.

Major Anderson of the American Office of Strategic Services (OSS) had requested that Karl and some of his top agents be assigned to the British Security Coordination (BSC) being assembled to train additional recruits for the OSS at a secret location in Canada to commence early July 1942. That intense training would continue through March 1943.

Arriving back at the camp, Karl had a pint in the lounge, catching up with some small talk with others doing the same thing. Monday morning at 0630 hours, Karl met with close friends Lieutenant Colonel Clive Knight and Major Bill Lowes, along with Major Andy Anderson of the OSS. Their objective would be to map out a strategic plan for the upcoming training in Canada. Over the course of several weeks, a strategic handbook was developed. In the months and years ahead, this would become the bible for both Intelligence services.

May was coming to an end, and life for Karl was becoming very repetitious. Most Monday mornings, Claire would drive him to the Hitchin Station to catch the 0630 hours' train to Kings Cross, and on Fridays, he would arrive home about 1830 hours. Other than a few weekends when he would stay in Slough for some meetings, his weekly schedule would be repeated. While in Slough, he would work long hours, sometimes into the early morning hours. Even when Bill discouraged working like that, Karl would just wave him off with sarcastic remarks like, "I don't know how to be a part timer, or too much to prepare for and not enough time to do it in."

Karl was never the office type, he missed those long voyages aboard the Tristian, stopping in exotic ports, raising hell at local taverns, and always a beautiful lady on his arm. Those carefree days would never happen again and thinking about them now was not the best way to keep up his spirits. "Karl, you're burning yourself out trying to do everything yourself. Why don't you have one or more of your office staff assist you?" asked Bill, only to be shut out by Karl.

Karl said, "Bill, our security is at risk; that's why I'm doing all this by myself." Karl was almost at a breaking point, which bothered his friends immensely.

Clive, hearing this from Bill, intervened one morning by calling Karl's office, "Morning, Karl, you and Bill will be joining Julie and me for dinner this evening, and don't try to give me an excuse. I've heard them all before. Karl, this is a direct order. By the way, an old friend of yours will also be joining us; see you both at 1830 hours!"

With great effort, Clive refrained from telling Karl that his partner on the failed Saint Nazaire mission would be the surprise guest. Major Jean Yves Jerva had arrived back in England the previous week. He had been recalled and assumed a position on the General Staff of General Charles de Gaulle of the Free French Legion. His experience operating with the French Resistance movement had given him a wealth of knowledge on how to combat the Nazi Regime. In his new position, he would be the French liaison between the English, Canadian, Americans, Polish, Czech, and the Free European Brigade, all of which were secretly training for the invasion of Europe still two years away.

Bill had previously accepted Karl's offer to become his best man. Now, with Jean back on English soil, that could change things. With Julie's approval, Bill and Clive believed the near death experience these two men shared had created a special bond between them— more like blood brothers. Bill approached Jean with the question of whether he would consider replacing himself as Karl's best man on June 5th. Jean was beside himself when hearing this, even though he knew nothing about Claire. Over a glass of wine, Julie had told him about Karl's transformation, falling head over heels in love with this exceptional lady.

Julie also told him how Claire had helped him through so many nightmares including a few that nearly put him over the edge. "We all love Claire so much, so when these two asked me my opinion about Bill standing aside, I instantly agreed. Of course, you haven't said yes to this yet, have you, Jean?" concluded Julie.

Like the good romantic Frenchman, he was, Jean lifted his wine glass and responded by saying, "It will be my pleasure and my honor. Bill, you are a true friend, and I can imagine how you must have wrestled with this. It will be an event I will always remember as a very special day but doesn't the final decision lie with Karl? One way or the other, I need to get my dress uniform cleaned and pressed."

Julie responded by saying, "Get me that uniform, and I'll take care of doing that for you."

Bill pulled his car up in front of building B-3, waiting for Karl to come out. A few minutes later, Karl came out in civilian attire. "Nice to see you out of uniform; casual suits you, old man. Tonight, will be wonderful; Julie is so creative working with limited food ration books. Karl, you must be looking forward to a relaxing evening, are you?"

Karl sat listening, a little rattled at being ordered to take a night off. "Bill, who is the mysterious guest tonight that supposedly knows me?"

Bill was enjoying the secret he was keeping, and with a big smile, he shrugged his shoulders. Arriving at the Knights' home, Bill reached over the front seat to retrieve a bag from the back seat containing two bottles of French wine. "Ready, Karl? I managed to liberate this wine earlier today. Come on, old man; let your hair down; you are with friends who care about you."

Standing at the front door, Karl pulled Bill back, saying, "Thanks, Bill, you're right; I need to be with real friends. I guess there's too much going on right now. This weekend, I will become Claire's husband, and I couldn't be happier. However, I continue to let the war bring me down, so my old friend, it's not right for me to take that out on you, especially when you're going to be my best man in a few days."

Bill looked at Karl, and as hard as he tried, he could not stop laughing. Karl looked at him with a perplexed look on his face. Clive opened the front door, saying, "Welcome, you two, what's so funny?"

Clive was grinning, knowing what Bill was laughing at. Walking into the sitting room, Julie walked over to hug them both. Then, taking Karl's arm, she led him to the couch, saying, "Karl, sit here, and please don't turn around." Karl complied, still having that confused look on his face.

A familiar French voice behind him made him stand up very quickly. Turning around, he responded in French, saying, "Jean Yves, my God, I can't believe it's you; what a surprise! When did you return to England?"

"Well, it was about a month ago when I received orders that I would be returning to England to assume a new position on General Charles De Gaulle's staff. What a surprise to learn about my Casanova friend meeting a girl and getting married. It was, to say the least, a real shocking surprise. I can't wait to meet this amazing tigress, Claire."

Karl embraced his friend before they sat back down again. Bill turned toward the two friends, saying he had an announcement to make and would they listen before responding. "Karl, when we found out about Jean's return, I asked the Knights here what they thought of having Jean be your best man instead of me. As much as I have looked forward to that monumental occasion, things have changed, haven't they? Considering Jean's recent return to England, it would make more sense to have him replace me by your side and become your best man. Karl, you two went through so much together. What better way of celebrating life by Jean doing this for you? I have already cleared this with him, and, speaking on his behalf, he feels the same. So, old man, what do you say?"

Karl took another slug of whiskey, then put his arm around the tall Frenchman and responded by saying, "Jean, I'm still in shock that you're sitting here next to me after such a long time, and yes to you being my best man. Bill, thank you for doing this. Both you and Clive have always stood by me through thick and thin, and now we have another brother in Jean. Even though he is a bloody Frenchman, I can't think of any other chap I would rather trust my life to. Julie, I'm assuming you have already told Claire about this, am I right? I still can't figure out why I'm always the last one to find out about things. Clive, can you wangle some extra time off for Jean ahead of the wedding so he can come home with me to meet Claire? I would like them to know each other ahead of that special day on Saturday."

As he said that, Karl looked at the eye play between the three of them, realizing what was going on. "Oh, I guess I'm slow on the uptake. She already knows we'll be heading home this Thursday if you can wangle the extra time, correct?"

"Well, sunshine, we all decided, in light of Jean's return, we should make this wedding weekend a special one by adding a few more days to it, old man. You're not going home this weekend by train. We're all going to Hitchin in Clive's staff car on Thursday morning," said Julie, beaming with a beautiful smile on her face.

Karl still smiling, reiterated, "I'm always the last to be informed of social activities."

"Unfortunately, Bill and Dorothy can't leave until later in the day but will be there in time for your bachelor party; he has a previous engagement that could not be broken."

Unbeknownst to Karl, there was another secret in store for him. Ronny and Clive had planned some entertainment for that bachelor party; yet another secret had been planned without him.

After dinner, Karl excused himself to call Claire from Clive's office, "Darling, how is my own devilish English spy doing?" Karl laughed as he said that.

"Oh, my, the cat got into the chicken coop. Did they tell you I practiced my poor French on Jean Yves earlier? And what else did you find out at dinner or before having cocktails?" asked Claire, playing with him to find out what other activities were planned for this wedding weekend.

"Claire, you already know we will be home Thursday late morning with Jean. Can we add another room for Jean? I'm assuming we reserved enough rooms at the Letchworth Hall Hotel. When is your sister arriving with David? Did she decide to leave the children in Oxford, or will they all come together? Julie also asked me over dinner if it would be alright to include their girls, and I told her absolutely—bring them along. Claire, I'm scared to ask you this; how many will there be at this wedding?"

Karl had not been vigilant in keeping up with the wedding plans until today. His BIS duties would always take precedence over those sorts of details. "Well, as of today, now, Karl, don't flip out on me. I know you really wanted to keep it small, but, well, Lover Boy, between us, we have too many friends and acquaintances who all wanted to attend."

Claire was cut off by Karl asking, "Just give me a number, Claire. I'm already nervous from the way you're beating around the bush."

Claire braced herself, knowing what Karl would say when she gave him that number. "Alright, I'll face the music, Karl; the total attendees will be two hundred and twenty-five that includes last minute people like Jean and several of my school friends." Claire waited while Karl processed that number. "Karl, are you still there, or am I in real trouble about now?" Claire waited for the blasting response she was expecting from Karl.

"Well, Claire, I'm relieved; I was expecting to hear you'd invited the entire High Command." Once over the shock, Karl laughed, then continued to speak, saying, "Claire, as of today, don't you ever call me a crazy Austrian again; you're really a Limey Nutter."

Claire sighed hearing this, he was rattled but over it. "Claire, you realize we will be paying for this wedding for years to come, don't you?" said Karl, now with a relaxed tone to his voice.

"No, we won't, Sailor. I've already paid for most of it." Claire knew, sooner or later, she would have to tell Karl her mother had left her and her sister a substantial inheritance.

"In those last few days, when she was terminally ill, she made me promise by saying, your heart is broken right now, Claire, losing Patrick as you did. One day, someone will bring sunshine back into that grieving heart of yours; my sorrow is I'll not be there to see it. Claire, when that happens, promise me you'll have a huge wedding, and to hell with the cost. Life goes on; please find that lost smile and love of life you had previously. It breaks my heart seeing you like this.

Karl was just about to read her the riot act when Claire cut him off, telling him all about her mother's last wishes. "Karl, this was my mother's parting wish, and you will not spoil it for me. Do you understand, Karl Vita?" Claire was becoming emotionally upset.

Karl could hear the change in her voice, so he calmly responded by saying, "Claire, I wish you would have told me about your mother's wishes ahead of today. We will make her proud of those plans she wanted for you; happily, they now include me. Forgive me, darling; I guess all the tension I've been carrying ignited that outburst. Please allow me to thank your mother this week. We should buy the biggest arrangement of roses in Hitchin and place them on her grave, and please allow me to tell her that she has a daughter who, when she gets excited, spends money like water."

Karl's dry sense of humor was kicking in again. "Karl, I so wish my mother could be there. She would love that warped sense of humor you have. By the way, have I told you lately how much I'm looking forward to being Claire Vita? Hurry home to me, Karl; I'm not really that good without you."

Hearing Claire's last statement sent a cold chill through Karl, thinking, this war is far from over. I hope I can live up to that statement. "Good night, darling; see you Thursday." Claire returned the phone to its cradle, thinking, no matter what happens, Karl always handles it in stride. Returning to the living room, Karl apologized for the lengthy phone call.

"That's perfectly alright," said Julie, pouring Karl another glass of whiskey. "I'm assuming she told you how many people will be at the wedding? She has been so nervous about telling you that. I told her that, at first, Karl would want to strangle her, then recover quickly with some sarcastic remark, am I right?" asked Julie with a wicked smile on her face.

"Julie, answer me this; do you two talk every day about what I'm either doing or saying?" Karl broke out laughing with Julie and the others joining in. "One other thing you can answer for me, Julie, who will I know in that mass of people?" Karl swigged back his whiskey, asking for a healthy refill. "I think I need this about now." That generated even more laughter; it was turning out to be a whirlwind evening.

The end of May was almost upon them, and Karl's extended leave was about to start. This coming weekend, he and Claire would make their wedding vows in front of families and all those friends. Wednesday afternoon, Karl's staff got together with a wedding gift.

Sally knocked on his office door, inviting him to come out into the main office, saying, "Sir, before you head out tomorrow morning, we would like to give you this small gift. It's our way of wishing you both a wonderful wedding and honeymoon. We all chipped in to buy this; it's not a lot, but it's from a staff that appreciates having you as their boss."

Karl was lost for words. He suspected they would not let him go without some parting gesture. "My, thank you so much for this. I hope you don't mind if I wait to open it with Claire, or should I say, Mrs. Vita. All of you have made my job so much easier every day, and on occasions, you go above and beyond what I expect from you. Today, I seem to be lost for words, so allow me to thank each one of you personally." With the brightly covered box in hand, Karl moved amongst them, giving each one a hug that conveyed what his heart was feeling at that very moment. "Now, one last parting comment, and I need to make it very clear: Get back to work, you lot, it's not a bloody holiday camp!" Karl turned and headed to his office with that last minute sarcastic remark, waving the box high above his head.

Sally had the last word, though, yelling, "Hey, Karl, don't wear it out next week!" The whole staff started laughing at this very saucy remark, including Karl.

Thursday, Karl packed his small case and headed down the hall to meet up with Jean, who was already having his morning coffee, and said, "Jean, you look relaxed; let me get my coffee, then we can talk about what's going on. Well, maybe we should just talk about the wedding and all those people neither of us knows."

Jean, sipping his coffee, just chuckled. "Karl, from what I've heard, you really hit the jackpot with Claire. Before I forget, I have a letter here for you from Monica. With all that was going on yesterday, I completely forgot to give it to you," said Jean, handing over the letter.

Karl took the letter, then asked Jean, "Would you mind if I take a minute while we are sitting here to read it?"

Jean stood up, saying, "While you read that letter, I'm going to get some of those terrible powered eggs and more coffee; shall I bring some for you as well?"

Karl moved his head in agreement; his eyes fixed on the letter in front of him.

Dearest Karl,

When Jean gave me the news that he was being reassigned back to England and would be seeing you, he also told me that you had gotten engaged. I am so happy for you. Since our first meeting back in 1936, your life has not been easy. In fact, it's been somewhat dangerous. I always had a crush on you, and that's not going to change anytime soon. No matter what you wish for, sometimes those dreams never materialize. They haven't for me anyway.

Must go; Jean is getting antsy waiting for me to finish this letter. I hope our paths will cross again, maybe after this war is over. Please give your fiancée my best wishes for a wonderful life as Mrs. Karl Vita.

Love always,
Monica

As he finished reading the letter, he thought to himself, another broken heart, but someone that helped me when I needed that help so very much. Yes, Monica, we will meet again under better circumstances; I'm sure Claire would like to thank you as well. Taking the letter, Karl put it into his briefcase just in time to receive that second cup of God-awful coffee as Jean sat down again. "Well, everything alright with you and Monica?" asked Jean with a somewhat cavalier look on his face.

"Yes, Jean, she is alright, even a little melancholy at hearing about my engagement. I will always think of her as a beautiful, friendly nurse that came to my rescue more than once. I look forward to introducing her to Claire after this war is over."

"Drink up, or Clive will get upset if we're not outside waiting for him. I think we both have a wedding to get to." Clive, as expected, was outside with his big Humber staff car. Julie and the younger daughter were in the front seat, the older one in the back.

"Morning, you two, glad you decided to join us." Karl and Jean just looked at each other, grinning profusely.

Arriving at the house in Hitchin, there were numerous cars parked on the street and in the driveway, "Looks like Claire is having a hen gathering," remarked Karl as he opened the car door. "Okay, let's introduce all of you, then we can decide what we're doing, or Julie, is that already planned?"

Julie looked at him as she also got out of the car, replying, "You're right, Major; get used to it; this is only the beginning." Julie blew Karl a kiss as she said that.

Inside, there were people everywhere, so Karl yelled, "Excuse me, is there a Claire McGivern in here? She has visitors."

Claire answered from the kitchen, "Only for a couple more days, you Austrian hunk. Get over here right now, or I'll be forced to embarrass you in front of these people."

Karl elbowed his way into the kitchen, finding Claire and her sister Caroline making sandwiches. Karl felt overwhelmed with a house full of mostly strangers. Claire moved toward him, excusing herself as she placed her arms around Karl's neck, giving him a very passionate welcome home kiss. Caroline came next, kissing her new brother-in-law on the cheek, saying, "Welcome home, Karl. Introduce me to your friends, will you? I say these chaps are worth being very bad over."

Claire, shaking her head, was waiting for her sister to be saucy in front of Clive and Jean. Claire introduced Julie and her daughters to her friends and old school chums. The next several hours were somewhat of a blur to Karl, trying to listen to and talk to those around him. "Jean, what say we get you checked in at the hotel? I'll ask Clive if he is also ready to leave."

Karl told Claire, "I'll drive Jean and Clive to the hotel, and you should plan on meeting us later. That will give you more time with your company."

Claire answered him, "Karl, no, you won't. The boys are taking you out tonight. Clive thinks if the party gets too rowdy, you can stay in our suite. Sorry about all this mayhem, darling. Blame Caroline: it was her idea. I would have much preferred spending more quiet time with you, darling, but as you can see, it's a madhouse right now. Sorry again, as you would say, it's a hens' evening. Freida is dropping Ronny off at the hotel before coming here; he'll be waiting for you at the bar. Jean and Clive are outside now waiting for you. Behave yourselves tonight. I think they have a very wild night planned. Boys will always be boys."

Karl was so pleased to get out of there. As much as he was happy to see Claire, there was absolutely no privacy in that madhouse. Arriving at the Letchworth Hotel, Jean could see Karl was starting to relax. "Here we are, old boy; let's get you chaps registered. I'm going to join Ronny at the bar for a very large drink. After being in that henhouse, I think I need one about now."

"Ronny, so glad to see you, such a sly dog you knew the house would be full of women; this is so much nicer. In all fairness, Caroline made sure all their old school pals and people that grew up with them in Hitchin had time to see her before we got married. She has been through so much over the last couple of years, so I won't complain about this get together." Karl pulling up a bar stool as he said that.

"Karl, you both have. It's your time now for happiness, and while we are on that subject, my scheming brother-in-law, less of the heroics from now on. Your first loyalty starting Saturday will be your wife. Karl, I shouldn't be pouring cold water on this auspicious occasion, but last week, I received new order to report to a training camp in Wales this coming July. I haven't told Freida or Mama yet, although they know it's only a matter of time before I'm shipped out. Karl, it's not going to be easy for either of us.

"We both know what's coming, and the preparation will be totally consuming. Our time at home will decrease, and the girls will have to rely on each other more. War is madness; I'm sure you'll agree. On a happier note, with that posting comes a promotion to captain; took long enough, didn't it?" Karl listened intently to Ronny, wishing he could share what was being planned for the summer of 1944.

Thursday evening, the bachelor party was every inch of Julie's prediction. Claire had reserved a private room at the Fox with good old Harry, introducing Bill as the party coordinator. Clive and Ronny had arranged for an entertainer to give the twelve or so gentlemen attending the party a randy evening of saucy fun.

The piano player was hilarious, getting everyone to sing along with the rugby song famous in the British Military and sports clubs. At about 2000 hours, two Royal Air force women entered the room. With a big grin on his face, Clive, almost three sheets to the wind, yelled out, "Go get them, ladies. That one is a Frenchman, and the other one next to him is Austrian. Show them how to fly the friendly thighs of the WRAF."

Karl, looking at Jean, yelled out, "What are these ladies up to, Clive?" "You're about to find out, chaps," answered Bill as he and Ronny put two chairs in the middle of the floor, commanding Karl and Jean to sit down and keep their hands firmly by their sides. Everyone was singing and yelling for the two entertainers to take it off. The piano player started playing a medley of music for the two girls to perform to. Circling the two victims, they slowly started gyrating to the music, removing one piece of clothing with each pass. Jean was laughing very hard, totally enjoying the treatment. Karl, on the other hand, was still holding back. When they were down to their lacy bra, panties, and nylons, they played around in front of them with hand gestures about who got who.

Karl, at this, letting loose, yelled very loudly, "If it's going to be torture, then let's get it on." Everyone joined in with more rugby songs. The two ladies, facing forward, sat on Karl and Jean's laps, grinding away, which caused everyone in the room to stand, clapping loudly at the two BIS officers who were making complete asses of themselves. The evening came to an end at about 2300 hours, with Karl and Jean thanking the two performers for making the evening so much fun. Karl politely continued to ask questions of them, "Ladies, what is your everyday occupation?"

"God knows, it's not doing this, darling," answered Ruby. "We both have jobs in Luton as switchboard operators. We only do this for extra money to take care of our kids and have a little fun with the lads. The pay the Army gives our blokes is not enough to get by on, so that's why we got hired to spice up your party tonight," continued Ruby.

Jean looked at Clive with a look that said, did you pay them enough for tonight's performance? Karl stood up on a chair, asking Bill to get him his cap, then said loudly, "Gentlemen, these ladies gave us all a randy good time tonight. Please, dig deep and show them how much we appreciated having them here tonight." Bill was next passing his cap around for a healthy tip for the piano players. Karl, still on a roll and quite wobbly on the chair, still with a very large glass of whiskey in his hand, continued by saying, "To all of you that made this such a mad, fun-loving evening, thank you from the bottom of my heart." Jumping down, he walked over to Ruby, the blonde, sweeping her off her feet and giving her a lip-smacking kiss, then followed by saying to Deborah, "Can't forget you, can I?"

Deborah answered, "Better make it better than you just gave Ruby then." Karl, quite drunk, laughed as he kissed her. Jean, with his French accent, yelled out, "What about me? I'm not getting married any time soon." Deborah grabbed him by the neck and slapped a big kiss squarely on his lips, followed by Ruby. Outside, they all tumbled into cars heading in the direction of the hotel.

Clive said, "I'm going to take Ronny home. Karl, come with me to give me directions, will you? Ronny, feeling no pain, his face covered in lipstick smudges, sat next to an equally inebriated Jean.

"Clive, you're not driving me home. I'm going to the hotel with you blokes. I'm in no condition to face Freida or Mama right now."

The following morning, Claire and Caroline drove over to the hotel to find out about the boy's wild party. In the breakfast room, they found Julie sitting with Dorothy having their morning tea. "Julie, what time did the boys finally return to the hotel last night? When I dropped you off last night, they weren't back yet."

Julie looked at them, finally saying, "Well, it's been a very long time since I've seen Clive like that. His shirt is covered in lipstick, and he reeks of smoke and whiskey. I guarantee you; they're all the same. As I said, I can't remember seeing Clive let go like this. Then again, in the line of work they're in, it may help release all that tension they carry."

Claire, the organizer, had taken Karl's luggage and dress uniform over to the hotel early Thursday morning to be ready for the big day Saturday. Friday would not be very convenient as everyone was getting together for a luncheon that day. "Is he in our room right now?" asked Claire.

Julie, with a grin on her face, simply answered, "Well, that's a good question. There are bodies in different rooms, some not even staying here, so I'm not really sure."

Claire started giggling, saying, "Well, ladies, it's not like we didn't expect these mad military blokes not to raise hell, but tell me more about that lipstick; what shade is it? I need some ammunition to use on him as he squirms, trying to get out of this episode. Ladies, between you and me, I love him so much that this wild party is absolutely fine by me. How about you two?"

Julie reached over to hold Claire's hand and responded by saying, "We should thank God for every day we have them."

Friday was going by fast. Claire looked at the other two ladies, then stood up, saying, "That's it, Let's go get them out of bed or off the floor. Otherwise, the day will be over; come on, ladies, let's do some damage." Claire took her key out of her handbag and opened the door to their room. All was quiet except there were no bodies. "What the bloody hell is going on?" said Claire, becoming rattled. Spinning around to the other two, she asked, "Am I missing something?" Dorothy couldn't hold back as she started laughing, followed by Julie.

"Go look out the window for your answer." Claire walked over to the window, pulling the curtains back, and there below were all the men, smartly dressed, holding a long sign made from cardboard that read:

Claire, we are sorry, can we go play now?

"You bugger, Karl Vita; you're going to be paying for this for a very long time, maybe years." Claire looked at her friends, then broke out laughing, saying, "You two are in on this prank. Whose idea was this?" Dorothy and Julie looked at each other, then pointed to the side of the door.

"I'm to blame, big sister; we all agreed you have been uptight the last couple of days, so I came up with this idea to loosen your knickers." Caroline approached her big sister, arms out straight, ready to give her a big hug all was forgiven. Lunch would be served on the terrace. The men were standing around drinking Champagne as their ladies walked out into the sunshine.

Karl, wearing a big smile across his face, approached Claire, then dropped onto one knee, saying, "Claire, I hope you're not overly upset with all of us. When Caroline called me early this morning with her idea, I totally agreed with her. You have been going nonstop with these wedding arrangements, so she thought a little scare tactic would go a long way to getting you out of it. Am I still in the doghouse, you sexy thing?"

Karl slid his arms around her legs, tapping her backside in jest. "Get up, you maniac. Put a bunch of you blokes together in a pub, and all hell breaks loose. Mr. Vita, you are pushing up my skirt! That, sir, will cost you dearly tomorrow night; now, let's go eat, I'm famished.

Standing next to Julie and holding her hand, Mama finally said, "Medicine comes in all forms; this one is by far the best." The rest of the day would be so much fun with the children running around throwing a football and playing catch, making the adults laugh. Claire pulled Karl to one side, saying, "Darling, tonight, don't go crazy again drinking. Tomorrow, I need your wits to be sharp as a tack. It's our wedding day, you crazy Austrian. Some of the chaps told me all about the two of you and the dancing, or should I say the striptease performance last night. What did you do with that lipstick smeared shirt? I need to see what color it was." Claire, laughing and holding him, thought, I could not be happier that the boys had that time to let their hair down.

"Claire, are you girls leaving now for your bachelorette party at the Crown and Castle?"

"Yes, Karl, we are. Maybe someday in the future, I'll tell you all about it. You realize it's Caroline and Julie that organized this, don't you?" Karl was laughing at her as she tried to tease him into believing they were planning some mischief.

Seeing Karl and Claire talking, Julie moved over to them, saying, "Karl, kiss her goodbye. It will be the last time you do so as Claire McGivern. Next time you kiss her; it will be as Mrs. Claire Vita."

Saturday morning, Karl, Clive, and Jean went for a sunrise cross country run. After all the drinking, they all needed to burn off that alcohol and maybe a few calories. Nobody really said much as they crossed the fields that lined the golf course, and it was the perfect way to tone their minds. As the men arrived back at the hotel, the staff was busily arranging the tables in the banquet room to get ready for the two hundred and fifty invited guests. Still in their running gear, Karl and Clive took a quick look inside, overwhelmed at all that was taking place.

"I think I'll call Claire before it gets crazy at the house. You know what women are like when there are no men around," said Karl.

"Karl don't ever lose that warped sense of humor; it's really contagious. Now, let's get bathed before we stink up the whole ballroom," remarked Clive. Walking toward his room, he started reminiscing about that Thursday morning when he and Bill met Karl for the first time on board the Clyde Princess docked in Dover. Karl was seeking political asylum from a war he wanted no part of but desperately wanted to contribute to its demise.

Wearing that striking dark blue maritime uniform, he had a commanding presence as he addressed both of us from the BIS. How far we have come since then. And look at the unbending friendship that has grown out of that first meeting. Today, all that womanizing comes to an end at 1000 hours as we witness his marriage to Claire, our English Rose, and an end to all those wild romances he has become famous for.

Karl had gone to the bathroom for a long hot bath and a shave. Back in the room, he put on his starched shirt and dress trousers, followed by highly polished brown shoes. His ceremonial tunic still hung from the wardrobe door, ready for him later. Karl inspected the insignias to ensure they were securely attached in the correct place and none missing, thinking, I must admit that tailor did an excellent job making this uniform. Claire, always the perfectionist, probably scrutinized every stitch he made.

Walking downstairs, he wandered out onto the terrace for some quiet time in the sun. Reclining there in the deck chair, he allowed his mind to take charge. Almost in a self-hypnotic state, he remembered all the ladies that had left an impression on him, especially Annie,

Kitty, and Hazel, and finally Claire, the one he would spend the rest of his life with, assuming he would survive this war. Thinking these things, he took a moment to ponder that he would never again live in Wien, his boyhood home, and that saddened him as he lay there thinking all these things. A soft squeeze on his shoulder brought him back into the sunshine. It was Jean, saying, "Karl, they sent me out to wake you; it's time we all got ourselves ready. Come on, my friend, we have a show, sorry, I mean wedding to attend."

Jean laughed as he took Karl's arm to pull him out of the deck chair. Looking at his friends in their dress uniforms made Karl do a double take. Sitting in the lobby from left to right were Lieutenant Colonel Clive Knight, Major William Lowes, Captain Ronald Whiting, General Arthur Jacks, Major Gunther Fischer, Captain Herbert Werner, and now joining them, Captain Jean Yves Jerva. Another surprise Karl was not expecting was seeing his second in command of his new division, Captain Hardy Meyers.

Yet another surprise, members from his crew aboard HMT Reese, his Second in Command, Lieutenant Ken Adams, now a captain, beside him stood two other survivors from Reese, Chief Petty Officer Charlie Brice, and Chief Petty Officer John Arnold. Karl stopped in front of the older CPO. Arnold was the sailor responsible for saving his life that fateful day off the beaches of Dunkirk. Karl took both his hands and quietly spoke alongside his ear, saying, "Thank you, Chief, for saving my life; I believe my new wife will also want to thank you as well."

Karl turned in front of this military gathering, and with both his hands grasped together, he shook his head and finally spoke. "My goodness, you all look so spiffy in your dress uniforms. I feel out of place amongst you all; what can I say?" Karl was lost for words.

"Finish getting your bloody uniform on, and that's an order. There's a young lady that can't wait to ground you for all your wild shenanigans!" yelled General Jacks, laughing as he said that.

Karl came to parade attention, replying, "As you request, Sir, may I have an extra five minutes for a last pee?" Saying that brought the roof down in a show of verbal abuse. Karl made a quick exit, running up the stairs two at a time.

Clive spoke, while they waited for Karl to return, saying, "Listen up, chaps; when you arrive at the church, remember you will be the ushers. After everyone has been seated, we form up five asides in front of the altar. General Jacks, you, of course, will be at the head with me on the opposite side. Gentlemen, remember, five asides. Jean, you will stay and travel over to the church with Karl. Ronny, I'm assuming the RAF Honor Guard will be on time to do the Ceremonial Saber Arch Salute; are your people here yet? And how about that flyover by the boys from Duxford in their Spitfires? Are you all set with that as well? Remember, they need to be on time as Claire and Karl exit the church. It's a little tricky, I know, but your flyboys are geniuses at doing this." Ronny assured him all the preparations were well in hand.

Karl returned to the lobby in his dress uniform, marched right up to General Jacks, came to parade attention, and, yelling loudly, said, "Major Karl Vita reporting for wedding duty, Sir."

General Jacks, playing along, approached Karl, saying, "Soldier, you think that tie is going to pass muster? And straighten that belt. Do justice to the uniform of a BIS officer. By the way, may I congratulate you? And, Karl, everyone here is so very proud of you today." Saluting Karl, he wheeled on his shoes, saying to the others, "what say we all head over to the church? We can't be late for this mission, can we? Mayor Lowes, if Karl even flinches an inch, you have my permission to block any attempt he may have of bolting," concluded General Jacks. The laughter was contagious; these fellow warriors were extremely happy and proud of their comrade in arms, especially on this bright and sunny Saturday.

Arriving in a convoy of cars, they all entered the church, the ushers taking their places on either side of the entrance to escort guests to their seats. The altar was decorated with so many flowers; it was hard to imagine a World War was going on. The priest approached Karl and Jean, saying, "I say this will be an amazing wedding with all you military chaps in this church. Now, Captain Jerva, I'm assuming you have both rings readily at hand, correct? Claire asked me to have you place them on the satin cushion the two ring bearers will bring you. I believe they are Lieutenant Colonel Knight's daughters?" Karl spotted Mama and Freida with Franchot entering. Excusing himself, he walked down the aisle to greet his mother.

"Mama, Freida, you both look so beautiful! Can you believe all these preparations that have been made? Mama, you have waited a long time for this day; may I escort you to the front?"

Mama, taking his arm, said as they made their way toward the front, "Son, I wish our entire family could be here; they would be so proud of their baby brother, especially your father if only he could see you in that uniform." Mama stopped talking; she could say no more. Those tears were of total happiness; she had waited and prayed so many years for this to happen, and today, it was all coming true. Taking their places at the front of the church, all the men in uniform stood at attention, waiting to turn toward the back of the church when signaled by the change in the soft classical music.

At 9:43 a.m., that change happened as Caroline entered, leading the two young ring bearers ahead of Julie and Dorothy. All three bridesmaids in beautiful pale pink dresses started down the aisle. All eyes now waited in silence for the organ to commence playing the Trumpet Voluntary. At precisely 9:45 a.m., the organist announced the bride's arrival, Claire, in her beautiful, cream colored wedding dress, wearing a short veil over her hair, which was up in her usual French twist. She entered the church, escorted by her brother-in-law David.

From his vantage point, Karl was beyond words as he watched his bride to be walk down the aisle. Jean whispered in Karl's ear, "You, my friend, are the luckiest man in England right now. I am so honored to be standing next to you as your best man."

Karl answered him by saying, "Jean, you have always been my best man." At the altar, David put Claire's left hand into Karl's waiting hand; her smile was simply radiant. In silence, they turn to face the priest. When the ceremony came to exchanging wedding rings, Caroline, holding the hands of the ring bearers, moved forward for Jean to accept the rings from the two young ladies. Karl and Claire chuckled at how cute the Knight girls looked.

Karl took Claire's hand as the priest asked them to repeat their wedding vows, that would bind them together as man and wife. Lifting Claire's veil, Karl locked onto her eyes as he placed the band of gold on her wedding finger, then Claire did the same for Karl. The tears she had controlled since entering the church now flooded her eyes, rolling down her cheeks as Karl squeezed his new bride softly. "Major, you may now kiss the bride," announced Father Gibson. He followed that with, "Karl and Claire, would you please turn to face the congregation," continued by, "Would all in attendance please stand and join me in congratulating Major Karl and Claire Vita, and please, kiss her again for all to see."

Karl turned toward Claire, his face against hers, saying, "Claire Vita, I love you so very much. I pray to God that our lives together will forever be blessed and, with His grace, so will our future family." Claire tried to reply, but her emotions would not allow her to speak, so she kissed him passionately, hugging him as tightly as she could.

As they stepped down from the altar, General Jacks called out loudly, "Attention and salute, Major and Mrs. Vita." Turning towards the rectory they proceeded to sign the marriage book. As the ceremony came to its end, the organ once again filled the church with the beautiful music of Wagner. This would be the signal for Ronny to excuse himself to call the airbase from the church rectory, giving the green light for the training flight of four Spitfires to take off to fly low over St. Mary's Church. Arm in arm, Claire and Karl stopped first to kiss his mother, then continued down the aisle, shaking hands and kissing loved ones. Finally, they arrived back at the entrance, waiting for the signal from the deacon to proceed outside into the bright sunshine of this perfect morning. Lined up on either side of the path, eight RAF honor guards raised their swords, forming the old military tradition of the Saber Swords Arch.

A loud command came from the Master Sargent, "Attention, Honor Guards, raise your sabers into an arch." With military precision, the men in blue extended their swords. Claire showed her excitement as she held Karl's arm, tightly passing beneath the shining silver sword blades.

"Karl, isn't this wonderful? Can you hear that sound overhead? It must be the planes from Duxford. Everyone looked to the sky to watch the formation of four Spitfires flying very low overhead in a diamond formation, then peeling off, flying in a straight line, one behind the other around the church. Finally, they performed a precise maneuver; flying overhead doing a barrel roll. Their parting gesture was to waggle their wings as they headed back toward Duxford. The crowd had gathered around the entrance to give their congratulations and take pictures.

Clive approached Karl, saying, "Time to get you into the car, old man!" Inside the 1936 Rolls Royce Limousine, they had twenty minutes to relax before the reception. Holding hands, they finally could talk to each other.

"Karl, my darling, I'm still a little overwhelmed by that service. It was a sea of military uniforms, and the honor guard arch was awesome, don't you think?" asked Claire, still very excited at all that was going on.

"Yes, it was how Ronny pulled off that flyover that is beyond me. Those flyboys really know how to impress a crowd, don't they?"

Claire got quiet, turning to face Karl as she spoke in a very deliberate tone, saying, "Darling, I feel so wonderful knowing that from now on I belong to someone, someone that will love and protect me. Thank you, darling, for giving me this day."

Karl sat listening to his new wife, and a silent smile told her what she needed to know: Karl would always safeguard their union. "I'm the one who should be thanking you, Claire. You're the light I look to when I'm not sure of where I'm going. I love you, Mrs. Vita; there is a Heaven here on Earth because of you." Karl wanted to lighten the mood, so he asked her a question to change that solemn look on Claire's face. "Now that you're a married lady, would you mind awfully if I rested my right hand under your dress until we get to the hotel?"

"Karl Vita, behave yourself. I've got a gold band on my finger that gives me the right to stop your foolery." Hearing her say that Karl leaned back in the seat, laughing his head off. Claire could not keep a straight face, so she too broke out laughing, grabbing his right hand, and placing it on her upper thigh. "There!" she said. "Will that keep you quiet for a while?" Karl wrapped his arm around her and kissed her deeply, his hand firmly placed on her upper thigh. On the other hand, Claire did not trust his motives, so she held that hand to stop any further advancement he may be planning.

The main ballroom was filling with guests, and Clive wanted to ensure the photographer had enough time for picture taking out on the terrace. The ones he took at the church were mainly Claire and Karl at the altar and many others of family and friends. Out here on the terrace, the pictures he took were more personal of the new couple. Music could now be heard as Claire and Karl cooperated with each pose, "Claire, don't we have enough pictures? I really would like that drink about now and a whirl around the dance floor with my bride," asked Karl, becoming impatient.

"Almost done, Major, just a couple more," said the photographer. With soft music playing, the luncheon commenced, surprising everyone how well it was prepared, considering the war time shortage of food supplies. As the best man, Jean stood up, calling for everyone's attention, then started to speak in his strong French accent.

"You know, Karl and I have shared some difficult situations, but for me, this is the one that is terrifying me, considering I'm French and am speaking English; well, I think it's English?" Everyone started to laugh as Jean continued with his story of how he and Karl became friends, careful not to mention the secure times. "You know; it was only last week I found out about Karl's engagement. Wow, what a surprise my friend, getting married. MonDieu, can this really be happening? Then, I met the charming, beautiful Claire. You know she needs to be very strong around this one; every day will be exciting that is for certain. I can say that because he is my friend. To be serious, I can't believe how wonderful a lady you are, Claire. Now, I can stop worrying about my crazy Austrian friend; thank you all for being here today. A toast to Karl and his new bride, Mrs. Claire Vita; may each day they are together be one of love, devotion, and eternal happiness. I will stop now as I'm out of English words."

Everyone was laughing at this comical Frenchman. Jean turned to Karl, kissing him on both cheeks before taking Claire's hands as she stood up to kiss him as well. Karl stood up next, and taking Claire's hand, he thanked Jean for leaving him with a bit of dignity intact. "Ladies and Gentlemen, let me add my thanks to all of you for making this the best day of my life. To my new bride, in front of all of you, let me say I will always put you first, and yes, General Jacks, that includes the BIS.

"To my family and my dearest mother and sister Frieda, your support has always been there for me, especially through those bleak times. To my father and brothers, who are not with us today, we look forward to a time when we can all be reunited. To my very English Brother-In-Law, Ronny, is the RAF still looking for those four spitfires that mysteriously went missing this morning? Claire and I thank you for making this such a wonderful day."

Claire added some words of encouragement for those who had family serving in the armed forces, along with her thanks to her sister, who made her bachelorette party such a success. "And, please, ladies, never tell my husband Karl about that fabulous evening; I would much prefer to keep him guessing."

Clive and Bill stood up next to toast Karl in the tradition of the English Military. The party went on all afternoon with much merrymaking, drinking, and dancing. After most of the guests had left, the ones staying at the hotel sat around until it was time to retire for the night. Ronny left, coming back with a piece of paper, saying, "I say, this looks encouraging from the latest weather report from my base."

"Read it out loud," said Clive with a big smile on his face. "Will do," replied Ronny. "It reads, as of 1900 hours today, Warm and Close Tonight, With A Little Son Later. Karl thought about that forecast, then broke out in a fit of laughter, followed by all of them.

Claire was laughing as well, but her eyes were on Karl, saying out loud, "That forecast is spot on for our future, Major Vita." Claire stood up, reaching for Karl's hand, and with a snicker said loudly, "Thank you all for making this so special. Now, let's go make that weather forecast an accurate one, shall we?" With that, the new couple retired to their room upstairs.

Clive, watching them leave arm in arm, turned to the others, saying, "Never thought I would see this day. However, I think you all would agree with me; they make a very striking couple." Clive and those still seated in the lounge toasted Karl and Claire one more time before they also retired for the evening.

Sunday morning, the guests still at the hotel gathered for breakfast. Bill drove Ronny to Hitchin to pick up the MG. When they arrived back at the hotel, Dorothy and Julie attached some empty cans and streamers to the honeymoon car, laughing as they did so. Back inside, they all sat enjoying breakfast and waiting for Claire and Karl to come down, unaware of the decoration to the MG.

"Morning, all," said Claire as they entered. Karl, now in civilian attire, and Claire in slacks and a jumper set, looked the part of the newly married.

"I'm really famished, and it smells delicious," said Karl, holding the chair for his new bride to sit down. Moving over to Mama and Freida, he leaned over to kiss both before sitting down himself.

Mama was holding Claire's hand and had a wonderful smile across her face as she said, "My wayward sailor has finally docked his ship, and that's all thanks to my new daughter and her little MG car. We love you so much, Claire; you have brought so much to our family; sorry for my poor English. Claire, when you come back from your honeymoon, perhaps we can continue with my English classes?" concluded Mama.

"Mama, that will be my pleasure with one condition; you continue teaching me German, or should I be specific Austrian German?" Claire leaned over to kiss her mother-in-law on her damp cheek; this was a delightful day.

Karl looked at his watch, then stood up, saying, "It's time for us to think about leaving, Claire. Thank you all again for making this such a wonderful wedding. Ronny, did you bring the MG over? If so, we should think about heading out; it's going to be a long drive." Karl helped Claire stand, then told her, "Stay here with the others while I get our bags and check out."

"All accounted for, Major; now, be off with you," said General Jacks as he came around to Claire and Karl. "My dear, I wish you both a wonderful honeymoon, but Claire, don't wear him out; we desperately need him back in the BIS." The general was laughing but meant every word of getting him back soon to the BIS and the training mission to Canada that he could not discuss.

Outside, the morning was a little cloudy but warm, and everyone congregated outside around the MG to see them off. Karl, seeing his little car with all the streamers flapping in the breeze, started to chuckle, saying, "So, you think I'm going to drive with those attached? Please, help me remove them, will you, Ronny?" Their bags barely fit behind the front seats. "Darling, perhaps we should take the Wolsey instead?" asked Karl.

"No way, Sailor; this MG is as much a part of this honeymoon as we are. We have hats, scarves, and gloves to keep us warm, and the new heater I had installed last week will help. Now, get that engine started, or we'll never make it to Looe, Cornwall at this rate." Waving goodbye, they stopped halfway down the drive, realizing there was a clatter coming from the back of the car.

Karl hopped out and quickly saw the cans attached to the spare wheel, shouting, "You buggers get me a knife to cut off these cans!"

Ronny ran over with the knife he had ready. "I thought you would have at least made it to the end of the driveway?" Still laughing, they turned out of the driveway, heading west, Claire navigating.

The drive was mainly uneventful. Traffic, however, would create traffic jams near Watford and Salisbury. The sun was getting low as they entered Cornwall. With the hooded headlights, driving became difficult all vehicles were required to hood their driving lights as a wartime precaution. Claire suggested to Karl that they pull over at a pub that had a sign saying rooms available. Karl agreed with her. No need to get stressed out on their first full day as man and wife. The Cider House Inn was an old sixteenth century coach stop.

Claire said, "Stay with the car, darling; I'll see if they, in fact, have a room available for one night." Claire entered the pub and immediately fell in love with its low beam ceilings and wonderful bar. Approaching the innkeeper, Claire asked if they still had rooms available for tonight.

"Yes, we do, young lady; come upstairs with me and decide which one you would like." Claire, impressed with the way the rooms were decorated, picked the one that overlooked the front.

"How much for tonight?" asked Claire politely.

"How does a guinea sound to you, young lady? That includes breakfast for two. I'm assuming that's your husband waiting outside in the little sports car, am I right?" Claire liked hearing the innkeeper referring to her husband; it had a comfortable sound to it. Claire paid the innkeeper, then walked outside to call Karl.

"Cor, she's a smasher, Ted; lucky bugger that got her, really classy must be from London," said one of the old timers sitting at the bar drinking cider. Karl retrieved their bags and locked the car. Inside, Claire guided Karl to their room.

"Well, darling, isn't this a delightful room? The bathroom is conveniently right next door. Let's head downstairs for a nightcap, shall we?" asked Claire, pleased that their first night would be in this quaint old inn. Claire's small alarm clock woke them at 7:30 a.m. "Come on, sleepyhead; let's get washed and go downstairs for breakfast, shall we?"

Downstairs, a corner table was already set up for them where they could smell the wafting aroma of bacon coming from the kitchen. "Morning," said Maud, the innkeeper's wife. "Sleep well, did you? By the looks of you two, I would say you're on your honeymoon, am I right?"

Claire reached for Karl's hand before replying, "Yes, we are heading for Looe when we leave here. This inn was such a find. We loved it; perhaps we will stop on the way home," answered Claire. Breakfast was a real treat, fresh eggs from the hen house and bacon from a nearby farm. The only thing missing was the coffee.

"How far will we have to travel to get to Looe this morning?" asked Karl, getting a strange look from Maud.

Claire saw that look and knew how to answer it immediately. "Excuse me; I should have mentioned that my husband is Austrian, a major in the British Intelligence Service since 1937." Claire took that opportunity to brag about her husband's rank.

Maud looked at Karl, then apologized for the look she had on her face, saying, "I'm so sorry; you must think I'm really rude. I did not mean to make you uneasy. My Wil and I have two sons servicing, one in the Navy and one in the Air force. We haven't seen either of them in over two years; we still get letters from time to time, though.

Now, from here, you're about ninety minutes from Looe. The weather on the radio this morning said it will be quite warm, typical weather for Cornwall this time of year." Saying that, Maud wished them a wonderful honeymoon, then turned, returning to the kitchen.

Claire stood first, straightening her skirt, then said, "Shall we get going? If we leave right now, we'll have most of today to explore Looe. Maybe tomorrow, if it remains this warm, we can go to Sandy Beach to soak up some sun?"

Karl stood up, agreeing with her, then, returning to the room, he grabbed their bags and returned the key to Wil waiting by the bar. "Have a nice stay in Looe, Sir, and congratulations on marrying that charming lady of yours."

Karl shook his hand, then proceeded outside. The sun felt wonderful. "Karl let's take the top off and enjoy the drive; what do you say?" asked Claire as she put her scarf around her hair.

"Sounds like the right thing to do on a day like this," replied Karl. In daylight, the narrow roads made driving an absolute delight, both thoroughly enjoying the lush scenery. Arriving at the Talland Bay Hotel, Claire beamed at the choice she had made, saying, "Darling, why don't you put the top up on the car and grab the bags? I'll get us registered, alright?" With a spring in her step, Claire entered the front door. Karl watched her as she walked up the path, thinking, she is such a spirited woman; her laughter and smile are so contagious, and she's easy on the eyes as well.

Karl walked into the lobby to find Claire talking with the girl behind the desk. "Darling, this nice lady is showing me some interesting places to explore; this is going to be so nice. Let's put the bags in our room, then go exploring, shall we?" Claire led the way, carrying the smaller of the bags. Opening the door to the Honeymoon Suite, they looked out over the Cornish coast. "Oh, my God, Karl, this is so beautiful. I can't wait to go exploring along that beach. The Honeymoon Suite had a big picture window that looked over the lawn, covered with colorful flower beds. Claire stopped talking. Slowly, she turned to Karl with tears rolling down her cheeks. Her arms around his neck, she squeezed him with all her might, saying. "Forgive me, Karl; all of a sudden, I feel so alive. I'm on a cloud of happiness being here with my husband. It's overwhelming me. You must think I'm a silly so and so."

Karl replied, "Claire, you're feeling as happy as I do. We have a life ahead of us to travel and enjoy being together, so go right ahead and let all those feelings come through." Karl's self-control was becoming weakened as he held Claire in his arms, thinking, why must I leave her for so long? Standing there, looking out the window, he could feel the presence of that dark cloud trying to push its way back into his mind. Taking control, he squeezed Claire tightly, thinking, not today, you're not. "Well, let's get changed into holiday attire and head for town, shall we?" said Karl, driving those clouds out of his mind and allowing the sunshine back in.

For the rest of that week, they floated on a cloud of happiness, enjoying, and exploring the surrounding fishing villages along the coast, romantic dinners, long walks along the beach, and sunbathing on the white sand. Claire told Karl, "I need to go home with a nice golden tan. It's easy for you; you get tanned right away, but I'm a fair skinned English girl, so we usually go red first, then tan."

Every day, they enjoyed each other, making love whenever the fancy took them. Claire would repeat in her mind many times over a line Karl had said at the wedding, and that was: There is a Heaven; it's right here on Earth with you. Claire could not feel more complete. She was a married lady, totally in love with her man, and that would never change. Thinking this, she felt a pang of anxiety, realizing that when this honeymoon was over, Karl would again enter a place where danger was a way of life.

To Karl, this was the way he always envisioned married life to be, and he could not dream of anything better. On their last evening, sitting on the lawn chairs watching the sun slowly go down through a golden array of whispery clouds, Claire reached over to Karl. Taking his hand, she looked at him; they were both thinking the same thing. Tomorrow, they would return home, and Karl would again leave her for his next assignment in Canada.

"Claire, I know what you're thinking because I was doing the same; put those sad feelings aside for now and let us enjoy this evening together. After this war has ended, I promise you we will return to this very hotel. Claire, keep this picture in your mind whenever you feel down; focus on this moment, enjoying this timeless sunset. Karl was trying to pass along the mind control skills that had aided him when his life looked like it would come to an end.

"Karl, darling, you're much stronger than I. It's this thought in the back of my mind that nags at me: What will I do if you are taken away from me? I wish we could escape to some neutral country and be safe away from these visions that crowd my thoughts almost daily." Claire had sunk into self-pity, which, under the circumstances, was understandable.

"Claire, stop this right now. Block those negative thoughts; we are still here with very little time left. This is not a good way to end a perfect honeymoon." Karl was feeling her pain, and, like her, he was dreading having to return to the dangerous occupation waiting for him back in Slough.

"You're right, darling; forgive me for spoiling this wonderful evening. Take me upstairs and make love to me; make me feel alive again, will you?" Claire needed him more right now, and she would use this memory to carry her through the lonely times ahead. In a few days, she would take him to the Hitchin Station and see him off. She needed this time to prepare herself to say goodbye again for a very long time. The drive home would be enjoyable but so much quieter than a week ago. They both had things to say, but the stress of separation was preventing that from happening.

CHAPTER 3

CANADA

They arrived home late on Saturday evening, unpacked, then drove the MG to the garage, exchanging it for the Wolsey. Claire suggested they spend time that evening at the Fox, which Karl agreed would be nice. Tomorrow, they would head for Baldock to see the family and say goodbye for what could be almost nine months. Mama welcomed them home, embracing Claire as her new daughter. They all had coffee and freshly baked cake in the sitting room, Claire telling them all about the honeymoon. Karl was somewhat subdued, eyeballing Ronny to make his announcement official.

"Now that you two are home again after that wonderful honeymoon, I have some news I would like to share with you both. I told Freida and Mama a few days ago about my promotion to captain, which means extra in my pay packet. However, what I'm going to share with you all now, I have refrained from announcing, as I wanted you all together when I did so. July 15th, I will be leaving Duxford for a new duty station in Kent as the Op's Director. I shall be commuting to work much like Karl has been doing. I felt it would be easier to make this announcement once we were all together as it changes so much for us living together in Baldock. Any questions?"

Everyone was quiet digesting Ronny's announcement. Claire spoke first, "Well, I can come over more frequently to drive you to the shops and any other errands that need doing. With Karl away on assignment for eight months or possibly longer, I would much prefer to be with both of you and spend more time with Franchot. Maybe a change of scenery occasionally would help break the monotony by

54

staying with me in Hitchin. God knows there's plenty of room in that big old house; I would really love that. What I'm suggesting is we three make plans for these challenges that lie ahead of us." Claire turned to Karl for his approval. "Darling, what do you think about my suggestion?"

Karl looked at his mother and sister, then answered, "Claire, I really like the idea of you three being together more often, especially on weekends, maybe a picnic or some other outing would cheer you all up?" answered Karl. It was now time to say goodbye; for Karl, it would be a long separation, and for Ronny, a new position to adjust to. "Mama, Freida, it seems like I'm always saying goodbye. This time, it is much harder because I will be far away from you all. Hugging his mother and sister, he told them how much he loved them and asked them to keep him in their thoughts.

"Freida, write me when you can, so I don't lose my ability to read German? Ronny, old man, congratulations again on the promotion. I know what that entails with the added responsibilities; please, stay in touch and let me know how it's going?"

Claire was dreading this moment, "Mama, can I come over tomorrow after I leave the office? You know how I get when Karl goes away," said Claire.

Mama took her hand and answered by saying, "Why don't we have Ronny drop us off, so we can stay with you for a few days? Would you like that?" answered Mama.

"Oh, please, that would be wonderful!" Those last few minutes pulled on Karl's heartstrings. How he wished that this damn war could be over so that life could return to normal. Waving out the car window as they drove around the corner back onto Letchworth Road, heading towards Hitchin, Karl's heart was sinking. The thought of saying farewell to his wife tomorrow morning would be a very emotional time for them both.

Arriving home, Karl went upstairs to start packing his big travel bag. Claire made coffee, then took two mugs with her upstairs, where she asked if she could help pack. "Karl, please take my scarf for when it gets cold. New Brunswick, I'm told, can get extremely cold in winter, and when you put this around your neck, it will bring us closer together."

Karl stopped what he was doing, saying, "Of course, darling, but you should know that I keep a picture of you always in my mind. Claire, how I love you! Let me finish packing; then we can have an early night as I want another vivid image in my mind of my sexy wife making love to me." Karl was trying to cheer her up as he continued packing.

Claire, hearing him say that, decided to give him a treat for that memory he mentioned. Karl had a hot bath, then climbed into bed, organizing some files he would take with him. The bathroom door opened, and Karl looked up to see Claire in that pink nightgown. Karl's reaction was immediate, with the files and briefcase landing on the floor as Claire climbed onto the bed, pulled the bedsheets back, and slowly kissed Karl's chest to arouse him.

"Darling, you are responsible for turning me into this new person I've become. I can't get enough of my husband; Karl, you complete me in every way." That night, they made love numerous times until exhausted, they fell asleep in each other's arms. The alarm clock went off at 0500 hours, and Karl banged the top to silence it. Getting out of bed, he went into the bathroom, where he shut the door to let Claire sleep a little longer. Drying his face after a close shave, he went back into the bedroom to find the lights on, the bed made, and the aroma of fresh coffee coming from downstairs.

Claire is always so efficient; why am I not surprised at this? Dressing in his field uniform, he proceeded down the stairs to find his wife in the kitchen, making her husband a hearty English breakfast. The table was set with mugs of piping hot coffee.

Claire, in her housecoat, was making eggs which was a real treat in war starved England. "Darling, sit down; I can't let you go off on an empty stomach, can I? It's almost ready."

Karl walked up behind her, kissing her neck as she worked over the stove. "Claire, you didn't have to do all this. Coffee would have been just fine." Karl could feel the tears welling up in his eyes as he looked at her. No matter what time of the day or night, she would always captivate him with her poise, even in her housecoat.

"Darling, my man will never go without anything. Didn't I prove that to you last night? Now, sit down, and let's have breakfast together, then I'll run upstairs to get ready." The drive to the station was quick, as usual, with Claire holding his arm tightly.

"Claire, I know I always say this, but today, it will be especially difficult saying goodbye, so why don't you drop me off? That's better than the two of us shedding tears."

Claire, moving her head from side to side, quietly replied, "Not a chance, Sailor. I want every minute I can get with you, so get that out of your mind!" Claire was trying to appear stronger than she actually felt. Karl purchased a one-way ticket to Slough, then, carrying his two large travel bags, proceeded through the tunnel to the platform with Claire at his side. The minutes seemed to drag by, making small talk difficult. In the distance, that familiar sound of the approaching train intensified the tension they both were feeling. "Karl, darling, please try not to worry too much about Mama, Freida, and me. We have each other to lean on. Oh, God, I am going to miss you! Why does it have to be so long and so far away across the Atlantic? Darling, kiss me; I need to feel your lips against mine one more time."

The emotions Claire was holding back could not be held back any longer. It was now time to say goodbye. Karl swooped her up into his arms. Feeling her tremble made him feel like those black clouds in his mind had now turned into a thunderstorm of mixed feelings. "Claire, my wonderful wife, how I'm missing you already. One last kiss, then I must board the train; I'll call you from Slough tonight." One final embrace, then he climbed into the compartment. Standing by the window, he tried to maintain a smile, but the anxiety of separation was making that very difficult.

The train shuddered, followed by the shrill of the conductor's whistle as the train gathered momentum out of the station. "Claire, please find time to write me every day, and I will do the same. Stay positive, darling; remember, you have a husband that loves you very much." Claire stood there sobbing as she watched the train leave the station with Karl waving and throwing kisses through the engine's smoke.

Arriving at the Slough Train Station, Karl carried his two travel bags out of the station to the waiting staff car. "Nice to see you, Sir, and congratulations on your wedding," said Charlie, his driver.

"Thank you, Corporal. I would like to say glad to be back, but that's not the case. I'm missing my new wife." Karl didn't wish to elaborate.

"Sir, they told me to drop you off at the gymnasium; that's the meeting place for those traveling today," said Charlie. In front of the gym, an RAF bus was parked, already loading luggage and equipment. "Sir, I'll give your bags to those chaps loading the bus if that's alright with you."

Karl nodded his approval as he exited the car. Inside the gym, people were milling around, drinking tea, and talking mainly about the flight to Canada. Karl looked around the gym until he saw his group, "Morning, chaps; ready for today's trip?" Karl was taking five of his best agents; his second in command would assume command of the division in his absence. "Captain Meyer, good morning; come to see us off, have you?" asked Karl.

"Correct, Sir, do you have any last minute instructions for me?" asked his second in command.

"I'm sure I'll think of something before we leave, but more than likely, I'll think of something halfway across the Atlantic. While we're waiting, I have a phone call I need to make. Please, excuse me." Karl needed to hear Claire's voice before leaving. Karl found an empty office and placed the call to Claire's office. The receptionist transferred him to Beverly. "How is the new Mrs. Vita this morning?" Karl was feeling Bev out to see how Claire was handling his departure earlier that morning.

"Good and bad, let me put you through, Sir," answered Bev. "Karl, darling, I didn't expect to hear from you so soon; is everything alright? Is your departure still on schedule?" Claire was putting up a good front, but Karl could sense she was close to tears.

"Claire, I had to call you before we leave because I am missing you so very much. These next eight plus months will be torture for both of us. Stay strong and positive, my darling." Karl meant every word. "Remember, mail could be up to a week, depending on airmail shipments. I just needed to hear your voice before we left. Must go, darling; I think they're about to start the pre-operations roll call. I love you, my sweet, darling Claire."

Karl was about ready to hang up when Claire said quietly, almost in tears, "Love you too, Sailor; write as soon as you arrive." Claire hung up the phone, then broke down crying.

Beverly came in carrying a hot cup of tea, saying, "Claire, drink this and take a few quiet minutes to regain your composure." Beverly closed the office door behind her, leaving Claire holding her picture of Karl in her hands.

Back in the gym, everyone had started to find a seat before Clive entered. A loud "Attention" came from Bill from the makeshift podium as Clive approached.

"At ease, chaps, we just want to go over some route details with you before you depart. From here, you will be transported to RAF St. Mawgan in Cornwall. Before you start complaining about this, let me tell you we are joining up with two other groups at that aerodrome.

"Air Command is stretched thin, so operations had to juggle things around to accommodate today's travel arrangements. From there, you will fly to Prestwick, Scotland. Once on the ground, one of the other groups will deplane, and some of our Northern chaps will join you. I'm led to believe the C-54 heavy transport aircraft will take on extra fuel and some extra cargo before the long flight out over the Denmark Straits to the next stop in Reykjavik, Iceland. Once you land there, you will change planes to another C-54 operated by the Royal Canadian Air force. This flight will depart on the final leg to RCAF Aerodrome Saint John in New Brunswick, Canada. Gentlemen, it will be a long trip, so try to be tolerant of today's route. Believe me, it will be worth it not having to travel there on a military transport ship.

Karl made his way over to Clive and Bill to make his farewell. "Are you worn out yet, Karl, hearing all about today's flight? By the way, Julie called me just before we all got together. She told me she and Dorothy are taking the train this Friday to spend the weekend with Claire. This all happened less than an hour ago after you spoke with Claire. The girls felt she should not be left alone on her first weekend. Julie's mother is going to watch our daughters, so you should be relieved she will have company this weekend."

"My mother and sister will have to put off staying in Hitchin for another week, I guess. Chaps, as always, I find myself thanking you both for always watching out for Claire and myself you're such good friends." Karl shook hands with his friends, then, stepping back, he saluted them before heading off in the direction of his group waiting by the exit.

The coach trip to Cornwall was uneventful but slow going through many villages and towns before arriving at the aerodrome six and half hours later. English double daylight savings made it feel like early afternoon instead of almost 1900 hours. Getting off the bus, it felt good to walk and stretch after that long coach ride. Karl and his group followed the RAF first lieutenant into the operations building; then, a sergeant made a roll call to ensure everyone was accounted for. Then, he led them into the cavernous hangar to meet up with the other group flying with them up to Prestwick.

"Gentlemen, please, follow me, and please stay together. There is a lot of activity tonight with planes moving around the dispersal area; we don't want to lose one of you to a propeller blade, now, do we?" said the sergeant. The four engine C-54 was relatively new, manufactured by the Douglas Aircraft Company in Southern California. Compared to the other aircraft parked on the ramp, it was very streamlined and so much larger. At the rear of the plane, a crew member waited to check them off as they climbed the steep stairs into the cabin.

"The officers' section is the first eight rows in the front, then open seating for the remainder of you passengers. Please, find a seat and strap in as quickly as you can; the captain would like to be airborne in the next fifteen minutes," said the Air Force air hostess. Slowly, the first propeller turned until a big blue gray puff of smoke was accompanied by the radial engine spluttering into life, followed one by one by the other three. The cabin noise was loud but tolerable as the cockpit crew completed their preflight tests.

The plane lurched as the captain released the brakes and proceeded out to the active runway. Waiting at the end of the runway, the crew performed their final engine run-up, then throttled back until given clearance to takeoff. Karl sat by the window, resting his head against his clenched fist. He looked out over the parked aircraft as they sped by, followed by the nose wheel rotating toward the heavens. Everyone was reasonably quiet, each one thinking of their loved ones left behind in war torn England.

The three-and-a-half-hour flight was surprisingly enjoyable; Karl had never been on an aircraft this fast or this big. Landing in Prestwick, the captain requested all those traveling on to Reykjavik remain seated as the time here would be short. Karl stood in the aisle to stretch his legs. Leaning over his seat back, he watched the group walk away across the ramp to the terminal entrance. Simultaneously, another group walked toward the aircraft. Karl strained as he focused on one particular lady wearing a captain's uniform. He continued watching her as she walked toward the boarding stairway. My God, it's Hazel; I forgot she was part of this detail. Well, at least I'll have someone to talk to on this long next leg; that's assuming she would like to sit next to me.

As the officers boarded, Karl remained standing with the window seat next to his unoccupied. Hazel entered the door, turning to walk down the narrow aisle. Looking up, she caught sight of Karl standing, facing backward, a big smile across his face. Is he expecting me to sit with him, or is he just happy to see me? She pointed toward her chest, silently asking, do you want me to sit with you? Hazel thought about her gesture to Karl. This bloke has just got married, and I'm still vulnerable anywhere near him. How ironic that I will see more of him over the next eight months than his own wife will. Blimey, what are the chances of this happening? I was a second once before; that won't happen again, but if he wants company on this flight, I can't see any harm in sitting next to him.

Approaching Karl, she smiled, seeing his head nodding and pointing to the empty window seat. "Karl, I don't seem to be able to avoid you. I'm assuming you're asking me to sit next to you, is that right?" Hazel could still feel the excitement of being with Karl, remembering those intense but too few intimate moments, never to be repeated.

"Hazel, so good to see you; now, the flight won't be so dull. Let me put your briefcase and coat overhead for you. Hazel slid over into the window seat. Karl sat down next to her, smiling as he buckled his seatbelt, "So, where shall we start?" asked Karl, feeling happier now that he had someone, he knew to spend this flight with.

Hazel turned her head to look at his left hand. She reached over and took his hand, running her index finger over his wedding band, saying, "Well, Karl, you did it. You're now a married man, so no fooling around anymore, or I'll have to tell Claire, won't I?"

Karl chuckled, knowing this once hostile relationship was turning into a true and lasting friendship, although those times together would remain locked away in both their memories. The hours passed with time for talk, sandwiches, and even time to catch up on some sleep. The overhead PA came on with an announcement from the cockpit. "This is the captain speaking; we are making our descent into Reykjavik, Iceland. Once we have parked this bird, remain seated until instructed by a crew member to deplane. For those continuing on to Washington, D.C., you still need to deplane while we refuel; if all goes well, we will be departing within the hour. Thank you."

Karl stood up first, then reached over to give Hazel his hand. "Hazel, you looked tired. It's been a long day so far," said Karl as he retrieved their things from the overhead rack. Once they were off the plane, a young Canadian lieutenant yelled for everyone's attention, standing by the aircraft boarding ladder.

"For all of you going on to Saint John's, follow me, and those flying on to Washington in this aircraft, follow that sergeant over there."

Karl's group walked across the ramp to a small wooden building, then they were instructed, "Please, wait in here until your aircraft arrives in about thirty minutes or so." Forty-five minutes passed, and still, no aircraft and no one in authority other than the accompanying sergeant to be seen. Karl was about to pull rank and demand an explanation when a Jeep pulled up with an American Air Force lieutenant who announced that they should board the buses pulling up in front of them. The bus took them over to another building on the other side of the dispersal area. Standing around once again, there was little to talk about other than how tiring this journey was so far.

"Sir, where did they say we would be flying to next?" asked Sergeant Michael Kleber.

"Sergeant, the original itinerary lists our final flight directly into St John's. Then again, that American lieutenant thought that there may be a modification to that itinerary; here he comes now, so let's listen, shall we?"

"If I can have your attention, sorry for leaving you here wondering where your aircraft is. Well, up until ten minutes ago, operations were going to reroute you through Gander, then on to St. John. By a stroke of good fortune, an inbound C-54 from Montreal was dropping off passengers to connect with the flight you came in on. It was scheduled to deadhead back to its base in Montreal. We are refueling that aircraft over on the other side of the field, and when that is done, we will transport you to it," said the very apologetic lieutenant.

"What about our luggage and equipment; where is that right now?" asked another member of the team.

"That luggage and your crates are being loaded as we speak; again, sorry for the confusion, and here come our buses."

The group boarded the C-54, sitting in almost the same seats as the first flight. "God, it feels so nice to sit on padded seats, doesn't it?" asked Hazel. "Karl, I don't mean to be rude, but I must get some sleep. I'm sorry for becoming a dull travel companion." Hazel took her bag and placed it against the window frame as a pillow, immediately falling asleep as the plane climbed out and headed southwest toward New Brunswick.

Karl thought about the next six plus hours of flying and the 1400 plus air miles before they would finally touch down in St. John's and the onward road trip to their new base in Milledgeville. How long *will it take to get from the aerodrome to our camp?* Thinking this, he also gave in to overdue sleep.

The announcement from the cockpit made Karl jump into full consciousness, his head against Hazel's shoulder and her head against his. "Hazel, time to wake up; we are on the descent into St. John's Aerodrome."

"How did we get so comfortable like this?" Hazel stretched her arms out and chuckled at what she had just said.

Someone in the back yelled, "Finally! For a minute, I thought we would be in the air for another bloody day!" Everyone hearing this started shouting with relief that they had arrived. Outside, the weather was very warm, even though it was 2000 hours' local time. The summers in this part of Canada, on average, ranged from the low 50s to mid-80s. Today, however, was exceptionally hot, near 90 degrees Fahrenheit.

Hazel, feeling the heat, said, "Bloody hell, it's really hot on this concrete, isn't it?"

Karl removed his tunic, then answered, "Better off without these wool tunics; you'll feel better, Hazel, if you take yours off as well," reaching over to help Hazel remove hers.

"Karl, you devil, the last time you helped me take off my tunic, you took off a lot more than that!"

First, Karl gave her a blank stare, then Hazel broke out laughing, causing Karl to do the same. "Hazel, I swear to God, when you put your foot into it!" Karl stopped there and decided it was funny but should go no further.

Inside the terminal, it was hotter than outside, so a few of them sat on a bench outside, drinking bottles of water and soda. Two military buses pulled up in front of them. The driver in the first bus took out his clipboard, then took a headcount, proceeding to call names for those that should board this first bus. Karl, being one of the senior officers, was told the front seat was reserved for him.

"Thank you, I'll board after everyone has boarded," answered Karl. One by one, they boarded, then the driver announced, "All the rest of you can board the second bus."

Karl looked at Hazel, asking the driver, "Why was Captain Collins not called?"

"Don't know, Sir; I just go by the list here." The driver was getting ready for the major with the funny accent to scream at him as he became more irritated.

"Is that seat next to mine taken, Corporal?" asked Karl. "No, Sir, it's left empty for your comfort."

Karl turned to Hazel and said, "Climb in and sit next to me; enough of this stupidity."

Hazel shook her head and said in a soothing voice that would cool Karl's erupting temper, "Sir, it's perfectly alright. I don't mind where they put me. Just get me to a hot bath; that's all I need right now." Hazel put her hand on his arm as she said this.

"Nonsense, now, get on board, Captain, and that's an order!" barked the reply from Karl. Hazel shook her head, proceeding as instructed, climbing into the bus. The fifty some miles did not take long at all, but the temperature in the cabin was stifling.

Even with the numerous fans running, everyone was sweating in their heavy wool uniforms. Hazel did not say much but needed Karl to understand he did not have to shield her like that, nor should he pull rank like that again. She just put it down to everyone being tired, and their nerves also frayed.

Hazel spoke to Karl quietly, "Karl, what you did back there was honorable; however, it will send the wrong signal. As much as I appreciate the gesture, please don't repeat it. We will be here for a long time. I, however, will be here even longer. When you all return to England, I will be heading to Washington and my new duty posting. Remember I told you in my letter that I was applying for an overseas posting?

"Karl let's make a pact right now on this bloody hot coach, and that is, we have found a place always to remain close friends, and I, for one, will cherish what we almost had before that. But that was then, and this is now. Karl, I was not going to say this ever again, but indulge me by letting me say this one last time. I will always love you, Karl, no matter where I go and no matter who I end up with. Wish the best for me, Sailor, and let's enjoy each other's company while we are here, shall we?" Hazel took his hand and squeezed it. "There, that's a load off my chest. Now, let's talk about tomorrow, shall we?"

Karl turned to look at her, then squeezed her hand back before answering. "Hazel, you know it was always that black cloud that held me back; the tragic memory of your friend and my love would not allow me to move forward. With Claire, there is no black cloud, no skeletons, and over the last six months, fewer of those dangerous nightmares. Hazel, you and I will always share that special bond. I'm pleased we have been able to find this new place to remain kindred spirits." Karl chuckled, then finally continued by saying, "Hazel, I should not be saying this right now, but sitting here with you makes me remember, you are one hot woman, and the lucky chap that finally places his ring on your finger better have a lot of energy."

First, Hazel looked at him with a smirk, then chucked. "Maybe, Karl, you could coach him because, Sailor, you are the best in that department." On a bus far from home, two people had discovered that there could be a bond, closeness, and tender friendship after being intimate lovers.

The next four months were filled with hectic, long hours and strenuous days and weeks training new recruits that passed through every six weeks. The pace and strain were starting to show on all of them. Most nights, Karl would have supper in the mess hall and maybe a drink in the lounge before retiring to his quarters to write his daily letter to Claire. The long days of summer were changing to the prettier days of autumn. Cooler, drier weather was setting in, preparing the people of New Brunswick for the long cold weeks of winter that lay ahead.

In one of those letters, he wrote about Hazel and the friendship they had found, a new place where they could remain friends. Claire's return answer had a comical theme to it about friendship. Karl knew he could tell her anything; that was the promise they made each other on day one. He always ended it with: Beyond the shore of another land, I send my devotion to my wife, my lifelong companion, and always my love, your husband, Karl. Good night, sweet dreams, only ?? days left.

Christmas was a trying time for the people of the BIS. They were far from home, and only the friendship of others in the same boat made it tolerable. The BIS and ATS girls made decorations for the mess hall, and some Canadian airmen supplied two very tall Christmas trees. The local church in Milledgeville very generously brought over decorations to turn those trees into things of beauty. Karl wrote to Claire, telling her how thoughtful the Canadians were. Their kindness and willingness to create a homey place were so very touching. Karl had not seen Hazel in over two months. The building her group trained in was on the opposite side of the camp, and from what Karl had heard, she was seeing an American captain assigned to her training operation.

On Christmas Eve, a big party was planned for everyone. Hazel's new boyfriend, Captain Steven Kowalski, pulled a few strings to have a Canadian Air Force band provide live music. The kitchen staff, with the help of the locals, made a magnificent buffet. The bar was well stocked, and the first hour was on the camp commander; that may not have been the best idea, but it surely created the holiday spirit.

Karl had booked a call home to Claire at 1500 hours to wish her and the family a Merry Christmas. Claire had sent Karl his Christmas gift in advance to make sure it would arrive a couple of days early. Receiving his parcel, he had written a long letter to her, thanking her for the extravagant gift of a silver cigarette case with his initials engraved in the center. Two weeks earlier, he had also sent his package containing gifts for the family and a larger package containing Claire's gift. The previous month, on his weekend off, he had taken a bus to St. John's to look for a suitable present for his classy wife—no easy task as she had about everything he could think of.

Walking along the main street, he came across a leather shop; the sign in the window said, all items hand made. Karl thought for a moment, then entered the shop, knowing precisely what he would buy her. "Excuse me, can you make a briefcase for me if I sketch it out for you? I would like it in oxblood leather with a detachable shoulder strap as well as a handle. Could you also make a matching handbag in the same color leather? I like the style of that brown one if you can copy it for me." Karl was on a roll and enjoyed every minute of it. The leather smith also agreed to add her initials to the center of the briefcase flap, embossed in a gold tone.

In his office, he waited patiently for the phone to ring. Looking at his watch, he saw he still had about two minutes to wait, so he poured another cup of coffee from the thermal carafe always on the corner of his desk. The phone rang at precisely 1500 hours. "One moment, Sir," said the operator. "The phone is ringing; go ahead, Mrs. Vita. Major Vita is already on the line." Karl was getting very emotional, hearing Claire's voice at the other end.

"Karl, darling, is it you? Oh, my God, just to hear your voice talking to me is wonderful and so very clear. Now, tell me everything, but before you do that, let me thank you for the gorgeous briefcase and handbag. You know my taste so very well. Thank you, darling, thank you. The gifts you included for your family were greatly appreciated. Franchot can't put that model airplane down needless to say, they all send their best wishes and love. Mama told me they were a little late sending your gift packages, so expect them shortly. Sailor, you are such a thoughtful man; I'm so lucky you're mine.

"Now, let me tell you about an unexpected phone call I received three hours ago! Would you believe me if I told you? Hazel Collings called me. She got my number from Mama. Karl, what a wonderful chat we had! She was so complimentary of how you took care of her on the way over to Canada. I bet you didn't know about her new boyfriend, did you? Probably not. She also told me she has not seen you in over two months, and you probably had no idea about her new friend, is that correct? She went on to say that she was looking forward to seeing you tonight at the party. Hazel is really looking forward to introducing you to Steven; that's the new boyfriend's name. She and I talked more about well, let's say, girl talk that may be told some other day.

"Darling, I enjoyed that chat so much that my conscience was starting to bother me, so I apologized to her for taking you away from her. She really is a wonderful gal with a very kind heart. As we talked more, and, of course, most of it was about you, I started feeling terrible. She guessed as much and told me it was meant to be, saying the relationship was rocky the day she left on that mission that none of you will ever discuss with me.

"Karl, she still loves you and is still very sad at losing you, but darling, in a strange way, she took comfort in knowing you and I found each other and got married. That surprise phone call made me feel so much better now that the ice between us is broken. Before hanging up, she closed by asking if one day after this war comes to an end, would we be open to a visit from her here in Hitchin. That, of course, would be with your approval, Major." Claire stopped talking, waiting for Karl's response.

"Well, darling, now you have come up for air; my news is relatively boring. Work keeps me busy at least ten to twelve hours a day. Other than a nightcap in the lounge, my life is not much without you." Karl continued by asking her how her sister was doing and what plans her family had for the Christmas holidays. He was pleased to hear that Mama and the family were staying in Hitchin for three days.

"Right now, they are in the living room by the fire. It's so homey all together like this, but one person is missing, and that's the man of the house. Ronny arrived earlier in the day, totally exhausted. Everyone in the office sends their best wishes and a safe journey home. It's time for us to hang up, my darling. Please stay safe and hurry home to me. I'm not much without you, Karl."

Karl was choked up as he listened to her saying goodbye. "Good night, my sweet Claire. I will try to book a call next week; kiss everyone for me." With that, he returned the phone to its cradle.

He returned to the party and found everyone having a wonderful time, drinking, eating, and enjoying the music. Many were out on the dance floor, raising hell. Karl stood on the sidelines, wishing he and Claire could also be out there dancing, but that would have to wait till next year. He felt a hand slide around his arm as he stood there, which made him react somewhat. "Down, Tiger, it's only me, Hazel. Are you mad at me for calling Claire? I hope not because I enjoyed our frank discussion so very much. I think it helped me understand more about what happened. As you have a habit of saying, the circle is almost closed. Now, put that drink down and join me on the dance floor. You must do this as I promised Claire. I also said I would drag you if necessary, and Karl, I will do this for her. I haven't yet met her in person, but I feel like I know her, and we'll be lifelong friends. She is so easy to talk to."

Hazel, taking his hand, guided him out on the floor, kissing him on the cheek, saying, "And that's also from Claire, handsome."

Karl looked at her, replying, "And this is from me." He turned her head, looked her in her eyes, and kissed her softly on the lips. In the middle of the dance floor, two people, once lovers, now friends, discovered that love that was would always be there but never again more than this.

"Karl, this is getting too weird. Come on; let me introduce my new friend, Steven. I think you will approve; he's sitting at our table over there." Hazel's heart was beating faster, thinking back to when she met with Clive and told him the chances of seeing Karl again would never happen. But here they were, dancing, and yes, he kissed her as a friend never to be repeated.

"Major Vita, say hello to Captain Steven Kowalski." The American captain immediately stood and offered his hand to his superior officer, saying, "Major, so very pleased to make your acquaintance. Hazel speaks of you often, and, quite honestly, it makes me wonder if I can live up to the standard she has set to become her friend." Steven was obviously very intimidated by the charismatic officer standing in front of him.

"Steven, first, drop the rank; the name is Karl. Secondly, my impression of you is that you are a polite, well-spoken Yank. Hazel, you have found yourself a very nice chap. I hope you have fun together, and Steven, remember this, put one foot out of line with Miss Collins, and you will have me to deal with. Now, let's you and I have a whiskey together, so I can give you the do's and don'ts when it comes to Hazel. What do you say?" Karl looked at Hazel as he said that, and she grinned with her unspoken approval, clearly loving every minute.

"I told you he would be sarcastic in his likable way, didn't I?" concluded Hazel.

On Christmas day, virtually everyone in the English contingency attended a wonderful lunch that had been prepared for them, then spent the remainder of the day relaxing and enjoying each other's company, drinking, and telling outlandish stories until it was closing time. The English tradition of Boxing Day was not observed; instead, it was treated as another day of training. For Karl, his day was filled with the tedious task of writing trainees' progress reports. How he hated doing this; he longed to be on a mission that would utilize his many skills in the cloak and dagger world of the Intelligence Service.

1943 came in with lots of conflicting reports from around the world. Karl's calendar was getting closer to the day when he would pack for the long flight home to Claire. He had not seen Hazel since Christmas Eve, which he expected. He was genuinely happy she had met Steven, and something in the back of his head told him that Steven would be the one for her. He continued booking a phone call to Claire every three weeks; most of the time, they talked about things going on in England but rarely about life in his camp. On one of those calls, Claire had told him about a long letter she had received from Hazel several weeks back.

"I'm so happy for her, darling; she reminds me of how I was when I met you for the first time. I was never a good single, and I think Hazel is cut from the same cloth as I am. After you two separated, she meandered along, going through the motions but never being whole. She told me how you intimidated Steven then made good friends with him. She said if Steven could pass the Karl personality test, that was a good sign to take the next step, whatever that meant." Claire finished by adding, "My away calendar is getting shorter. Only ten or so weeks until you are home again, darling. These will be the longest ten weeks for me. Good night, remember you have a lady back in Hitchin pining for her man to be home."

By mid-February, the change of command was being implemented. Only a few weeks to go, and Karl's group would be returning to Slough and then home for a deserved leave.

Daydreaming about that last day, Karl was brought back by the phone ringing. The receptionist on the other end announced, "Captain Collings calling on #3, Sir."

"Thank you, put her through," Karl's spirits were heightened hearing this. "Hazel, nice to hear from you. How are things going for you? Keeping busy, I'm sure." Karl's sixth sense told him she was calling to say goodbye.

Hazel waited before speaking, "Karl, this is a sad and good day for me. In three days, I will be leaving for Washington and my new duty post. This mission originally flustered me, wondering how you and I could work together. Thankfully, it worked out just fine, didn't it? I'm leaving with a new level of confidence that I'm finally happy with. Claire gave me that, and you were always watching out for me, even if you won't admit it. You scared the hell out of Steven. By the way, he will be posted back to his home base in Baltimore when you all leave, so that's working out nicely. He has invited me to spend a long weekend with his parents sometime in May." Hazel went quiet, waiting for Karl's response.

"Hazel, I'm actually very relieved at this news. You know I will always worry about you. Tell me; is this relationship with Steven getting serious?" questioned Karl, knowing the answer already.

"Karl, you bloody Intelligence bugger, you already know that answer, don't you?" Hazel would always know when his line of questioning meant he already knew the answer. "Karl, when I leave for my new assignment in Washington, I'm not sure when we will see each other at least until after this war is over anyway. Can we have a goodbye drink tonight, just you and me, so we can talk openly?" Hazel was feeling somewhat sad, knowing it would be many years before she could meet up with Karl again and meet her new friend Claire.

"Absolutely, Hazel, how about 1830 hours in the lounge?" replied Karl.

"See you there, handsome." The phone went dead with Karl still holding the receiver to his ear. Sitting there, he allowed his mind to go on one of its journeys into the past. Returning the phone to its cradle, he smiled, thinking how everything has a funny way of working out. I'm willing to bet Steven has already asked her to marry him, and that's the real reason for getting together tonight. I'm also inclined to believe that matchmaker wife of mine, Claire, has given her advice on how to proceed. Women, they are always scheming at something! With that, he chuckled, returning to the stack of files in front of him. The hours ticked away the afternoon, and soon it would be time for Karl to head to the officer's lounge. Looking at his Lecoultre watch, he stashed the pile of files in front of him in his overnight safe, then headed to the lounge.

Sitting at a private table in an alcove, he ordered a bottle of Molson Canadian beer. Taking a long swig, he could feel the cool liquid going down his throat. Unlike the English, Canadians drank their beer chilled, and Karl was starting to like it more with every bottle. Feeling a lot more comfortable, he unbuttoned his tunic and reclined in his chair, enjoying his beer. Almost at the point of falling asleep, he jumped at the sensation of a soft kiss on his cheek and a familiar fragrance filling his nostrils. He looked up at Hazel, who was smiling down at him.

"Karl, I did not mean to startle you like that. You looked so peaceful sitting there with your hand firmly around that bottle."

Hazel sat down next to him, and Karl asked, "Beer or whiskey, you good looking lady?" Returning with two bottles of the same Molson beer in frosted glasses, he said, "Here you go, Hazel. Let's drink to times gone by and better times yet to come." Karl, saying that, was setting the stage for her to share the troubles she was wrestling with. "Hazel, I know why you're here, so relax; I'm here for you." Karl took her hand, and he could feel her tension. In a comforting voice, he asked, "Hazel, correct me if I'm wrong or out of line. You asked to see me tonight, not so much about you leaving in a few days, but you're really looking for my advice on whether to accept Steven's proposal of marriage, is that correct?" Karl looked at her troubled face, then watched it change as she nodded in agreement.

"Karl, your rabbit ears are at it again. Is there nothing you don't second guess? I've never been able to surprise you. Obviously, you're right. I'm so confused. It's like I've been in the same position too many times before, and God knows, being that close with you has made me very leery about making another commitment. If I accept his proposal, I will end up living in the States. That's a big sacrifice for me. You know how I love England and the place I grew up in." Hazel turned to Karl before continuing, "Tell me, Karl, what shall I do?"

Karl thought quickly before answering her. "Hazel, do you love him? If you do, is it strong enough to make America your new home? You realize this is the same problem I had to wrestle with, knowing I would not be returning to Vienna after the war. This is a sensitive question that I will now ask you and let me apologize in advance if it's too painful for you. Hazel, is this love on the rebound? Don't answer that if you prefer not to. Hazel, talking to you like this reminds me so much of Claire in many ways.

"You know, one of the first things she told me was that she really does not like being single but is very much the marrying type. Remember, Hazel, I know you intimately, and let me add to that, when I was all banged up, you fussed over me like a mother hen. You pulled me through, Hazel, and that will always bind us. No matter where we are, nothing will ever come between us. Again, I ask you, is this really love or a powerful need to settle down with just one man?"

Hazel looked down at the floor, composing her response. She looked up with tears in the corners of her eyes, "My darling, Karl, you are blunt, aren't you? I believe I am in love with him, and if I must live in Newport, Rhode Island, I will. But know this—my true love will always be you, but you already know that don't you, my psychic Intelligence officer. Admit it; you already know these things."

Hazel stood up, straightening her uniform, not taking her eyes off Karl. "I guess you have told me what I'm going to do. Promise me, Karl, we will always stay in touch. It would devastate me if I lost that thread. By the way, Claire has promised me that she would like Steven and me to visit you in Hitchin after the war, and that is something you can bet on. She also told me I should pour my heart out to you as she also did not so long ago. Well, Karl, time for us to part again. Give me a big hug and damn military politeness, kiss me goodbye. Claire gave me permission if you're wondering."

Karl scooped her up in his arms, kissing her farewell. Everyone in the lounge started whistling and cheering. Little did they know this was the last farewell for Hazel and Karl. Walking back to his quarters, he thought more about the advice he had given Hazel. Was it the right thing to say? His conscience was bothering him, filling his head with guilt at the course of events that were now torturing Hazel. Leaving England would be difficult for her, and his fear was it would throw a wrench into a marriage yet to be consummated.

Wednesday morning, Karl rose early, putting his parka on to ward off the piercing wind. He walked over to the American main building to inquire if Captain Kowalski was still in the building. The receptionist answered, "Sorry, Sir, he left about thirty minutes ago to take his girlfriend to St. John's Aerodrome. Is there any message I can give him when he returns?" Karl took a pad out of his jacket and wrote: Steven, would you like to have dinner with me this evening if you're free? Cheers, Karl Vita.

Karl got a call late morning that Steven would be glad to join him after 1830 hours. Sitting in the mess hall, Karl took his time to write his daily letter to Claire. As he sipped his beer, he did not see Steven enter. "Major, glad you invited me to join you tonight. I really could do with the company."

Karl smiled, then flagged the steward to get two beers. "So, tell me, how was it seeing Hazel off this morning? Not a show of tears, I hope. Steven, the main reason I asked you to dine with me this evening is selfish on my part. I'm not sure what Hazel has told you about us and the rocky road we have traveled."

Steven stopped Karl, saying, "Karl, not to interrupt you, but Hazel has told me just about everything concerning your relationship. She said this morning that she would consent to marry me; however, she was emphatic that I knew she still had strong feelings for you, Sir. Correct me if I'm wrong, but that also applies to you, am I right?"

Karl looked directly at the young captain and replied, "Yes, that is correct, and by the way, my wife Claire is also aware of the bond Hazel, and I share. When we were training in Scotland before the outbreak of the war, her closest friend at the time, my fiancée, was tortured and killed in a deliberate crash by resistance fighters trying to save them from reaching a Gestapo interrogation center while on a mission in Germany.

"Unbeknownst to me, Hazel was also on that mission and shared with Kitty that she was in love with me. Kitty was sympathetic to how she felt; she was that kind of friend. Several years later, we met again in a field hospital after I lost my ship off the beaches of Dunkirk. I was badly injured. Hazel, along with others, pulled me through, and I will be eternally grateful for that. Helping me the way she did turned into a love affair that would go nowhere. I was still in love with Kitty, which led to the breakup, this I did not handle very well. That guilt will always be with me. I'm trying to tell you that this bond will always be there, and you must believe me, it will not interfere with your plans to marry her. Hazel may appear to be confused and maybe a little frail right now. She is facing a big decision to leave everything she loves about England, including her family, for a new life in far off Rhode Island. This is not easy for her. Is her love for you strong enough to carry her through those times of homesickness?"

Karl stopped talking, taking a big swig of his drink, "Well, Steven, I hope I haven't upset you too much, and please excuse my being so blunt. What happens to Hazel is very much my business, and I hope you can live with that."

"Sir, I can see that you are trying to protect Hazel. I do appreciate that in times of war, relationships take on a different meaning. As I said, she has bared her soul to me, and I believe, with time, I can help her find a better place, a place where she will enjoy all that our lives together will produce. You have my word on that, Sir. As for England, I will make sure we visit every year, so expect a visit from us in Hitchin." Steven moved forward, stretching out his hand for Karl to grasp.

"Steven, my instincts about you are right on. I just needed to clear the air and make sure you are alright with me protecting Hazel. So, my new Yank friend, pull out your wallet; you're buying the next round or maybe two."

"Not to burst your bubble, Karl, but Hazel did warn me that you would try to unhinge me. That was a really good hosing."

Karl's face became stern. "I'm glad you took it the right way, my new Yankee friend," replied Karl.

CHAPTER 4

HOME SWEET HOME

The final day brought much excitement for the twenty plus BIS members returning to their home base in Slough, England. It had been almost nine months since they arrived. Steven had left the day before, anxious to return to his base in Baltimore. He had told Karl he would meet up with Hazel that weekend in Washington. Karl had taken the time to see him off, asking him to give Hazel a letter for him, "I would have been surprised if you didn't give me a letter to carry, Karl. I just want you to know how much I admire the dangerous things you have done to defend England. It makes my career look a little tame in comparison." Steven held out his hand to Karl. To his surprise, Karl moved forward, wrapping his arms around this tall American.

"Goodbye, Steven. I look forward to seeing you one day when this world is free from tyranny. With that, Karl saluted him, then walked back in the direction of the main building.

The BIS group gathered cheerfully by the buses waiting to take them back to St. John's Aerodrome. Karl went inside to thank all the local Canadian staff for the excellent assistance they had provided them and to tell them good luck with the incoming command. Back outside, his group was starting to board the buses. "Sargent Blackwell, make the roll call for each bus, then join me on the first bus," instructed Karl, taking a last look at the building he had called home for such a long time. When they arrived at the aerodrome, their C-54 was waiting, taking on last minute supplies and fuel for the long flight home. Karl boarded first, telling everyone to get comfortable and catch up on their sleep or read a book from the box in the galley. It would be a long day of flying.

Back in Hitchin, Claire had managed to take the following three days off, so she could meet Karl when the coaches arrived back in Slough. She had arranged to stay at Julie and Clive's house that evening, and Clive had told her the transports should arrive about at 1400 hours, all going well. Julie and Dorothy had planned to get together that morning to catch up and have lunch together before Claire headed off to the camp to meet Karl.

After many hours of listening to the steady droning of four big Pratt & Whitney engines, the pitch changed as the pilot started his approach into Langley Aerodrome. Two bounces on the runway, and the C-54 started slowing down. Karl could see the two outboard engines spooling down as they taxied toward the hangar. With a squeal, the brakes were applied, then the inboard engines also spooled down into silence. Over the PA, the pilot announced, "Welcome home, you chap on board from the British Security Coordination and British Intelligence Service. This crew thanks you for what you are doing for the war effort. Listening to the captain, Karl thought, *I must thank him for those kind words.*

Walking forward to the cockpit, Karl spoke loudly to the captain and first officer. "Captain, on behalf of my entire division, let me thank you for a smooth flight home. Moreover, I would like to thank you for recognizing our contribution to the war effort." Karl touched the corner of his cap in a casual salute. Without waiting, he turned to walk toward the back of the aircraft and down the ladder to be on English soil once again. This aerodrome was much closer than the one they left from in Cornwall, so the drive was relatively quick. Karl looked around at the smiling faces as they approached the main gate. Standing up in the narrow aisle, he announced loudly, so those in the back could hear him, "Well, chaps, in a little while, you will all be reunited with your loved ones. I would like to take this opportunity to thank everyone for the tremendous work and the long hours you have put forth during these long months away from home. Wherever I serve in the future, I will always think of each of you fondly; thank you all again."

As Karl turned to sit down again, a corporal stood up, yelling, "Let's have three cheers for the Gaffer."

The sound inside the coach erupted into a loud cheer followed by, "Hip, hip, hooray for the finest Major in the BIS. God bless ya, Sir, and don't wear out the misses tonight." The group was letting off steam because they were finally home!

As the coaches entered the parade ground, the camp military band played a song so very near and dear to all the people in England. The White Cliffs of Dover made popular by England's own sweetheart, singer Vera Lynn. Karl looked at his men as the sound came through the open windows of the coach. There was not a dry eye to be seen. As the group commander, Karl was the first to step down from the coach. Looking into a sea of faces, just one caught his eye as Claire ran forward to throw her arms around his neck.

"Karl, you're finally home. This is the best day! Kiss me, you fool, and squeeze me as much as you want." Claire was so excited; he could feel her trembling in his arms.

"My darling Claire, what can I say when words are nowhere near enough to tell you how much I've missed you. I never realized until now what a half person I have been without you."

Karl threw his cap on the ground and swept her off her feet, kissing her like there was no tomorrow. He was home!

The PA made an announcement, "Would all members of the returning detail form ranks in the parade ground."

Now what?, thought Karl, obviously rattled by this announcement.

"Come on, chaps; let's get this over with," barked Karl sarcastically, looking toward Claire and kissing her again before joining his group. "Back in a few minutes. This is just a formality to welcome us back."

Claire was all smiles as she watched her husband lead the small detail to form ranks, with Karl and his second in command out in front. The camp commander, Major William Lowes, along with three other officers, entered the parade ground. "Attention," yelled Captain Hardy Meyer.

The detail came to attention, followed by "Salute." Bill, facing Karl, spoke loudly, saying, "Please, rest." The detail came to parade rest, hands behind their backs. Bill walked up to Karl, trying to remain formal. "Gentlemen, today, we are proud to have you back amongst us after that long deployment in Canada. We thank Major Vita for providing the leadership and commitment needed to train our new allies and their contingency from the OSS. The training you gave them will save countless lives in the months and possibly years that lie ahead of us. Shortly, we will disperse for an extended leave, so I won't detain you any longer than necessary." Bill saluted Karl, then winked with a silent, welcome home, my friend.

"Attention, commanding officer leaving," yelled Captain Meyer as Bill returned to his building. Karl shook hands once again with his group, wishing them all an enjoyable three weeks leave.

Karl returned to Claire, standing on the side, proud as a peacock, watching her husband. "Claire, I must see Bill before we depart; is that alright with you, darling?"

Claire linked her arm around Karl's, saying, "Whatever you want, darling. I'm too excited to have you home, so lead on, you good looking spy." Karl shook his head and smiled at her. For a moment, he thought about Hazel not being here with the rest of the group. There will always be a special place for Hazel in my heart, but not like the love I have for Claire. She alone is the one that owns this heart. In that flashing moment, Karl had closed the file on Kitty and bid farewell to Hazel, remembering what he had promised himself when they got married, my life from here on would be the love for my wife, Claire. Karl stopped in the middle of the parade group. Throwing his arms around Claire, he drew her to him, and in a soft voice, said, "Claire, my wife, my closest friend, my everything, I just need you to know I never want to be apart from you unless this bloody BIS sends me off again. You alone own the key to my heart." Karl, flooded with emotion, was pouring his heart out, looking for the words that would express how much he loved her.

Claire, searching his face, was trying to sense the feelings he was struggling with and trying to convey to her. "Karl Vita, you are such a romantic. Whatever you're feeling or trying to say, you need to know those feeling is the same for me. You must know that. How on earth did I get so fortunate? Thank you, Lord, for making my life so perfect."

Arm in arm, they entered the command building. As they rapped on Bill's office door, they heard Bill say, "Come in, you two." Karl opened the door for Claire. As they entered, there was Bill with a big smile on his face holding three tumblers of whiskey between his outstretched hands. "Come on in. It feels like an eternity since you left for Canada. Before you hit the road, let's celebrate your return." Putting the tumblers down, he walked around to the front of his desk to hug his friend, then kiss Claire on her cheek and give her a big hug. "Welcome home, Karl; you have been missed. Clive called me at least five times this afternoon to find out if you were back yet. Well, drink up, and be off with you. See you in three weeks." Bill swigged his drink down, then hugged them both again, wishing them a relaxing leave.

Leaving Bill's office, they walked arm in arm to the parking area to find Karl's luggage already in the back seat of the Wolsey. "When did this happen?" asked Karl.

"That nice corporal asked me for the keys when you were on the parade ground," answered Claire. "Now, let's get you home, Major, shall we?" Karl opened the passenger door for Claire.

Sitting down, she swung her legs into the car, making sure she was teasing him with a view up her skirt, a wicked smirk on her face, throwing him a kiss that made her intentions for later very clear.

Karl chuckled, walked around to the driver's side, and slid behind the steering wheel. On the other hand, Claire was displaying that side of her wanting to make the drive home a little more mischievous by moving her leg alongside the gear shift. "Darling, when you put the car in gear, remember my leg is right next to it." Claire always loved to tease him, knowing that it usually turned into something more.

"Claire, ever since we met, you have turned into a real vixen, but I know how to satisfy that look you're giving me when we reach home!"

Claire moved closer, wrapping both arms around Karl's left upper arm. Placing her head on his shoulder, she was at peace once more. Karl was home, safe and sound. "Darling, why must they send you away for so long?" asked Claire.

"I'm one of the lucky ones, Claire. There are people in the BIS that are deployed for years, not months. Hazel will be in Washington for a long time, and now, with her new boyfriend, it could become her new home. Like you, she loves the English way of life. It's going to be a real heart wrenching decision to accept Steven's proposal of marriage because, when she does, that door to returning to England will more than likely be closed. Before departing for Washington, I did my best to advise her. I know what it's like to face the reality of not returning to the place of your birth, in my case, Vienna."

Claire, hearing this, hugged him even tighter, saying, "Karl, wherever you want to go, I go too. Like Hazel, I am really English, but since I married you, I'm a Vita, which means more to me now than anything else, including this country.

Please, keep that in consideration if you feel we need to move." Claire could not believe she had just said that, but she also knew her marriage to Karl meant so much more than their home in Hitchin.

"Claire, we are getting too serious. I've been away too long; we need to think about how I intend to ravish you once we arrive home."

Claire reached over and kissed his face. "Welcome home, my darling; whatever your heart desires are fine with me." Claire did not tell her husband about the letter she had received only yesterday from Hazel, and right now was not the time to mention it. They spoke no more. Claire closed her eyes and soon dropped off to sleep, still holding onto Karl's arm.

Arriving home, Karl pulled into the driveway to see Ronny's new car, a 1937 Morris-12. It was much larger than his little Austin-8, which they had outgrown and desperately needed additional room. With his promotion and added duties, they could now afford the luxury of a bigger car. "Claire, wake up; it looks like we have company. You didn't tell me they would all be here. What a nice surprise. Come on, sleepyhead; let's go."

Claire was still groggy from all the excitement of the welcome home ceremony at the camp and the tumbler of whiskey. "Oh, Lord, we're already home. Some wife I turned out to be, falling asleep on you like this."

Karl looked over at her. Lifting her head, he kissed her forehead, saying, "Darling, you obviously needed that nap. Come on, straighten your hair; it's kind of flattened from leaning on my arm." Claire looked up with a look that made him laugh. Karl unloaded his luggage, and with Claire carrying his briefcase and topcoat, entered through the kitchen door to an overwhelming welcome from his family.

"Welcome home, son," said Mama, followed by Freida, Ronny, and finally Franchot.

"Franchot, you are growing up so fast, young man. You're almost nine, is that correct?" Karl put his cap on his nephew's head. After a wonderful dinner, they sat around the fire, sipping coffee. Karl got caught up on what everyone was doing. Ronny didn't say too much, and Karl could tell he was knackered just like he was.

"Ronny, I think you and I should get some shut eye. We're both running on nervous energy right now, so let's call it a night, shall we?" Karl was saving Ronny from saying the same thing.

Ronny chirped up, agreeing with Karl. "Is it that obvious, Karl?" remarked Ronny.

As they left, Karl yelled to Ronny, "How do you like the new ride? It's so much larger than the little Austin. See you Sunday."

Karl and Claire went back inside, Claire saying, "Darling, have a brandy, and let's go straight upstairs. You can shag the hell out of me tomorrow morning when your battery is recharged.

Karl chuckled, following her upstairs, then said, "Claire, you have never said that before. What happened to my proper English wife? You've been talking to Caroline too much; she loves that word, shagging. You are becoming a fallen woman, I fear."

Karl stopped halfway up the staircase, looking up at Claire as she turned, saying, "You bugger, it's all because of you turning me into a lusting woman, so it's all your fault, Karl Vita." Claire always enjoyed the way they bantered at times like this.

"Darling, you use the bathroom first. I need to separate the things going to the cleaners' tomorrow. This is going to be a whopping bill, Sailor," said Claire, already thinking about what had to be done.

"Claire, leave it till tomorrow. No need to do this tonight. I need my hot bloody vixen next to me; that will help me sleep so much better for the first time in so many months." Karl was thinking, I pray to God I don't have another one of those nightmares tonight. They are becoming more and more frequent. I was hoping after all this time; they would go away.

The following two weeks were like an insight into what life would be like in post war peace. Claire would leave for the office about 0900 hours, returning home about 1600 hours. Karl would see her off, then organize his day, starting with at least an hour on the secure phone with his people in Slough. He had started a maintenance log of things that needed repair or replacement around the house. He always looked forward to driving his little MG car to Baldock to be with the family; that was always a treat. Occasionally, he would take his sister Freida to a pub for lunch. The time alone gave them time to talk frankly. The news about their father and brothers was very sketchy from the limited information they could obtain.

Freida asked Karl, "Is there anyone in your network who could make contact with them, Karl? Surely, there's a way?"

Karl, taking a sip of his beer, looked at Freida before giving her an answer. "Freida, there is information I cannot tell you, even though I would like to, so take this as highly confidential information. Our agents in Italy are working with high-ranking officers in the Italian military who are planning to overthrow Mussolini. If that happens, the Italian military will capitulate and join the Allies. Only then will I be able to find out more through our network about our father and brothers. Freida, we are very confident this will happen very soon, maybe before Christmas. Please, you cannot disclose this to anyone, including Mama, Ronny, or even Claire. Make me that promise to keep this confidential between us." Karl took his sister's hand as he told her this information.

"Karl am I to believe that other branches of the military have no knowledge of this development?" asked Freida with a surprised look on her face.

"So far, this information is on a need-to-know basis," replied Karl.

When he returned home to the bungalow, Mama told him Claire had called and asked for him to call her back as soon as possible. When he heard this, his sixth sense told him something was going on. "Excuse me, Mama; I'll call Claire's office right away." The operator answered the phone, recognizing Karl's accent immediately. "Major Vita, please hold; I'll put you right through to your wife."

"Karl, I did not want to spoil your day, but I received a call from Clive. He tried to call you at the house, but, getting no answer, he called me to see if I knew how to get ahold of you. It sounds important, Karl; you better call him right away," said Claire with a tone of fear in her voice.

Karl rang Clive's office using the secure phone still in the bungalow. "Clive, what's this flap going on? Claire said it sounded very important." Karl was becoming tense, waiting for Clive to answer.

"Karl, I'm sorry to disturb your time off, but headquarters is calling for a general meeting in Cambridge next Tuesday. You and Gunther will be accompanying me. Do you think Claire will mind if we bunk in at your house Monday evening? That way, we can leave early in the morning to get there by 0730 hours," asked Clive, deliberately being vague.

"Clive, why are we going to some meeting? Care to enlighten me?" asked Karl.

The answer from Clive was abrupt, "You know better than to ask me that. I will call you tomorrow on your secure home line. Sorry again for disturbing your afternoon." Karl returned the phone to its cradle, then asked Mama for some coffee. He was trying to act like the news was unimportant, but Mama knew so much better than that.

Claire returned home to find Karl had been busy in the kitchen. The aroma of an Austrian dish filled the downstairs. On the way home, Karl had stopped at the farm to see his friend John Brown, a local farmer, to convince him to part with some pork, eggs, and some home preserved vegetables. John had been a school friend of Claire and Caroline and at one time dated Caroline. Although the whole country was on food rationing, occasionally, there were still ways of bartering for extra food supplies.

"Karl, that smells wonderful. You should stay home more often." Over supper, Karl explained Clive's request for him and Gunther to stay at the house while attending a General Headquarters meeting the following Tuesday. Claire, of course, had no objections to having houseguests.

"Karl, how long will this conference last?" Karl was not sure but would know more in the morning. Claire sprang into action, saying, "Alright, my house boy, you and me, this weekend will get the two spare bedrooms ready. How many nights should I plan for? I'm looking forward to seeing Gunther again. We haven't seen him since the wedding."

Outwardly, Karl showed no signs of concern, but inwardly, his brain and stomach were all a jitter. His sixth sense was telling him this meeting would include danger. Friday morning, the secure phone rang, and, of course, it was Clive. "Morning, Karl, are you alone right now?" asked Clive.

Karl replied that Claire had already left for the office. "Clive, I know you will not tell me too much, even on a secure phone. I'll wait till we are face to face, but I have one high security question for you. Claire needs to know how many nights you and Gunther will be staying at Hotel Vita."

Clive let out a loud laugh, saying, "Oh, how I miss that sense of humor of yours three nights at max. Will that be alright? And seeing as you are hosting us, I will be picking up dinner, so think about places to dine. Karl, every branch of the Allied Military will be in attendance, the British, American, French, Canadian, Australian, New Zealand, Norwegian, Dutch, Greek, Polish, Czech, and the combined Free European Brigade. Karl, I believe you are following my line on where this call is going, so I won't say any more until we see each other Monday. One other thing, Gunther is bringing you some salami and wurst sausage; don't ask me how he acquired it. I don't really want to know. See you Monday afternoon about 1400 hours."

Karl sat, staring at the picture on the wall, his mind in overload, thinking about what Clive had just told him. I'm willing to bet they have been planned meetings about whatever this conference is about for a long time now. I believe and am ready to speculate that we are going to hear about returning to Europe.

The back door opened, and in walked Claire with her new briefcase over her shoulder and a shopping bag under her left arm, calling, "Karl, darling, I'm home. Where are you? Come look what Beverly was able to barter some legal time for."

Karl entered the kitchen to see a big pot of freshly made beef stew. "Shall we have this tonight, or are we going to the pub? It is Friday when all is said and done," said Claire. Looking into his face, she could sense his mind was in a BIS mode, and that could not be a good sign.

"Whatever you like, darling. Remember, though, we will be out with Clive and Gunther Monday through Wednesday evenings. On that note, Clive wants to know where we should take them for supper." Over the weekend, they went to Baldock and spent another evening with an old school friend of Claire's who lived in the next town of Letchworth. Before leaving for work on Monday, Karl asked Claire what time she expected to return home.

"Karl, if you three need some time alone, I have plenty of work still waiting to do. So, shall we say around 5:30 p.m.? Will that allow enough time?" answered Claire.

"Darling, you should have been in the BIS with that ability to read people like you do." Karl enjoyed her way of asking questions to gauge what people were really thinking.

"Have you forgotten that I'm married to an Intelligence bloke? Some of the things he does are rubbing off on me, can't you tell?"

Karl moved over to her, then kissed her with nothing else but love in his heart for this wonderful woman, saying, "You got me beat, darling."

Monday at lunchtime, after Claire had returned to the office feeling so much more relaxed after Karl had worked her over, she would stay at the office until Karl called her with all clear signal. Karl was pacing the living room like a caged lion, processing what his instincts told him he knew. The sound of car doors closing told him they were here. "Clive, Gunther, so pleased to see you. Clive gets nervous when I'm not in camp is that right?" smirked Karl. "The rooms are at the top of the stairs; you decide who gets which room, then come back downstairs, and I'll make coffee. Clive, would you prefer tea?" asked Karl, already in a BIS mindset.

Gunther came downstairs first, carrying a box wrapped in brown paper. "Karl, I thought you would enjoy sampling this. I'll bet it's been quite a while since you savored this kind of cured meat. Take a sniff."

Karl pulled a slice of salami out and gulped it down in one bite, saying, "Oh, God, I've missed this stuff. I won't ask how you acquired it."

Over coffee, they sat in the living room, mainly talking about the outcome of the Canadian mission. "Clive, Claire will be coming home at 1700 hours, so why don't you dispense with the small talk and get to the reason we are heading to Cambridge tomorrow morning, shall we?" asked Karl bluntly.

"Always abrupt and to the point, aren't you, Major?" replied Clive. "Alright, let's talk about why we are attending this meeting tomorrow along with attendees from every Allied government and their Armed Forces' representatives. Early in March, a new committee known as COSAC was formed. It stands for Chief of Staff Allied Commander Designate. It was established to start planning for the return to Europe. Would it surprise you if I told you that we have been secretly preparing for such an operation since the latter part of 1941?

"The time is rapidly approaching for the Allies to take this war to the Germans, fighting them for every mile back to Berlin by sea and air, landing troops on the beaches and countryside of Western France. This massive invasion force will be the likes of which the world has never seen before. However, once committed, we must follow through or face certain disaster. The logistics and implementation for such an operation will be the focus and purpose of this conference in Cambridge tomorrow. Now, that's enough for today. By the way, Jean Yves will be attending for the French contingency. He is looking forward to seeing you two again in the morning."

The sound of the back door opening ended the discussion about the Return to Europe. Claire entered, carrying her briefcase and a shopping bag. She called out to notify Karl she was home, suspecting they were still talking about very sensitive issues. Looking every inch, the businesswoman she was, she entered the living room, receiving a very warm welcome from Clive and Gunther. Speaking in her very best German, she welcomed them to their home. Gunther was the first to respond, also speaking in German.

"Claire, since I saw you last, your German is almost perfect. I do detect the Austrian influence, though."

Claire hugged him as she laughed with her approval. "Have you finished your business, or should I make myself scarce?"

Karl moved over to her side, saying, "Darling, these two requested to stay here, not to see my mug, but to enjoy your beautiful presence."

"Karl Vita, you always know how to charm the ladies, and I'm the biggest sucker. Look where it got me, right into your bed."

Karl looked at Gunther and Clive before breaking out laughing at what Claire had said. "Darling, you're giving my secrets away again. Remember, these are comrades, not trainees." Claire had a way of blending into any conversation or gathering.

"Karl, I'm going upstairs to get changed. Shall we go to the Fox for supper, or would you prefer the Crown? It's your call."

Karl answered her by saying, "The Fox will be just fine." Over dinner, they talked mainly about absentee family and their wonderful wedding right up the road at the Letchworth Hall Hotel.

Clive looked at his watch, announcing, "We have an early start tomorrow, so we should think about heading back to the house. Claire, do you have an idea where we may treat you tomorrow evening for supper?"

Claire thought a moment, then answered, "Do you think your conference will be done by 6:00 p.m.? If so, I will meet you at the George and Dragon; it's so much closer to Cambridge than Hitchin. When you leave Cambridge, just call the house, and I will make my way over there, alright?"

The following morning, Claire's side of the bed was empty. Karl knew his wife so well. He thought she must be downstairs, making coffee and tea. Entering the kitchen, Karl saw the three of them talking quietly amongst themselves.

"Morning, old man, Claire here was just about to get you out of bed. Drink up, so we can head to Cambridge. Claire, I will call you when we are about to leave, alright?" said Clive, drinking what was left of his tea. Gunther was already waiting for them by the hall entrance. Claire poured coffee into a thermos mug for Karl, then wished them all a rewarding day.

The drive was relatively quiet, almost too quiet, each of them pondering the outcome of today's meeting. Entering the enormous hall, they were shocked to see the sea of uniforms milling around, drinking tea and coffee. Registration was two long tables manned by RAF personnel. "My God, how many do you think are here?" asked Karl to Gunther.

"We were told about 120 from all branches of the Allied forces." They signed in next to their names, then pinned their labels to their breast tunic pockets.

Looking into the hall, Karl spotted Jean Yves walking toward them. "Gentlemen, such a nice surprise to see you all so early in the morning. Major Vita, how is that charming new wife of yours? I'll have to visit soon. Well, maybe that will be on hold until we get through this year and maybe next year as well." Jean looked at them like he had already been briefed on what to expect from this conference.

"Gentlemen, please find your designated area. My name is Brigadier General Norman Larwood. Over the next three days, you will learn how the combined Allied forces have been planning, since 1941, to return to the European Continent. Gentlemen, it's time for us to fight the Germans on European soil!"

Loud cheers resounded throughout the hall. "*Operation Overlord* is what we are here for today. Although we are more than likely a year away from implementing such an invasion, we have much planning to do. The learning curve will not be easy, nor will the buildup of troops and training them. The massive acquisition of equipment will tax manufacturers here and abroad. You will hear more later about how we are planning to ramp up that requirement. The code name for the invasion from here on will be referred to as D-Day, called this for lack of an actual date. Let me also caution you on discussing this openly beyond these walls, other than when you are in a meeting directly connected to this operation. It should be treated as top secret. Any violators to this secrecy will find themselves in the brig for a very long time. Please, stand now for the invocation given today by Father Donald Rumen, then remain standing for Lieutenant Colonel Reginald Murray, the organizer of this operation."

The colonel took the podium. "In early 1942, we assessed three different operations. The first is Bolero, the build-up of Allied forces in Britain. The second, Sledgehammer, will establish a defensive salient on the French Cotentin Peninsula with the intent to pin down German Forces. The third is Roundup, in which broad beachheads will be seized on the French Channel coast, enabling a breakout into German occupied France. The code name D-Day is an outcome of the Arcadia Conference held in Washington D.C. toward the end of December 1941. *Operation Neptune* is currently our biggest challenge, amassing sufficient vessels to land troops and equipment for this landing. Without question, this will be the largest seaborne invasion in modern history.

"The General Staff has estimated the maritime requirements will be in excess of 6,800 vessels, that including combat and merchant shipping. Now, that's a lot of ships. Well, considering this, we will be equipping and training over 160,000 troops for this landing. This will include an airborne assault in advance of the D-Day landing. To launch this airborne assault, the air ministry estimate we need to amass over 425 transport aircraft to drop approximately 24,000 paratroopers. In addition, we are currently manufacturing gliders capable of carrying as many as 13 men and their equipment. The air ministry believes the C-47 will be the aircraft of choice to tow these gliders. This will also be discussed more in detail at tomorrow's meeting."

At 1630 hours, Colonel Murray called for an adjournment for the day, saying, "Gentlemen, I believe today was productive. See you all tomorrow morning at 0730 hours."

Driving back toward Baldock, the mood was one of being overwhelmed by this aggressive plan to land a massive army on the beaches of western France. Karl broke the silence by remarking, "It was so easy before the war to go over the channel to Europe, and now, you need a massive army to get there." That did it. Karl had got them to loosen up as they arrived at the George and Dragon to meet Claire.

Walking into the lobby, Karl spotted Claire sitting on a highchair at the bar, her head in a magazine. "Claire, sorry to keep you waiting. Have you been waiting very long?" asked Karl, kissing her on the cheek.

"Not at all; your timing was perfect; I only just sat down." Claire hugged Karl, then Clive and Gunther. "You know, people will talk, seeing me pick up three handsome blokes in uniforms," said Claire, sensing that this high security meeting had drained them, so getting a laugh out of them would make them relax for a little while anyway. "I'm assuming you'll be leaving at the same time tomorrow. Is that right, Clive?" Claire addressed Clive as the senior officer.

"Correct, I'm sure tomorrow will be another marathon." Claire looked at them, then asked, "Chaps, how about we have supper at the house tomorrow evening? You look like a relaxing evening would do you all good."

"Claire, that sounds like an awful lot of work for you," said Gunther.

"Nonsense," replied Claire. "I will enjoy fussing over you three. Now, let's get a stiff drink before dinner. By the way, you look like you need one about now." Karl beamed with pride and linked his arm with Claire's, leading the way to the lounge. Clive and Gunther smiled with approval for the strong-willed lady that had captured the heart of their friend and comrade.

Day two brought more focus on the logistics of such a massive invasion. After a box lunch, Colonel Murray introduced Commander Billy Michaels of the American Navy to talk about potential ports in the south of England that were being considered for the invasion. "Gentlemen, I can see your eyes glazing over at hearing all these details. Well, I'm here to tell you how we will deliver our forces onto those beaches. We are presently considering four deep water ports. Although we believe these ports will be the actual ones used in the final plan at this juncture, we are not prepared to name them yet. Once again, the meeting was adjourned at 1630 hours by Colonel Murray, summarizing what will be covered tomorrow, the final day of the conference.

Clive, after a while, said, "Chaps, before Gunther and I head back to Slough tomorrow afternoon, I think we should do something special for Claire, our hostess; any suggestions?"

Gunther spoke first, "We could have roses delivered to her office or maybe buy her something personal, but what can we buy? The shops will be closed by the time we get out of the meeting."

Karl thought about the question, then said, "I think delivering roses would be a wonderful gesture. I have an account at Harkness Roses, so let's stop there on the way home. I think Charlie will still be around there. I think those flowers should come from you two, as you're the guests. I'm just the husband." Karl's witty sarcasm made them laugh.

Charlie was still busy making flower arrangements for the following day. "Major Vita, nice to see you; what can I help you with?" Charlie worked quickly, arranging the dozen roses in a tall crystal vase. Clive paid Charlie, thanking him for accommodating them while they waited. Sitting in the front seat, Gunther held the big arrangement, careful not to break any of the stems. Claire was busy in the kitchen, preparing supper. Hearing the car door slam shut, she went to open the front door. What a pleasant surprise, she thought, as well as being thrilled by the colorful arrangement being carried by Gunther.

"Gunther, you blokes didn't have to do that. They are beautiful, so thoughtful; thank you so very much. I guess I'll make you all a special cocktail to take the edge off, shall I?" said Claire as she took the vase from Gunther, kissing him then Clive on the cheek, followed by a big kiss for Karl, saying, "Welcome home, Lover Boy. You all look a little happier than yesterday." Claire was stepping lightly on that statement. Dinner was marvelous, Claire outdoing herself to give them a relaxing evening with good home cooked food.

"Nothing like a home cooked meal, don't you think?" said Clive as he polished off the last piece of chicken. Gunther had a sad look on his face, and both Karl and Clive realized he was thinking of years past when he could have a meal with his family. That look was more than that he had no idea where they were hiding in Germany.

The following morning, Karl once again found the three of them sitting, drinking coffee. "Morning, old man, ready for another day of frying your brain?" asked Gunther as he poured Karl the liquid that would jolt him into the new day.

"Karl, Claire just proposed an idea for when we are finished today, and what she has in mind is fine with us. So, Claire, tell your husband what you have in mind," suggested Clive.

"Well, I was thinking earlier that Freida, and I like to shop in Cambridge. When you adjourn your meeting, you can drop Karl off at Lyons Tea House around five, and we will meet you there. It will be much quicker for you to head back to Slough from there. It's always slow going through Hitchin that time of day. What do you say?"

Claire was always planning and organizing, thought Karl. "That's fine with me, and it will make things easier for you two, I suppose," replied Karl.

Back in Cambridge, they gathered in the large meeting hall. The atmosphere seemed more upbeat, and there was an air of confidence for an operation of unprecedented proportions that would finally happen sometime in 1944. Most of the day was spent on questions and not too many answers to when the preparations would commence. One question was asked about landing all the equipment, supplies, and vehicles such as trucks, tanks, and bulldozers to clear the beaches.

"I'll take this one," barked Lieutenant Colonel Murray. "In the planning stage, we wrestled with how to land the projected massive amount of equipment in the event deep water harbors would not be available to us on D-Day. Thanks to the creative mind of Prime Minister Winston Churchill, he proposed making portable docks that could be built here in England, then towed over to specific landing beaches and sunk into place. The corps of engineers could then bolt on decking, forming a pier. These concrete floating caissons are already being built in the Portsmouth dry docks. From now on, we will refer to them as Mulberry artificial harbors. I hope that satisfies your line of questioning." Sitting back down, Lieutenant Colonel Murray looked around at all the blank faces, thinking, I bet they never saw that one coming.

The last topic of the day was the diversionary methods being considered to mislead the German High Command about where the landing would take place. Every effort will be made to mislead the Germans that an invasion would take place on the beaches of the *Pas-de-Calais*. This ranged from dummy camps, fields full of inflated dummy tanks, airfields with hundreds of wooden planes, and lorries and Jeeps parked in various places to confuse the German reconnaissance aircraft. If this deception worked, two whole divisions of German Panzer Tanks, artillery, and thousands of infantrymen would wait for an Allied invasion that would not happen, not in the *Pas-de-Calais* anyway. The RAF and American Army Air Corps will start intensive bombing of German radar sites as early as a month before D-Day. We need to make sure their eyes are permanently shut for *Operation Overlord.*

The closing speech was delivered by Brigadier General Norman Larwood, driving home the need for total secrecy. "We can deliver the Germans a crushing blow. However, loose tongues over a pint of beer could cost thousands of our boys their lives as a result of that carelessness, so speak to no one about what you have heard. Thank you all for attending; safe travels home."

With that, a loud cheer brought the conference to a close. Everyone attending was ready to return to their posts with a new feeling that the tide would finally turn on Adolf Hitler and his henchmen.

Clive dropped Karl off at the Lyons Tea House in Cambridge, where Claire and Freida were standing outside waiting for them. "Clive and Gunther, it was really nice to spend time together. Poor Frieda and Mama really did not have any time to socialize with you at all. Maybe we can have a weekend together soon. We need to work on that." Claire and Frieda kissed them both on the cheek, then stood back from the curb as they drove off back to Slough.

In the Wolsey, Freida mentioned how it seemed like yesterday that she met Clive and Bill in Dover when they first landed in Dover back in 1936. "Time goes by so fast; it seems like this blasted war will go on forever, doesn't it?" Freida looked over her shoulder at her brother, hoping he would shed some light on Allied progress. Karl kept looking out the window, displaying no expression or reaction to her question. Then again, Freida really did not expect any response from her brother.

On the last day before Karl returned to Slough, Claire announced she was taking the day off to be with her husband and would do so each time he left from now on. She adopted this practice because his times away were getting longer, which, in her mind, was leading up to one thing and one thing only: The Allied Invasion of Europe. Even though she would never ask him about his work, she was a solicitor with honed skills in identifying the story behind a straight face. There was another reason as well, and that had to do with making their family larger than just the two of them.

"Karl, it's your last day today. Tomorrow, you will be leaving for God knows how long. Is there something you would like to do other than shag the hell out of me before you go off again?" Claire knew using slang like shag would annoy him, and that's why she did it.

"Claire, I swear to God, your language is becoming really horrendous. What happened to that proper English lady I fell in love with?" Karl, looking at her, could immediately see there was a reason for her needling him like this.

"Karl, darling, I'm sorry; would you allow me to make it up to you before we go out to lunch?" With that devilish look in her eyes, Claire sat on his lap, taking his hand placing it on her knee, then with deliberate action, spread her legs for Karl to make the next move, which did not happen. Claire looked at him, saying, "Darling, I'm inviting you to ravish me; don't you want to?" Claire was processing what he was up to. Karl always did things with deliberate actions, so what was he doing this time?

"Claire, you will have to convince me differently from this," said Karl, now enjoying the interplay going on between them. Claire stood up and pushed him back onto the couch, not saying a word. She knew exactly what he was suggesting, and that person inside her that was once so strait laced when she met him was no more. Claire, with slow movements, removed his trousers and underwear and kissed his chest, working her way down to his erection.

"Will this do it, my prince?" As her hand gently encircled him, the look on his face told her he was waiting. Claire continued to hover

over him, driving him to push up toward her lips. Claire continued to tease him, and just as he was going to ask her to continue, she moved her mouth over him, which made his breathing even heavier. "Karl, that's a deposit on making love to me. Now, show me how you plan to do that," said Claire, swinging her legs over him. Claire was still praying for that miracle that would begin her journey to motherhood.

Karl rose earlier the following day; he wanted time alone to gather his thoughts. With all we learned over the last few days, it's a safe assumption that my division will be heavily involved. That will make it very difficult if Claire becomes pregnant and I'm away when the baby comes. Caroline, Freida, and Mama will be there for her, but to miss the arrival of our first child would be very difficult for me. I will have to work on that. Entering the kitchen, he made himself another cup of coffee and one for Claire. Carrying them upstairs, he quietly sat next to his sleeping bride, thinking how peaceful she looked.

"Claire, darling, it's time for you to wake up. I've got a train to catch in ninety minutes."

Claire rolled over, and, reaching up to hug her husband, she softly said, "Karl, it's not fair. It would be so nice to cuddle in bed, drinking our coffee instead of dropping you off at the station. I love you, darling, more so now than ever. I'm praying you can come home this weekend." Claire was already sad, never knowing if he would return at the end of the week or many weeks later, which was becoming the typical case.

Claire dressed and got ready for the office. She hated returning to an empty house, so on those days when she took Karl to the station, she preferred to get an early start at the office. Karl watched her as she slid behind the steering wheel of the Wolsey, thinking, what a striking woman. She seems so proper if only people knew what a vixen she has become. Thinking that brought a smile to his face. They both hated these Monday morning goodbyes. The empty, lonely feeling of separation was always difficult. Kissing her and squeezing her as if it was the last time, Karl finally spoke, "Claire, I love you so much. It seems like with each passing month, my need to be with you all the time keeps pulling at my heartstrings. How I now resent having to follow orders." Taking her face between his hands, he looked into her eyes, searching for that certain look she had whenever they parted.

"Karl, you always know what I'm thinking, so you know what I'm praying for now, don't you? May the Lord keep you safe and return you to me this Friday. Karl, I'm a mess; forgive me. I don't need you to leave seeing me like this. It always seems to happen I try so hard to keep a smile on my face, but that is becoming harder to do." Claire walked him to an empty compartment, then kissed him goodbye as he hugged her tightly for one more minute. From the carriage window, he stood with a silent thought going through his mind: *I love you, my sweet Claire. Stay strong; the road is going to become very rocky as we get closer to D-Day.*

The war was turning against the Germans. The first crushing blow happened in February of 1943 when General Paulus surrendered his army in Stalingrad to the Russian forces, resulting in thousands of German soldiers being taken captive. In May, the Allied forces took back North Africa, and thousands of additional prisoners faced captivity. On May 17th, the three dams in the Ruhr Valley were destroyed by RAF Lancaster heavy bombers of the 617 Squadron, led by Wing Commander Guy Gibson, using a revolutionary new bouncing bomb that was the brainchild of inventor Barnes Wallis. The U-Boat war in the Atlantic was also turning against Germany, thanks to the codebreakers at Bletchley Park and the new Allied radar equipped long range aircraft.

At last, the Allies could deliver a crushing blow, finally sinking these sharks of the North Atlantic in alarming numbers. This shift caused Admiral Karl Donitz to withdraw most of his larger submarines from the North Atlantic. Italy finally surrendered in early July and joined the Allies against the Germans, paying a very high price for that decision. Daily, the news would flood into the Intelligence Service in Slough, changing the doom and gloom from prior years to positive feelings of gaining the upper hand.

Karl was able to get home on an average of once every two weeks. Although the news was encouraging, they were far from winning the war, and the preparations for D-Day were becoming even more demanding. The first week of August, he was given a four-day leave to spend at home with his wife, and it was like a dream come true.

"Claire, it's Karl! Darling, I've got wonderful news. I'm coming home Friday for four whole days! I can't wait to hold you, but I must go; I've got another meeting to attend."

Karl was on cloud nine. It had been almost twenty-two days since he saw his wife. For once, the train from Slough was empty, so Karl took the time to relax and read a book he had been reading on and off for almost six months. The routine was second nature to him now; it was like he was on autopilot, changing to the Kings Cross station for the short ride to Hitchin. He stopped at the flower stand to buy flowers for Claire, and in his briefcase, he had another gift for her, which Julie had picked up for him in Slough. He had ordered the gold bracelet two weeks before, although it was still two months before her birthday. He just wanted to spoil her, and this bracelet would do just that. The familiar bumping of the buffers signaled the train was slowing, making its entrance into Hitchin Station. Karl's excitement was getting himself nervous with anticipation. The brakes squealed as the train came to a stop.

Karl strained to see where Claire was on the platform. There she was in a floral flared dress, her fair hair blowing in the breeze. Once she spotted him, she started walking quickly to close the distance, and Karl jumped onto the platform almost in a sprint to get to her. Throwing his strong arms around his wife, he spun her around and lifted her legs clean off the platform.

Embracing, they were oblivious to everyone around them. "Steady on, you crazy Austrian; from now on, you'll have to be a little more careful," yelled Claire.

Karl loved the way she was talking to him. Stopping abruptly, Karl put her back down. He could see she had a different look to her, she was simply glowing, but why? "Major Karl Vita, it looks like you're going to be a father next year—probably early March."

Claire's original plan was to tell him once they arrived back at the house, but seeing him so excited… what better way to announce they were pregnant than here on the platform of Hitchin Station?

"Claire, what did you just say?" asked Karl, holding her by the arms.

"Darling, we are going to have a baby. I just couldn't wait to tell you; you know how I get. Karl, can you believe it? You're going to be a brand-new papa; we need to celebrate." Claire was floating on a cloud after worrying all this time whether she could conceive. Losing her first baby at only two and a half months back in her university days had given her reason to be concerned, but those thoughts had now passed.

"Claire, who else knows other than Dr. Burgess?" asked Karl. "Just Julie and Caroline. They've helped me a lot. Once Dr. Burgess confirmed I was indeed pregnant; I didn't want to announce it to the family until you were here by my side. I called Freida and told her we have some exciting news to share with them on Sunday. I can't wait to see Mama's face; you know how she loves children. I've asked them to join us for lunch; is that alright with you, darling?" asked an excited Claire.

"Of course, my new little mama has shocked the heck out of me. God, you have a way of making an announcement, don't you?" Karl stood there, then yelled out at the top of his lungs, "I'm going to be a dad!" People on the platform started clapping and congratulating them.

"Karl, we're in a public place, and you're making a spectacle of yourself," remarked Claire, half laughing and half self-conscious about the way her husband was reacting. "Let's go home, darling, shall we?" asked Claire.

"No, we're not; let's stop at the Crown to celebrate. Claire laughing at his enthusiasm. "How about a bottle of champagne," asked Karl. "White wine will be just fine darling," replied Claire.

Sunday morning, Karl was jittery, walking around the house and thinking about what the reaction from the family would be to their announcement. Mama will be so excited to have another grandchild. War may be hell, but sometimes the announcement of a new baby brightens the day for everyone, thought Karl.

When they arrived, Karl welcomed them at the front door with hugs, kisses, and words of happiness, asking them to go into the living room to join Claire. There were more hugs and kisses, followed by Karl asking them to take a seat. Claire stood up going into the kitchen, returning with flutes of Champagne. This brought looks of confusion to Freida and Ronny, but not Mama. She stared at Claire; as a mother and a grandparent, she knew what that Champagne toast was all about!

Karl took Claire's hand, saying, "Today is such a wonderful day! We're so glad to have you with us, and you're probably wondering why we are celebrating with Champagne." Putting his arm around Claire, he kissed her forehead before continuing. "Claire made me a very happy returning soldier yesterday when she met me at the train station because she announced we are to have a baby. So, raise your glasses to toast another Vita coming into our family."

Karl kissed Claire again, then kissed his mother and sister. Lifting Franchot in the air, he said, "Franchot, you are going to have a new cousin next year!"

Ronny and Freida both kissed Claire, then hugged Karl, with Ronny saying, "This is such wonderful news! We're so happy for you both." Karl kept looking at his mother, sitting with a different look on her face.

"Mama, you are happy about this, aren't you?" he asked, sitting down next to her with his arm around her shoulder.

"Oh, don't mind me, son; I couldn't be happier! I was just thinking about your father and brothers; they would be so thrilled to receive this wonderful news. You must also be thinking, why am I so sad then? Well, son, your father and brothers have never seen or met our wonderful Claire, nor were they at your wedding. They would be so proud of where you are today, married to a wonderful, successful woman, a major in the army, and now expecting your first child. Karl, all these things they have missed, so, as happy as I am, there is sadness because of what they have missed." Mama, while saying that, reached out for Claire's and Karl's hands, tears welling up in her eyes.

Freida, Ronny, and Franchot moved close, so they all could hold each other tightly in a bond of love and trust. "War is hell; it separates families and creates pain and anxiety, but through all that comes the news that a new baby will be born into our family, giving all of us hope for a better tomorrow!" concluded Mama.

Soon, it was time for his family to return to Baldock. Tomorrow, Ronny would head to the station, and it would be three weeks before he could return home. Karl would also be heading to the station in three days, returning to his camp in Slough. But today was Sunday, and once again, they had this evening to enjoy making love, although Karl was acting differently toward Claire a little nervous now that she was expecting.

Claire laughed at him, saying, "Karl, I'm having a baby; I'm not going to break. Now, Sailor, send me around the moon. You know exactly what I need for those long, lonely nights ahead, don't you?" Karl smiled at her as he moved over her. Claire willingly parted her legs, so he could enter her, their passion building with every thrust he made, closing the window to a troubled world outside, for this one evening anyway. Monday and Tuesday, they spent shopping in Luton and Cambridge for the baby's room. Karl questioned if they were a little premature with buying all these things, but then again, Claire never waited too long for things to happen, did she?

Returning to Slough, Karl was congratulated by all his friends and staff. Julie had invited Karl, Bill, and Dorothy to dine with Clive and herself at the Charter Arms to celebrate. Clive, as always, spoke first, saying, "Karl, today you have delivered on all your promises. Look, my friend, I know how difficult these times are for you, but be assured that you and Claire have close friends that will be by your sides, so if you are worried about Claire and having this baby, don't! She has a support network that will always be there for her, and Karl, let's also remember how strong a woman Claire is." Clive was assuring his troubled friend that he should only be looking forward to the exciting arrival of the new baby.

On his second night back at the camp, Sally and John had invited him to join his staff for an after-hours party at a local pub, also inviting many of Karl's closest friends. It was a sea of khaki uniforms at the bar, all happy to escape, even if it was only a night at the pub. Besides socializing in the officers' lounge and occasionally joining others at the local pub, Karl buried himself in work, preparing for D-Day and always ended the evening writing to Claire.

It had been almost a month since he was home. He missed Claire so very much, and he needed to see her. With Bill's help, he was able to get a three-day pass for this coming weekend. "Claire, darling, I'm coming home. I can't wait to be with you. Pick me up at the usual time, and darling, how do you feel about heading down to the Fox for a plowman's and a pint? How does that sound? I need to relax with my beautiful wife. How does the bump look?" asked Karl, excited to return home and have a few days away from planning to send his men into harm's way.

Claire had a few days before Karl would return home. Her conscience had been bothering her for some time about seeing Patrick's parents and his siblings, so she announced that she would not be in the office on Friday. Calling Dorine on their home party line, she asked if she could visit them Friday morning at about 10:00 a.m.

The Cooks lived in a council house in the Henlow Grange estate, so driving there would only take twenty or so minutes. Parking on the street, she reached over, picked up the flower arrangement and box of freshly baked biscuits, then walked up the short path to the front door. Using the polished brass door knocker, she announced herself. Dorine opened the door, very excited to see her former daughter-in-law, boisterously saying, "Claire, I'm so pleased to see you; it's been quite a while, hasn't it? Come in. Dad is in the garden, cutting the grass. He is going to be so happy you're here."

Claire walked out into the small fenced in garden and was immediately welcomed by Patrick's father. "Claire, you're a sight for sore eyes. Am I allowed to hug the expecting mother?" asked Donald, a proud veteran of the First World War and now in the home guard, still serving his country. In the small lounge, they sat drinking tea and eating the delicious biscuits.

"Claire, you look radiantly happy again, and seeing you pregnant is wonderful for us to see. Patrick would be relieved to see you have moved on. As much as we miss Patrick every day of the week, we will always feel sadness knowing the child you carry won't be our son's, nor will we be that's child's grandparents. Promise us you will bring the baby over to see us when time permits; that would mean so much to us both."

Claire's heart was breaking, and she felt very guilty at not visiting or calling them more often. They had been her in-laws not that long ago; neglecting them this way was not the right thing to do. "Dorine and Don, I will not neglect you like this again. I won't make excuses;

please, forgive me. If you're up to it, perhaps you could meet my husband Karl next time he's home on leave. That's, of course, if you're not uncomfortable with that suggestion?"

Dorine reached for Claire's hand, saying, "We would love to meet your young man."

Don asked Claire a pointed question, "You mentioned on the phone that he was in the Intelligence Service, is that correct?"

"Yes, he is, Don," replied Claire, not wishing to add more than that. "I suppose you are not at liberty to tell us what his duties are? Could I ask you this then, what is his rank?"

Claire, hearing this question smiled, and diplomatically replied, "Karl is a major in a special group; more than that, I can't say." She could feel herself feeling very proud of the man she had married, and as much as she would always love Patrick, Karl would always be the only one to own her heart. No matter what might happen, she would always have a part of him in their child she was carrying. "Sorry to run; I'm picking Karl up from the train station in a little over an hour. It was delightful to spend this afternoon with you." Claire stood and hugged them both, then, at the front door, kissed them both.

Still holding onto her hand, Don asked, "Claire, could you please thank your major for us? What he does is probably dangerous, and I can only imagine what that entails. He must miss his homeland very much. We would welcome a visit when you can fit us in." Don walked her to the car, saying, "Still driving the Wolsey, I see." Taking her hand, he carefully tapped her stomach before kissing her cheek and opening the car door for her.

Driving to the station, Claire thought about what they had talked about. *Did I do the wrong thing by telling them he was an Intelligence officer? I hope not, but I won't mention it to Karl. I know how sensitive he gets about what he does. Well, I will have to because if I introduce Dorine and Don, he will surely be asked about the Intelligence Service. I can't think about that now. I'm almost at the station.*

Parking in the same area she always parked in, she fixed her hair, freshened her makeup, and proceeded through the tunnel to the opposite platform to wait for the train from Kings Cross.

Standing there, she was still thinking about some of Don's comments. One question came to mind that she had never really thought about before, and that question was, why did I change my surname back to my maiden name of McGivern after Patrick was killed. I wonder why? Deep in thought, a loud whistle announced the arrival of the King's Cross train entering the platform, and just like that, she put those questions aside because she could see her husband Karl waiving from the carriage window.

Like so many times before, Karl ran down the platform and swept her off her feet, kissing her passionately. One last thought crossed her mind; he will always be the reason I'm happier. Whenever I see my bloody foreigner jumping down from the train, I feel safe once again! With his arm around her waist, Karl was looking for some sign that her belly was growing.

"Claire, do you think we're going to have a boy or a girl? Lately, I find myself thinking about that all the time," asked Karl.

"Darling, you'll just have to wait like the rest of us. For once, your sneaky Intelligence stuff won't work here; isn't that right, Sailor?" Over a pint for Karl and lemonade for Claire, she told him about visiting Patrick's parents and how guilty she felt.

Karl, always a softy when it came to matters like this, answered her by saying, "Claire, you did the right thing. Remember, they, like my family, are thrilled to see you pregnant. They sound like wonderful people, and I would really like to meet them one of these days."

Claire took his arm and squeezed it, then, with her head on his shoulder, answered, "I kind of told them we would visit, and, Karl, forgive me, but I bragged about you being a major in the Intelligence Service. Please, don't get mad at me; you know how proud I am of you. Forgive me, darling; my mouth was rattling again." Claire turned her head to look into his eyes. Waiting, she could see he was processing and taking advantage of her nervous fidgeting.

"Claire Vita, I don't know what I'm going to do with you. That mouth of yours could be better served on something else." Karl could not hold back any longer, and he burst out laughing, saying, "Claire, no harm done, but I love it when you think you're in the doghouse.

That side of you could melt an iceberg another reason I love you so much. So, when do you want to show me off to Patrick's family?"

A thought flashed through Claire's mind, my bloke is always so understanding and always ready to help others. God help anyone, though, who gets on the wrong side of him; it's not a good place to be more like downright dangerous. Driving home, Claire sat in the passenger seat, telling him everything that had gone on since he was home last. Karl was driving, smiling as she talked. His mind, however, was still in BIS mode, wrestling with sending twelve young men on dangerous missions to many parts of Germany, young men that may never return to a special someone waiting at the station to welcome them home. These tough decisions would haunt Karl by day and night.

"Darling are you listening to me or is your head still in BIS mode?" asked Claire, knowing her husband so very well when that smile was on his face. Karl needed sleep and relaxation; he was mentally drained. So, the weekend was low key, only venturing out to visit Baldock to spend time with the family.

July was a beautiful time to be in England. The Germans were losing on many fronts. Like an injured lion, they were still very dangerous, though. Their newer weapons were far more destructive, with power that created revised defensive methods for those living in England. By month's end, Italian dictator Mussolini had escaped, and his reign of power was no more. Within two months, Italy would surrender to the Allies, and, after being shot, Mussolini would be hung by his feet along with his mistress, a fitting end to an evil dictator.

Karl now had a way to locate his father and brothers still hiding in the Dolomite Mountain village of Madonna Della Rose. Over six weeks, Karl had numerous discussions with the American OSS, scouring the mountain towns and villages, looking for German and Italian soldiers. With the help of Major Andy Anderson, a team of American soldiers entered Madonna Della Rose, only to find marauding Italian deserters had ransacked it.

The town's people fought back with whatever weapons they had but escaping into the mountains was their only salvation. The rebuilding had started when they returned to their village.

At the home of Silvio Suave, a squad of Mountain Rangers located Karl's brothers, working hard with their uncle to repair his house. The sad news was that Karl's father had died five months before of heart related complications. With no doctor or medicines to help him, he grew weaker, eventually sliding into a coma, never to regain consciousness.

Once again, Major Anderson pulled some strings to transport the two brothers back to England to be reunited in Baldock with their family. Karl and Claire met them at the Tilbury Dockyard. Seeing them coming down the gangway, Karl was beside himself, tears flooding down his face. Both his brothers were waving madly. In his major's uniform, Karl pulled rank, bypassing the gangway guards climbing halfway up the gangway to hug his brothers. Claire, standing at the bottom, felt they needed this time alone together.

"Ardie, Ello, meet your sister-in-law, Claire, my very pregnant wife." Ardie took both her hands. Crying tears of joy, he embraced Claire, followed by Ello.

Claire, speaking in German with that Austrian dialect, shocked them both by saying, "Welcome to England, dear brothers; we are so delighted to have you safely home with us. Mama, Freida, Ronny, and young Franchot are anxiously waiting for you both back in Baldock. Do you have luggage to collect?" Claire, asking that, looked at them and how they were dressed, both carrying cardboard boxes containing some clothes and essentials given to them by the people in the village before they left.

Claire immediately realized that was a stupid question. Turning to Karl, she commanded, "Karl, tomorrow morning, you and I will pick up some new clothes for them, or would you rather take them by yourself?" Karl simply responded by saying, "Darling, your tastes are always better than mine."

After meeting with the British Customs agents and the local police, they walked to the Wolsey parked nearby. All the way back, they fired question after question, and seeing their baby brother wearing the uniform of a high-ranking officer was quite the shock. For a moment, there was silence before Ello reached over to Claire. Taking her hand, he asked, "Claire, you must be a very strong woman to keep the attention of our brother. Needless to say, you are a beautiful lady, and from listening to you talk, so much smarter than he is. Do you have a secret as to how you did this?"

The three brothers all started laughing at this question, Claire answering, "Yes, I most certainly do, but that will have to remain my secret."

Karl, reaching over the front seat to take her hand, said, "Brothers, she is the captain I rely on to keep my ship on a steady course. I'm so pleased to see you approve. Just remember, she's my pregnant wife."

Claire was enjoying herself immensely, finally being in the company of Karl's big brothers. The news from Meno was that he would remain in Trieste with his son, Fritz, for the time being. His wife, however, was somewhere in Austria. Where? Nobody knew. Other than Ardie mentioning that their father had passed away, they all stayed away from discussing that painful topic until they were home all together with Mama.

Karl honked the horn as he pulled the Wolsey into the driveway. The front door flew open and outran Mama and Freida with Franchot in tow. "Mama," yelling Ardie, "I never thought this day would ever come. I can't believe we are together again."

After all the driveway excitement, they made their way into the bungalow. Claire went into the kitchen to make sandwiches and coffee, leaving Mama and her sons and daughter on their own in the lounge to talk about the demise of Papa. Through the open kitchen door, Claire could hear Mama crying. She thought, this is a very hard reunion. I think I'll go outside and play with Franchot, maybe take him up to see Tuff, his favorite horse up the road in the big field.

Mama settled down, sitting in between Ello and Ardie. Regaining her composure, she finally spoke, "Your father and I talked about these matters many times before the war. Karl, when you arrived in Wien to pick us up back in 1936, you never asked me, nor did I volunteer why he was not there to meet you and see us off on that long trip to Ostend. Well, now, I'll tell you. He was at our farm, burying assets. He was able to make numerous trips using the company lorry, and that's why he was not there when you arrived. Karl, when the Allies finally overrun upper Austria, it will be up to you and your brothers to find and retrieve those assets. I have the instructions to where the cave is located and how to find the entrance, which was filled with rocks and plants to hide it," concluded Mama, relieved finally to answer that nagging question.

"Mama, I must confess that I suspected that might be going on, but now we all know, don't we?" Karl, saying that, was also thinking, my parents should have joined the BIS, considering they have kept this secret for all these years. A smile crossed his face before he continued, "Mama, do not tell me or show anyone else the location to that cave. The war in Europe could continue for years. Assuming we are successful in setting Europe free, which could be years from now, we can consider going together, alright? After which, we can also give Papa a proper gravestone," concluded Karl.

Claire had returned, entering the lounge carrying a large tray of sandwiches and a big pot of coffee, saying, "Here you go; you must be famished by now."

Karl looked at his wife, beckoning her to come to sit down next to him, saying, "Claire, what do you think about what we have just discussed?" Karl needed her legal input in this discussion.

"Karl are you asking me this question as your wife or are you seeking my legal opinion?" answered Claire, sitting there holding Mama's hand.

Freida responded before anyone else could, "Claire, your part of this family. You are also its solicitor, so, yes to giving us legal advice."

Claire stood up to address them, saying, "From what I overheard, you are all concerned about hidden family assets, correct? Well, the weak link to this is Mama herself. God forbid if something should happen to her, that secret will more than likely be lost as well." Turning and smiling at Mama, she continued by saying, "That will not be the case, I'm sure. Mama, does the caretaker of the farm have access to that location, and how well can he be trusted?" Claire was mentally compiling the facts.

"Claire, Arnold Bucker has been a trusted employee for almost twenty-eight years, and yes, he helped Papa seal that cave. I can assure you he would never betray us; Papa trusted his life to Arnold. Claire,

I can see by the look on your face that you're about to give us your opinion, so don't worry; we won't attack you."

Claire smiled, then answered Mama. "If you are comfortable with Mr. Bucker, that's fine. As for the information you have hidden away in this house or your safe deposit box, I propose that information be transferred in a package sealed with my company stamp, then stored in my company's record vault. This way, there are two methods to locate the cave. Again, it's your decision, Mama, not ours." Claire looked to Mama for her answer.

"Thank you, Claire. My question is, would that safe be secure in case of fire? Although, these days, it's more than likely a stray bomb would hit the building."

"Good question, and yes, our vault is below the basement, buried in heavy concrete. My father always felt we needed our own vault as well as the banks, so yes, it's very safe," answered Claire.

"Well, next week, let's put that package in there, shall we? Is there room for an additional box of documents I brought with us when we left Wien?" asked Mama.

Claire walked over and kissed Mama on her cheek. Laughing, she told her, "You could have dinner in there; it's so big." The mood lightened as they sat drinking coffee and talking about the old days. Karl kissed Claire on the cheek, then announced it was time for them to head home.

In the car, Karl kept smiling as he drove. "And what is so funny, Karl?" asked Claire.

"I'm smiling because, as I look at you, there are so many facets to your personality. You're beautiful and very classy, you're a successful solicitor in your own company, you're a wonderful lover, you're an incredible wife, you're almost a mother, and the bonus to me is that you're all mine."

Claire, hearing this, slid over to his side and whispered in his ear, "Darling, all that flattery is going to get you anything you want once we are home."

Karl took his left arm off the steering wheel and put it around his wife's shoulder, thinking, *I love being her husband.*

Karl spent as much time with his brothers as he could, Claire joining him on those days she did not go to the office. Through the local council, Ronny arranged for the brothers to work in the maintenance department. The pay was minimum but keeping busy was therapy for these men that had lost everything. Like all the times before, Karl's time at home was almost at an end.

Leaving was becoming very stressful for both him and Claire. Leaving his very pregnant wife and never knowing how long it would be before he could return to her was making him increasingly resentful of his commitment to the BIS. The planning for the D-Day invasion was building at an alarming rate. The equipment stockpiling was increasing and hiding all of it was a mammoth undertaking along with the deceptive dummy equipment.

Karl and his staff were working almost around the clock with the Americans, the French, and all the other nations that would make up the Allied Invasion Force. Each beachhead would have its own BIS squad to handle the interrogation of prisoners and assist the military with communication with the local population, not a simple task. All these responsibilities were thoroughly documented for every contingency during the early planning meetings.

The months dragged on, and on those weekends that Karl managed to head home, he was always surprised by how big Claire had become since seeing her last. Jumping down from the train, he would look at her, love written all over his face. "Claire, you lovely blimp, let me look at you. This pregnancy really suits you, and you're simply glowing with happiness. Can the bloke who did this to you get a huge and a kiss?" Karl, holding her, was finding it a little more difficult with each visit.

"Karl, darling, I can always rely on you to make some stupid remark. Don't ever stop acting like this, darling, because you know I love it so very much." Arriving home, Karl got comfortable, finally out of his uniform and into a loose-fitting shirt along with a pair of summer slacks. Claire had taken a tray out into the garden with a pot of coffee and sandwiches, placing it between the two deck chairs. "Come, sit down, you good looking man," said Claire.

Sitting there, catching up on things that had happened while he was away, the first question Karl asked was, "What does Dr. Burgess say about your condition, and what date should I burn into my brain about our new arrival?"

Claire, still beaming, replied, "We are still on track for the early part of March, and he is very happy about my health and the state of the baby. My back is starting to give me problems when I go to sit down, and when I get up, it will start aching. Dr. Burgess said that's normal considering this weight in front of me; still, it won't be long now, will it, Papa?

"Karl, I'm a little concerned about when the baby comes. Do you think there will be a problem with you getting away for a few days? I don't want to add any more stress to what you already have. I just need to have all my ducks in order just in case. Caroline will be coming to stay with me the week before the baby arrives, and Freida and Mama would like to stay over just in case my sister can't make it, so it's not like I'll be on my own if that's what you're worried about." Claire saying this was also sending him a message: If his duties were to become an issue with getting leave to come home, as much as it would be sad, he should think of seeing his child for the very first time whenever he could return home.

"Claire, there is very little that could stop me from getting home to see our baby. One way or another, I'll find a way; this I will promise you!"

Claire looked at her husband's face, knowing that look of determination. "Karl don't do anything stupid; it will only ruin the arrival of our baby. Please, Karl, I know how you get once you have the bit between your teeth." Claire poured more coffee for them both, taking this time to change the subject to how his brothers were holding up and living in Baldock.

The hours passed by with much small talk before Claire said, "Come on, you; let's get an early night. You look like you could do with a whole night's sleep about now." Karl was beyond tired; however, his mind was spinning with the thought of not being home when the baby arrived.

Sunday, the whole family came over to Hitchin for a lunch party out in the garden. Ello was enjoying himself, helping Mama and Freida in the kitchen making an Austrian Apple strudel for dessert. Claire was assisting but mainly watching Mama work her magic. Having a family gathering was what she loved the most, and by the look on Karl's face, he felt the same. After lunch, Karl and Ronny strolled off down the garden to talk shop. Claire could see Ronny's lowered head moving from side to side. This could not be a good discussion they were having; it must be about the activities they all talk about in secret. The afternoon turned into early evening, and it was time for the family to return to Baldock.

"Karl, I don't know when I will see you next; please, be careful doing that dangerous thing you do. I could see Ronny was telling you about his new posting to a training squadron in Scotland. He leaves in two weeks, but Freida has been expecting this for quite some time. Try not to worry, my son; we ladies and your brothers will watch out for each other while our men are away. Karl, I will stay close to our Claire, so try not to worry about her; she is in good company." Somehow, they all squeezed into Ronny's car, then waved out the windows as they drove off toward Baldock.

Claire woke Karl early as she always did on Monday morning, saying, "Karl, while you get yourself ready, I'll make coffee and an egg sandwich for you downstairs, alright?" Karl got dressed in his field uniform, and carrying his travel bag, proceeded downstairs. In the kitchen was Claire, smartly dressed in her maternity outfit, ready to go to work after she dropped Karl off at the station.

"Darling, what time did you get up? It's only 0630 hours right now." "Karl, you ask me that every time you leave for Slough. You know I can't sleep too well with this big bump parked in front of me, and my internal alarm clock always goes off early each time you leave," answered Claire as she busily continued making breakfast. "Sit down, you handsome spy; we will have to make it a quick breakfast to get you to the station on time." On days like this, when Karl would return to Slough, they talked but never brought up what was really bothering them most: long periods of separation and Karl's dangerous command in the BIS.

Once more, Claire walked Karl through the tunnel to the platform. Holding each other was heart wrenching; they both wanted to say so much, but words would not come. Claire was thinking, *will he return soon?* Karl was thinking, *with what I'm involved in, will I be there to see Claire give birth to our first child?* They had one last kiss and a tender embrace before Karl climbed up into the compartment, thinking this gets harder and harder each time. Karl waved to the lonely lady standing there through the open compartment door, lost in her grief and once again on her own. Silently, she stood there watching the train disappear into the smoke trail behind it.

The station master came up to her and, with a sympathetic voice, spoke to Claire. "Mrs. Vita, I always see you watching Major Vita leaving on the early morning train to King's Cross. It reminds me of when I used to leave my wife back in 1916. It still makes me sad, seeing young ladies like you doing the very same thing; let's hope he can return in a few weeks, shall we?"

Claire smiled at him, and, kissing his cheek, she answered, "Let's pray he'll be alright, and let's add another prayer for all our lads in uniform around the world." Walking back through the tunnel, how could Claire know that, on his return to Slough, her husband would be confined to the camp and would not be there at her side when baby Nicholas finally made his presence known.

December was a hectic time for the Vita family. Karl only got away for Christmas Eve and Christmas Day but had to return that evening. Ronny was much luckier; he got one week off. That year, 1943, came to a thundering end. The Allies were finally gaining footholds in many parts of the territories formerly controlled by Germany. Italy surrendering caused the Germans to regroup, sending many divisions into Italy in a last-ditch effort to hold onto it.

The U.S. forces overcame the Japanese at Guadalcanal in the Pacific, continuing success after success in the Aleutian Islands, New Guinea, and the Solomon Islands. The British and Indian troops began their guerrilla campaign in Burma with growing success, liberating towns and villages that the occupying Japanese forces had starved. The Russians advanced with a growing conviction to defeat the Hun on the Eastern front, recapturing Kharkov then Kiev.

Allied bombing continued around the clock over Germany, the English Bombing by night and the Americans by day. Some of these raids had as many as a thousand aircraft dropping thousands of tons of bombs at one time. The second front in Europe would continue being planned and, on numerous occasions, postponed. This would all change in 1944 when the final plan became the bible for the D-Day invasion.

Karl was constantly working; restrictions continued to the point that getting a pass for leave was out of the question. His position and the work he did still allowed him the occasional phone call to Claire. By February, with heightened activities around England, camp overcrowding was a big problem. An even bigger problem was the many makeshift tent camps everywhere, which made security almost impossible. But with strict controls in place, they managed to keep the lid on this massive invasion force. The Allied Command became increasingly concerned about potential leaks getting fed back to the German High Command.

Karl, very much at the center of all this preparation, had become bitter, torn between duty and family. His constant anger increased the closer it came to Claire's due date. The thought of not being able to travel home to be with his wife with only a few days left before giving birth frustrated him immensely. Trapped in this position, he formulated a plan to make it back to Hitchin before a total lockdown was enforced at all military facilities throughout England. D-Day was only a few months away it was that close.

Lying on his bed, he considered what such a plan would cost him, and would it have any repercussions to his wife and family? He could face a court martial or possibly something much worse. The thought of seeing their new baby was compelling him to want to break the rules. What if something happened to him once the invasion started? Then he would never see the baby, nor his wife, Claire. If that happened, it would scar Claire indefinitely. Damn the rules and restrictions; he was going over the wall back to Hitchin and the Lister Hospital!

CHAPTER 5

BABY NICHOLAS

Karl walked over to the motor pool to find his driver, "Morning, Charlie, I have a question for you. As you know, my wife is imminently expecting our first child, and I was wondering if I could obtain a pass, could I use one of those Hillman utility vehicles?" Karl was putting his plan into place, and by the look on Charlie's face, he knew exactly what this major was planning to do.

"Well, I guess if you had a pass, that one over there is usually available. We keep it ready with a full petrol tank, and the ignition key is always kept under the driver's seat, so we don't misplace it. No need to find me, Sir; I'll make a notation in the vehicle log if I see it's gone. I'll assume it's being used or out on a test drive just in case someone needs to know where it is if you know what I mean. Whenever you need it, you know what to do." Charlie smiled. Saluting, he turned and walked away; his parting words over his shoulder were, "Make sure I get a photograph of the new baby, Sir; good luck to you."

Karl knew Charlie would help him with transportation. Now, how to secure a pass? Entering the main office building, he proceeded down the hall to Bill's office. Knocking on the door, he waited for the familiar answer. "Come in!" came the response.

"Karl, I've been looking for you everywhere. Sit down; we have some celebrating to do. I just received a call from your sister, Freida. Karl, old man, you are now the proud father of a healthy baby boy. Freida also said Claire is doing marvelously well and is as happy as a new mother could be. Sit down while I get a bottle out of the cabinet in the other room. We need to toast Nicholas Vita. Karl, I can see that look on your face. Don't be thinking anything stupid. You do realize

I cannot issue you a pass, and if you attempt to leave this camp, you will be picked up and will probably face court martial charges, don't you? Now, let me get that bottle and two glasses," threatened Bill as he left the office.

Karl sat there, burning up inside with anger, when he noticed a pad of blank passes on Bill's desk. The top one had been signed with no other information on it. Karl sprang into action.

Reaching over, he peeled the pass off, noticing the next one was also signed. Smiling, he knew Bill could not issue a pass, but he had signed the two blank ones the top, ready to be dated. Bill returned with the bottle and glasses. As he placed the bottle next to the pad, his eyes quickly noted that the top one was missing. "Well, my good friend, here's to you taking on a new role and responsibility as a new father. A toast to Claire and Nicholas. I hope it won't be too long until you can see them both."

Bill, smiling, was also thinking, I hope he makes it to the Lister Hospital before someone notices he's missing. I'll have to talk to Clive about saving his skin. "Karl, you've been working almost around the clock. Why don't you take the rest of the day off to catch up on that lost sleep, now that you know mother and child are in good health? You have much to be thankful for now that the waiting is over. I'm sure your staff won't miss you until tomorrow afternoon; they'll understand. When you leave here, why don't you stop by to give them the good news and tell them about your need to get some needed sleep? Is there anything I can do for you right now?" asked Bill, putting the day pass pad back into the center drawer of his desk.

"No, Bill, giving me this amazingly wonderful news and a good glass of whiskey is more than enough. I will take your advice, though, about retiring to my quarters for a long overdue rest."

Bill walked around the desk to hug his friend, whispering very quietly in his ear, "Kiss them both for me!"

Karl waited until the motor pool was on a break. Carrying his briefcase, he marched boldly over to the Hillman. Reaching under the seat, he found the ignition key, then quickly started the engine. Approaching the main gate, he presented his ID card along with the pass, which he had filled out, showing a noontime departure with a return date for the following morning. The guard saluted, then entered the guardhouse to enter the departure time and return date. Returning, the guard wished him a good day, then saluted as Karl drove through the barrier and out onto the main road.

Driving as quickly as he legally could, he covered the forty-five miles in one hour and forty minutes. Before reaching Lister Hospital, he stopped to buy a dozen roses for Claire, then proceeded to the rear of the hospital to park the Hillman. Karl walked around the building toward the main entrance, only to be met by two military policemen. God, I didn't even make it to the entrance, he thought. "Major Vita, we've been waiting for you," said the sergeant. "We're told your wife just gave birth, is that correct?"

Karl, standing in front of them, flowers in hand, replied, "That's correct. Look, I know I'm here without permission, but all I want is to spend some time with my wife and son. Please, allow me that. Just give me an hour, and I will return without protest."

The two military policemen looked at each other, smiling; the sergeant answered, "Sir, you have us confused. Colonel Knight called us to intercept you with instructions that you are to return to the camp in Slough no later than 2000 hours this evening, not 1200 hours' tomorrow, due to the heightened security restrictions. The colonel also instructed us to stop at Harkness Roses and buy a dozen roses, charging them to your account. He said you left in a hurry and probably wouldn't have time to stop. By the looks of it, your wife is now getting two dozen roses, isn't she? Sir, may we add our congratulations as well, and Sir, I was told to ask you, as an officer, to abide by the revision to your pass. Do I have your word on this, Sir?" asked the sergeant again.

"You have my word. I will be back in the camp no later than 1930 hours, probably earlier, though. Thank you again for your understanding." Karl felt very relieved that he was not branded as a deserter. Entering the lobby, he asked the receptionist for Claire's floor and room number. The excitement was building as he waited impatiently for the lift. Getting off on the third floor, he marched quickly to room #305. Outside in the hall, he could see Freida and Caroline talking. Seeing a khaki uniform and two big bunches of roses hiding that person's face, they both walked toward him.

Being her witty self, Caroline said, "Oh, Karl, you shouldn't have bought those for Freida and me." Both ladies hugged Karl, congratulating him on being a new father.

"Where is Mama? Is she still here?" asked Karl, hoping she was in with Claire.

"Mama left less than an hour ago in a taxi. The neighbors next door kindly volunteered to watch Franchot so that we could spend time with Claire. Mama is going to be so disappointed to find out you turned up unannounced. Karl, you will have to wait here with us until the nurse has finished attending to Claire, but it should only be a few more minutes."

The door finally opened, and out came the nurse, saying, "You, must be Major Vita, is that correct? Congratulations, Sir; your wife and son are doing marvelous; go ahead and introduce yourself to your son, Nicholas."

Karl was feeling nervous. As much as he was a man with nerves of steel and an Intelligence officer, he had no practical skills handling a new baby.

"Go ahead, Karl, and don't look so nervous! Nicholas is a baby; he doesn't know how to be a Vita yet," said Freida, looking at the troubled look on her brother's face. Slowly opening the door, Karl quietly entered the room. There was Claire, sitting up in bed with baby Nicholas in her arms.

When she saw Karl, her face beamed with joy and happiness, and she said, "Nick, say hello to your dad. I knew he would get here one way or another. Nothing can stop your crazy Austrian father, and here he is. Darling, isn't he beautiful? He has your eyes. Thank God, though, he has my nose. Come here and kiss me now, kiss us both."

Karl, with tears of happiness, crossed over to the bedside, hugging and kissing Claire. "May I hold him, Claire, or is it too early for that?" Karl, feeling out of his comfort zone, kissed her again.

Claire, with a big smile on her face, answered, "Of course, you can; put your hand under his head when you take him." Karl nervously took the baby from Claire, and, for a split second, he felt he had passed into another place; the connection with his new son was overpowering. Walking around the room, Karl kept kissing the soft skin of his son. Tears flowing freely down his face, he looked up at Claire, who could feel the love and bonding between her two men. Nick's little hand was now holding a finger of his father's big hand. Karl slowly moved it side to side.

Karl returned to the bedside, returning Nick to his mother. Karl finally said, "Thank you, darling, for giving us this most precious gift, our son." With emotions running high, Freida and Caroline joined them, all sitting around Claire's bed, totally in love with Nick and enjoying their time together. The nurse obliged them by taking pictures with Karl's camera.

Freida and Caroline announced they were leaving, saying their goodbyes, giving the new parents some private time, knowing Karl was also close to leaving. "See you tomorrow," said Freida as they left. Karl looked at his watch, then at Claire, silently telling her it was time for him to depart, returning to the stress that faced him, commencing from tomorrow until long after D-Day.

"Claire, I hate to do this to you, but I made a promise I would return later today. If I leave now, I should be able to meet the curfew time. On my return, I have two very close friends to thank, and another one, my driver, Charlie. Those three made it possible for me to be here today." Karl held Claire and Nicholas for a few more moments, knowing it would be a long time until he could do this again.

"Karl, I don't want to put any undue stress on you right now, but I must ask you this, when do you think we will see you again?" Claire was always careful about asking that type of question, but today, she had a gut wrenching feeling that this would be the last time for many, many months to come.

Karl looked at her as she asked this question. How could he tell her he already knew the answer but could not say more due to security? His heart was breaking, and it would, in fact, be many months before he could return home. With luck, maybe he could come home by August, assuming he lived through those first few weeks after D-Day. Karl stood up, holding her hand, again telling her how much he loved her and Nicholas. Then, he walked toward the door. Turning in the doorway, he threw a parting kiss before returning to his car and his stressful duties in Slough.

CHAPTER 6

THE LONGEST DAY
D-DAY JUNE 6TH

1944

Karl drove up to the guardhouse, presenting his ID and pass. "One moment, Sir, while I log you back in," said the guard, saluting before opening the barrier and waving him through. Parking the Hillman in the exact parking place he had taken it from earlier that day, Karl walked toward the main building, thinking, I wonder if any of my chaps are still in the lounge? I think I'll stick my head in while I'm here. There, at their usual table, were Bill, Clive, Gunther, and Helmut.

"Look what the cat just dragged in," said Gunther with a big smile on his face. "Come, sit here; you have a lot to tell us!" Karl looked at Bill, then Clive, a broad smile on his face that told them he was very thankful for putting their careers on the line for him.

Being the senior officer in the lounge, Clive got preferential treatment, ordering a cocktail for his friend. Then he asked the steward to open the box of cigars he had brought with him. Once the drinks arrived, Clive stood, asking everyone in the lounge to stand.

"Gentlemen, please raise your glasses and join me in welcoming baby Nicholas; may his years be blessed with good health, good fortune, and to his parents, may their years ahead be filled with love for their new son. Congratulations to you, Major Vita, and your wife, Claire." Clive slugged down a large gulp of whiskey, then sat back down again with everyone in the lounge still clapping and cheering.

The air was now full of cigar smoke as they all enjoyed the camaraderie of those around them. Karl was asked to tell them all about his visit and how Claire was doing before he left. The strain of the day was catching up to Karl. Feeling very tired, he thanked them all again for the congratulations. "Gentlemen, would you please excuse me? I need to head to my quarters to write to Claire and then get some way overdue sleep."

Gunther was the first to speak after Karl had left. "I still can't grasp the change in Karl. He has changed into a very responsible husband and now a new father, and let's face it, Claire is an absolute gem and loves him completely. Hazel wrote to me recently, telling me how he watched over her while they were in Canada. She also said when her American boyfriend proposed marriage, it was Karl she turned to for advice. I promised her I would write her once the baby was born. I don't know if you are aware of this, chaps, but Hazel and Claire have become good pen pals. In a sad way, it's a pity because Hazel is still very much in love with Karl and has been since the training camp back in 1938. I guess it was never meant to be," concluded Gunther.

The following two months were very chaotic for all the planning groups, organizing the disbursement of thousands of troops to five ports along the south coast of England, directing where the massive armada of ships would be moored and berthed.

Keeping track of the thousands of tanks, half-tracks, heavy artillery, Jeeps, trucks, and all sorts of other equipment was a monumental undertaking. Keeping all this from the spying eyes of the Germans' surveillance aircraft was a massive task for the Intelligence people. During this buildup, the job of keeping the Germans away from the English Coast would be the responsibility of the combined Air Force Command, maintaining around the clock aerial patrols in the channel area and embarkation ports, discouraging any Luftwaffe probing. In addition, the coastal command would provide day and night patrols along the coast of England and the narrowest part of the channel for any U-Boats lurking there, hoping to catch ships entering these southern ports.

Part of Karl's contingency had been assigned to support the American offensive that would go ashore on Omaha and Utah beaches. Their orders would be to go ashore on the second day, then push inland to set up their interrogation site nearer the front lines. The Allied High Command needed to assess troop movements along the Western Coast of France, and Karl's people were highly trained in making that assessment. Mid-May, Karl was asked to attend a meeting with old friend Major Andy Anderson of the OSS and Bill Lowes, the Camp Commander in Slough. Others in attendance were officers of the British and American commando's brigades.

General Jacks called this meeting, and in attendance with him were members of his staff, including Colonel Clive Knight. "Gentlemen, we are all here today to discuss *Operation Overlord*. We have been concerned about German tank and heavy artillery movements in and around *Pas-de-Calais* for quite some time. To date, our deceptive measures have been working with thousands of blow-up tanks, trucks, and wooden airplanes all centered in East Anglia, making the Germans believe, if an attack is made, it will be in the *Pas-de-Calais* region. If we had any sense, we would blow those inflatable tanks up with helium and launch them in the direction of the German forces; that would mess them for certain. Can you imagine being attacked by an armament of flying Sherman tanks?"

His dry humor made everyone start laughing out loud. "Seriously, if those Panzer tanks were to be deployed to Normandy, they could deliver massive firepower onto all five landing sites. Let me now unveil one of our plans to make sure that does happen. Gentlemen, we intend to grab a high-ranking Panzer Commander, Major Gustav Jagger, to gain vital information about tank strengths and their present locations. This plan will be to land commandos about ten days in advance of the D-Day landing, capture that officer, then, with the help of the French Resistance, move him to a safe hiding place. Major Vita will assign two of his top agents to this mission. It will be up to them to obtain the information we absolutely must have prior to D-Day. We are confident that the methods developed by Major Vita and his team will get the answers we are looking for. If that fails, we will revert to brute force.

"Extraction of the commando unit will be by submarine; if that fails, they will make their way toward Normandy to meet up with the main force when they come ashore. As for Major Gustav Jagger, well, the people at MI-5 are anxious to continue his interrogation. He will be extracted from France by airlift back to England as soon as the BIS chaps are done with him.

"Major Vita, you and your agents attached to Major Anderson's command will ship out with him on the Heavy Cruiser, the USS Augusta CA-31, already berthed in Portsmouth. Major Anderson, your OSS command will assist the BIS chaps.

"A platoon of American Rangers will be accompanying the Intelligence people until relieved by a regular division of infantry. The French Resistance has secured a deserted farmhouse about eight miles inland that will be used during the early days before the push inland, once it is safe to move the interrogation group away from the Omaha Beach area. If all goes according to plan, that will be within eight days of the first wave gaining control of the beach."

General Jacks now turned the meeting over to Colonel Knight to explain further the details of the mission. Karl and his twenty agents would land on the second day, boarding the landing craft at 0630 hours', assuming the beach has been secured. Karl, hearing this, felt relieved, knowing he would not be in that first wave. Early projections forecasted casualties would be at their highest on that first day. The commitment he made to Claire was ringing in his ears like a loud bell. He was torn now between duty and family, which wasn't something he had ever had to deal with previously.

The meeting went on all day, continuing through the next three days. After this combined meeting, each one of the groups broke off to rehearse and perfect their mission objectives. Next came training with the commandos that would grab the German tank commander and their extraction plans.

Karl and Andy worked diligently with their groups, rehearsing and perfecting their plans on how to interrogate prisoners. "Chaps, once we have established an interrogation center, we need to move quickly, keeping our troops abreast of German troop locations. First on the list, other than name and serial number is to find out what division they are from; their uniform insignia should provide this detail. Remember, you must try to trick them into divulging their last position or general location before being captured.

You need to be convincing, even cocky, that you already have information on their troop locations and tank strengths. Those insignias on their uniforms will help down the road when other prisoners start arriving, wearing the same ones. It could well provide us with tools to trick them further. This will be a good place to start. Remember, move quickly, and don't give them time to think about your line of questioning. Try to establish a link between their surnames and dialect; this will help define where that prisoner originates from. Information like this will assist us in getting them to make a slip.

Also, remember that what we are really after is divisional strengths and how many divisions are hidden in and around the areas our troops are advancing toward. These same interrogation methods we can use on other Axis prisoners as well. These are just a few of the methods we will perfect each day until we have a fool proof plan," concluded Karl. The Allied High Command was still very concerned about how many heavy Tiger tanks were already in the area and that nagging question, when would the German Commander Marshal Erwin Rommel expect reinforcements to start arriving from the North?

In whatever spare time he had, Karl would socialize with his friends in the officers' lounge after work. Because of the restrictions placed on everyone in the camp, the officers' lounge was becoming much busier. Men and women clogged the lounge. Because of heightened security, these nightly get-togethers were the only outlet they had to relax and blow off steam from the daily stress of training for that big day. As for Karl, when he returned each night to his quarters, he would write his letter to Claire. In his latest, he included the photographs he took of Claire and Nicholas at the Lister Hospital. The camp photography lab was more than willing to make six sets for him to send home. All incoming and outgoing mail was subject to censorship, so no saucy content other than cleverly disguised phrases could be written.

On May 24th, many of the BIS units would ship out to their respective deployment units. Two days before shipping out, Karl had time with Clive and Andy to review their orders once again. Clive and his team would be supporting the British force leaving from Shoreham by Sea; their landing beach code name was Sword. His contingency was divided to support the second British invasion force departing from Southampton; their landing beach was code named Gold.

Karl's second in command, Captain Hardy Meyer, would lead his contingency, supporting the Canadian force already in Portsmouth; their landing beach code name was Juno. The American forces would depart from Dartmouth to their landing beach code name Utah. Karl's contingency would leave with Andy, heading to Portsmouth to board the heavy cruiser, the USS Augusta.

Before leaving to their designated embarkation ports, the commanders got together for the last time in the lounge. Clive, now in field attire, looked so much different than his usual uniform. "Gentlemen, in a few hours, we will head out to different ports to join the biggest armada in history. As much as we are all excited about returning to Europe, we must remember, we are also going into certain danger, not as much as the infantry hitting those beaches on the first day, but, nevertheless, expect to be in constant danger most of the time, so please, think about that before you do something stupid. Make General Jacks and myself proud by the actions you take.

"Major Vita, you have a reputation as a risk taker; I know I can rely on you to do your duty, but remember, there's a youngster that would like to get to know his dad in the years that lie ahead of him. Major Lowes, I know how disappointed you are about having to remain here in Slough. Unfortunately, that bum leg of yours is not the liability we can chance. Sorry, old man, I know how much you wanted to be included in Operation Overlord. Gentlemen, it's time for us to depart. One last thing, have you written letters to your loved ones, just in case you don't return? Give them to Major Lowes before you depart today." As Clive looked around the lounge, he could see the looks on their faces as he reminded them about that last letter.

Boarding the American coaches and transports, Karl sat next to Andy. The mood was upbeat, probably due to the nervous energy they all had. In Karl's head, he was considering all the scenarios that could disrupt their objective. "Andy, once we get ashore, stay to our plan of splitting into two groups as a precaution. We will be under attack, so if one of us goes down, the boys will still have a leader. I have been in two dangerous situations before; things happen very quickly. We can refine this more once we get our division together on the ship." Karl's mind was processing all the things that could go wrong in those first few hours.

"Karl, I'll follow your lead; whatever you think is best is good with me." Andy's nervousness was obvious. Having never been in a really dangerous situation before, he would rely on Karl when the time came. The group gathered around Karl and Andy on the pier with all their equipment in waterproof bags, ready to climb down those boarding nets into the landing craft. "Bloody hell, it's a big bugger, ain't it, Sir?" asked one of the BIS agents.

"Yes, she is, Corporal; it's old, but she can still pack a big punch. CA-31 has been in service since 1931. We are fortunate to be crossing the channel in a heavy cruiser; other chaps are not so lucky. The weather is turning nasty, so we are definitely in a better place; let's get aboard, shall we?" said Andy. Little did Andy realize how that bad weather would set back the actual D-Day.

Thousands of troops were jammed into all types and sizes of ships, waiting day after day for the order to set sail. The constant orders to stand down were having a negative effect on the thousands of troops, their nerves on edge waiting for the launch command. Many heated argument would explode due to this confinement. Karl and Andy followed the sailor as he guided them through the labyrinth of corridors. Karl was used to narrow passages on ships but never a warship of this size. Typically assigned to two officers, their quarters now had four small bunks, one above the other jammed into the cramped space. The tall Andy would learn to sleep with his legs hanging over the end of his bunk and almost into poor Karl's face. With his usual dry sarcasm, Karl informed Andy, "From here on, you are instructed to wash your big feet every night before turning in." They both sat laughing, trying to make the best of this tight sleeping arrangement.

"Put your gear on your bed, so the two other blighters joining us will know these two are taken," suggested Karl before leaving the cabin to find their team berthed someplace on a lower deck.

"Karl, you're the seaman; why don't you guide us to berthing section #103? I think that sailor said it was aft of this cabin," remarked Andy.

After making numerous wrong turns, they finally found the open area designated #103. Bunks stacked four high on each side ran the length of the compartment, giving new meaning to the term overcrowding. "Better not say anything about our cramped quarters, Andy; one of these blokes is likely to take a swing at you," said Karl, laughing but realizing many days would pass before they finally could vacate these quarters.

Finding their group, they both felt saddened seeing how the team was forced to endure such accommodations. "Major Vita, are we allowed to go up on deck? It's stifling down here," said one of the younger agents.

"I see no harm in doing that; don't get in anyone's way, though. These blokes running this big tube are rattled enough already," replied Karl.

The following day, Karl found a quiet spot to write to Claire while they were still dockside.

My Darling Claire,

How I miss you. I would love to be home with you and Nicholas about now. I hope you show him a picture of his dad each day, so he knows who I am when I return home. I find myself thinking back to our honeymoon by the sea. How I would like to be back there right now. I'm still very busy; paperwork was never my strong point. Hopefully, this will change sometime soon. Having this evening alone makes me think back to when I was an officer on a merchant ship. Those were wonderful times but now shadowed by my life with you and our son. I will write when I have more time but don't get angry if I don't write for a while. You know how forgetful I can be.

Kisses to you and Nick.

My love always.
Karl

Karl read back his short letter to Claire, thinking, I hope she connects the dots. She's sharp as a tack when it comes to a hidden message. The days dragged on, and boredom was becoming routine. June 2nd, a meeting was called onshore by all commanders landing at Omaha beach. "Gentlemen, it now looks like we will ship out within the next several days. The weather is not on our side, but that may be an advantage, as the Germans will not expect any type of invasion in such conditions. The armada of aircraft and gliders are on standby for immediate deployment once General Eisenhower throws that history making switch.

"The American forces comprising the 82nd and 101st airborne divisions and the British 6th airborne division will be the primary assault units; others will include French and Polish units. Their objectives are to secure all roads and bridges leading to Normandy, and others will push to secure the port of Cherbourg. Once we set sail, we will join the main body, heading for our assigned landing beach, Omaha. Right now, a big concern is towing the Mulberry floating docks across the channel to Omaha and Gold beaches in these heavy seas.

"Expeditiously getting equipment ashore will be critical to the plan. The builders have assured us that these massive concrete docks will be able to weather that storm, and I pray to God they're right. Now, most of the first wave will board the landing craft from the transport vessels right after the Naval bombardment ceases. That will be around 0615 hours. You guys will be going ashore on the second day. Hopefully, the shore batteries and artillery positions will have been eliminated by that time.

"You will still have to move with extreme caution and stay on the marked pathways. Our minesweeper will mark those that have been swept clear leading off the beach. We can't be sure of the areas around them, so pay attention! From now until then, take this time to get your affairs in order. Thank you; we will meet again once we are committed to a sailing date," said Lieutenant Colonel Michael Wells of the U.S. Navy.

June 4th, the order came down; they would set sail after midnight on June 5th, arriving on station in the very early morning hours before dawn in the company of over 6,800 other vessels that made up the armada of transports vessels and landing craft loaded with tanks and other vehicles. The massive firepower of 1,213 Naval vessels would start the bombardment in the predawn hours. In that opening bombardment, the *Augusta* would fire fifty-one 230mm shells, the range being provided by overhead U.S. Navy VOS-7 spotters aircraft flying English Super Marine Spitfires.

The landing commenced precisely at 0630 hours', with the first wave of landing craft hitting the beaches under a hail of German MG42 rapid firing machine guns that could fire up to 1,500 rounds per minute. Also, along that beach, eight heavily fortified concrete pillboxes with menacing 75mm caliber artillery guns were bombarding ships and landing craft as they attempted to land, turning many into flaming wrecks. All along the beach, landing craft dropped their boarding ramps pushing into the sand, exposing the forward infantrymen to a hail of lead, their lifeless forms falling inside the craft, never making it to the beach. Bloodied bodies lay everywhere, but still, these determined young men pushed forward, seeking shelter on the shore behind the steel Czech hedgehog anti-tank obstacles. If they were fortunate enough to make it to the protection of the high sand dunes, they would be protected for a while anyway.

The long beaches and the lapping seawater turned red with the blood of young soldiers that would never see the sunset on this day, June 6th. Andy found Karl on the railing, watching all the activity taking place below. "Karl, come with me. We have been invited to the bridge by Captain Jerald Brennan, adjutant to Admiral Alan Kirk," yelled Andy over the constant bombardment from *Augusta's* main battery and other warships close by to them. "Why are we being invited to the bridge? Don't you think they're kind of busy about now?" Karl yelled back to Andy. Arriving at the bridge wing, the sight that unfolded in front of them was beyond words. Smoke and burning wrecks were all along the beach and bodies everywhere, and still, the landing craft kept coming, the larger ones carrying tanks, heavy artillery, and trucks, the smaller one's landing infantry. Entering the bridge, Karl was immediately impressed at how much larger this bridge was compared to what he was used to; it was a heavy cruiser, after all.

"You must be Major Vita, is that correct?" asked Brenner.

"That is correct, Captain. Thank you for inviting Captain Anderson and myself to your bridge."

Captain Brenner, like Karl, had been in the merchant service before America entered the war. "Your friend here told me all about you last night, and I understand you served with the Langstaff Shipping Company, is that correct?"

"That is correct; it seems like a lifetime since I wore that maritime uniform, though." Karl was thinking, why on earth is he interested in my previous carrier?

"Well, I was just interested; that's all. What was the last ship you served on? Let me guess; was it the *Tristian*? Am I right?"

Karl's defenses went up, almost in lockdown, with Brenner smiling back at Karl. "Well, I have an old friend that was with you on the *Tristian* right up until you left it unexpectedly in 1936."

Karl continued to stare, waiting for that name. "Gentlemen, you are welcome to watch the progress from up here. Help yourself to coffee over there." Captain Brenner turned to rejoin the staff officers out on the bridge wing with General Omar Bradley in the center.

Karl called after Brenner, "Captain, before you leave, aren't you going to tell me the name of your friend from the *Tristian*?"

Brenner stopped briefly; turning around, he said with a broad smile, "Does the name Giovanni Sauvé come to mind? We'll talk later!"

Karl froze, completely stunned. He could not believe what he had just heard. Brenner knew his old captain. Turning to Andy, he was lost for words, "What are the chances of meeting someone on a warship standing off from the beaches of Normandy in the biggest invasion in modern history who knows the captain of the *Tristian*?"

Andy, shaking his head, answered, "I found that out last night when I was in a meeting with Captain Brenner. He asked me what I knew about you before joining the BIS. I hope you are not rattled that I told him about your time in the merchant service; it was only what you told me. That's when he informed me that he knew all about you and was looking forward to meeting you today. He also asked me not to say anything as he would like to do that himself. Now, you know why we received the invitation."

Karl's head was spinning. There would be time to reminisce later, but right now, he wanted to return to the bridge wing to witness the carnage taking place all along the Normandy beaches. All around them, the constant loud explosions, gunfire, and antiaircraft guns hammering at enemy aircraft trying to break through with an attack were constantly vibrating throughout the ship. Smoke and poor visibility, along with the constant wind, were not ideal for this invasion, but it did make it difficult for the Germans. By the afternoon, the beach was strewn with wrecked vehicles of every type, some still burning. In the water were wrecked landing craft, some beached, some half sunk. The lapping waves were crimson with the blood from thousands of young dead warriors.

Much later that night, activities on the beach became quieter as the night sky, heavy with clouds and smoke, made visibility a challenge, a Godsend for the weary troops waiting for the dawn to start the fight all over again. Karl had just completed an intense rehearsal with his group for their strategy in the morning. Satisfied, he told his group to get some rest as they would need their wits about them when they hit that beach. Karl was wound up, visions colliding in his mind, thinking about the following day.

Entering the officers' mess, he found Andy sitting at a long table with some officer from this morning. "May I join you, gentlemen?" asked Karl as Andy slid over to the next chair, making room for Karl.

"How are you guys holding up, Karl?" asked Andy, making small talk.

"As well as can be expected. For most of them, being this close to so much danger is probably playing on their nerves. They may be young, but they are shouldering their responsibilities really well. Tomorrow will be the making of all of them. Anyone seen Captain Brenner or is he still on the bridge?" asked Karl, really wanting to find out more about how he knew Captain Sauvé.

Excusing himself, Karl made his way up to the bridge, the lights dimmed from the red night lanterns.

"I thought I'd find you up here, Captain; mind if I join you?" asked Karl.

"Glad of the company, Major. Can we dispense with the formalities of rank for a while? Please, call me Jerry; if you have no objections, is that alright Karl? I am assuming the real reason you came up here is to ask me about my old friend, Giovanni Sauvé; is that correct?

"I first met Gio in 1938 when he was in Havana, Cuba. My ship, the Gabriel, was on the opposite side of the dock. That first night, I went ashore to find a quiet bar to have a drink. There at the bar, I met Gio—also alone. We talked for about two hours, and a friendship started. I'm not sure how it came up, but he started telling me how he had lost his first officer and close friend in Marseille back in 1936. I could tell he missed you very much. Using his words, he said if you had made your intentions clear, he would have tried to talk you out of leaving. He also said he prayed that you made it to Vienna, and from there, managed to get your family out of Europe. He went on to say, if only I could have kept in touch with Karl, I would have felt much better. I have no idea where he is or what he is doing, other than I pray he is safe in England.

"We saw each other four or five times more before the war started. I have his address in Genoa. I'm not sure if he is still there, but it could help you find him after this damn war comes to an end." Jerry reached into his breast pocket, pulling out a folded piece of paper. "I hope this will help you, Karl. I, too, would like to meet up again with that noble gentleman. Karl, you should head back to your quarters and try to get some sleep. Tomorrow will tax your energy to its limit, but I'm glad we had a few minutes to talk. As they say, to be continued."

Karl stood up, and, shaking Jerry's hand, he left the bridge. "Officer leaving the bridge!" said a sailor standing by the entrance. Karl sat outside under a night lantern, protected by a high metal partition that sheltered the light being seen from the shore. Opening his leather binder, he started to write letters to Claire; one he would give to Andy in case he didn't make it.

My dearest Claire and Nicholas,

I pray this letter will never be delivered to you because, if it does, it means I have fallen doing my duty. We both knew the risks we were taking, hoping that I would make it through this terrible war. Claire, you and Nick are always at the forefront of my thoughts. I love you so very much, and hopefully, that comes through in this letter. When you look at Nick, my blood is running through his veins along with yours; that is something I will always treasure. I'm so pleased you pushed me to the realization that we needed to bring Nicholas into this war-torn world. Now, I can go on my mission to someplace with that vision in my heart. Chances are, you have already received the latest news about what we are doing. Like Patrick, I only have two wishes for you now: Be happy, my darling; don't be bitter, and let those wonderful memories we made be your strength. I always knew the dangerous line of work I was in could, and now it has taken me from both of you. I'm saddened that I won't grow old by your side and watch our son grow up into a fine, handsome man. The other wish is for my wonderful son, Nicholas, to know all about his dad, the good and the bad alike, and Claire, remind him of my love for the sea. Perhaps he could continue where I left off, wishful thinking on my part. Claire, I could go on, but deep inside me, there is a thought and a prayer that one day I will be sitting next to you as we read this letter together, the war a distant bad memory. After that, we can burn this letter, never to think again of the devastation it could have caused if delivered. My darling, I pray this is what happens. Then, we can look to a brighter future as we head up the Western Hills with our son Nicholas on a peaceful sunny day's hike.

I Love you always, Claire.
Your Husband,
Karl

Karl read it several times. Satisfied, he sealed it into an envelope, and he wrote in bold letters on the front: Only to be delivered if I fall doing my duty. Major Karl Vita.

That night, Karl studied the maps that Captain Brenner had given him. Karl was always very thorough in his planning. Satisfied, he climbed up into his bunk to get some sleep.

At 0500 hours, Karl got dressed, then strapped his .45 caliber pistol to his right leg. Checking his Bren gun to make sure it was operating correctly, he checked one more time his ammunition packs before putting on his forage cap, his helmet hanging from his backpack. "Well, Andy, I'm about as ready as I will ever be. I hope to see you in a couple of days when we are set up. Remember that letter that's with the rest of my stuff. With any luck, you will be returning it to me sooner than later." Karl and Andy made their way down to deck three to meet up with his group.

"Morning, chaps, did you all have a hearty breakfast this morning? I don't think we will find a restaurant that's open en route, do you?" Once again, a loud cheer came from his group, along with the young American Rangers that would provide their protective cover. "Andy, we will try to stay in touch by radio; don't bank on it, though. Bye for now, old friend." With that farewell, they proceeded to the lower deck, ready to climb down the boarding nets. One last look up to Andy on the upper deck, then over the side, he lowered himself down the boarding net.

Karl quietly prayed, *Lord, give me the guidance to protect these young men I'm to lead into extreme danger.* As he thought that, a phrase came to mind made by General Omar Bradley the day before as the first wave of troops gathered to board the landing craft.

BRAVERY IS the capacity to perform properly
even when scared half to death.

CHAPTER 7

LIVES IN PERIL

The waiting landing craft was bouncing wildly alongside the Augusta's hull. Karl and his men lowered themselves down the wet, scrambling nets, but coordinating the boarding was tricky as the waves lifted the landing craft up to meet them, then fell away again. "Now!" commanded Karl as the craft raised itself on the next wave. Each time the craft rose, six more would jump into the craft before it rode the wave back down again. Once onboard, their equipment was lowered down to them. Then, with a loud command, the mooring lines were cast off, and the landing craft got underway, banging into the waves as it pulled away into the dawn of June 7th.

The boat's coxswain yelled down to those below, "Guys, remember to stay low and get off this tub as quickly as you can. Today will not be like yesterday, but remember, there are still snipers present. God be with you." The coxswain rammed the blunt bow of the craft through the surf as it lifted, then ground through the sand onto the beach.

Karl yelled one last time to everyone, "Okay, lads, when that ramp goes down, head straight up the beach. Remember, stay inside the markers in the sand." The craft made the last push with a grinding sound, followed by the ramp dropping into the surf. "Okay, lads, let's get up the beach; stay low, your weapons cocked and ready. Now, go, go, go!"

Around them, sporadic gunfire could be heard, kicking up the sand as they ran to the shelter of the sand dunes. High velocity shells could be heard as they passed overhead, then exploded into the dunes farther down the beach. Out of breath, Karl called Lieutenant O'Brian of the Rangers for a headcount. "All here, Sir; it looks like we're in luck, making it to the dunes before it really got light."

Karl turned to the radio operator, yelling, "Sparky, send a burst to Command: all okay, waiting for the resistance chaps to arrive." O'Brian was a mere twenty-one years old, but Karl already knew he could count on this cool, nervy, lanky Texan. Huddled in the dunes, Karl whispered to him, "Would you mind if I refer to you as Number One? I'm an old maritime officer; I hope you don't mind."

"Sir, it would be my honor to have you call me that. Thanks, Boss." Karl, grinning, could feel the bond of trust they were creating. A movement on the opposite side of the dune brought all the rifle hammers to the ready. The recognition signal to be used was three handclaps, then a brief silence, followed by three more claps repeated twice. All eyes were on the top of the dune watching a body crawling over the top, whispering, "Where are you, you mad Austrian?" It was Gunther. "We were expecting you before dawn; what happened?" asked Gunther again.

"Sorry, I didn't get the telegram, so I had one last pee." Karl was truly happy to see his old friend.

"Come on; we need to move off this bloody beach really quickly. Are you all here?" asked Gunther.

"All accounted for, Major," replied O'Brian.

"Don't call me or anyone else by their rank, alright?" demanded Gunther. Karl's Number One had just received his first lesson in spy operations. Moving quickly, they joined the French Resistance group that would guide them to their first stop at an abandoned farmhouse. Gunther could now welcome his old friend properly, saying, "Yesterday, I asked permission to join this operation, knowing you would welcome the addition of a Kraut to accompany you and this motley group. So, here I am, volunteering to join you. I must really be a glutton for punishment." Karl grinned at Gunther's last remark. "I came ashore at 0400 hours this morning and met up with Claude Archambault and his team of resistance fighters. We made the trek together, and he knows this area so very well.

O'Brian, I apologize for snapping at you a few minutes ago force of habit, again, I'm sorry." Gunther was feeling bad about mouthing off that way.

"That's perfectly alright with me, Corporal," replied O'Brian, loving the look on Gunther's face. Crawling off the dunes, they came across a platoon of infantrymen who gave them advice on how to proceed and not to be shot at by friendly forces. Claude skillfully navigated them away from the roads, already heavy with troops and equipment heading inland.

"Karl, I suggest we circle the abandoned village of St. Michele. The Germans pulled out yesterday, but you never know about booby traps and snipers that may still be in hiding, waiting for any advanced troop movement. If we follow the tree line along that cow path until we reach the farmhouse, I think we could make it by 1430 hours, all going well," advised Claude.

"You're in the lead, Claude, so move out; the rest of you stay alert," whispered Karl. After about two hours of stealthily moving along the path, they came across a broken sign lying on the ground.

"We're only two kilometers from St. Michele, so far, so good. I'm a little concerned that we haven't run into any Allied or German troops. Other than the artillery gunfire off to the northwest, we appear to be alone." Claude was still leery that the Germans were close, hiding until the forward divisions of American troops would run right into an ambush. Circling the bombed-out village, they continued until Claude announced, "Here, look through my binoculars across that field to the left. See the farmhouse? That's our destination. I'm sending two of my men to notify the rest of my group that we're coming across that field and not to fire on us."

Gunther, hearing this, interjected, "As a former German infantry officer, I would caution you that such a move would not be a wise thing to do. What if they're caught out in the open by enemy aircraft or even an armored column hiding in that tree line waiting for precisely something like this to happen?" Gunther was right, of course, so they took the long way around to reach the farmhouse, remaining safe.

Approaching the farmhouse, Claude made the recognition signal with his cupped hands, then made himself visible to the rifle barrels pointing through the broken windows. A few resistance fighters came out to greet them, ushering them inside in case of prying eyes in the nearby woods. Claude spoke first, "As soon as it's dark, we'll leave you to return to our group up north. It was our privilege to guide you today; stay low and safe, just remember the Nazis could well be closer than you realize. Your transportation and equipment should be arriving in the morning. By then, the roads will be packed with convoys and infantry." Claude shook hands with Karl, Gunther, and Will before moving out behind the farmhouse, back into the safety of the tree line. Will jumped into action, directing a perimeter defense around the farmhouse. The platoon of Rangers took up their defensive position, digging foxholes. Once that was done, the heavy, rapid fire machine guns were installed, and the first watch was set.

This first night would be long, with nobody attempting to catch up on sleep. Their adrenaline kept them on edge and wide awake.

"Such young chaps, Gunther, most of those youngsters have never been far away from home like this. It makes me feel like an old man, and I'm assuming you feel the same," said Karl as he and Gunther rested up against the farmhouse wall eating K rations. The dawn was breaking, and already, the sound of heavy caliber guns was shattering the quiet of the countryside.

O'Brian entered the farmhouse kitchen, no longer recognizable as a kitchen. Taking his helmet off, he sat down next to Gunther, saying, "Sirs, we have just received a radio blast that the rest of your detachment will be arriving shortly. Major Anderson will be relieving you, Major Fisher, and you will return with us. The detachment of regular infantry on those trucks will replace my guys as your protection.

The Rangers were already gathering their gear, ready to move out once the transports arrived. "Well, Karl, it looks like we part again. I'm not sure when we'll meet again, someplace in Germany, I would imagine." Gunther gathered his kit in preparation to depart. Moving outside, they waited patiently, looking down the lane for the first sign of the trucks.

"I understand this Intelligence detachment will remain here before moving up again in a couple of weeks, is that correct?" inquired Will.

"That sounds about right, and Will, thanks again for the protective screening," replied Karl. Off in the distance, they saw the column kicking up dust as it made its way up the hill to the farmhouse.

"Gentlemen, this where we part company. Safe travels to your next location. Gunther, drop me a line when you find a quiet minute." Karl was feeling melancholy about his friend's imminent departure. In the lead Jeep, Andy was the first to climb out and head up to the group standing by the farmhouse door. "Good to see you, Andy; how was the drive here?" inquired Karl.

"Considering it's only been three days since the invasion, it was relatively quiet for the first four or five miles, after which we ran into a gun battle. We had to seek cover behind a hedgerow. A forward detachment from the 101st airborne had cornered a squad of Germans in the village of Saint Michele. Luckily for us, the Germans retreated after that skirmish put them on the run. That's why we're late. Have you made radio contact with HQ yet? I was told they have five German officers we can expect later today," said Andy as they walked out toward the trucks being unloaded.

"Finally, we'll have some tables and chairs to work on, and those cots look inviting. So, if we're to interrogate these Krauts, let's get set up, shall we?" snapped Karl.

"Goodbye then, old friend; stay in touch and pass along my regards to Clive when you catch up with him." Karl gripped Gunther's hand, refraining from hugging his friend in front of these new, young troops.

"Karl, don't you have something for me to post? Like that letter you wrote to Claire last night?" inquired Gunther.

"You are so right; wait one moment while I get it." Karl walked swiftly back into the farmhouse, returning almost immediately. "Here you go; I hope it doesn't take too long to reach Claire. Bye again, and please stay safe," said Karl as Gunther climbed into the Jeep. He waved as the small convoy made its way back down the lane; it would be many months before they met up with each other again.

CHAPTER 8

THE LONG MONTHS APART

Claire sat in the living room, playing with baby Nick. She was hoping the postman would deliver a letter from Karl; it had been almost a week since she received his last one. Instinctively, she knew receiving a letter would be nearly impossible for the time being but wished it anyway. Lying on the floor with Nick, she kept staring at this little bundle of joy, thinking, darling, I can feel your presence in our son. Life was more tolerable having Nicholas as her company while Karl was away.

Each morning, she would rise early to take care of Nick, then get herself ready for work. Claire had arranged to pay an old school friend living only five minutes away to take Nick during the daytime; then, she picked him up again after 4:30 p.m. Sheila's husband was also in the military. Unfortunately, he was only a corporal, so money was always tight. When Claire had offered to pay her to watch Nick, Sheila jumped at the chance to earn extra money.

On the weekends, Claire would spend most of Saturday with Mama and Freida. Franchot would wait patiently to see his aunt pull into the driveway. If the weather was dry, he would always ask if they could go for a walk with Nick in the pram. On Sunday, she would dedicate the day to time with Nick. The Sunday before, she had taken Nick to visit Patrick's parents, taking a shopping bag of food supplies she had gotten on the black market. Karl's old friends always had items that were not on the grocery store shelves and were always obliging when it came to taking care of Karl's family. This evening, she sat at her desk, Nick sleeping in his playpen next to her. Claire had beautiful italic handwriting, and she pondered a moment before starting to write to Karl, always sensitive not to include any problems or things that could make him anxious.

My Dearest Karl,

I hope this letter finds you well. Even though you can't tell me where you are, I can only imagine what it must be like. The news we see in the newspaper and hear on the radio is so very frightening, as well as very graphic. You, my darling, will perform your duty in those places, and we both know you are performing your duty to the max. Your son, Nicholas, is growing up so quickly. As young as he is, certain mannerisms are all his dad's, and that is exactly what thrills me to watch. Karl, you can be proud of our little man we brought into this world. Mama talks to him in German, and Freida and I speak to him in both languages. I hope we don't mess up his speaking abilities. Sheila is wonderful with Nick. I sense him getting excited when I drop him off on weekdays. I can't help getting a little jealous, knowing he spends more time with Sheila than with me. Oh, well, just call me a spoiled brat for being like that.

Darling, as we agreed, I wrote to Ronny, asking him and Freida to be Nicholas's godparents when you boys eventually return home. Freida is thrilled. She did ask me, though, wouldn't some of your friends in the BIS be disappointed at not being asked? Guess who just woke up and is looking for his next feed? It's amazing how large my breasts have become. Julie and I were laughing our heads off the other day on the phone, talking about what you are missing. Time to go. Nicholas is like his dad when things need to occur; there is no waiting.

Karl, how I miss you being right by my side. As I always tell you, I'm not too good without you, darling. Please, please, please, stay safe. You have a family that can't wait to have you home safe and sound. I hope you enjoy the pictures I'm enclosing.

Love and Kisses from your adoring wife and son,
Claire and Nicholas xxxxx

Claire read her letter over again to make sure it would pass screening, then, folding it, she placed it into an envelope addressed to the military forwarding department. "Come on, young man, time for bed. Kiss your dad's picture goodnight; then, we'll go upstairs, shall we?" Claire did this every night. Holding Karl's picture close to Nick's face, it was more like a peck than a kiss, which always made her laugh. Claire also kissed the picture before returning it to the desk. Even now, a tear would roll down her cheek as she kissed a finger, then touched Karl's lips in the picture.

Later that night, her phone rang just as she was closing her romance novel, ready to get some sleep. "Claire, I'm so sorry to call you this late, but I needed to talk to someone close to me who would understand my situation. Earlier today, I got a call from Bill with news about Clive. Claire, he has been wounded. Bill said he's conscious but in a lot of pain. He went through surgery yesterday to the left side of his back. It's bad enough that he's being shipped back tomorrow, arriving in Portsmouth after 2:00 p.m. I have no idea where this happened, but Bill said he would update me when I see him Tuesday morning. Bill will be driving us down. God, I hope it's not going to stop him from walking. He would be devastated not to remain in the BIS." Julie was in a bad place, sick with worry about her husband.

"Julie, what can I do to help? Do you want me to go with you and Bill?" asked Claire.

"As much as I would welcome your company, I think being driven down to Portsmouth by Bill is already a blessing. So, thank you, my sweet Claire; pray for my Clive. Maybe it would be best to keep this from Karl; you know how close those boys are. Sorry again for calling you at such a late hour; I just had to talk to you. Good night, Claire; I'll try to call you from the hospital."

Claire returned the phone to its cradle, shaken by the news. Claire remembered how she was informed about Patrick's body being found floating in the English Channel back in 1940. Her thoughts now focused on the welfare of her second husband, Karl, not knowing where he was or if he was in imminent danger. Uncontrollable tears started rolling down her cheeks. Sobbing, she turned the light off, crying herself to sleep.

Wednesday afternoon, Claire was almost ready to leave the office and drive to Sheila's home to pick up baby Nicholas when her office phone rang. Picking up the receiver, she answered, "Yes, Bev, who is it?" Claire suspected it was Julie calling from Portsmouth.

"It's your friend, Julie Knight. Shall I patch her through?" Claire waited until she heard Julie speak.

"Claire, I'm glad I caught you before you left. Can you speak?" Sitting back down, ready to listen to the news about Clive, Claire became tense. "Well, Clive is conscious, but he's in a lot of pain. He said they were in a convoy when a German patrol attacked them as they scrambled out of their vehicles to run for cover behind a high bank. Before he could reach safety, he felt a searing pain just above his waist on the left side. As he fell, he hit his head on a large rock; then there was nothing as he hit the ground, unconscious. Two grenadier guards dragged him to safety behind that bank. A fierce gun battle followed, and many of Clive's people were injured and many more killed. Of the forty-six soldiers in those trucks, only twenty-two survived. The Germans suffered about the same, retiring to the safety of the nearby forest.

"Clive's doctors are confident that the wounds, although quite bad, will not hinder a full recovery. Clive also asked me to tell you not to mention this to Karl. We're heading home right now, so it will be a long night. I'll call you in the morning. Clive is being transported back to Slough by ambulance in two days.

Claire, it would mean a lot to him if you could come to visit him once he's back in Slough. You can stay with me at our house. It would be wonderful having you here. That's only if it doesn't disrupt your hectic schedule."

Claire quickly looked at her diary, then said, "For you two, I would move Heaven and Earth, so count me in. Give Clive a big kiss for me; see you soon." Claire hung up the phone, thinking, *it sounds like he's going to be all right. I hope my Karl is lucky enough to get through this war in one piece; he already has his share of battle wounds. I'll call Bill later after I pick up Nick.*

Returning home, Claire called Freida to explain that she needed to drive to Slough for one or maybe two nights to be with Julie and visit Clive in the hospital. She asked if it would be alright to leave Nick with them for a couple of days.

"Would we mind? You are kidding; taking care of little Nick will be so much fun. Mama will be over the moon with happiness, and Franchot will probably wear the tires out on that pram. When are you planning to drop him off?" answered Freida.

"Would after work tomorrow be alright? That way, I can get an early start the following morning. Thanks a million for doing this; I'll see you tomorrow then," replied Claire, hanging up the receiver. That night, she put together an overnight bag for herself and another for Nick's clothes and toys. Lying on the bed with her little man cuddled up alongside her, she tried to envision the conditions Karl and his men were enduring, week after week.

She did not know where they were. The newspapers had indicated that the losses on the first day were high, but for security reasons, they did not print how many were injured and how many poor lads lost their lives on that first day, June 6th. She found herself praying, sending her beloved Karl a message to remain safe. Tucking Nick into his crib, she crawled into bed and turned off the bed stand light. She lay there in the dark, fighting back the tears from what she kept thinking.

CHAPTER 9

RETURNING HOME

By the end of June, conditions were barely tolerable. Karl had grown a full beard; fresh water was a big issue, so growing a beard was an easy solution to preserving their precious water supply. When the Germans had bombed the farm, one of those bombs had knocked out the well. However, conditions in the farmhouse were still better than the conditions experienced by the infantry in their foxholes.

Karl and Andy worked diligently on perfecting a strategy to obtain German infantry strengths and Panzer locations. That strategy did not yield meaningful information from the prisoners that had arrived, most being from the German officer corps.

After a few days of little success, they would be shipped back to England; some eventually would be transported to the United States and Canada for the duration of the war.

In the time they had been at the farmhouse, they had interrogated forty-five German prisoners of war. The ones that wore the uniforms of the S.S. and Gestapo were a real problem. Their arrogance was almost intolerable. Even though they were now prisoners of war, they responded to their captors as if they were second rate soldiers. Their elaborate plans to trick these officers were not working, and Karl's temper was becoming frayed almost to the point of exploding and doing something he would later regret.

"Guys, we are getting absolutely nowhere with these Krauts. We can't bang them around; that's against the Geneva Convention for captives in uniform. If the shoe were on the other foot, I very much doubt these Krauts would give a damn about that Convention. I can assure you that not all our guys who are taken prisoner are treated humanely. We, however, are handcuffed to that damn rulebook. We must isolate them from each other; that's the only way we stand a chance of tricking them into making a slip.

"What might help us is the new orders we just received. We will be moving closer to the front lines. General Patton's 3rd Armored Division is in a fierce battle with the German 7th Army to secure the bridges over the Mayenne River. Those bridges are vital to our continued push to the East and the German border. If our boys successfully secure that town, we will be moving up with the 90th Infantry Division. They will more than likely make their headquarters in the medieval castle overlooking that river, which, at this point, is still in German hands.

"Recently, the RAF bombed it heavily, and the eastern side is in ruins. However, we are told the west side is still intact. Assuming those Krauts don't blow it up before evacuating to the east, we might have a new location to operate from. Our forces are advancing at an astonishing rate. Finally, those Krauts are getting a taste of their own medicine. I have explained my concerns to command. They assure me our next site will be more amenable to our needs. We will relocate to that castle with 15th Corp, so until then, it's business as usual," said Andy as he looked at Karl and the rest of the team, all becoming frustrated with the results of their interrogation methods. He needed to boost their confidence that present conditions would change for the better very soon.

The weather was changing to clear sunny, hot days. Whenever possible, Karl would sit outside, soaking up the sun and enjoying whatever time he could get to relax. He continued his daily ritual of writing letters to Claire, never sure if they would be delivered to her maybe she would never get them. Writing, however, gave him an escape from the monotony of interrogating reluctant Germans, day after day.

They processed another sixty-five Germans during July, many from the 362nd Infantry Division and 2nd Panzer Division. This painful interrogation process was not really yielding any information of value until American troops obtained highly classified battlefield reports written by Lieutenant General Freiherr (Baron) Von Luttwitz.

These reports finally gave the Allies insight into the movements of the 2nd Panzer Division and the 362nd Infantry Division. Once translated, it was widely distributed to all Allied field commanders, called the Weekly Intelligence Summary No. 42. Karl and Andy now had ammunition to use against their prisoners, with results coming quickly after that. Finally, after many weeks of fruitless interrogating, they could map out German activities and the locations of those menacing Panzer tanks.

The weeks dragged on, and by the end of August, the farmhouse would change hands from the Intelligence Division to the new field headquarters of the 358th and 359th infantry regiments. Two days before the Intelligence Division and the 15th Corp were preparing to move to Mayenne, Andy called Karl into the farm kitchen. "Karl, I have some news that might brighten your day.

The BIS is requesting you be returned to Slough at the earliest opportunity. That request came from General Jacks himself. Don't ask me why, but I suspect they feel my group is up to speed, and therefore, your talents will be better served back with the BIS." Andy, saying this, had a slightly sarcastic tone in his voice.

"Andy, this is preposterous. Now that we are getting proficient in our interrogation methods, those buggers are pulling me out. I need to contact HQ and get that order rescinded." Karl was more than agitated at hearing these orders.

"Karl don't be ass you are being ridiculous. You're not using your head, man. Have you forgotten you have a wife and child back in Hitchin that haven't seen you in how many months? God, I wish they would send me those orders. Believe me, I would be over the moon. Karl, we all have worked hard at this frustrating job—you more than all of us put together. I am responsible for your temporary assignment to the OSS; I think we can stand on our own two feet from here on." Standing up, the tall American major addressed Karl, saying, "Major Vita, you are hereby relieved of your assignment. I will inform my command that you have done an exemplary job assisting our operation. I will have transportation ready for you at 0630 hours' tomorrow morning. On behalf of this OSS command, let me thank you and all those on your team."

Andy was having a hard time putting Karl in his place. As close friends, they had been through a lot together, and discharging him like this was one of the hardest things he had to do.

Karl stood up, saluting Andy responding by saying, "Major Anderson, I have overstepped my position. I have a habit of doing that, my apologies. I will do as ordered." Karl stood there waiting for Andy's reply.

"Karl, you know I'm right. Don't worry, old friend; we will meet up again very soon, maybe in Berlin. That really would be something, wouldn't it?" Andy walked over to Karl. First, he saluted, then, with both arms, he hugged his friend, feeling that if Karl was being recalled, there must be a new assignment waiting for him in Slough.

Karl slapped Andy on the shoulder, then walked out of the kitchen. In the doorway, he stopped and turned around, saying as a departing gesture, "Thanks, Andy."

Packing his things into his kit bag, Karl started to realize that in a few days, he would be reunited with his wife and child and see his family in Baldock. It would be a relief after such a long separation. At 0530 hours the following morning, Karl got a large mug of coffee, then sat down at the bench in the kitchen with his kit bag alongside as he pondered how he would be sent home.

Andy entered, looking happy but sad at saying goodbye. "Morning, Karl. I see you're ready to go. I need a favor from you. Could you post these letters for me once you arrive back? Sending them from here will take weeks, and here's that letter you gave me to hold for you should something happen to you. By the way, your team will travel back in a couple of days. I'm not sure why they're being held back here, though."

Karl, smiling, could not resist a little sarcasm as he answered, "Well, Major, you realize that all mail is to be censored. So, what parts should I turn a blind eye to?"

Hearing this, Andy laughed out loud, replying, "Karl, old friend, how I am going to miss that razor sharp tongue of yours. I will have to owe you for the stamps. With any luck, you can collect that whenever and wherever we meet again. Give Claire a big hug for me and tell Nick his American uncle is looking forward to seeing him soon. When you see Clive, have him drop me a line. Would be nice to catch up with him." Andy looked at his watch, then said, "I think I hear the transports outside. Let's be off, shall we?"

Karl picked up his kit bag and followed Andy outside. There, in front of the trucks, were many of the supporting infantry, along with members of Andy's division and the BIS team to see him off.

"Attention," called a sergeant as they walked closer. "Gentlemen, I have never served with such a ragtag, undisciplined bunch of misfits in my entire military life." Karl stopped to look at the faces in front of him, then proceeded by adding, "From this day forward, I will always think of my time serving with you all as the most gratifying experience I have ever had. I hope you clobber those Krauts now that you know their battle plans. Thank you for putting up with me, and to your commanding officer, Major Anderson, I will be forever in your debt for requesting my assignment to this division." Karl saluted the men in front of him, then proceeded to shake hands with as many as he could. Andy watching this charismatic officer as he moved amongst the men.

"Major Vita, I believe it's time for you to climb aboard that half-track."

Karl nodded his head and picked up his kit bag, throwing it into the back, then climbed into the cab for the drive back to Gold Beach in the remains of *Arromanches-les-Bains*.

His assignment was over.

Driving through the narrow roads with their high banked hedgerows, the column of vehicles passed by many burned out tanks, trucks, cars, and even motorcycles, and so many dead storm troopers. Most of the American dead had already been recovered. Eventually, the Germans would be picked up and buried nearby. Karl sat, watching the changing scenery as they closed the distance to the coast. He was thinking, so many young men on both sides obeying orders killing and being killed because some power mad tyrant decided he would turn all the people of Europe into cheap workers and slaves. I pray to God we catch the damn Fuhrer and enslave him, so he gets a taste of his own cruel medicine. The driver finally announced they would be arriving within a couple of minutes.

Driving through the remains of the town was very distressing. How would the townspeople rebuild from this pile of rubble? Turning down a ramp, they approached the beach. Karl was in complete shock at all the vehicles and equipment lined up as far as the eye could see along the beach. From the beach, steel gratings led out to the temporary harbors invented by the English. This feat of engineering, known as the Mulberry harbor, was made up of 73 individual prefabricated concrete caissons, some standing as high as a five story building, stretching out into the sea, some seven miles in all. On top of these caissons, prefabricated steel tops were bolted down to create piers and jetties.

Karl could not believe his eyes, and he kept repeating to the driver, "This is unbelievable. We had heard about this harbor, but really, you must see it to believe it. When we landed on the second day, none of this was here. God, these engineers are incredible, aren't they?"

The driver smiled, then answered, "I guess Rommel and his Atlantic wall of troops had no idea what they were up against, did they, Sir?" Karl nodded with a big smile on his face. "Sir, that Jeep over there will drive you out to your ship once the traffic officer clears you to proceed out onto the ramp. I hope the drive was not too uncomfortable for you. God bless you, Sir. From here, I will escort the prisoners in the trucks behind us down the beach to a landing craft. For those guys, the war is over. They don't know how lucky they are right now." The driver gave Karl a friendly salute as he jumped down into the sand.

"Thanks, Corporal, for getting me here. Have a safe return to the farmhouse." Karl swung his kit bag over his shoulder, then walked over to the waiting Jeep. The driver saluted Karl as he approached. "No need for that," said Karl as he threw his bag into the back of the Jeep. "How far do we have to drive that I need a ride out to the ship by Jeep?"

"It's a hike, Sir. Your ship is a big freighter; that's why it's on the end." Karl was still in awe as they made their way down the dock. "Driver, what is the name of the ship I will be traveling back to England on?" asked Karl.

The driver looked down momentarily at his clipboard, then replied. "The ship you are boarding today, Sir, is named the Clyde

Princess." Karl froze in his seat hearing this. What were the chances of this happening?

"Oh, my God, I can't believe this. By chance, do you know the name of its captain?" asked Karl.

"Sorry, Sir, I don't," replied the driver. "I wonder if it could be Captain McKinley. I met him back in 1936 when I last boarded that very ship it's a small world, getting smaller," concluded Karl as they approached the end of the dock.

"This is as far as I can take you, Sir. Have a safe trip back to England," said the driver as he pulled up to the end of the dock. "Your ship is over there on the left of us, Sir."

Thanking the driver, Karl walked down the dock toward the boarding ramp. Visions of leaving that ship eight years earlier were making him melancholy reliving that fateful day when he left Ostend in Belgium. Two armed sailors were stationed at the bottom of the boarding ramp, and Karl saluted. Showing his papers, he waited while they checked his kit bag, then one of them told him to follow him up the ramp. The Clyde Princess was a shadow of her former self with rust stains along her hull and her teak decks dark and buckling from neglect. The sailor led him to the officers' wardroom. "Sir, you can wait here. We will be leaving in about three hours."

Karl looked around at the shabby conditions of the compartment, then asked the seaman, "By chance, is Captain McKinley still the skipper?"

The sailor looked at Karl before replying, "Yes, Sir, he is. How would you know that?" Karl smiled, then asked if he could visit the bridge as he knew the captain from years back and had also sailed on the Clyde Princess before. "Well, blow me, Sir; he'll be pleased to see you again, I'm sure."

Karl walked down the deck toward the ladder leading up to the bridge deck. Opening the door, he said in a very stern voice, "Permission to enter the bridge. I'm Major Vita, and I would like to see Captain McKinley."

The officer of the watch replied, "Permission granted, Major. Have a seat, Sir. I'll send someone to find the captain." Karl looked around the familiar bridge and remembered images of a time when he stood right here, wearing the marine uniform of the German Langstaff Shipping Company.

Those memories flooded his brain. So much had transpired since that time long ago. Karl, lost in those memories, did not hear the bridge door open. With his back to the door, he was immersed in those memories until a familiar voice behind him announced Captain McKinley, wearing the uniform of a Royal Navy Reserve Captain. "Karl, I can't believe my eyes. When my number one announced there's a Major Vita of the BIS asking for me on the bridge, it did not dawn on me that it could be you."

Karl smiled at hearing that Captain McKinley had not forgotten him. "Come, let's have some tea; we have a little while until we leave for Portsmouth," said James McKinley.

In the small day cabin, Karl gave him a condensed version of all that had happened since leaving the ship in 1936. "Now, Jim, I couldn't help noticing you're wearing a Royal Navy uniform. What transpired to bring about this change?" inquired Karl, sipping his tea.

"Karl, if you can remember, I told you I was a reserve officer in the Navy. I was the skipper of a mine sweeper until about eight months ago when I was reassigned back to the merchant service. The lack of qualified captains was becoming a big problem, so many had been lost in the Atlantic convoys. So, when I got recalled, I got the shock of my life. My new command would be my old girl, the Clyde Princess. The invasion fleet was building up, and the serving commander of the Princess was sent to a training site in Scotland. That left this ship without a skipper. Being very familiar with her, I was asked to resume my old job as her skipper. So, here I am again, and now so are you," concluded James.

"Captain, the harbormaster is requesting we prepare to cast off once the final batch of prisoners comes aboard," concluded the first officer.

"Thanks, Number One. Karl, why don't you join me? It will be like old times for you, I'm sure." Captain McKinley was in high spirits as he directed the departure procedure. Clearing the entrance to this amazing manmade harbor, like those times long ago, Karl was giving orders in his mind, remembering the maneuvering procedures he would give aboard the *Tristian*.

Several miles off the harbor, they were joined by two other merchant ships returning to England, escorted by a Navy Corvette and a minesweeper.

Karl walked out onto the deck, looking back down the length of the ship to the stern. The smell of salt water filled his lungs, and taking deep breaths was like being rejuvenated this was the medicine he needed. Sitting on a deck box, Karl drifted off into a relaxing sleep, probably the most relaxing he'd had in a long time. A gentle nudge to his shoulder made him jump as a steward woke him, saying, "Sorry to disturb your snooze, Sir. The captain would like you to join him in his day cabin for a late lunch." Karl thanked the steward, then returned to the bridge. Lunch, it's kind of late for that, he thought, looking at the cloudy sky overhead.

The two friends enjoyed their late lunch, swapping more stories. Karl told in detail about his command during the Dunkirk evacuation and how the HMT Reese had met her demise that fateful day.

Captain McKinley listened intently, then told Karl he was also part of the evacuation aboard the Clyde Princess. "What a pity I did not hear about your ordeal. It sounds like you are extremely fortunate still to be alive; there were wrecked ships everywhere. This old girl came close to being blown to kingdom come when a bomb hit the water very close to the hull amidships; it rattled her keel bolts. Karl, I hate to leave, but we are close to Portsmouth, and I'm needed on the bridge. Why don't you join me for maneuvering?"

Karl agreed knowing he would enjoy that very much. Safely docked, Karl retrieved his kit bag and thanked Captain McKinley for the second time, promising to stay in touch with no excuses. As he walked down the gangway, an old instinct stopped him halfway down. Turning, he looked back, and, just like that first time back in 1936, Captain McKinley was saluting him as he watched Karl disembark. Returning the salute, Karl could feel the comforting feeling that he was almost home.

Walking along the dock, he stopped for a moment to watch the German prisoners being filed down the stern gangway. He thought, not so cocky now, are they? Well, at least they won't die in action. Of course, they would never admit to appreciating that, arrogant bastards.

Karl presented his ID card and received a salute from the officer behind the long table in the clearing hall. "Welcome home, Sir." Karl nodded with a tip to his cap, thinking it was a little different from the first time he landed in England. Walking down to the end of the hall, he inquired about train service back to Slough and asked if the station was nearby.

"Excuse me, Sir; are you Major Vita?" asked a kindly corporal. "Yes, that's me," replied Karl.

"Your driver and car are waiting for you outside the terminal." Karl stopped momentarily, thinking, how the bloody hell did they know I was arriving today? It must be that cagey Bill that arranged this.

Outside, he followed the corporal down a line of army trucks. As they turned the corner, there stood a familiar face next to an all too familiar Humber staff car. It was Charlie! "Welcome back, Sir. It's really good to see you home safe and sound." Charlie was obviously happy to see Karl again.

"Charlie, how did they know what ship I was arriving on?" Karl was a little dumbfounded. Portsmouth was not exactly around the corner from Slough.

"Well, Sir, from what I heard, it was Colonel Knight who arranged it. Don't quote me on that, though." Charlie and the guys in the motor pool usually knew more about what was happening than most in the camp.

"Charlie, are we returning to Slough, or can I make it home today?" Karl was becoming anxious to see Claire and Nicholas now that he was back.

"Sorry, Sir, my instructions are to drive you straight to Slough," replied Charlie. The drive back was long and, at times, slow. Besides a stop for petrol, the drive was very boring for Karl, so he excused himself, rolled up his uniform jacket against the window pillar, and went to sleep. Charlie occasionally checked the rearview mirror to see if he was still sleeping, thinking, poor blighter—I can only imagine what he's been through.

Pulling up to the guardhouse, Charlie quietly presented both his and Karl's IDs, saying, "The major is out cold, Bill; best not to wake him just yet. See you later." In front of the main building, Charlie shut off the engine, then walked around to the rear left of the car. Carefully, he opened the door, then gently moved Karl's arm until he stirred.

"Charlie, we're already back in Slough? I guess I slept most of the way back. I didn't realize I was so exhausted. I'm so sorry for not being better company." Karl got out of the car, and Charlie walked behind him with his kit bag.

Inside the lobby, familiar faces greeted their returning warrior. "Welcome back, Major; let me announce your return to Major Lowes," said the receptionist.

"No, my dear, let me shock him by walking into his office." Karl turned to Charlie, saying. "Thank you, Corporal; you can leave my kit bag out here. I'll pick it up when I leave. Thanks again for driving me back."

Walking down the hall toward Bill's office, Karl became melancholy, knowing he was one of the lucky survivors from the Normandy invasion. His eyes welled up with tears, and everything that he had been holding back was now flooding into his brain. He stopped momentarily, putting his right arm against the wall to steady himself, then, without provocation, he started crying uncontrollably with his head against the hallway wall.

"Karl, let it go; you have witnessed too much. Clive had a very similar reaction when he returned. You can't keep that sort of stuff bottled up inside. God, I remember how I was when I returned after being banged around by the Gestapo." Bill had walked out of his office to greet his friend, only to find him leaning against the wall, crying.

"Bill, please, forgive me; I'm so sorry for this outburst. Walking down to your office, I started thinking how lucky I was not to be in that first wave hitting the beaches on D-Day. As I thought that, a terrible guilty feeling came over me. I didn't see this coming, and now I feel very stupid, or should I say embarrassed. I'm glad to be back and happy to see you, old friend." Karl recovered quickly, following Bill into his office.

"How about a wee toddy for the body, Karl? It will make you feel much better."

"Sounds like a plan, Bill. How long are you going to keep me here before I can go home?" inquired Karl.

"I'm planning on returning you to Hitchin in the a.m. I thought it would be better to surprise Claire instead of a telephone call. It's your call, though, Karl? Clive already called this morning to find out what time we would be going over to visit them. I told him later this afternoon after you have had time to wash away that dirt from months of not washing. You still have your room in the officers' quarters. How about a nice hot bath, shave, and for God's sake, change that uniform? The one you're in looks pretty bad. You could grow potatoes on it, so changing it would be a really good idea, wouldn't you say? Drink up and meet me back here, say in about an hour." Bill, while talking to Karl, was watching him carefully. The ordinarily cocky Austrian was looking shabby, thin, worn out, and a look of defeat was across his face. This was not like Karl; he very rarely showed any sign of discouragement.

"Karl, do you need a sharp razor to hack away that beard?" Bill was trying everything to snap Karl back, and that last remark did it.

Karl stood, looking at him for a long minute, then burst out laughing. Bill's sarcastic remark was all it took to get him out of his current state. "See you in an hour. Call Clive to let him know we are coming over. Will this turn out to be a debriefing?

Knowing you two as I do, there's always an underlying reason. Both of you are always doing something secretive. After that, you can tell me why I have really been recalled. You thought I wouldn't bring that up, didn't you?"

Karl walked out, feeling more like his old self. Bill smiled, thinking, that's the old Karl we all like. Walking down the hall, Karl stopped first in his old department to say hello to his staff, followed by retrieving his kit bag from the lobby. After a hot bath, Karl took a pair of scissors and as instructed, hacked off his beard, followed by a close shave. Thank God he left his spare field uniform hanging in the wardrobe. He was starting to feel human again well, almost. His boots had caked on mud, so with a wet rag, he cleaned them up as best as he could, then took a final look in the mirror before walking back to the main building. He would take everything in his kit home with him tomorrow to be washed. After months of continuous wear, the contents of that kit bag had a definite stale odor to it.

Bill and Karl drove the thirty minutes to Clive and Julie's house. Karl was getting excited to be back amongst his friends again. No sooner were they in the driveway than the front door opened, and out hobbled Clive with two walking sticks to support him. "You, old bugger what the hell happened to you? or are you trying to take the mickey out of Bill with those sticks? Really Clive is there something I was not advised of?" yelled Karl as he walked up to Clive, both his arms outstretched.

"Well, you two have gone through carrying walking sticks, so I decided to join you. Karl, welcome home; it's so good to see you back. We have much to discuss, but that will be later."

Clive still had difficulty walking, but he was determined to greet his friends out in the driveway. In the garden, they met up with Julie and their two daughters. Seeing Karl, Julie and the two girls wrapped their arms around him, tears of joy in Julie's eyes.

"Karl, it's so wonderful to see you home safe. You know, I was on the phone with Claire earlier today; she misses you so much she will be over the moon to see you tomorrow. Is that when you're returning to Hitchin Karl? Claire has no idea you're back from France, and I haven't said a word to her, so she still believes you're over there. I would love to be there with my camera to get a picture of her seeing you again after all these months. Nicholas has never seen you, other than when Claire gave birth. He is going to be so shy seeing you for the first time. Enough small talk, today, you are going to eat home cooked food with a bottle of wine. How does that sound to you?"

"Julie don't ever change. We all love you just the way you are," said Bill, enjoying this reunion. After a delicious dinner, Julie took the girls into another room, leaving the spy blokes to talk. Clive taking this time to tell his friend all about how he got injured.

"Karl, I know what's on your mind, so let's get that out of the way. General Jacks was responsible for your immediate recall because of information Gunther has been feeding back to us about a new weapon the German scientists are trying to perfect. From the intelligence Gunther has received, he believes, at the rate they are developing this bomb, that could be operational in the next few years. That statement is unsubstantiated; it's pure conjecture at this point. The lack of scientists and specific materials is the reason for the slow development. The problem is finding out what type of bomb it is and where they are doing the development.

"So far, Gunther and his team have been running up against a brick wall. We believe it could be a similar design to the one in development in Los Alamos, New Mexico. This new type of bomb is the brainchild of Robert Oppenheimer, and it is called an atomic bomb. It is so powerful that it could flatten a city the size of London with just a single bomb. Karl, we have no real information to go by, so we are trying to find the names of the scientists involved in this project. To date, we have been completely unsuccessful in finding out anything that will substantiate that they have something for us to be worried about. Remember, we are talking about those brainy German buggers, so we can't discredit anything at this time. When you return after your leave, you will work with Gunther and his team to find out more. We need definite proof that this weapon will not see production before we can end this war." Clive stopped short of telling Karl any more about the Intelligence plan to steal anything that could shed light on the project.

CHAPTER 10

HITCHIN HIS HOME

Friday morning at 0500 hours, Karl was already washed and dressed to leave for Hitchin. Smiling again at the pass that would give him ten days' leave, he was finally on his way home. "Morning, Charlie, sorry to get you up so early, but I can't wait to see my wife and a son I only saw once when he was less than one day old." Karl's excitement was contagious.

"That's alright, Sir. I'm delighted to drive you home this morning," announced Charlie. This early in the morning, the drive was a mixture of stop and go traffic, but Karl could care less; he knew Claire would be at home. Julie had called Claire the evening before and told her Karl would be calling her. She wasn't certain of the time Julie had been very convincing.

Driving past Saint Michaels College, Karl said to Charlie, "Almost there." As always, he thanked Charlie. "Here, please take this fiver and buy yourself a good breakfast." Charlie simply waved that was not necessary, but Karl would not have it. "Please, Charlie, this is nothing to all you do for me, so please, take it." Charlie put his hand over the seat, taking the money.

"Thank you, Major, see you in ten days."

Karl almost leaped out of the car. Grabbing his kit bag, he walked toward the front door. Claire was in the kitchen, making beef stew, when she heard a car door slam. "I wonder who that could be, Nick. Let's take a look, shall we?" Picking up her son, she walked to the front door. Opening it, she froze in her tracks. There, in front of her, was her husband with his kit bag over his shoulder. Before she could say one-word, strong arms encircled her and Nick. Almost screaming, Claire yelled out, "Karl, oh, my God, I can't believe that you're home! Am I dreaming?" Trembling, she kissed Karl again.

Regaining her composure, she held Nick out in front of her. "Say hello to your Daddy, Nicholas. I told you he would be home soon. Isn't your daddy handsome?" Karl had not been able to say a word; Claire was talking a mile a minute.

"Claire, I'm home at last. You are the picture I have kept in my mind throughout the time I was away. I never thought it possible to miss someone as much as I missed you. Nick, you are a chubby little chap, aren't you?" said Karl, hugging and kissing his son's cheeks as he swung him around. The little guy started crying; he was not used to this big man handling him like this.

"Easy, Karl, you're scaring him. Remember, he has never seen you before, and right now, he's probably wondering who you are. He will be fine by tonight, but remember, darling, he is only a little over five months old. Karl, he has your eyes, and as young as he is, he is just as obstinate as you are. You bugger! why didn't you call me? Julie, that sly one, told me to stay close to the phone because you would be calling me today. Claire, holding Nick again, started to laugh. "You were all in on this, weren't you? As you always say… bloody spies. She's just as bad as the rest of you."

"Claire, you look marvelous; as always, you're perfectly dressed. How lucky am I," said Karl as he followed her into the kitchen. "What smells good? I'm famished. Army food is so bad that the rats won't even eat it." Karl, saying that, laughed loudly, setting Nick off again. "Claire, I think you're going to have to educate me on how to be a good dad."

Claire, standing in front of the stove, looked back over her shoulder, saying, "Try talking to him slowly and quietly. It's not a bad idea to use small words until he gets a few months older and hold his hand softy. He will respond to you; there's that bond between a father and his son, so go ahead and try it while I prepare lunch."

Karl took off his tunic, rolled up his sleeves, then turned his chair toward Nick, sitting in his highchair, not taking his eyes off this strange man in front of him. "Claire, is this the highchair we bought used in Letchworth? I did a nice job repainting it; I almost forgot about it." Karl put his finger out in front of Nick's tiny hand. That first touch of his little hand wrapping around Karl's finger sent all of Karl's senses spinning. In a very soft, slow voice, he started to talk but could not finish his sentence, "Nicholas, my son, your daddy loves you."

Karl broke down, crying freely; he put his head down on Nick's serving tray. Claire stopped, and in silence, watched that little hand reach for Karl's ear, then with excitement, he started pulling it. Karl looked up, tears still in his eyes, leaning forward so Nick could grab his nose. Claire was emotionally charged, seeing her two men starting to bond. Walking over, she put her arms around them both, whispering, "Karl, it's our own little family. We love you so very much; thank you for all you are doing to keep us safe." Claire and Karl had their wishes granted but only for ten days! After lunch, Claire said, "It's a nice day. Go put on some civvy clothes so that we can go for a walk in the park. Nick gets excited when he sees the birds flying around in the trees."

To Karl, walking behind a pram was strange. It's not like he hadn't been around one before; it just felt different because it was his son on the inside. Claire, walking by his side, was beaming with pride. This was the vision she'd had for so many years, and now, it was a reality. "Karl let's stop at that bench for a while; we haven't had time to share stories since you got back. Clive told me you were with Andy at Omaha beach. He told me that you both went ashore on the second day; was it as bad as the papers tried to indicate?" Claire knew from experience that if Karl did not get those demons out by talking about them, they would manifest later in those frightening nightmares she had already witnessed.

"Claire, words cannot describe the carnage all along those beaches, mutilated bodies of young soldiers, vehicles of every description blown up or still burning, ships half or totally sunk close to the beaches, and fires burning out of control on other ships. The smell and sounds will forever haunt me, and Claire, I was one of the lucky ones."

"Karl, I really shouldn't be bringing this up on the day you have just returned to us. If you have been prematurely recalled, then the

BIS must have some sort of special assignment for which your type of expertise is required. Am I right, or should I mind my own business? Karl, I'm a solicitor, and any secret information will remain strictly confidential between us." Claire, now silent, reached for his hand, waiting for his response.

"Claire, you keep digging for information which you know I can't tell you other than it's an area we in the BIS are rather concerned about as it could affect the outcome of this war in Europe. That's about as far as I'm willing to go. Now, tell me about what has gone on since I last saw you two at the Lister Hospital?" Karl could not tell her how severe the outcome of this new bomb could be if Gunther substantiated its development.

Changing the topic, Karl spoke up by saying, "When we return home, I must call Mama; she will be shocked to hear I'm back home."

Claire, with both arms around him, said, "Karl, we should go home and drive over there right now; let's go." Standing, she pulled him to his feet, only to be shocked when he quickly wrapped his arms around her, kissing her passionately and then squeezing her backside. "Karl Vita, we are in a public park; behave yourself. I'm not a call girl or a one-night stand; I'm your wife and the mother of your son." That done, they both started laughing profusely.

"Darling, I miss your mischievous ways; they keep me alive. So, when we return from seeing the family, and after Nick gets his bath and is tucked away in his crib, you can show me just how much you miss me. Is that a deal?" Claire was enjoying this game they were playing.

Karl pulled the Wolsey into the bungalow driveway. Shutting the engine off, he walked around to the passenger side. He took Nick from Claire's arms, and, holding Nick in his left arm, he helped Claire out with his right hand. "Here we go. You do realize it's been the best part of nine months since I was here. Look at it this way; I'm still alive and in one piece." Even though Karl was joking around, he really was thinking that yes, I'm still alive.

Hearing the door knocker, Freida walked to the front door, expecting to see Claire and the baby. "Karl, oh my God, when did you arrive home? Claire, I'm surprised you didn't call us. If you were trying to shock me, well, you did that and more." Claire took the baby so that Karl could hug his sister closely.

"I arrived this morning unannounced. So, like you, Claire was shocked as well."

"Mama, come look what the cat dragged in." Freida was relieved to see Karl was in one piece and very much alive.

Mama opened the kitchen door, saying, "Freida, what are you yelling for?" She could not finish that sentence. Stopping in the hallway, her hands over her mouth, she froze, seeing her youngest son in the doorway with his arm around Frieda's waist. "Karl, is it really you? My prayers have been answered, and you're home! Oh, my God, come here and kiss your mother. I swear you will give me a heart attack turning up like this."

Mama cried with joy and relief from the worry she carried in her heart for all the other family members scattered in so many places. Karl walked up to his mother with open arms, throwing them around her and kissing her on both cheeks. He could feel her shaking and so very thin, thinking, it must be the constant worrying we are putting her through.

Mama, regaining her composure, turned toward Claire, saying, "Where is my grandson? Karl, he has your eyes; I hope the rest he gets from my daughter-in-law, Claire. Come here, Nicholas; let your grandmother hold you."

Claire, all smiles, kissed her sister-in-law, then, transferring the baby to Mama, she kissed her on the cheek, saying, "I couldn't think of a better surprise than having our two boys here for you today." Claire looked around the room for Franchot. "So, Freida, where is the little terror? I haven't seen him in over a week."

Frieda, looking at the wall clock, then said, "He should be here shortly; he walks home with his other school friends. As soon as he sees your car, he'll leave his friends to run right in. He absolutely loves playing with his Aunt Claire and pushing the baby around in the carriage. He'll be another one that's shocked when he sees his uncle."

Karl looked around to see what carriage Freida was talking about. "Oh, Karl, I bought this one from my old school chums so that we could keep it here. I got it for five quid; that's a steal for a

Marmet pram." Claire, saying that, felt like she had to explain to Karl why she bought another pram. Karl, being Karl, simply smiled with approval for her purchase. Seeing that smile on his face, Claire shook her head slowly, thinking he never sweats the small stuff, but then again, that's one side I love about him.

Staying only a couple of hours, they sat around drinking coffee, waiting for Karl's brothers to arrive home from work.

"Karl, you might as well hear it from me first. Your brothers have both volunteered for duty in the Free European Brigade; they will be reporting for training in two weeks," said Mama.

Karl had a look of anger and worry across his face. "Mama, they didn't have to do this; war is not a game. The chances of being killed are very high; let me talk to them."

Claire put her arm around Karl, saying softly, "Karl, they are grown men and older than you. This decision was not arrived at lightly. In fact, we all challenged their announcement, but they are determined to have their own justice against the Germans. Ello told us if our brother can do his part for the freedom of Austria, then so can we." Karl, his head in his hands, had mixed feelings, knowing so much more than anyone in the room about the hell that war could be.

The front door opened a little after 5:30 p.m., and in walked Ello and Ardi. They were shocked at first, then elated to see their younger brother, the major. Excitement erupted once again as the three brothers hugged each other, "Karl, who would have thought you would be sitting here when we walked through the front door? What a wonderful way to arrive home," said Ello as he took off his work jacket.

"What's this I hear about you two idiots signing up for military service? Do you have any idea what the survival rate is these days? I'm talking from experience; this is a total commitment. Are you listening to me?" Karl could see he was talking to a brick wall, so he stopped by saying, "When I return to Slough, I'm going to find out where you will be training and where your first assignment will be. These bars I wear carry some clout, so I'll get you posted to somewhere I can keep you safe."

The two brothers responded by saying they would prefer he did not interfere. As much as they appreciated his concern, they did not want anyone to think their high-ranking brother pulled strings for them. Karl, listening to them, shook his head, finally replying, "I understand and will honor your decision, even though I know what you both will be exposed to. It's your necks that are at stake." Once more, he reached for them with tears in his eyes. He was thinking, our poor mother, how much of her family will be here when this war finally comes to an end? They have no idea what strings I can pull without them knowing it's me that will establish their future, so let them believe what they want to for now. Karl, looking at his mother, winked at her. She knew exactly what he would do, and for that, she was thanking God for her high-ranking son. Ronny would arrive home from Scotland three days after Karl returned to Slough, so they would not get to see each other for another eight months.

The days were going by quickly; Claire had taken this time off from the office, unsure when she would see her husband again. So, they would spend the next nine days together with their son. Sitting in the garden, Claire loved watching Karl playing for hours with Nicky. The bond was so different from only a few days ago. Karl, lying on the blanket, was bouncing Nicky, who loved playing like this.

In her deck chair, Claire was thinking, this is how it should be, not this bloody war and Karl doing those dangerous things. I have my family at last, and my girlhood dreams have come true. I hope we can expand our family before Nicky gets too many years on him. A telephone ringing from the security phone snapped her out of those daydreams. Its unique sound always brought on stress for Karl and Claire whenever they heard it. "Darling, take Nicky for me while I answer that bloody phone," said Karl.

Walking quickly, he entered the house, picking up the phone, "Vita here," announced Karl with a distinctive rattle in his voice.

"Clive here; sorry to disturb your day, old man. How is Nicky doing with his dad? I'm willing to bet you're having the time of your life. Claire must be thrilled to have you turn up unannounced like that. Karl, you know full well when this secure phone rings, it usually means something serious is happening. As always, I'm sorry to call you when you are on leave, but I need to share some information with you. Yesterday, Gunther and Herbert arrived back from Germany. They have been actively following the rumor about German scientists designing a new bomb based on atomic fusion. I'm not sure if you've heard anything about this science, but we are heavily involved in the same development in a joint program with the Americans in the desert of New Mexico.

"From what they have been able to ascertain so far, it's in the early stage design and development and something we need to know more about before anyone else does. Just one of those new bombs mounted to a V-2 rocket could annihilate a big city like London. Karl, I am asking you to volunteer along with Gunther and Herbert to be part of a new, top-secret division being set up to go after this new bomb, its scientists, and their technology.

This new group's objective will be to gather as much information as possible about Kraut advancements in atomic warfare. Karl, a word to the wise, this is not to be shared with your American friends, is that understood? The Germans are not on their knees yet; however, they are desperately trying to perfect this weapon, hoping to turn around the war's outcome. Our mission will be to stop them dead in their tracks. Finally, I must ask you this, Karl, are you up to this mission? I know things have changed for you over the last several years, and no one would blame you if you declined. I will be assuming this command under General Jacks, who has instructed me personally to approach you three to spearhead this new division."

Clive stopped talking, giving Karl time to process the question being asked of him and the dangers of saying yes to joining this secret division. Karl stood, listening, his allegiance torn between family and loyalty to the BIS. "Clive, how soon do you need an answer?" questioned Karl. "I need to prepare Claire if I'm to accept this assignment." The old Karl would not hesitate; the new Karl now considered a young man out in the garden that wanted to grow up with his dad, not with his memory, and there was Claire to consider. She had already lost one military husband to this war. These questions weighed heavily on Karl's mind through the next few days.

Claire knew her husband so well. At first, she had decided she should confront him, but then again, he was an Intelligence officer and would not tell her any secret stuff anyway. "Karl, that call you received from Clive the other day has been bothering you since he called. I won't ask you any secret information, not that you would tell me anyway, but Karl, there is something that has me concerned. That look on your face, darling, can only mean one thing another dangerous mission, is this correct?" Claire, the solicitor, was careful how she should approach him.

"Claire, my sensitive wife, you always know how to ask me a question about what is bothering me, don't you? Come, sit down next to me; I need you to help me make a very difficult decision." Karl, in confidence, told her what he could divulge without specific details. "Darling, I've been asked to become a member in a top-secret division being formed right now. I can't tell you too much but let me say this: if this new division cannot stop the development of a new German superweapon, we are all in danger here in the British Isles. We have been gathering intelligence on this new weapon that concerns us enough to warrant in-depth investigation. If perfected, it has the potential to destroy a big city with just one of these devices.

"Claire, you and Nick are my life; I can't allow any harm to come to you. I will do whatever I have to in order to keep you both, my family, and those dear to me safe. This is what has been troubling me."

Karl put his arms around Claire, and he could feel her shaking with fear. "Karl, why is it always you and our friends in the BIS that are asked to go continuously into harm's way? I've already lost one husband to this damn war. Now, I've got to let you go back into that hell you live in, hoping you will come back to me in one piece." Claire was sobbing profusely as she spoke.

Regaining her composure, she kissed him, then with both arms, she squeezed him, saying, "My darling spy, one selfish side of me is screaming no way, and the other side is praising you for putting your loved ones ahead of your own safety. If you think this is something you must do to keep us safe, I will not try to stop you. Just promise me you will not do anything so reckless it could make me a widow once again."

Claire continued squeezing Karl, knowing he had confided in her for her approval. Even though it was his duty, he did not want to leave without her knowing he may never return home to her. Karl emphasized again that this information had to be kept totally secret. No one is to know about it, not even people like his family, including Ronny, and none of their American friends.

"Promise me this right now; getting that off my chest is a big relief. How about a glass of wine and maybe a promise for something special later?"

Karl walked over to the secure phone, dialing Clive's direct line. "Clive, is this bomb concerning you enough to risk your life to stop its development?" Karl waited for Clive's response.

"Yes, Karl, I have included myself in this operation. You know I would not ask you unless it was that grave of a situation.

Gunther and Herbert are already infiltrating the secret locations we know about, but those could well be fronts for the real locations. I'll tell you more when I see you. Can I assume the answer is yes, then?"

Karl answered, "I think you already know my answer!" Clive, hearing this, hung up the phone, not wanting to upset Karl any further than he already had. Returning to the garden, Karl sat down in the deck chair next to Claire. Looking her in the eyes, he could see the stress that comes from knowing her man would leave in a couple of days. Would he ever return home to Hitchin?

"Claire, all of us in the BIS signed on years ago with one objective: stop Hitler from enslaving every country they conquered. Right now, we have been successful at pushing the Krauts back toward their own borders. This new threat could annihilate thousands more. Realistically, that could be in the millions should that threat become real. Having no countermeasures, the Allies will have to consider a conditional cease fire. Better that than to continue the carnage this new weapon could bring. That's why I can't say no, even though I would like to."

Claire had sat quietly, holding his hand, then said, "Karl, one of the first things I loved about you is your honesty and commitment to duty. All the other attributes were icing on the cake. Darling, of course, I will worry, cry, and probably swear at Clive and all the other members of the High Command for sending all of you on this mission. Pointing toward Nicholas, still rolling around on the blanket, Claire said, "It's for him you're doing this, so whatever happens, your blood and personality will flow through him. Karl, I'm close to breaking down, so let me get us some wine. That will give me enough time to regain my composure." Claire stood up, and, leaning over Karl, she kissed his forehead; there was no need to say more.

After supper, Claire gave Nick his bath, which always made her laugh. Karl, leaning against the bathroom door with his arms crossed, was enjoying how Nick would splash the bathwater, making sounds of excitement. He was thinking, now that she has this baby, it will make my leaving more tolerable. He turned and went downstairs, returning with two glasses of sherry. After Claire had put Nick to bed, she entered the bedroom to find Karl still dressed, sitting upright on the bed, candles sending shadows against the wall. Holding out the two glasses, he softly asked Claire to join him for an evening aperitive.

Claire, smiling widely, climbed onto the bed, snuggling up to her husband. "So, Major, are you sending me a message that you need this body of mine to have your way with?" Karl always loved this foreplay they engaged in on most occasions before making love.

"Well, it had crossed my mind that you need some relaxing, and darling, I know exactly what to do to make that happen."

Karl placed the glasses on the nightstand. Pulling her close, he moved his left hand down over her skirt, and with deliberate, slow movements, he pulled her skirt up, stopping above her stocking tops. Claire's breathing was becoming heavier with the sensation of his touch. He always knew how to get her aroused, and right now, she was more than ready for his next move.

"Karl, you're such a tease; you always get me into this state, leaving me powerless. Darling, please make love to me right now."

Karl smiled into her face, quietly responding, "It's the uncertainty that you love, so guess what's next?" Karl moved his hand under her panties, finding her more than ready. Claire willingly spread her legs, helping him place his fingers over her now very moist sensitive mound. Claire started moaning as he circled. Finding the right spot, he increased his motion with gentle pressure.

In a labored whisper, Claire said, "Karl, not yet. I need you inside me so that we can come together." Hearing this, Karl rolled her onto her back, removing her underwear. Then, he removed his trousers and shorts. Kissing her deeply, his arms around her, he slid into her, then stopped, waiting for Claire to thrust against him. When that happened, he started moving slowly. Getting very close, he was fighting back that sensation of letting go.

Again, he stopped. Feeling Claire quiver and push against him, he thrust into her, and together, they exploded in an intense orgasm. "Claire, that may have started baby number two. It was that powerful," said Karl in a labored voice.

Claire, holding onto him, snuggled up to his neck, kissing him. With tears in her eyes, Claire said softly, "That suits me fine, you wonderful lover. Feel like doing it again to make sure you sleep well tonight?"

Karl, hearing this, smiled, replying, "My conservative English lady is always in quiet control and always proper, if only they knew what a vixen you can be when it comes to making love."

Claire tugged at his shirt, replying, "Come here, you animal. I want you naked, skin to skin before we do anything more." The winds of war may be all around them, but here in the confines of their bedroom, there was only the moon and stars over a scented field of lilacs.

CHAPTER 11

THE LAST DANGEROUS MISSION

Like all the times before, Karl's time at home was coming to its end. Although Karl and Claire did not outwardly show it, the fear of his not returning was at the forefront of their minds. Karl spent as much time with Nicholas as he could. His son would beam whenever Karl entered the room, and Claire would sit smiling and watching her two men play on the floor, hour after hour. Nicholas had bonded with his father very quickly; it was like Karl had been there every day since his birth. Claire felt the tension building as she looked at her watch. It was getting close to 10:30 a.m., and Charlie would be here shortly to drive Karl back to Slough.

"Darling, sorry to interfere with you two having so much fun, but it's getting close to Charlie arriving. Maybe you should think about getting ready?" Claire always got nervous each time Karl had to leave, and today would be extra difficult because she knew Karl would definitely be going back into war torn Europe, which made saying goodbye a real challenge.

Promptly at 1030 hours, a sharp rap on the front door announced the arrival of Charlie. Claire opened the front door, saying, "Charlie, you're getting to know Hitchin quite well. Come on in; I'll make you a nice cuppa before you head back. Feel like a crumpet with that tea? The major should be down momentarily."

Charlie removed his cap as he entered, following Claire into the kitchen. Now wearing his field uniform, Karl gathered up the remainder of his kit, neatly arranged on the bed, cleaned, and pressed by his proficient wife, Claire.

Returning to the kitchen, Karl greeted Charlie with his usual smile, "Charlie, good to see you, although I prefer it when you're dropping me off, not picking me up. Have you seen baby Nicholas yet?"

Claire answered, "I put him down for a nap. Stick your head in, Charlie; he's all Vita, I can assure you. The three of them quietly entered the lounge. Nick, lying on his back in his crib, his thumb in his mouth, was staring at the crib toy Karl had made for him a few days back. When he saw them, his little legs started kicking, and his arms were reaching to be picked up. Karl lifted his son so that Charlie could see him.

"Quite the little lad, Mrs. Vita; he must keep you going all day long, does he?"

Claire, holding Karl's arm, simply answered, "Nights as well. Charlie, please, start calling me Claire when there is no one else here."

Charlie could sense they needed time to say their goodbyes, so turning, he excused himself, saying, "Thank you for letting me see young Nicholas. Let me take your kit bag, Sir; I'll wait for you outside in the car. You need a few minutes to say your goodbyes alone." Charlie was very special to Karl; he had always been there for him, and now, when it was time to leave, he knew Charlie would be there for him again.

"Claire, this is what I hate; there is no good way to say goodbye." Lifting Nick in the air, he said, "My little man, you will be walking when I return. I seem to be missing all the most important times. I hope your mummy takes lots of pictures to send me." Karl put Nick back down in his crib, then with arms outstretched, he folded them around Claire, saying, "Claire, my ray of sunshine, words always fail me when I have to say goodbye, so let's make this short. Neither of us can handle these times. I love you so very much, and our little family means more to me than anything else. Try not to worry too much; that will only stress you out. I know it's easier said than done but try to keep that stiff upper lip that you English ladies are famous for."

Karl needed to leave; the tears were now flowing from Claire's eyes. Looking into his eyes, she said, laboring with each word, "Darling, we both know this mission will put you in grave danger again. Please, please, take extra care of yourself; we need you so much." Claire stopped talking as she could not say any more. With one last kiss, Karl broke away and headed for the door.

With the rear door open, Charlie waited for Karl, but that inner feeling made him stop and turn around to look at Claire, stressed and crying at seeing him leave maybe for the last time. "Wait one more minute, Charlie," said Karl as he walked quickly back to the front door. Once more, he wrapped his strong arms around the love of his life, Claire. "Give me a lasting kiss that will stay with me; make it a really good one," said Karl. Claire kissed him passionately, her tongue deep in his mouth.

Pulling back, she smiled at him, asking, "Will that do it, you sex crazed Austrian?" Karl, with a renewed smile, turned and walked back toward the car. As he lowered his head to enter the car, he threw her a last kiss. Claire stood there in the doorway until the car had driven off. Back inside, she scooped up Nick, then sat on the couch, crying profusely.

Almost shaking, she looked at Nick, then said under her breath, "Bugger it, Nick, we are going to see your grandma. Staying alone here in this house is not any good for either of us. Come on, little man; let's get you ready, shall we?"

All the way back to Slough, Karl said nothing. His mind was in another place, a place where war was not an issue and happiness was all around him, rolling in the grass with his son, his wife Claire laughing as she laid on the blanket, watching them together. These images were the reason he would continue putting himself in danger. These thoughts were the only reason to continue in this dangerous occupation. He needed to hang onto the belief that, when it was over, he would never leave home or his family again. That's assuming he did not get injured or killed in that dangerous line of work he operated in!

"Charlie, drop me off in front of the main building, then take my kit bag to my room; that's a good chap. Thanks for driving me back; I really appreciate it." Karl was also thinking; I hope I'm still around for you to return me to Hitchin one day.

Entering the lobby, he was about to sign in when the ATS receptionist asked him to go straight to meeting room A-2. "Thank you, Corporal. It must be an important meeting to use that big conference room; any idea what's going on?" Karl thought more about that question. *You idiot, that was a stupid question to ask that corporal. How could she know about the secrets being discussed behind those doors?* Removing his cap, he tucked it under his arm before opening the meeting room door. Inside, long tables were arranged in a horseshoe configuration. All branches of the armed forces were present, including Karl's friends, Clive, Bill, Gunther, and Herbert.

"Major Vita, welcome, come and have a seat next to Colonel Knight. We are about to start; we're just waiting on two more from the RAF to join us," announced General Jacks, sitting in the center of the middle table.

Whispering into Clive's ear, Karl asked, "Is this meeting anything to do with the telephone call you made to me a few days ago?" Clive did not answer; instead, he simply nodded, placing his index finger over his lower lip. Karl reached over to shake Gunther and Herbert's hands, pleased to see them back in Slough again. A simple nod from both told him the feeling was mutual.

Standing, General Jacks thanked everyone for rearranging their schedules to attend this first of many strategic planning meetings, followed by, "Please, refer to the folders in front of you. The first page should tell you why we are all here today. The Germans may be losing this conventional war; however, that doesn't mean they're finished far from it! Their weapons technology is quite amazing, and that, right now, is concerning the High Command. Since 1939, German scientists have been secretly designing a new type of bomb that utilizes atomic fusion.

"Our people, until recently, believed they were far from having a working prototype. In fact, they believed the war could well be over before having to face that threat. More recently, our sources believe their scientists are beyond the preliminary design phases and are now building an atomic bomb with aspirations of having it ready by October of this year. Yes, gentlemen, you heard me right October! As of last week, we got confirmation that this first test will be scheduled for test firing on a small island in the Baltic Sea where that location is, we are still trying to identify. Sadly, the Intelligence team assigned to this top secret mission were all shot trying to outrun the Gestapo.

They burned the documentation they were carrying before being overpowered by the Gestapo.

"Gentlemen, we are here today to address how to find that island. How do we obtain additional information on the status of this bomb, and finally, how do we destroy it before it can be unleashed on our homeland? The intelligence brought back by Major Fisher and Captain Werner confirms the existence of a long new range heavy bomber that has successfully been tested with the sole intent of detonating an atomic bomb on a city somewhere on the East Coast of America we suspect New York to be that target. This is even more reason to believe they are much closer than we were led to believe.

"That Junker JU-390 six engine bomber is ready to deliver that bomb, from the safety of their hiding place in the nearby woods, they observed this aircraft at its manufacturing site in Dessau in Germany. Major Fisher's team witnessed its ground maneuvering through their binoculars and finally saw it taking off into flight. If that's not enough to scare you, we now have information about a new type of U-Boat for the Kriegsmarine, code named Vergeltungswaffen, which means V-weapon. This new submarine has been designed to launch a rocket carrying an atomic warhead. These new weapons only add to the growing belief that they are buying time till they can wage a new kind of terror to gain the upper hand and turn this war back in their favor."

Silence fell on the group as they listened intently to a new phase that the Wehrmacht intended to wage war on the allies. Hands shot up, looking for answers. General Jacks said, "Gentlemen, I can see you are looking for answers, but today is not the day we will be addressing them."

One Naval captain stood up, ignoring the general's request, "Sorry to ignore your last statement, but my question is short and to the point. Do we have any information that confirms the Germans are planning on sharing this technology with the Japanese?" The Naval captain sat back down, looking to General Jacks for a response.

"Captain, we have every reason to believe the Axis Powers will share whatever technology they have for weapons of mass destruction to gain the upper hand in this World War."

Standing, a Naval Commander instructed all the attendees, "Your folders have a group code on the front. Please go directly to that meeting room assigned to your group. This meeting is now over, and your specific meeting will continue there."

Clive looked at the others around him, saying, "Well, chaps, let's adjourn to meeting room B-6, shall we? There's a lot to plan for, and time does not appear to be on our side." Clive led the way. As the men took seats around the oval table, Clive opened a large binder, taking out support documentation that they would be using. Clive gave a brief overview of what each group was tasked to do. "I have been fortunate, or should I preface that statement by saying, the High Command has given me a directive. Gentlemen, this assembly has been charged with the following assignment: to find out more about the heavy equipment needed to manufacture this bomb and where that secret location is. From the information Major Fisher brought back, we believe it could well be somewhere close to Kiel; so much legwork needs to be done in this area.

"We can assume that when this equipment and machinery are completed, it will be transported to that island in the Baltic that General Jacks mentioned, but from what port? Gunther you, and Herbert will return to Germany next week to set up an advanced Intelligence site. Karl, you and I will start to organize the resources we will need. The other three groups have been charged with identifying routes that could be used. Knowing the Germans as we do, I'm sure this will include some deceptive dead ends. Finding the location of that island will require many reconnaissance flights by the RAF and countless hours of reviewing the film they bring back. Finally, we will have to assess any land routes that would be considered to transport additional equipment to some port which may have limitations, assuming the Germans have already identified the high risk of shipping by rail.

"The Allied domination of airspace is too much of a risk to consider that; therefore, let's assume it will be by sea from the original shipping point. Karl, you're our resident expert on shipping and port capacity, so you take the lead in this area. Now, what do we have so far?" asked Clive as they commenced digging through the mound of support documentation.

"I have a question for you, Clive," said Gunther. "Why are we not including the Americans in these meetings? They are our allies when all is said and done." Clive looked around the room at the group, which now had questioning looks on their faces.

"Good question, and one I have only limited knowledge of, so let me answer this way. The Americans are already on the ground, looking for German Uranium Oxide. Thousands of tons of this precious material are buried or hidden in many German laboratories, most of which are underground. The Americans desperately need that material for the Manhattan Atomic Bomb project being developed in New Mexico. Gentlemen, our job from now on is not about conventional warfare; it's about the most destructive technology known to man. The Americans are cooperating in certain areas, but this division under General Jacks is operating autonomously for reasons that are not our concern.

"As for our other allies, the Russians, well, from what we can ascertain, they are rushing to capture as many German scientists and their equipment for the same reasons as the rest of us. By the way, Major Vita, it's your friend Major Anderson who is heading up that American push to find those stockpiles of Uranium Oxide. This war could be close to an end; let's pray those German geniuses don't get any further with their atomic bomb and its delivery methods. Gentlemen, that is our job to make sure they don't." The meeting went on about another three hours, then adjourned till the following morning.

Karl was tired, so he bowed out of having a drink with the others, electing to return to his room before supper to call Claire. Telephone use was becoming an issue, and censorship of all calls made sensitive discussions almost impossible. But at least they could hear each other's voices, and with crafty use of select words, they could get their point across. Every other day, Karl would write her a letter again, censorship limited the freedom of its contents.

As planned, Gunther and Herbert would return to France in two weeks, then link up with the underground fighters, who would get them back into Germany. Once there, they will start their mission to find the locations of those secret manufacturing sites, then confirm the port to be used. When signaled to do so, the underground fighters were preparing to sabotage rail lines heading North and East.

Daily reports were leaning toward the heavy equipment being shipped out by ship from Keil to that Baltic Island, but when? And did the Navy have a plan to stop that ship from reaching its destination? Clive, Karl, and the other group members worked almost around the clock, piecing together a clearer picture of what had to be done. The data and aerial images received daily from all sources started to point toward the need to know more about that ship in Keil. Was it a Naval vessel or a cargo ship?

"Chaps, I think we are all in agreement. The next phase of this operation must be shared with the Admiralty in London before going further. Let me set that meeting up in the morning with their senior Naval Intelligence chaps. Our plan is extremely dangerous, so expect opposition from that bunch. This is not the sort of operation the Royal Navy likes to endorse; that's why we need to do this face to face." Clive looked at the faces around him, fully aware that some of these chaps would not return home if approved. The stakes were that high.

The drive to the Admiralty was uneventful. Each member on that bus was either fine tuning their part for the upcoming meeting or daydreaming of someplace else maybe with a loved one or their children. They all knew the risks, and in that quiet place in their minds, they were considering the consequences.

The Admiralty was a place Clive and Karl were quite familiar with. Their proposal today would ruffle many of the Navy attendees because it would require many types of warships and aerial patrols, fighter aircraft, and submarine chasers to make this a successful mission. Walking down the long corridor, they saw paintings of famous Royal Navy vessels, sailors of all ranks, and famous battles that would forever revere the Royal Navy as the world leader in sea power. The young lieutenant showed them into the meeting room, already occupied by ten high ranking officers representing the Royal Navy and the Royal Air Force.

Commodore Benjamin Wriggles, standing at the head of the long conference table, walked around, approaching the visitors gathered by the entrance. In a cheerful voice, he said, "Gentlemen, thank you for traveling up to today. Colonel Knight, from your telephone call, it would appear this meeting pertains to a serious new threat to the British Empire, is that correct? First, let me introduce this panel for today's meeting."

Standing to one side of the group, Karl looked around the room, thinking, such a lavish conference room compared to the ones back at BIS headquarters. It makes ours look very shabby in comparison. "Before we commence, can we provide a beverage and light pastries?" asked the commodore, pointing to the sideboard. The group zeroed in on the pastries and hot tea then sat down across from the others. Over the next several hours, the BIS officers detailed the looming danger from German weapon developments. Then, they waited in silence for questions that would surely follow.

Hearing this latest update on atomic development, Commodore Wriggles sat quietly in his chair, hands together in front of his mouth, deeply concerned this weapon could be launched before the war comes to an end. Everyone sat quietly, waiting for his response, which came loudly, "My God, I was starting to believe this damn war would be over in a few months. We are all aware of this atomic bomb, but quite honestly, the Admiralty thought the American program was the one closest to completion. You must be confident in the accuracy of this latest information, or you would not be here this morning."

Clive stood up again, detailing the BIS proposal to the panel, emphasizing that their plan was already in motion.

"Are we hearing you correctly, Colonel? Are you proposing we hijack that freighter carrying equipment and machinery for this atomic bomb program? Is that correct?" asked the commodore, shaking his head in shock at hearing about this dangerous mission.

Clive stood up once again to explain how they arrived at this plan. "The original plan was simply to find out what port that ship would sail from, then sink it with a massive aerial attack. However, that would not help our scientific people understand more about this new design and how it works, so that would not work. Then, Majors Vita and Fisher came up with an alternative plan, and that was to hijack that ship and sail it back to Scotland. Major Fisher and Captain Werner are both former Wehrmacht officers and very familiar with German military tactics.

"Major Vita is a former German merchant marine officer; he is very familiar with most German ports and the waters around Germany and Norway, including ports on the eastern shores of England. Although the island in the Baltic is still unknown to us, that test cannot take place without the equipment on that ship. From our limited intelligence, we believe the ship will more than likely be heading for Oslo or maybe Stavanger; another destination that can't be ruled out could well be as far north as Bergen.

"From these Norwegian ports, we believe that cargo will travel by road or rail, or both, to a site we don't have details on yet. There is a possibility that equipment is destined for a new secret heavy water facility close to any of these ports.

"The main facility in Vemork, just outside of Rjukan, was producing hydrogen for the German war machine until February of this year. Norwegian commandoes sabotaged it, so it's safe to assume that Oslo is not a destination for that ship."

Clive and his team had covered every avenue. Their plan, although extremely dangerous, had about a forty percent chance of delivering that ship to Aberdeen in Scotland, the closest Allied port.

"Thank you, Colonel, for a very detailed plan. Assuming we proceed with this, what part do you expect the Royal Navy and Air Force to play in it?" asked the commodore apprehensively.

Clive asked Karl to continue the briefing as it pertained to the ship. Karl was prepared, and Clive had been in many meetings with him, so he knew it would be polished and very detailed. "Well, assuming we can take control of the ship, which we can discuss later in the briefing, we would head north from Keil through the Great Belt and the Samco Belt Straits, up the Danish east coast to Frederikshavn. Up to this point, it will appear the ship is following the intended course. Turning west, it would still be on course to prying eyes on the shore or from aerial surveillance. This is where you blokes must be ready to jump in to protect us once we are abeam of Kristiansand.

Instead of heading on a corrected course NNW, we will commence our dash toward Aberdeen that's over three hundred miles in open waters. We will need Naval warships such as destroyers, maybe heavy cruisers to take up stations around us, and as many sub chasers as Coastal Command can spare to keep U-Boats at bay.

"Gentlemen, from this point on, the German Kriegsmarine will be out to sink that ship. RAF fighters from bases in Scotland need to be at the ready to engage the Luftwaffe, stopping them from bombing and strafing us. If we can deliver that ship to our scientists, they will be able to get a firsthand look at that cargo. In addition, assuming we can make Aberdeen, we must be ready for additional attempts to blow that ship up from long range fighters and bombers once we are docked. A comprehensive plan must be in place from when we change course off Kristiansand. Gentlemen, there's a lot at stake, and every arm of our military must be ready to participate if we stand a chance of pulling this off." Karl nodded to Clive, who thanked him for his presentation.

"Question for you on taking command of the ship, Major Vita? How do you intend to do that?"

Karl turned toward Gunther, asking, "At this juncture, Commodore, Major Fisher is in the best position to address that question, Major."

Gunther stood, thanking Karl. "As Colonel Knight has already told you all, both Captain Werner and I are former German Army officers. This puts us in a very good position to masquerade as German officers in charge of protecting the cargo. Each one of the twenty-five S.A.S. troops have volunteered for this mission; some are former German military; most have a Jewish background. We have labored over an elaborate plan to send the officers and troops assigned to protect that cargo to Hamburg instead of Keil. Our inside people have changed their orders, so by the time they arrive at that dock in Hamburg, we will have sailed from Keil, assuming we are successful in this phase of the mission. In the interest of covering all the other details associated with this mission, I can assure you that we have not left one detail to chance." Gunther was always to the point and always instilling confidence in success.

Commodore Wriggles called for a recess to evaluate the contributions and risks that would be needed to pull off this risky operation. "Thank you, Colonel Knight. I propose we take a short recess for this panel to discuss this operation in private say thirty minutes or so. My adjutant will show you to another area for refreshments; thank you again."

The commodore walked around to shake hands with each presenter. "Well done, chaps. We'll try to make this a quick as possible."

Walking down the hall, Herbert asked Clive, "How do you think we did in there?" Clive, smiling back at him, raised his finger over his mouth in a sign they would talk more once they were alone. Along the back wall of the meeting room, a table with plates of sandwiches, pastries, and an urn of hot coffee was quickly devoured.

"Well, Herbert, to answer your question, I think the first reaction was one of shock. However, their questions led me to believe they are deciding how many ships and aircraft will be needed to pull this off. Does that answer your question?" said Clive as he bit into a cucumber sandwich.

Punctually, thirty minutes later, a loud rap on the door was heard, followed by Clive yelling, "Come!"

Announced the return of the Adjutant, "The commodore sends his compliments and requests you and your staff return to the meeting room."

"Okay, chaps, let's find out if we have a mission or not," said Clive as he led the group back to the meeting room, all of them wondering about the outcome.

Back in Slough, the rain was making the morning miserable as Karl, Gunther, and Herbert walked over to the main building to meet up with Clive and his staff to commence the intense planning for *Operation Thunderstorm*, named by Commodore Wriggle because of its limited chances of succeeding.

Clive brought the meeting to order by saying. "Well, that meeting went well, even though we had to make concessions to having sappers and a couple of atomic scientists assigned to the mission. I, for one, was not happy with their demands for those chaps to rig the ship with explosives in case we are unable to break out into the North

Sea. Now, let's start with how we will get all involved to arrive at the safe house near Keil at the same time. Right now, our people on the ground in Keil are trying to identify which ship it's going to be." For the next five days, the group planned their deceptive trap to steal this German ship, working into the early morning hours until every detail was as foolproof as it could be, and they were ready for what could be viewed as a one-way suicide mission.

CHAPTER 12

OPERATION THUNDERSTORM

The night before they were due to leave, Karl sat in his room at his small desk. Pen in hand, he stared at the blank sheet of writing pad in front of him, thinking how he would word this letter of goodbye to Claire and his son Nicholas. The previous goodbye letter was on the desk; a reminder he had been in this same place before.

My Dearest Claire and Nicholas,

If you read this letter, it will mean I have been taken prisoner, which is highly unlikely more like killed doing my duty to King and Country. There is no way to say how sorry I am for putting you in a position to face the sobering fact that I will not be returning home ever again. Claire, what we do in the BIS is always dangerous. This you have always known, and even though that cloud has hung over our marriage, we always knew there was the high risk of a mission taking me. There will never be perfect words to describe how much your love and now our son Nicholas have made my life worth all the danger I can't escape from. If there is a hereafter, I will be watching over you both. As for your life, Claire, never give up on a new romance. As you always remind me, you're not good at being single.

Please, make sure you include me in all those talks you will have with Nicholas as he grows up into a Vita, I would be so proud of. It would mean the world to me if he knew all about his dad and the brief wonderful life we had together.

Claire, my wish right now is that you never read this letter alone. I pray we will read it together after this madness ends hopefully, very soon. If all goes well, Bill can return this letter to me after this, my Last BIS Mission! God willing, it will be successful, and I'll be home once again safe in your arms.

With all the love I can send to you and Nicholas,
Your devoted, loving husband,
Karl

Tomorrow, the team would leave in groups of four and five by various routes and transportation to arrive at their hiding place outside of Keil. The hiding place, an operating farm, was the front for this operation. Karl, Gunther, and four of the S.A.S. troops would land at the docks in the French channel port of Cherbourg, now under Allied control. Another team led by Herbert and his S.A.S. Officers would parachute into Germany not too far from Keil. From here, they would make their way by night to Keil. Three other groups would make their way into Germany via a beach landing from a Navy submarine.

The channel crossing was extremely rough, with most of the passengers getting seasick. However, to Karl Vita, it was invigorating that blasting salt air was blowing all the cobwebs out from his brain. Looking back at the disappearing coast of England, he sat outside, wondering if he would ever see it again. God willing, he would survive, even though there was less than forty percent chance of that happening. A strong hand on his shoulder made him jump, and he looked up to see Gunther standing next to him, rocking with the movement of the ship.

"Karl, I know what's going through your head about now. May I sit with you, or would you prefer to be alone right now?" asked Gunther, looking at the solemn face of his friend.

"Gunther, that would be nice; come, sit next to me. Have you heard more about your wife and children? The last time I brought that up, you believed they were somewhere in Norway. Is that still the case?" Karl carefully asked that sensitive question. Gunther was very much the German officer, keeping everything like this safely locked away.

"Karl, forgive me for not conveying the latest on my family; you know how I am about that subject. Right now, I can tell you they are finally safe with my wife's family near Gothenburg." Gunther had never shared with Karl that his wife was originally from Sweden.

"Your wife is Swedish? Gunther, you never told me that, but then again, you never really told me that much, did you?" Karl, looking at Gunther with a smile across his face, continued. "Gunther, you don't have to answer this question, but did you have a hand in making that happen while you were on your last mission to Germany?" Karl looked at the expression on Gunther's face; no words were needed.

Entering the battered port of Cherbourg, their transport tied up alongside a similar transport vessel. The port was very crowded with ships offloading supplies, vehicles, and military personnel. From here, they would be met by a guide, then travel by road northwest toward the front lines between France and Germany.

In the bombed-out village of Dinan, approximately twelve miles from the front line, Karl and Gunther's group was met by a German freedom fighter who guided them through the lines into Germany. Now dressed in their German uniforms, they traveled by truck toward Keil, staying away from main roads and any military buildups. Two days later, they arrived at the outskirts of Keil. Waiting for the protection of night, they drove carefully to the farm. Stopping by the gate, the driver flashed his headlights once, then waited five seconds to flash three more times, followed by one more to complete the recognition signal.

The return signal flashed, so they drove up to the open barn doors. Without stopping, the truck drove straight into the barn, the doors closing quickly behind them. All but two teams had arrived. Grouped in the back of the big barn, they all shook hands, pleased that the first part of the mission was now behind them. Sleeping in the hayloft, a noise from below made them all jump to their feet, Sten guns at the ready. The last two teams had arrived; the time was 0230 hours. There were greetings all around, followed by Gunther asking them to get some sleep. They would need all their faculties to be sharp for tomorrow's mission.

Karl and Gunther were up at the crack of dawn, already going over the objectives for taking over the ship, which had been identified by the freedom fighters and the shortwave radio signal from Slough with the proceed signal (the weather could have thunderstorms later today). "Well, Karl, are we ready? It looks like the Gustav III is our next stop." Gunther gathered the squad that would accompany Karl, wearing his maritime uniform, for a final review of the operation.

"We will accompany Major Vita, or I should call him Commander Vita until we are safely in control of the ship. The guards at the main gate are by now our own people; the original guards disposed of. The ship will have armed sailors at the boarding gate. Commander Vita will board ahead of us once he has shown his documentation. We will follow close behind, showing our documentation before boarding, which may take a little while.

"We are trying to plan our arrival three to four hours ahead of the cargo arriving. The latest intelligence informed us that the trucks would arrive sometime after 1900 hours. By then, we should be in total control of the ship. Once Commander Vita and I are aboard, we will go straight to the bridge with four troopers. Our job will be to convince the captain that he is aiding the total annihilation of many cities and the painful death of thousands of people by delivering that cargo. With any luck, he will recognize the demise of the Nazi Regime and join us willingly. I will clarify that I will shoot him if he resists, and Karl here will take over command; that order also applies to the others.

"Johan, you and your squad will go straight to the radio room. That must be in our control from the very start. Keep the operator with you until we have the rest of the ship secured. The other squads will follow that rehearsed procedure, taking up stations throughout the ship and engine room. Now, when the cargo arrives, we will act as the protective guards, lining up along the ship's railing and around the cargo hold. Our scientific members will be ready to inspect the cargo once it's in the cargo hold. Whatever you do, make it your priority to take as many pictures as you can. Remember to have yourselves or guards stand next to that equipment for size.

"If we fail to break out into the North Sea, our instruction will be to blow the ship out of the water, so those pictures will be all we have. So, keep that in mind; any questions so far?" asked Gunther.

"I have one, Sir; how do we handle guards and civilians traveling with the cargo? What are our orders?" asked one of the sappers.

"Good questions; we are moving very quickly on this mission. Chances are, they won't suspect you at first, so take the initiative to make the first move. Remember to shoot first if challenged; we can't afford a gunfight. Hopefully, they will already be discouraged and will surrender to you. Any other questions before we head out?"

"Sir, one quick question, when do we receive Naval and RAF protection?"

Karl replied, "We are on our own until we are headed west and away from our last land sighting of Kristiansand at the southern tip of Norway. Our protective coverage will rendezvous around us from there. Good luck, chaps; God be with us," concluded Karl. Everyone now took time to relax, catch up on sleep, play cards, or do anything to keep their minds off the dangers that lay ahead of them starting later that day.

At 1500 hours', Gunther yelled out loud, "Alright, you lot, let's get this show on the road." The German Mann trucks were lined up ready outside, and Karl and Gunther climbed into the Mercedes staff car. When the trucks were loaded, the convoy headed out of the farm complex and into certain danger.

Herbert and his two squads had arrived at the dockyard earlier that morning, their job to eliminate the guards as they changed watches. Once they had done that, they would remain on guard until all the trucks had passed through. The dock being used lay behind a badly damaged warehouse. Two of the massive cranes were leaning or collapsed completely, hanging into the dark brown waters of the harbor. The pier itself had two large bomb craters near where the ship was berthed. The anti-aircraft battery positions were at either end of the pier, with four more further down the pier.

A truck mounted crane was already in position, ready to lift the precious cargo from the trucks into the ship's hold. This crane truck had been brought in as the dock cranes were all out of action. Herbert and his two squads would remain at the ready in case suspicion by dockhands and anti-aircraft guards created a confrontation. If all went well, they would remain diligent until after the ship had departed, then drive back the way they had come, rendezvousing with Allied troops at a prearranged location. With any luck, they would arrive back in Slough, God willing, within a week.

Approaching the main gate, everyone had their weapons at the ready in case Herbert's squads were unsuccessful in overpowering the gate guards. The guards came out of the guard shack.

Speaking loudly, they asked for identification and orders, going through the motions in case prying eyes were watching. Handing back the documents, one of the guards winked, then in a low voice said, "Good luck," as he waved the convoy through.

So far so good, thought Karl, still with his hand on his weapon. Navigating around the large crater, the Mercedes pulled up in front of the boarding ramp. Karl and Gunther got out, casually saluting the driver, then waited as the trucks unloaded the guards. One of the sergeants yelled to form lines once the trucks were empty. Standing at ease until the trucks and staff car had left, Gunther saluted Karl as they went through their rehearsed performance. Approaching the armed sailors, Karl presented his documentation, followed by Gunther and the squad behind him.

One of the sailors looked suspiciously at Karl and said, "State your reason to board this ship."

Karl, taking the high road, barked back at this guard displaying visions of grandeur. "You have my documentation and my ID. Who gave you the right to talk to a superior officer in that condescending tone of voice, and what happened to saluting? You can expect repercussions for your insolent behavior." Karl stood with his left hand out for his papers.

"Sir, please, forgive me. I meant no disrespect. We are all a little on edge after the bombardment several nights ago." Karl took back his documentation, then approached the boarding ramp. Gunther, along with their squad, were quickly waved through. Karl and Gunther stepped onto the deck and turned to watch the rest of the group make their way up the boarding ramp.

"Karl, you're a marvelous actor. You scared the daylights out of that insolent sailor. That scolding seems to be working in our favor, though; look how fast they are boarding our chaps," said Gunther as they approached the bridge.

Opening the door, Karl spoke with a precise voice and said, "Permission to enter the bridge?"

"Enter," came the response from the watch officer. The captain and navigator were leaning over the chart table, making notes for the upcoming voyage commencing later in the day.

Once they were all inside, the armed S.A.S. troops moved quickly to secure both entrances and the doors that led out onto both maneuvering wings. Gunther moved over to the captain and navigator, saluting them in a sign of respect. Startled by these intruders, the captain stood, facing Gunther.

"Sorry to alarm you like this, Captain, but I need you to pay close attention to what I'm about to tell you. We have boarded your ship with over thirty-five crack, S.A.S. troops. At this very moment, all your crew members are facing down the barrels of MP-40 rifles. Captain Hoffmann, we intend you no harm, and that applies to your officers and crew if you agree to cooperate with us. After you have heard the reason behind this hijacking, we are hoping you will join us in delivering this ship and its lethal cargo to the safety of an Allied port. I am a former proud German officer, and Major Vita here is a former German maritime officer.

"This war was forced on all of us, you included, by power crazed Nazi's. This war is all but lost to the Germans. This cargo you are transporting, if delivered, will be used to create a weapon so powerful it could destroy large cities and thousands of civilian lives with just one bomb. Thousands more would be severely injured for the remainder of their lives. Do you really want that on your conscience? Captain, you look like a loyal German. Help us stop that madman, Hitler, and his thugs from using this debilitating weapon once and forever.

"Hitler and his scientists are developing this new weapon to turn this war in their favor, and they cannot be allowed to continue. One day soon, you will hear about the millions of Jewish people and many others who resisted the Nazi indoctrination forced upon them. Help us now to restore our Fatherland. By the way, all of us here are German, other than the major here, who is Austrian." Gunther turned to Karl to add more.

"Captain, I was a former first officer for the Langstaff Shipping Company's ship, the *Tristian*. My assignment on this mission is to ensure the delivery of this ship and its cargo to an Allied port. In the unfortunate situation that you and your officers refuse to assist us, I will take control of this ship, which I'm more than capable of doing. If that should happen. What will happen to you and your crew, simple we will shoot you, then feed you to the fish. Twitch one muscle in the wrong way, and these crack troopers will shoot first, then ask questions later. I don't particularly like violence or killing, so I hope you will consider our request to join us."

Karl stepped back, sitting at the navigation table, waiting for the other officers to be brought to the bridge. As the other officers entered the bridge, Gunther pointed to the back of the bridge for them to line up. Over the next forty-five minutes, Gunther and Karl told them all about the potential for unleashing the deadliest weapon ever to be used against humanity. Waiting for an answer, Karl and Gunther waited in silence until the officers and their captain were ready to answer.

Captain Hoffmann approached Gunther, a smile on his face that indicated he and his crew would cooperate. "Major, we totally agree with everything you have told us. In fact, we have talked amongst ourselves about taking this ship to the closest friendly port. The biggest problem we have faced to date is that all of us would be treated as traitors, and our families would pay the price with their lives. So, let's tell the rest of the crew that we are now prisoners of the English who have taken command of the ship. The biggest problem I see will be stopping them from smiling and cheering.

"Soon, that cargo will arrive with its own guards to ensure it gets delivered, so that's going to be the biggest problem. I will try my best to convince them that the added storm troopers have been boarded as a precautionary measure." The captain and his officer, with outstretched hands, now welcomed their new comrades.

Taking the captain and first officer aside, Karl sent a guard to find Gunther, then bring him to the bridge. "Gentlemen, right now, I need to know more about your orders starting from here in Keil."

The captain beckoned for them to gather around the chart table, then, with a pointer in hand, started detailing this mission. "The High Command felt the best way to transport this cargo would be to keep a low profile, with very little military presence to many prying eyes around these docks. Leaving under cover of darkness, we are to proceed on the predetermined course and speed to each of the recognition points; the code signal is A.D.Z.F.G. All going well, we are to proceed NNW toward Kristiansand.

"From there, we will maintain the same course until intersected by three Kriegsmarine destroyers. By then, we should have air cover from Luftwaffe fighters, more than likely FockeWulfe-190s with extended range drop tanks. From there, we have no idea where we will be heading, other than we have been instructed to follow the lead warship with the other two on our flank," explained Captain Hoffman.

"So, you have no idea where that final destination will be?" asked Karl, somewhat confused.

"Major, this has been kept from us in case of destination leaks." Karl turned to the navigator, saying, "Let's you and I start working on our breakaway course and bearing, shall we?"

Meanwhile, Gunther had lined all his troops along the rail and around the ship's cargo hold. Spotting the insolent sailor guarding the boarding ramp, Gunther, walking over to him, asked him, "I'm assuming your outburst earlier today was a sign of contempt for the Nazi party, is that correct?"

The sailor, nodding his head, looked at Gunther, saying, "How was I to know you were here to take control of the ship? Now, I feel terrible. That officer must despise my behavior, and I hope I have a chance to apologize to him. I'm sure Captain Hoffmann has told you we wanted to defect many times, but fear for our families has stopped us from doing that. Sir, I hope if we can pull off this dangerous voyage, you'll find a way for the Nazis to hear about this crew's brave resistance to being taken prisoners, won't you, Sir?"

Gunther patted the sailor's shoulder and answered, "Consider it done; you will become heroes of the Fatherland."

Captain Hoffmann stood on the bridge wing with Karl at his side, watching the line of guards along the rail as three heavy trucks arrived alongside the Gustav III. Gunther, looking every part the high-ranking German officer, walked back and forth along the ship's side as the crane was positioned to lift the components of that deadly cargo into the ship's hold. A German Gestapo officer, in the traditional black uniform, approached the third officer standing next to Gunther, barking, "Who is in charge here?" while slapping his leg with his swagger stick.

"That would be me, Sir. I'm the load officer; do you have the manifest for me to sign?" Lieutenant Bremen despised the arrogance of this Gestapo thug; his facial expression was giving him away.

"Get my luggage out of my car and have it sent to my state room right away, and who are you?" he said, turning toward Gunther. "A major, I see. State why you are here and are traveling with the ship?"

Gunther was steaming on the inside, thinking, I could shoot this prick right now; his arrogance reconfirms why I joined the English Military. "Captain, state your name and why you think you have the right to address a superior officer this way, with no regard for the fact that he outranks you. Now, address me correctly, or I'll have you shackled once you get on board this rust bucket." Gunther's temper was getting the better of him.

"My name is Captain Helmut Grucker, and let me remind you, I'm a Gestapo officer. I can make things very uncomfortable for you if you keep this up."

Lieutenant Bremen examined the documents, then asked the Gestapo officer to follow him up the boarding ramp onto the ship. From the bridge, Karl and the captain looked down at the show unfolding below on the pier. There was anger on both their faces and fire in both their eyes, with Karl thinking, once we are underway, that pig will regret the day he was born. Two hours later, the cargo was securely strapped into the ship's hold. They were now ready to cast off the dock lines and head out into certain danger. Two tugs were standing by to maneuver the old ship out of her berth.

The powerful propeller churned up the water astern as the ship started making headway out into the harbor of Keil. The bridge door opened, and in walked Grucker, announcing, "Captain, my name is Captain Grucker, and I will accompany the cargo to its final destination. My men have taken up stations around the cargo."

Little did he know, those troopers were already dead, killed by crack S.A.S. troops. "You will provide my men and me every courtesy. I want this voyage to go smoothly without any incident. It is imperative we deliver this cargo; is that perfectly understood? The Luftwaffe will provide limited aerial protection most of the way. Fuel is becoming a big issue, so we can't expect a whole wing of fighter support."

Looking at Karl, he barked, "Who are you? Are you part of this ship's complement?" Grucker was addressing Karl almost in his face. Karl, with hate in his eyes, stood nearly nose to nose without saying a word. With his left arm, he beckoned to the guard at the rear of the bridge to approach, weapons at the ready.

"Who am I? Well, my presence on this ship will shock you. My name is Major Karl Vita of the British Intelligence Service. As for you, Captain Grucker, you're an arrogant excuse for an officer.

As of right now, you're a prisoner of His Majesty's military." Karl was close to slapping Grucker across his face. Restraining himself, he had already made up his mind that this one would not see the dawn of tomorrow morning.

"Guards, arrest this insolent imposter masquerading as a Kriegsmarine officer. I want him shackled in the hold right now."

Karl could not contain himself any further. Grabbing Grucker by the throat, he screamed, "You pompous ass, are you so dense that you haven't figured out that everyone on this ship is going to England, and now so are you? As for your men, well, let's say their presence has been eliminated. Guards, get this idiot out of our sight, and if he puts one foot out of line or says one wrong word, shoot him in the head, then throw him overboard." Karl was still trembling as the guard pulled and pushed the screaming Grucker off the bridge. Captain

Hoffmann, watching quietly from the side, approached Karl. He spoke in a calming voice, saying, "Major, I have waited a long time to witness something like this. What you said earlier is so true. The people of Germany need to cleanse themselves of these warmongers, and with God's help, regain its dignity with all the people of Europe, if that's possible."

Karl looked at this kind man's face, replying, "That will be a long road, but if you are all willing to face the scorn from millions that at this point hate the atrocities conducted by the German military, then with time and real retribution for those acts of violence, there could one day be hope for a new, kinder Germany. Right now, we need to get ready to make our way through the Great Belt," concluded Karl.

"Navigator, have the signalman ready to flash the recognition signal as we pass the headland off Odense Funen Island; repeat that signal when we pass the peninsula off Grena. The last recognition signal will be at Skagen at the point off Aalborg Island. From there, our course will be out into the Skagerrak Straits. From there, Major, I'm sure the fun would commence if we maintained our original course. We would be close enough to flash the starboard recognition signal to the Kristiansand Tower."

"If that tower does not receive the signal, they will notify the Kriegsmarine and the Luftwaffe. Do you have a frequency for us to tune into, as we are going to need air cover from that point on? Be assured; the Kriegsmarine will dispatch all available warships they can muster. Can we rely on the Royal Navy and Air Force to be ready to move in to protect us?" asked Captain Hoffmann.

"That has been planned, so the only thing we must do is constantly flash this signal code every time we see one of our aircraft. The other thing we need to do is raise the British Maritime white ensign from the stern and a code pennant I'll give you, which you will display on the yardarm. The RAF and Coastal Command have been given a copy of that pennant and signal code. Coastal Command will be patrolling all around us, looking for U-Boats with Sunderland Flying Boats. I believe the Germans refer to them as flying porcupines because of all the armament they carry. If all goes well, they will outnumber all the German fighters and bombers dispatched to sink us.

"As for the Royal Navy, we can expect at least five to six destroyers and at least two light cruisers. Does that give you a more comfortable feeling about this voyage?" Karl reached inside his uniform, producing two pennants for later. The night was moonless, so, using dead reckoning, they steamed up the course, arriving at Skagen in the predawn hours.

Over the ship's PA system, Karl announced, "Gentlemen, we have been lucky until now. From here on, we will be running the gauntlet, so all weapons to the main deck. Major Fisher, make sure all photography has been done, and the film sealed in those waterproof bags, then join me on the bridge."

"Major, from here on, this bridge team and I will take instructions from you. God willing, this will be over soon." Captain Hoffmann reminded Karl so much of the Tristian's captain in the way he handled himself.

"Navigator, are you ready with the new coordinates I gave you to steer to? It's imperative that we arrive in the general area to rendezvous with the Royal Navy. Captain Hoffmann, can you make sure the pennants and stern flags are raised after we clear the Norwegian coast?" asked Karl in rapid order.

Gunther entered the bridge, saying, "Reporting as requested, Skipper." Gunther enjoyed seeing Karl in his element as a marine officer; it was that obvious that he was a natural seaman.

"Ah, Gunther, my sarcastic friend, did we dispose of those bodies as we planned? Hopefully, your chaps removed all dog tags before sewing them into those sea bags."

Gunther answered, "Yes, we did; however, that arrogant Gestapo chap was amongst them. We found him in the cabin we had locked him into with his throat slashed. He made a real mess of the furniture, sorry about that," explained Gunther, not really showing any remorse.

"What happened?" asked Karl.

"It appears one or more of the seamen took it upon themselves to have him meet his maker ahead of schedule; no real loss there." Gunther fluffed it off as a necessary thing that needed to happen.

The dawn was slowly coming up. Karl walked over to the chart table.

"Where are we now? Show me on the chart." Karl was totally focused on the job at hand.

"Alright, Captain, time to change sides; raise that ensign and pennant. Gunther, get everyone on deck with as much ammo we have with us. I believe our German friends will be looking for us shortly."

Gunther picked up the PA mike and announced, "Alright, it's show time on deck; close all watertight doors in readiness and ditch those uniforms." Each man had a British uniform in his backpack; the only thing missing was the English helmet, so this combination of English and German looked uniquely different.

About an hour later, four Coastal Command aircraft approached, flashing the recognition signal, which was quickly returned from the ship. The big Sunderland Flying Boats wagged their wings as they flew off, taking up their stations about eight miles away. Shortly thereafter, the first wing of RAF Hawker Typhoon fighters approached, taking up stations around the ship.

The radio crackled on the bridge with the sound of a muffled voice, "Able Baker One here; do you copy, over?"

Gunther picked up the mike, saying, "Able Baker One, we read you loud and clear; how long will you be on station around us, over?"

A short pause, then, "We will be circling you for about ninety minutes. We will withdraw as soon as the next wing arrives to relieve us. Don't worry; we have other wings that will maintain aerial coverage over you, ready to chase the Jerries away if they try to cause trouble. Expect the Royal Navy to rendezvous with you in approximately two hours. From their last transmission, they are sending a flotilla to protect you. We'll keep this channel open so that we can monitor those Navy blighters, over."

Feeling better than a few minutes ago, Gunther replied, "Thanks, chaps, Able Baker Two standing by, out." Gunther turned to Karl and Captain Hoffmann, saying, "Captain Hoffmann, we included a few guardian angels when we came aboard your ship." Everyone on the bridge laughed loudly, releasing the tension of all those hours during the night when their hearts were in their throats.

The radio crackled into life once more, "Able Baker Two, please respond; this is Rescue One, over."

The radio operator, hearing this, called the bridge, "Sir, we have Rescue One standing by; will you take it on the bridge?"

Gunther picked up the mike, replying affirmatively, "Rescue One, go ahead; Major Fisher here, over."

A strong English accent replied, "Commander Derek Manson here; we are at flank speed to rendezvous with you in less than two hours. We're expecting the Kriegsmarine to engage with a sizable force about the time we arrive; our coast watchers have signaled they left Stavanger in the predawn hours. Maintain your zigzag course until we take up stations around you."

Commander Manson, on the light cruiser, Aurora knew if he did not arrive before the Kriegsmarine warships, there could be little hope for the Gustav III to escape their guns, even with RAF aerial protection. The Sunderland Flying Boats were vigilantly scanning for U-Boat activities, now joined by five long range B-24 submarine hunters with similar scanning equipment and weaponry, extending the perimeter shield some twenty-four miles out from the Gustav III. Gunther and the navigator constantly monitored the radio traffic for any updates.

Karl looked at his watch, thinking, still about ninety minutes until we see those Royal Navy ships. Luck is on our side so far; the ships of the Kriegsmarine have not found us, not yet anyway! Taking his binoculars out onto the wing, he joined the other six sailors scanning the skies for aircraft and the horizon for telltale signs of hostile shipping. A loud yell made him jump as an excited sailor called out, "Contact bearing 030 degrees about eight miles out!" All eyes now focused on that direction, scanning the heavens in fear of approaching enemy aircraft.

"Able Baker One, can you identify those bandits approaching out of the northeast yet? Are they friend or foe?"

A muffled voice answered, "Engaging, looks like they're FW-190 fighters protecting a formation of bombers, estimate about fifteen, over." Everyone listening braced for the attack that would be on them within minutes. The skies above now swarmed as the two opposing fighter forces collided into a wild, noisy dogfight, flaming wrecks falling from the sky. The German bombers took advantage of this dogfight by pressing home their attack on the defenseless merchantmen below.

Karl rushed back into the bridge, yelling as he entered, "Helmsman, continue zigzagging maneuvers; we can't let those bombers get a fix on us. Get your helm over right now." He braced himself against the ship's annunciator as the fighter/bombers dove down on them. "Take cover; those three on our port side are coming in fast."

The German Messerschmitt ME-410s released their deadly bombs, while above them, the slower Heinkel HE-111 bombers opened their bomb doors, ready to commence the second attack from a much higher altitude. Karl, with fear on his face, stared at the swarm of incoming aircraft. On the deck below, Gunther was running toward the bow, pointing and yelling for his men to concentrate their firepower on the lead German aircraft. Their Bren machine guns answered his command, rattling like peashooters toward the lead bombers. Three RAF Typhoon fighters broke off their attack on the German fighter to engage the attacking bombers, diving down their lethal wing cannons spitting 50 mm shells into the lead Messerschmitt. Those piercing shells easily finding their mark mortally ripped that aircraft from nose to tail. The aircraft, shuddering, slowly rolled over on its back as pieces of its left wing flew off behind it; in a final dying maneuver, it cartwheeled into the ocean below.

The Typhoons, one of the deadliest of all Allied fighters, pressed home their vengeance on the two remaining bombers, sending them into the icy waters of the North Sea. While the Typhoons were dispatching those Messerschmitt's, the four Heinkel's about released their bomb load before turning to the north to make their escape. Most of those bombs hit the water, sending massive plumes of water across the Gustav's deck. The next string of bombs found their mark, exploding on the bridge and aft superstructure of the defenseless Gustav. Another bomb hit the bow close to the waterline, buckling the steel plates. The aerial dogfight continued overhead. There were not enough friendly aircraft to protect the ship and engage the enemy fighters. All those on the decks and superstructure watched in slow motion as the bombs rained down around them; this was Hell on Earth.

Wham! An ear-piercing shudder, sent bodies and equipment in all directions. Gunther, blown off his feet, clambered back up against the railing just as a second bomb exploded on the side of the bridge, hurtling giant pieces of metal over the side of the ship. Having chased off the remainder of the German fighters' cover, the remaining Typhoons tore into the lumbering Heinkel's, which were no match for these fire spitting lions of the RAF. What remained of the German force quickly withdrew, their number severely mauled and diminished, outmatched by the RAF.

"Able Baker One, Delta Three above you at 10 o'clock. Nice work, chaps, we will take it from here, over." The aircraft of Able Baker One, low on fuel, flew low in formation over the stricken ship, rocking their wings in a sign of good luck. The new wing of Spitfire fighters circled low over the damaged ship below them before taking up their protective cover.

"Able Baker Two, are you able to transmit? Delta One, standing by to receive, over."

On the bridge, the mangled remains of the steering station and navigation table lay beyond recognition. Sailors at their stations when the bomb exploded now lay dead, their bodies broken in pools of blood. Others, mortally injured, lay crying for help, their pain excruciating. No other movements in those brief few minutes were being made in the twisted remains of the bridge. Slowly, those still alive stirred, painfully trying to regain their stations if they still remained. Yelling out for help and instructions, Karl dragged himself to his feet, his left arm on fire and bleeding. A big gash along his forehead was bleeding into his left eye. God, not again, he thought as he tried to compose himself. At least my neck was not injured, he thought as he remembered the attack on the Reese back in 1940.

"Get a runner down to the aft emergency steering station, and tell them the bridge station is out of action. Maintain course and speed; we must close the distance to those Navy escorts." Turning to the radio compartment at the rear of the bridge, Karl called out, "Sparks, are you still able to transmit and receive? If so, make to Rescue One: badly damaged, still maintaining course and speed; stand by for a status update, Able Baker Two, clear."

The bridge door was blown off. Although not serious, Karl's injuries slowed his movements as he painfully moved out onto what was left of the wing deck. Looking down, he saw Gunther tending to his men, blood running down his injured arm. Grabbing the bull horn, Karl called down to Gunther, "Major, are you alright? How many have you lost? Can you manage on your own while we make emergency repairs to the steering station? It's in really bad shape."

Gunther looked up with a wave that told Karl to take care of the ship. "I'll have a runner try to round up a few extra people to assist you." Karl dragged himself back into the bridge. Looking around, he caught sight of Captain Hoffmann sitting upright in his bridge chair.

"Sir are you alright?" yelled Karl as he approached. Seeing the front of the captain's black uniform soaked in what looked like blood gave him his answer. With lightning response, he yelled once again, "Somebody, find the medic; the captain is badly hurt. Sir, can you hear me? Where is your injury? Can you show me?"

Slowly, the captain opened his blazer. What Karl saw before him told him the captain did not have much longer to live.

Signaling Karl to come close, the captain, in a voice laboring with pain, whispered, "Major, save my ship and crew. Tell my wife I died trying to save my country. I'm done for; go help others that need your help. Leave me here in my bridge chair; please, let me go with dignity. Thank you for all you have done for us." Captain Hoffmann's head slowly lowered, and with his eyes closed, he passed over into Valhalla.

Karl limped back into the radio room when he heard the only remaining speaker announce an incoming message. "Rescue One to Able Baker Two, can you copy, over?"

The radio operator handed Karl a mike to respond, "Rescue One, we are receiving you loud and clear."

The speaker once again crackled an incoming message, "Able Baker Two, are you in imminent danger of sinking? Can you maintain steerage? Are your pumps capable of keeping ahead of the seawater? Stand by for the next message from the command ship. Note, your new recognition sign will be Rescue Two, over."

Karl stood in the radio shack as a medic ripped his blazer sleeve to attend to his wounded arm. At this point, Karl had paid little attention to his wounds; his focus was too intent on saving the ship and what remained of its crew.

The safety of night fell, quickly surrounding the Gustav limping along at a mere eight knots. The ship's pumps were holding their own against the cold waters of the North Sea. On the bridge, the German engineers worked with determination to restore the steering station. Karl watched with admiration of their determination; these sailors were the Germans he admired so much, strong, determined, and loyal to their dead captain's promise to deliver the ship and crew into the safety of the Allied forces.

The warships of Rescue One now took up their protective stations around the limping Gustav, maneuvering close on either side and astern of the ship. Using signal semaphore to communicate, the command warship flashed a message: Stop engine; we are sending launches to evacuate all your wounded, stop. The Devon is sending a relief crew to take the ship into Aberdeen, stop. Requesting the engineering crew, if not wounded, remain on board to assist relief engineering crew, stop. Lower your boarding ladder, stop.

Gunther walked into the bridge, saying, "It looks like we're being taken off. Do you need help getting your wounded down onto the boat deck? For a time there, I really thought we were on our way to Davy Jones Locker, didn't you?" said Gunther, relief written over his face.

"I guess you could say that Gunther. At least, this time, I'm walking off not like Dunkirk when I got taken off the sinking Reese unconscious on a stretcher." Karl thought once more about the time before when he returned to England severely wounded. Sailors arrived with stretchers to remove the wounded from the bridge. At the same time, a burly seaman carefully lifted his dead captain, another wrapping a blanket around the limp form of their commanding officer.

Three launches came alongside, unloading the Royal Navy relief crew and medical supplies. Another launch lay alongside while the Gustav's derrick lifted two portable pumps onto the deck. First off, the launch was Lieutenant Roy Adams, who saluted Karl and Gunther, then said, "Lieutenant Adams, here to relieve you, Sir.

Are your people ready to be taken off? We've brought three German speaking sailors to assist with the ship's engineering crew. What is your advice for steering the ship in its damaged condition?"

With a sarcastic smirk on his face, Karl looked at the young officer, finally answering him by saying, "We were able to restore it to operating condition. Tell your helmsmen to be careful of wood splinters; that helm is a little battered from the attack." Karl's sarcasm was in full form as he answered. Down below, all the wounded were now in the launches, ready to depart. Armed Royal Navy sailors assumed their stations around the ship with heavy anti-aircraft weapons in case the Germans sent another wave of bombers. Above them, additional Coastal Command and Royal Air Force aircraft formed an impenetrable umbrella over the damaged ship.

Standing in the stern of the Navy launch, Karl and Gunther stood in silence, looking back at the Gustav as she got underway once again. Gunther finally spoke, "This German crew has given me hope for a new Germany, one I will be proud to help rebuild. Karl, this was the Nazis' last opportunity to wreak havoc on the people of Europe. I will return as soon as possible, but first, Hitler must be brought to justice for all these atrocities, wouldn't you agree? Is it safe to say you will reside in England after this is all over? I can't see Claire agreeing to move to Wien."

The motor launch bounced alongside the command ship, Karl and Gunther waiting patiently until the last of the wounded were carefully carried up the boarding ladder before boarding themselves. Stepping onto the deck, they looked in surprise to see members of the ship's company standing at attention as they were piped aboard. "Welcome aboard, gentlemen," spoke Commander Manson, "I wish we could have arrived sooner to help you. I am truly sorry for not being here to protect you." Derek Manson was the epitome of a senior Royal Navy Commander, honesty written all over his face.

Gunther answered before Karl could say a word. "Commander, all of you that took part in this rescue mission are to be praised for what you have done. Most of us are alive because of those brave pilots above us. Now, your force is on station. I, for one, feel relieved that I'm not a casualty of this war." The two officers from the BIS returned the salute as best they could, their wounds restricting their movements.

Down in the cramped sickbay, corpsmen attended to their wounds. Karl's arm was now in a sling, his forehead in a bandage. Gunther's arm did not require him to wear a sling, as his injury was below his elbow. Both his cheeks had bandages covering the gashes he had received from pieces of splintering teak decking exploding from the bullets unleashed from the Luftwaffe aircraft. Karl walked to the stern of the destroyer to be alone. Humbled, he thanked his maker for delivering them from almost certain death. With tears in his eyes, he thought about all those that were not so fortunate. Willingly, they gave their lives in the hope of a new free and peaceful Germany. Then, he returned to the wardroom to meet up with Gunther.

Dawn was breaking as the light cruiser slowly entered the crowded harbor of Aberdeen, Scotland. Commander Manson approached the BIS officers, standing quietly in the bow. "Gentlemen, your mission is finally over; ambulances are standing by to take your wounded to a Naval hospital close by. As for Captain Hoffmann's body, it will be transported to the Naval mortuary here in Aberdeen. Be assured; I will make sure he is given a fitting burial for a fallen hero. We have arranged for a car to take you both to Dyce Aerodrome. Transport Command will fly you back down to RAF Stanwick; your base has been contacted to lay on ground transportation from there."

Karl searched Gunther's face before replying to Commander Manson. "Commander, how far out is the Gustav at this time? No disrespect, Commander, but our mission will not be complete until we see her alongside a dock here in Aberdeen." Gunther smiled, instinctively knowing Karl's response.

"At her present speed, it could be another five or six hours before we can berth her into that dry dock over there."

"Well, I think you need to cancel that aircraft until tomorrow morning as Major Fisher and I will remain here until our mission is truly completed," replied Karl.

Commander Manson smiled at these determined Intelligence officers, then replied, "Of course, I should have known better than to arrange your transportation back to Slough so soon. May I add how impressed we all are at the show of strength and sheer determination you all have shown. Let me arrange for a day berth to be made up, so you both can get some sleep while you wait. Please, excuse me while I attend to that." Manson returned to the bridge.

Karl laid on top of his berth, his mind going a mile a minute. Falling asleep was not going to happen; instead, he just relaxed. Closing his eyes allowed his mind to wander back through the events of the last two weeks. *This could well be my last mission, and what will happen to me and all the others in the BIS when this war is finally over?* A knock on the door made him jump; those thoughts returned to that compartment in his mind.

"Sorry to disturb you, Sir. Commander Manson sends his compliments and said to notify you that they are towing the Gustav III in right now."

Karl sat up. Pulling his sea boots on, he walked quickly to the bridge. Gunther was already there, watching the tugs maneuvering the listing Gustav toward the entrance of the dry dock.

Heavy duty hoses attached to portable pumps continuously discharged thousands of gallons of seawater over the side; the ship's appearance looked like a derelict instead of the former proud ship she had been only a few days before. Watching this sad scene, most of the ships in the harbor started blowing their loud horns in respect for the battered vessel passing by them. In response, the Gustav's crew waved and screamed from the railing. Karl looked at those on the bridge, saying, "Gentlemen, our work here is done. On behalf of the Gustav III crew, let me thank you again for delivering her safely to Aberdeen." Those watching from the bridge saluted and clapped loudly, humbling the two BIS officers.

At 0530 hours' the following morning, Karl and Gunther said their goodbyes before proceeding down the boarding ladder to the waiting staff car on the dock below. The flight back to England was uneventful, the brown box of hundreds of films and documentation from that secret cargo locked securely behind their seats.

The pilot came over the aircraft's PA system, "Gentlemen, we are on our approach to RAF Stanwick; please, make sure your safety restraints are securely fastened."

Gunther looked over to his friend as the announcement came over the PA. "Karl, we are almost home, and, my friend, we are still alive; moreover, we are still in one piece well, almost. Welcome home, Major." Karl was beginning to choke up as he listened to Gunther. In his mind, Karl was thinking, *I will live to see my son grow up with my wife, Claire. It's time for me to embrace a future. For once, I'm optimistic about a life outside the military Intelligence Service.*

The American built Lockheed Hudson slowly taxied toward the hanger. Winding up the port engine, the pilot spun the aircraft around; then, after winding down the big radial motors, they were home. Gunther climbed down first, the copilot carrying the brown box. Next came Karl, still with that sling around his left arm. Both Gunther and Karl were in Naval jackets, their shredded uniforms discarded after they had boarded the cruiser.

Standing in front of the Humber staff car, Clive and Bill waited until their friends were out of the aircraft. Walking over to greet them, they could see that both had suffered injuries on this mission. Their arms outstretched; they hugged the two returning warriors. "Gunther and Karl, thank God you're back safe, but maybe not so sound; let's get you back to the camp. The very first thing we need to do is get a thorough medical examination on both of you, then a really good supper before an early night," said Clive, happy as a clam to have them back alive. As the mission commander, he had feared that all he had done was to send his friends on a one-way suicide mission.

"Wrong!" replied Karl. "The first thing I need to do is call my wife, Claire; then, I'm all yours." Karl was flexing his will and not really interested in anything else until he had done that.

"Of course, Karl; we should know better. Claire has been calling almost every other day for an update; she is going to be over the moon when she hears that Austrian accent of yours," replied Bill.

Arriving at the camp, Karl felt a wave of relief coming over him. He was safe once more, and the threat of Nazism was finally coming to an end in Europe. The threat of an atomic bomb that would have given the Nazi regime a rebirth to their quest for domination was no longer viable. Earlier, on February 20th, 1944, the Norwegian resistance had sunk the ferry carrying the last shipment of heavy water in the deepest part of Lake Tinn. Now, with the replacement machinery and equipment in the hands of the Allies, all hopes of atomic dominance was at an end.

Once again, he could dare to embrace a future, watching his son maturing and being with his wife, Claire, in a new, free world. All those memories of so many lost weeks, months, and years away from home, operating in harm's way, far away from that wonderful woman that had turned his life around, would be gone. Karl could feel his heart starting to race as he looked forward to seeing Claire the following day. The suppressed thoughts he feared to believe were now flooding his brain. A skittish big smile took over his face; he was going home.

Back at the camp, Karl thanked Clive and Bill for meeting them at the aerodrome. Turning to Gunther, he said, "My old friend, let's pray this was the last mission for us. I'm running out of arms, legs, and eyes to injure."

With a stern look on his face, Gunther stared at Karl, then broke out laughing loudly. Karl was somewhat surprised at his friend's outburst of laughter, a side of him rarely seen.

"Alright, chaps, I'll catch up with you later." Karl headed to his office to place his call home, receiving many greetings from the staff as he entered the bullpen. Karl sat quietly for a few minutes, composing his mind before lifting the receiver and dialing nine for that outside line, then the home number.

"Hitchin 4567, who's calling please?" came that sweet answer. Karl, choked up at hearing his wife's voice, answered, "Claire, darling, it's me. I'm back in Slough. We accomplished our mission, and I'm coming home tomorrow morning for an extended leave. Claire, that mission was my last. Your days of worrying about my whereabouts are over. Did you hear me, Claire? They're over!"

Karl went silent as he waited for Claire's response. "My darling spy, I have prayed every hour of every day for your safety. You're coming home; that's all that matters to me right now. Wait until I tell Nicholas that his dad will be here tomorrow. Karl, Clive called me this morning to let me know you and Gunther were back safe and sound. He also told me that you had a few scrapes but nothing serious. Darling, I could sense from the tone in his voice that he is relieved that he will not be ordering either of you on any more field operations. Those days are done. Karl, my darling man, how I have dreamt of our future. Can this really be happening? Can you believe this terrible war is finally coming to an end? Sooner than later, let's hope that happens. Karl, I'm so excited! I've already called Bev at the office to cancel my appointments for the next few days.

"Mama and Freida are going to be so excited to hear this news. See you tomorrow, Lover Boy; throw me a big kiss, and I'll decide where I'm going to put it. Karl, did I mention that your family loves you so very much? I'm so proud of you, darling." Claire, happy again, hung up, leaving Karl listening to the empty dial tone, his mind still racing. Placing the receiver back into its cradle, he slowly lowered his head into the palm of his one good hand. All those suppressed thoughts and feelings he had bottled up for so long now erupted uncontrollably. Those black storm clouds in his head were slowly dissipating, turning into tears of overwhelming relief. Struggling to regain his composure, he started to shake as he dried his eyes.

This reaction was brought on by not having to think any more about that last goodbye letter he had recovered from Bill earlier. Karl stood up, picked up his kit bag, and headed out of the office to his quarters and a hot bath that would wash away the grime from this last mission. With difficulty, he shaved before putting on his fresh field uniform. In the medical center, he caught up with Gunther, already getting checked out. "Karl, you are looking so much better than this morning. Was Claire excited and relieved to hear from you?" asked Gunther as he put his uniform back on.

"Gunther, it was wonderful talking with her. You know how excited she can get. I could hardly get a word in sideways, but I loved every minute of that call."

With help from the nurse, Karl removed his tunic, allowing her to examine his wounded arm. "The doctor will need to see this wound, Major. Those stitches are holding but not very well. Your head wound looks worse than it really is, so I'll go ahead and dress that first."

Karl sat calmly as the doctor numbed around the wound on his arm. The young doctor then removed the old stitches, replacing them with new ones. "There you go, Major, good as new. I'll write you a prescription to have them removed at your local doctor's office in about ten days." Karl could now put his tunic back on without the need for a sling. Thanking the medical staff, he walked out, down the hall toward the officers' lounge.

All his friends were sitting at their usual table, Clive in the center. "Come, sit down next to your partner in crime, Gunther. You two are quite the heroes around camp. Bill has told everyone you were both safe; of course, they had no idea what you were up to or where you landed. Tomorrow, we will make the debrief short, then send both of you off on leave. I don't want to see those faces at the camp for the next thirty days. Gunther, great news for you, my friend. The Red Cross has delivered a bunch of letters and a large box that looks like they're from Sweden. I had them delivered to your quarters," said Clive, showing signs of relief that this extremely dangerous mission was finally behind them.

Gunther's face was now beaming; he finally could catch up on his family. It had been many long months since he had arranged for their escape into neutral Sweden. As much as he knew they were safe, he missed being part of their daily lives. The atmosphere in that lounge was very upbeat.

"I'm buying; who's ready for a refill?" asked Bill.

The following morning, Karl and Gunther met for an early breakfast to review their debrief notes. "By the way, I forgot to mention last night about Herbert's team. They will be arriving back in two days; thank God, there are no casualties to report. I'll wait for them to return, then Herb and I are going fishing up North. I think this will be the most relaxing holiday I've had in years." Gunther reached into his briefcase, producing a brown envelope. "Now, I can show you pictures of my wife and kids." With pride in his eyes, he handed Karl each picture, explaining as he did so.

"Gunther, you've never shown me a picture of your wife before; she's a knockout and your son and daughter, what a handsome family. Gunther, I know the hell you have lived, not knowing if they were safe. You would never have told me anyway, you old Kraut; I'm so very happy for you. One day, perhaps we can all meet up. Will you return to Hamburg when this is finally over?" asked Karl, enjoying this time with his friend.

Gunther, putting the pictures away, answered, "I'm not sure, Karl; there is so much destruction, and quite honestly, I'm not totally ready to forgive and forget just yet. Hazel's last letter suggested I should consider emigrating to America. It would be a real big commitment on my family's part. Her husband has offered to sponsor the family if we should decide on doing that. She did say I would be a perfect fit in the diplomatic service and would help me apply if that's of interest to me. My kids would have better opportunities over there than in Germany. It's a big decision. A part of me wants to make sure Germany rebuilds itself as part of the new free, peaceful Europe. As I said, we have big decisions to make. Hazel, of course, asked about you, Claire, and the baby. Sadly, that flame she carries for you is still there. Well, Casanova, let's get this debrief behind us, shall we? Because there's a special lady waiting for her man in Hitchin."

CHAPTER 13

ALL THAT ENDS WELL

Karl, a new spring to his step and the mission debriefing behind him, waved goodbye to Clive, Bill, and Gunther as he walked out of the main building toward the waiting staff car. "There goes a chap who has put gray hair on all our heads," said Gunther as they watched Karl march toward the waiting staff car. "But when the chips are down, who would you prefer to have at your side on a mission? With all honesty, all of us here can say we have experienced his courage at different times in this damn war. Now, look at him, a family man on his way home to his wife and son," concluded Gunther as they returned to the main building.

Karl opted to sit up front with Charlie instead of sitting in the back seat. Today, he was more than happy, thinking about the end to the hostilities, which was very close to happening. Out on the main road, Karl struck up a conversation by asking his driver, "Charlie, have you given any thought to what you will do when this war ends?" Karl asked casually.

"Well, Sir, I kinda like the Army life. At my age and considering there will be thousands of younger blokes getting out of the military, let's face it; what chance do I have applying for the same jobs? No, Sir, I'm staying in if they'll give me that opportunity. While we are on that subject, Sir, could you write a recommendation for me, or is that too much to ask?"

Karl smiled, then looked at his driver before replying, "Absolutely, I will do that for you, Charlie. In fact, I will recommend to Colonel Knight and Major Lowes that you have indicated your desire to make the Army a career and let me add my own endorsement for a promotion to boot. I'm always happy to repay the many times you have driven for me; how does that sound!" replied the very cheerful Major Vita.

"Well, blow me down, Sir; that's more than I asked for." Charlie was feeling confident that he would now have a future. "Major, do ya feel like listening to the Armed Services Network while we're driving? The American Big Bands are on about now," suggested Charlie.

"Why not, Charlie? Today is a wonderful day, so go right ahead and turn it on." Karl was in the mood to be merry.

Arriving in Hitchin, Karl's heart was beating fast, the excitement building as they turned into the driveway. "Here we are, Sir; have a wonderful time with your misses and son. Just let the motor pool know when to pick you up again, and Major Vita, let me thank you for helping me. You're really a terrific bloke for doing this." Charlie jumped out, opening the passenger door with a big smile on his face.

Karl, still in the happiest mood he had been in since Nicholas was born, reached over, and laid on the car's horn. Charlie, watching this, started laughing, knowing Major Vita was relieved to be alive.

The front door flew open, and there was Claire with Nicholas under her left arm. "Charlie, you have brought my crazy Austrian husband back home to me. Thank you; thank you; don't leave just yet. I'm going to make you a cuppa and cheese sandwich before you drive back," yelled a jubilant Claire as she threw her right arm around Karl's neck, with poor baby Nick being squashed between them. "Darling, how long do Nick and I have you for this time?" Claire had tears of relief on her cheeks for those countless days and nights she worried about the possibility of being a widow for the second time.

"Bill told me not to return for a month; can you believe that?" Karl reached out to take Nick from his mother with happiness all over his face.

Claire started kidding, "Charlie, that's a long time. Will you pick him up early if he becomes too much of a handful?"

Charlie, enjoying every minute of this reunion, replied, "Sorry, Miss; he's yours for the next thirty days. No early returns, so enjoy this time to retrain him, and that may not be easy to do." Charlie continued making wisecrack remarks. Over the years, he had become really attached to this officer who always treated him with respect, even those times when he was heading out on another dangerous mission. Claire linked arms with Charlie, leading him into the kitchen for that cup of tea and sandwich.

Standing in the driveway, Karl and Claire waved goodbye to Charlie as he backed out into the street. Honking the horn, he drove off back to Slough.

"Darling, Bill told me about your arm. I guess you threw away that sling. Am I surprised? No, I'm not. Does it still hurt you? Come here; let me see that bandage on top of your head. Is that why you haven't taken your cap off yet?" Claire knew her husband so very well, always making out it was nothing to worry about.

"Claire, Clive told me before I left this morning to tell you everything, in confidence, of course. So, my good looking wife, let me first call Mama and Freida, after which I'm getting out of this damn uniform. I don't want to see it for the next four long weeks. After a hot bath, we can enjoy a glass of wine together. Then, I'll tell you about that mission from Hell." Karl felt the energy of relief as he said that.

"Nicholas, kiss your daddy; you haven't seen him for such a long time," said Karl as he held Nick high above his head. Nick was enjoying this, kicking, and waving his arms, making loud baby sounds. His parents laughed as they watched him.

Claire pulled Karl's good arm, saying, "Let's go in, darling; you're home at last. I've cleared my calendar for the next six days. Do you realize this will be the first time we've been together for this long in I don't know how long? Are you ready to be a civilian for a little while?" Claire was relieved and happier as she reflected on what Clive's parting words were earlier that morning.

"Claire, his days of being a field agent are over for the remainder of his time in the BIS. He needs to tell you everything about this last mission because we both know how he keeps everything inside. Doing that will start him experiencing those violent nightmares all over again. On a lighter note, Julie and I are taking you up on that invitation to come to visit you both in a couple of weeks. It will be great fun, watching our two girls with baby Nicholas. Claire, I also have a surprise for both of you when we see you. Bye for now."

Later that day, when Nicholas was having his nap, Karl sat down next to Claire, his good arm around her neck. "Claire, what I'm about to tell you might be upsetting, so just stop me if it's too much for you, alright?" Holding his hand tightly, Claire listened intently, visualizing the graphic picture Karl was painting for her, leaving nothing out.

"Claire, we lost many good men on that ship, including its captain. The loyal German crew was trying to escape from the Nazi hell their country was locked in. Our action of taking control of the ship was a blessing in disguise for that to happen. During the attacks, they remained steadfast at their posts. I'm praying those that were not killed will be taken good care of. The irony to what happened is that they will be viewed as heroes by the German military. Overpowered by a much larger enemy force, they lost control of their ship, becoming prisoners of war in England. Little do the Nazis know how brave those men were, fighting off their own countrymen in that attack."

Karl turned to face Claire, "Darling, in the heat of that battle, I was saying goodbye to you and Nicholas. I really believed our fate was sealed, and we'd be going down with the ship. From now on, my days of being an agent are over. I've been wounded too many times on too many missions. On my return to Slough, my group and I will have a new objective to train for, preparing for an end to hostilities. Hopefully, that will be in the not too distant future. Our new purpose will be to round up all those Nazi war criminals, wherever those spineless bastards are hiding. This will be a joint task, with our Allies participating in that mission. I'm quite looking forward to undertaking this new role. Keeping my temper will be a challenge if I recognize any of those Nazis. Darling, sharing this nightmare with you is such a relief. Thank you for listening to this long story; I hope I did not scare you too much," concluded Karl, feeling relieved that what he had to keep secret for so long was now out in the open.

Mama and the family were ecstatic at having Karl back home again. As he entered the bungalow, the look on his face sent his mother and sister a message that he was all done with those dangerous missions. Mama, hugging her youngest son with tears of relief and happiness across her face, guided him to the couch while Claire and Freida went into the kitchen, giving them some private time to talk.

"Karl, you look more like your father each time I see you come through that door. Sit next to me and give me my grandson to hold. He is so strong; he'll be crawling around very soon. We heard from Ronny yesterday; he will be returning home in another week. He's really looking forward to seeing you. It's been over a year since he saw you last. During those times you were away, Claire visited us almost every Saturday so that we could have quality time with Nicholas. Karl, it has been so hard on her. I could always see that strain in her face; it's hard not to notice, even when she was putting up a brave front, trying to hide her fear that you may not be returning to her." Mama was conveying what her son should know about his wife's mental anguish, which she suffered daily.

Freida and Claire entered the living room, carrying a pot of hot coffee and a plate of Karl's favorite strudel. Claire sat on the floor, her arm resting on Karl's leg while playing with Nick. "Freida, when Julie, Clive, and their daughters arrive next Saturday, we would love to have everyone over for lunch. Will Ronny be home by then?" asked Claire.

"I believe so. I'm not sure of the exact day yet, but I think it will work out alright, though," replied Freida. Claire, realizing that the conversation was about to return to her husband's dangerous line of work, tactfully changed the subject to a family concern. On the other hand, Mama knew precisely what Claire was doing, so she returned to playing with her grandson.

Karl looked at his mother, asking, "Mama, have you heard from my brothers lately? I haven't been able to stay in touch with them since D-Day. When I left, they had been assigned to a supply division up in the midlands," inquired Karl, feeling guilty at not staying in touch.

"Glad you asked," replied Mama as she moved over to the sideboard. She returned with some recent letters. "Here, read these letters I kept for you to read." Karl immersed himself in reading his brothers' letters while the ladies gossiped about rationing issues and other things that governed their daily lives. Karl read all the letters, then returned them to the sideboard, relieved that they were safe.

Standing, Karl walked over to Nicholas, sleeping on his blanket. Franchot was reading a book next to him on the floor. "Franchot, shall we take Nick up to the field to see Tug?"

Karl was enjoying this new sense of relaxation, maybe for the first time in many months. Carefully, he picked up Nick, kissing him softly on his cheek, then, cradling him under his good arm, he walked to the front door. Franchot opened it ahead of him, and Karl announced that he was taking the boys out for a walk. Outside, Karl took Franchot's hand, smiling at his nephew as they started to walk slowly up the road. From the kitchen window, the three ladies stood, watching Karl.

"Look at him; he looks so happy with the boys. Finally, my Karl has found peace, and it makes me so proud to see the man he has become," said Mama as they watched.

"Mama, when Clive arrives with his family this Saturday, he told me he has a big announcement for Karl. He is to receive a commendation for his brave acts of courage in the face of danger on so many occasions since this war started." Both Mama and Freida, with surprise on their faces, were feeling overwhelmed with a feeling of pride.

The following Saturday morning, Claire woke to find Karl already gone, but that was not a big surprise to her. Putting on her housecoat and slippers, she looked at Karl's side of the bed, so happy to see the sheets all ruffled up. He was home. Karl was always up at the crack of dawn. Going downstairs, she said loudly, "Where are my two boys?" as she entered the kitchen.

"In the living room, darling. Grab some coffee and join us," replied Karl. "Claire, what time did Julie say they expect to arrive today?" yelled Karl, lying on the floor with Nick.

"If all goes well, around two, maybe a little later if they get caught up in traffic. Do you want more coffee before I pour the rest down the drain?" Claire was starting to get their home ship shape for their guests. "Darling, I'm going upstairs to make the beds and make sure their bathroom has fresh towels and accessories. Care to help me, or are you having too much fun with your son?"

Claire smiled as she looked back into the living room. It was so nice to have her husband at home. She was thinking, this is what our future will feel like now that this war is coming to an end. Karl and I should think about expanding our little family before Nicholas gets too much older!

CHAPTER 14

New Objectives for the BIS

Clive and family arrived at 2:50 p.m., honking the car's horn as they pulled into the driveway. Karl, carrying Nick under his good arm, followed Claire out through the front door to the waiting arms of the Knight family. "Julie, you're here! It is so wonderful to have you all in Hitchin; let us help with all those bags, and you two young ladies, give your Aunt Claire a big hug and a kiss. It's been so long since I saw you last."

Karl gave Nick to his Aunt Julie, "So you can help your pal unload the car."

Karl replied, "For a corporal, you are throwing orders around like a sergeant major. Did Clive promote you without asking me first?"

In that driveway, two families came together, enjoying each other's company. "Major, I believe you're junior to me, so you can carry that big case with your one good arm, and I'll carry these two."

Clive jumped into the ribbing going on around the car. Karl responded with, "Like buggery; you're not the chief around here."

Claire interrupted them loudly, laughing while she replied, "You're so right, Major Vita. I am! Now, go take that case up to their room."

Karl looked at Clive with a devilish grin of surprise before the two friends broke out into laughter and embraced each other, Karl quietly saying, "Welcome, my old friend." Inside, Claire had made a late lunch, which they would have in the garden solarium.

Before their guests arrived, Karl had warmed this cozy area with a portable electric heater; no other form of heating was available out there. "Julie, it's a little chilly, so Karl heated up the solarium earlier.

It should be very comfortable about now; shall we all go out? It's nice and sunny, and with all that glass, it will be very pleasant to enjoy our lunch, don't you agree?" remarked Claire, leading the two girls outside. Claire, ever the perfectionist, had laid out a wonderful spread of sandwiches and other cold cut delights, served on fine china and cutlery. The presentation was laid out on a beautiful hand embroidered white table cloth, a gift to Claire from Karl's mother.

During dessert, Clive tapped his water glass with the back edge of his knife for attention. Then, standing, he announced, "If I may have your undivided attention for just a few minutes, no interruptions please. I have an announcement to make. Occasionally, someone comes to us who gives new meaning to the term "above and beyond the call of duty." Such is the case today. With profound gratitude for service to His Majesty King George VI, it is my honor to announce Major Karl Vita will receive a commendation for the many dangers he has risked his life for during this war. Karl, my dearest friend, you are to receive the Military Star and War Medal at a ceremony next month in Slough. Your good friend General Jacks will be presenting. Also receiving the same commendation is your good friend, Major Gunther Fisher. That last mission you both were on will contribute to the early demise of Chancellor Adolf Hitler and his band of thugs. Gunther was asked to join us here today, but fishing appears to be more important to him right now, which is understandable. He will, however, be at your side at that ceremony." Clive concluded by reaching out for Karl's hand, his eyes wet from the emotion he was feeling for these two foreign agents that saw corruption and brutality and decided to do something about it.

"Congratulations, Major, I can't think of any finer officers to receive such prestigious medals." Clive sat back down, waiting for his announcement to be processed by a dumbfounded Karl.

Claire stood and walked around the table; with tears of happiness and pride, she hugged her husband, followed by Julie. Karl, still saying nothing, was having a hard time wrapping his thoughts around Clive's announcement.

Finally, Karl stood, and turning to Clive, he labored a reply, "Well, old friend, you have given me indigestion with that announcement. What can I say except, from the bottom of my heart, you have humbled me? I never thought of myself as a hero or someone special enough to be awarded such prestigious medals. I will wear those medals all the time, including wearing them to bed. Well, there could be times when they might get in the way, so not quite all the time." Karl's humor was returning as they all toasted this very special day.

The weekend was flying by. Mama and family arrived Sunday morning, Ronny having arrived late Saturday from his base in Scotland. "Ronny, it's been too long since I have seen you, and I believe even longer since you saw the Knight family," said Karl, hugging everyone as they entered the house. With the help of Julie, Claire had prepared a wonderful buffet, a wiser choice considering the gathering of grownups and children.

Claire, beyond excited, announced to Ronny about Karl's commendation. Ronny shook Karl's hand and, with a two armed hug, said to Clive, "This brother-in-law of mine never fails to surprise me with the things he does. Can you make sure you send a request to my commanding officer for me to attend that ceremony? I just can't miss this one." Ronny was so proud and happy to know Karl would receive such an award.

"Ronny, consider it done. Can you get a jump seat on a plane heading south close to Slough? I'll arrange ground transportation to pick you from the aerodrome," said Clive. Before walking back into the solarium, the three men had time to talk privately.

"Karl, I know all about that secret mission you were on. Those fighters protecting the Gustav III were from my base near Aberdeen. I did not know at the time, nor did I even consider that you were one of the blokes involved in that firestorm. Some of the returning pilots told us that the Luftwaffe pilots were throwing themselves at that ship. As they banked away to return to base, they saw the badly damaged bridge and foredeck. They further reported it would be a miracle if anyone survived that pounding. Little did I know, my own brother-in-law was down there. God, Karl, you are one lucky blighter," concluded Ronny.

By 5:00 p.m., the party broke up. Ronny returned Mama and family to Baldock, and Clive and family headed back to their home on the outskirts of Slough. Both tired at all the excitement, Karl and Claire put their baby boy to bed. Both exhausted, they went straight to bed, falling asleep in each other's arms. It had been a wonderful weekend.

The weeks clicked by with Karl enjoying this life of a stay-at-home husband and father. But the calendar was counting down the days until he would once again return to his base in Slough, and that thought was weighing heavily on him with each passing day. On their last weekend, Freida had offered to take Nicholas overnight to give Karl and Claire a break so that they could have an evening out on the town. They dropped him off on Saturday morning, then went home to pack to get ready for his Monday morning departure. As much as they were looking forward to a romantic Saturday, they both felt a part of them was missing after dropping Nick off at the bungalow.

"Well, darling, without our screaming baby boy, what proposal do you have up your sleeve for your wife?" asked Claire, a mischievous grin on her face that left little to Karl's imagination. Karl reached over, taking Claire's hand as they drove home for a romantic interlude before heading out to dinner. "Karl, why don't we go out this afternoon in the MG? You really haven't used it lately. That little car is very much a part of this family, so let's swing by the garage and get it, shall we?"

Karl immediately agreed, heading for the garage on Bancroft Street. Returning home, they left the MG in the driveway, heading upstairs to change into warmer clothing for that open air drive. Claire removed her blouse and skirt, then laid out a pair of tweed slacks and a heavy wool jumper with a loose fitting cowl collar. From the wardrobe, she placed her stylish boots at the end of the bed. Bending over to put her slacks on, she felt a strong arm surround her waist, and another unclip her bra. Karl had watched her as she undressed, and the sight of her in her undergarments stirred him enough to think, no rush to go driving, but being alone like this is an opportunity too good to pass up.

"Karl Vita, what are you doing? I thought you wanted to go for a drive, or has that idea evaporated because you knew I would never say no to you?" Claire, by his actions, was feeling aroused, and he had a way of doing that almost on demand. Karl turned her around, allowing her bra to fall to the floor. In her underwear, this vision was all it took for Karl to sweep her off her feet. Turning, he placed her softly on the bed, then removed his own clothes. Claire lay staring at her husband, waiting for him to make a move, which did not happen. Instead, he stood there, his hands on his hips with that stare that always unhinged her emotionally.

"Karl, you're teasing me again. You started this; now deliver, or I'll drain that weapon of yours in some other way."

Karl was enjoying this game. "So, what do you have in mind, my sweet?" teased Karl.

"You bloody spy; come here and let me show you. Two can play that game of yours. I've been married to you long enough to know the game very well." Claire reached over and, putting her arm around his backside, pulled him close. Looking up momentarily, she grinned, then with her other hand, she guided his erection into her waiting mouth. Karl, breathing deeply, continued to stand naked in front of his wife, enjoying the moist feeling of her lips as she circled his penis with her tongue, then slowly moved up and down its length. Claire, doing this, was enjoying the power she had over her husband whenever she did this.

This afternoon, those juices would not be wasted as she pulled away, pulling him down between her open legs, saying, "Karl, let me feel you inside me. It won't take me long, so start thrusting that weapon of yours." Karl was at the brink, but then again, so was Claire.

"Darling, I'm going!" The powerful eruption stopped her from speaking further as they fell into a powerful orgasm together. It had been a while since they had made passionate love like this, and it was almost like their first time all over again. Still lying on top of her, both sweating, Claire was drained by the intensity, even shaking a little as the feeling subsided. "Darling, why do I get the feeling you're pulling out all the stops to give Nicholas a baby sister or brother? Would I be correct in thinking that?"

Karl knew they would try for another baby, but this soon. He thought, *it makes no difference to me; I love being a family man, especially being married to Claire.*

"Karl, you're being coy again. You know what I need for both of us very well, so if I can conceive again before our Nick gets much older, I will be the happiest lady in England. Come here, you animal, and do it again. And don't stop until I feel your deposit." Karl, with a grin on his face, obliged his wife. In each other's arms, they drifted off to sleep till late morning.

"Alright, you sex mad woman, let's get washed up and head out to the Fox in William for lunch and a pint; how does that sound to you?" Karl was remembering it was there that they both felt that magnetism that had started within hours of meeting each other.

"That sounds like a wonderful idea, darling. Let's save time; you use the guest bathroom, and I'll use ours. Now, let's make it snappy," replied Claire, feeling on top of the world. Karl went outside and put the roof down on the MG. Removing the side curtains, he placed them behind the front seats, then went back inside to get his leather driving jacket and cheese slicer cap.

Yelling upstairs, he called to Claire to hurry up. "Right behind you, Lover Boy." Claire surprised him by coming out of the kitchen. Bundled up, they drove off, waiting for the little car heater to start blowing warm air over their boots.

"This was a wonderful idea, Claire. How can you not love this car? It almost talks to you. It will always be in our family, and when we can't use it anymore, well, Nicholas can continue the love affair, does that sound right?" yelled Karl over the engine and wind noises.

Arriving at the Fox, they entered the lounge and decided to have lunch at the bar, reliving all the times they sat enjoying this old inn and the intimate conversations of young love. "Karl, I believe you are hoping we are pregnant again. It's all over your face, and I didn't have to convince you in any way. You're becoming an old softy as you get older. I must say, I love what we do to make it happen. You always turn me into putty when we make love. God, Vita, what did I do to deserve a man like you? Kiss me, Sailor, right here, right now."

Claire was ecstatic that her man would not be involved in any more dangerous missions and very much into expanding their family.

"Claire, can I suggest, only if you agree, that is? Why don't we stay until closing time, then go for that drive after? I would really like to swing by the bungalow and pick up Nick, then head home for a quiet evening just the three of us. What do you say to that idea?"

Claire sat looking at her husband, tears of happiness slowly running down her cheeks. Her heart was overflowing with love for this man she had fallen in love with right here at the Fox. Reaching over for Karl's hand, she lifted it, kissed the back of it, then pressing it against her cheek, she simply nodded with approval. "Harry, can I use your phone to make a local call?" asked Claire.

"Of course, you can, Miss Claire. Before I close the registry, do you two want another round?" asked Harry as he placed the telephone on top of the bar.

"Why not, Harry? It's a good day to enjoy another mild and bitter," answered Karl, his gaze on his wife.

"Freida, it's Claire. Would you mind awfully if we picked up Nick at about 4:30 this afternoon? His dad is missing his little man, and so is his mummy. I'm sorry to mess up your plans." Claire got her answer immediately.

"I was wondering about you two being away from the baby that long. Of course, that will be alright."

Claire replaced the receiver, then turned to Karl, saying, "Your sister is not surprised, so we can go for a drive, then stop off at the garage to swap cars again, then head for Baldock. That's our plan, alright, Sailor? I'm really not in favor of driving with our baby in that little drafty car just yet anyway," said Claire, taking a big swig of her beer. Pulling into the driveway of the bungalow, Claire started to smile at Karl, then, with laughter in her voice, said, "So much for a romantic dinner out on the town with my Lover Boy. I much prefer your idea. We had our dessert first before a nice lunch, so why bother going out?" Claire was enjoying her day and could not care less about going out to dinner.

"Mama will be home soon. She is up the road with Franchot; he loves pushing that pram with the baby in it. They'll be back real soon. What can I get you to drink, hot or cold? You two look like you have had a wonderful time so far today. I can only imagine what you were up to, lucky buggers." Freida could not resist saying that, but she would be seeing Ronny the following weekend. The front door opened, and in came Mama, carrying Nick, with Franchot pulling the pram through the open door.

"Mama, we've changed our minds. We decided we would stay home with our little Nick. I hope you're not too disappointed?" said Claire, walking over to hug and kiss her son.

"I'm not surprised, maybe a little disappointed. Make every minute count, Karl; soon, you will be returning to Slough." Claire waved to Mama and Freida as Karl backed the Wolsey out of the driveway.

"See you next week!" yelled Claire, holding up the baby for them to see. Sunday, Claire and Karl took Nicholas to church. Claire wore a brightly flowered dress with a white wool short jacket, and Karl decided to wear casual sports jacket and trousers, even though Claire had asked him to wear his dress uniform.

Karl's answer to her question was, "Tomorrow is coming soon enough for me to return to wearing a uniform. So, no thanks, lady."

In the afternoon, they strolled the main street of Hitchin, then, returning to their home, they made a nice dinner, enjoying each other's company, both becoming a little melancholy knowing tomorrow morning he would leave once again.

Charlie arrived at the house promptly at 0830 hours to find Karl all dressed, with his small travel case packed and ready by the front door. "Darling, it's time for me to leave. This month went by all too fast. I'll be thinking of you and Nick every hour of the day until Charlie drops me off once again. Claire, come here and give me a kiss that will last the whole week."

Karl, taking Nicholas from his mother's arms, kissed and hugged his son. Thinking it was a game, Nick started squealing and hammering his father's shoulders, enjoying being in his arms. "Karl, you're keeping Charlie waiting. As much as I want you to stay here and ravage me all morning, it's time you got on the road." Like all the times before, Claire was suppressing the tears she always had each time Karl left. This time it would not be dangerous, so she'd been told.

Waving goodbye through the open car window, Karl could see his wife was already feeling sad. Claire, dressed in a bottle green business suit, would drop off Nick at the babysitter before returning to her life as a solicitor. Karl sat, thinking, God, she is such a professional looking woman. She's way too good for a chap like me, but I'm very happy she's mine. I hope Nick grows up with her brains and her pedigree.

Karl decided to drop off his case at his quarters before returning to his department to review the new briefs. "Good morning, Sir," said Linda as she gathered the folders for his review.

"And a very good morning to you all." Karl was pleased with the new addition to his staff. John and Sheila added to the morning's welcome. In his office, Karl dove into the files that needed his signature before looking at the schedule, which Linda had brought in with a steaming mug of coffee.

"Linda, is this today's schedule? If it is, I'm supposed to be in a meeting at 1100 hours, and that's only twenty minutes from now. I guess I'll head out. Leave this mess on my desk until I return; see you later."

Out in the hall, he met up with Bill, coming out of his office. "Karl, glad to have you back. How is the family? I bet that little terror kept you busy, didn't he?"

Karl responded by saying, "I hope he doesn't grow up like his dad!" Approximately forty or more officers were milling around in the main conference room, drinking morning tea and coffee. Clive was standing with General Jacks to the left of the head table; two long tables on either side completed the configuration.

"Gentlemen, please take your assigned seats. We have a very busy schedule to cover over the next several days," yelled Colonel Knight over the noise generated by the groups of senior officers. Major John Abrahams made the roll call as they all took their seats.

"Gunther, Herbert, glad we are sitting together. Any idea what this is all about?" asked Karl as he opened his briefing folder.

"Karl, all of us here will be preparing to find those Nazi criminals that have plundered Europe since this war started. I believe it's safe to say all of us here have been looking forward to this day for a very long time," replied Gunther, a big smile on his face. Hitler's thugs would soon pay the inevitable price for the atrocities they have been responsible for.

General Jacks stood to address the group, "Gentlemen, today is a day I have looked forward to for many years. We have waged war against Hitler's forces for too long. Today's objectives are to create Intelligence teams to find those individuals, wherever they run to and hide, as we circle their remaining forces. We are confident that the might of the combined Allies force will obtain an unconditional surrender within the next several months.

Whatever your responsibilities were up to now are about to change from Intelligence duties to investigators of military crimes. Colonel Knight will now describe the various groups that will prepare for that surrender." Colonel Jacks turned the meeting over to Clive.

"All of you here are amongst our top Intelligence officers. That's why you were invited to this meeting." Clive turned to the big board behind the head table, removing the cover. The big map of Europe was broken up into zones and group numbers.

Flags for each Allied country were also displayed; they would be operating their own teams in those zones as well. Clive, with his pointer, first tapped Norway, referring to the group assigned to operate there. "Once you have established your command center, move quickly. Those Huns will be planning escape routes to save their filthy necks. Our latest Intelligence reports have uncovered an alarming statistic; the Roman Catholic Church is helping high ranking Gestapo and S.S. officers escape to South America. It's hard to believe the Pope could endorse such a policy, hiding and funding these criminals.

"We have also uncovered that the Vatican is supplying new identities and travel documents to these thugs. We will discuss that further in tomorrow's meeting. Now, refer to your group number, then refer to this board to see your operating zone. We will adjourn for an hour, so you can acquaint yourselves with others assigned to your zone, many of whom you know or have operated in the field with before."

Clive stood and walked over to the group assigned to B-34. "Alright, chaps, we will be working together again. I must be really dumb, signing on with this group. On the other hand, I wouldn't have it any other way. Gunther, you and Karl will focus primarily on Kriegsmarine activities, which will call for you to cross into other zones. Also operating in our zone will be teams from America, France, Norway, and a small team from Belgium.

"Major Anderson, who you all know, will be here tomorrow to start coordinating the American plans, along with your old friend Major Jerva for the Free French. Right now, we don't have the names for the Norwegian and Belgian representatives. I guess we'll find out tomorrow, won't we?"

Returning to the head table, Clive asked everyone to return to their seats. "Gentlemen, the containment of escaping war crimes' personnel is paramount. We need to move faster than they will, and that's the topic for this afternoon," concluded Clive, turning the meeting over to another interrogation speaker.

More and more teams were now operating all over Europe, gathering vital information on the whereabouts of the growing list of Nazi war criminals. Since D-Day, the Allied forces had waged war against Germany, giving them a taste of their own evil medicine. With the noose closing in around them, the policymakers at the top of the Chancery knew they would be held responsible for thousands of atrocities that would forever stain Germany's history.

Supplies were pouring into Europe with the major victory on June 26th, 1944, when Allied troops liberated the French port of Cherbourg. The Germans, in full scale, retreated toward Germany. Another milestone happened on August 25th, 1944, when Allied troops, with the help of the French Resistance, led by General Charles de Gaulle, liberated Paris after four years of occupation.

Planning in Slough was now at an all-time high as the teams worked around the clock, planning and dispatching Intelligence personnel throughout Europe, discovering where Nazi leaders had moved to or were hiding, knowing the end was very near. In many cases, high ranking officers changed their identities and ditched their colorful uniforms, sneaking through the lines as regular soldiers, denying the Allies justice. This added a layer of investigation that was more than frustrating for those searching for known war criminals. The final surrender was still a month from happening, and yet so many of Hitler's thugs were escaping with new identities; they simply disappeared.

Clive directed the activities of his team around tediously compiling the ever-growing war crimes list. His concern now was that the end of 1944 was less than thirty days away. The Christmas disruptions would mean many of his group would be returning to their homes. Feeling happy for those leaving, he was growing overly concerned about the monumental task they would return to. *Could they move quickly enough to arrest those German leaders trying to escape the hangman's noose? This would not be easy.*

Acutely aware of his men's needs, he asked for volunteers to remain behind to continue the investigation. The European members immediately answered that request. Their families were still in occupied Europe, so they had no homes to go to. With that issue somewhat resolved, the remainder of the group had a Christmas party in the officers' lounge for the poor chaps who would remain in Slough, Gunther and Herbert included.

Like so many times before, Karl packed his small case and headed out to find his driver, Charlie, waiting for him at the curb. Karl was more than ready for this time alone time to unclutter his mind. And this train ride would help him achieve that state. "Charlie, have a wonderful Christmas with your family. I have not had time to buy you a gift, so please accept this envelope to buy a suitable gift for your wife." Karl placed the envelope on Charlie's lap.

"Sir, you don't have to do that. You have always been so generous in all that you do for me," replied Charlie, feeling somewhat embarrassed as he looked at the envelope.

"Charlie, it's not a fortune. It's my way of saying thank you," said Karl, thanking Charlie again at the station, then with a casual salute headed for the ticket counter. Charlie waited until Karl had disappeared into the station before he opened the envelope. Inside, he found four five-pound notes and a note from Karl.

Charlie, wishing you and your family a wonderful Christmas. Take this time to embrace the best in all those you hold dear. Sorry, I did not have time to find a suitable gift, but you know how life is in the BIS. See you on December 28th.

Your friend. Major Karl Vita

As the train started to slow down, Karl heard the familiar banging from its bumpers as it entered the station. Looking through the smoke and steam, Karl strained to see his wife and son on the platform. There she was in casual attire, holding Nicholas under her left arm and waving with her right hand so that Karl would see her, jumping down onto the platform. Karl walked quickly, closing the distance to Claire in seconds.

"Darling, kiss me, you bloody Austrian. Your son and I have missed you so very much, and, Major Vita, your son has something to tell you. We have been rehearsing in your absence. Nicholas, what do you want to say to your father?"

Karl took Nick from his mother's arms. Holding him close, he kissed Nick's cheek, squeezing his little man. Claire prompted Nick once again to say da-da. Karl, holding his son face to face, was bouncing him, which Nick loved. Little screams of joy were followed by Nicholas's first word, "Da-da!"

Hearing that first word sent Karl's senses reeling. His son had said his first word here on the platform of the Hitchin Station. Claire was beaming with pride as she hugged her two men. "Come on, Sailor, let's go home and have a glass of wine to celebrate Nick's first word. Karl held Nick on his lap as Claire drove them home.

Christmas Eve, the family came together in Hitchin and repeated their new tradition of a feast and gift opening in front of the fireplace, the big Christmas tree flickering with lights.

Christmas morning, Claire and Karl got dressed in their Sunday best. Claire dressed Nick in new trousers and a pullover, then the coat that Mama had bought him. The three headed to church, then home for a relaxing day playing with Nick until he tired.

Claire carefully carried him into his bedroom for a midday nap. Downstairs, she found Karl lying on the floor, watching the flickering embers crackling as the dry wood burned with vivid flames. "Darling, seeing as we are not going out again other than you picking my sister and her family at six from the train station, l think I'll go up and change into something more comfortable. In the meantime, we have a few hours to ourselves. So, Sailor boy, do you have any more Christmas presents you'd like to share with your wife? Once my sister arrives, we won't be alone again, and after that, you will be leaving again on December 28th. That's only three days from now." Kneeling next to him, she slid her arm under his head and softly whispered in his left ear, "Wouldn't you prefer I undress here in front of the fire instead of going upstairs to do that?"

Claire was determined to take advantage of these precious few hours to make love to her husband, knowing that when he left, it could be weeks or even months before he returned home. The fear was still with her, even though the war was winding down. There still lurked the possibility of danger when the BIS agents returned to the Continent. Standing back up again, she waited for Karl's reaction to her question. Karl reached up to her, a big grin on his face. "Well, my sweet thing, if it's lovemaking you're hinting at, why don't you try to entice me?"

Still in a light blue and white striped skirt with a pale blue blouse, Claire looked down at her husband. Slowly shaking her head, she simply smiled and replied, "Sailor, if you want it, come and get it." Karl stood up in front of Claire. He lifted her head, and his eyes were looking for that sign on Claire's face that told him she was more than ready. Standing there, she felt that familiar quiver in her thighs, feeling those eyes of his stripping her naked, which he could do so very easily, unhinging her each time he did it.

With slow movements, he pulled her close, then kissed her tenderly, lingering as he opened her mouth with his tongue. Claire responded immediately. Karl moved to the fasteners on Claire's skirt, then, letting it drop to the floor, he unbuttoned her blouse. Kissing her shoulders, he slowly removed that as well.

Claire now stood in front of him in her slip and underwear, her chest rising and falling with each movement he made.

"Karl, you always know how to get me going. It scares me each time you do this. Darling, I've waited long enough. Now, give me what I go without all the time you're away." Claire knelt in front of the fire, pulling Karl down by her side. In the glow of that fire, they made love until they were both spent and content in each other's arms.

From upstairs, Claire could hear Nick moving about in his crib. "Back in a minute, darling; your son needs attention. Claire returned to the living room with Nick in her arms. "Karl, here you go; take your son while I get us both a glass of wine." Still on the floor, Karl bounced his son on his chest, and Nick let out little squeals of enjoyment.

Claire returned, carrying the white wine, "Darling, he loves it so much when you do that. Karl lay the baby back down between them as they sipped their wine.

Without any warning, Nicholas looked at his parents, then yelled out "Dada" twice. Claire and Karl broke out laughing with joy at their son's new word.

"Claire, you will have to work on his next word of Mama while I'm away. Darling, our little man is growing up right before our eyes; this is wonderful. Now, I must be off to pick up your sister and her family at the train station."

Karl parked the car, then casually walked up onto the platform. While he waited there, he started thinking about having to say goodbye to Claire right here on the platform in two days' time; that thought weighing heavily on him as he stared down at the concrete, allowing his mind to enter that world he lived in for so long with the near-death experiences he had narrowly escaped on many occasions and the demanding responsibilities he faced daily, sometimes around the clock. Off in the distance, the sound of the approaching train brought him back to why he was here.

The column of smoke drifted away from the approaching train as it squealed to a stop, steam escaping from below its carriages, and compartment doors flying open, discharging holiday travelers. "Karl, over here," yelled Caroline in an excited voice. Karl walked quickly toward his sister-in-law, her two children between her and husband David as they closed the distance.

Caroline's son Brian, seeing Karl, broke away, running ahead to greet his uncle. "Uncle Karl, Uncle Karl, I have missed seeing you!" Karl, seeing his nephew, reached down, lifting the young boy high over his head. They were both excited at the reunion. Caroline lifted her daughter Dianne to kiss her uncle, then kissed Karl's cheek as well.

"God, Karl, it's so wonderful to see you before you head out again. When Claire told me you couldn't stay for New Year's, I told David we needed to take a break and spend time with my big sister." Caroline was still hugging Karl, excited at this reunion.

"David, it's really wonderful you could get time off. It's been over eighteen months since we visited you in Oxford, or has it been longer? Here, let me help you with those cases. Now, if you're ready, let's get you home." Karl, a case in one hand and Brian holding the other, led them back to the car. This reunion had lifted Karl's spirits again, relieved that Claire would have company for New Year's. The following two days were magical for Karl, with both families spending each day together.

Mama watched as the children played in the living room, "Karl, we are looking at the next generation. Let's hope they won't try to destroy this world like the Germans and Japanese were trying to do." The morning of the 28th came too quickly for Karl. Rising early, he got himself ready; packing his small case before going downstairs wearing his field uniform.

"My handsome spy are you ready for coffee?" asked Claire, hiding her sorrow under a cheerful smile.

Wishing the family, a Happy New Year, Karl picked up Nicholas, and, with a heavy heart, he finally spoke, "Next time I'm home, I'm sure you'll be saying many new words. Make sure one of them is Mama. I miss you both already." Karl squeezed Nick one more time, then kissed his cheeks before returning him to his aunt.

"Well, darling, I guess it's time to say farewell again. I will call you once I'm back in Slough." Karl held his wife very close for that final minute or two. "I'm ready, David, whenever you are."

Karl picked up his case, stopped for one last kiss, then was out the door.

Claire took Nick from her sister and held him close, feeling alone once again. Caroline, with tears in her eyes, put her arm around her distraught sister. Resisting the urge to break out crying, Claire finally spoke, "You must think I'm a weakling crying like this, but it's the not knowing that hurts. Each time Karl leaves, I always wonder if this will be the last time, we will see him. He is such a proud man; he always tries to hide the pain he carries each time he leaves us for who knows how long. Caroline, I love him so much. I can't help getting scared at the mere thought of never seeing him again."

Caroline knew her sister still harbored that fear after losing Patrick back in 1940. That black cloud always reappeared each time Karl returned to the dangerous duties of a BIS officer.

Driving up to the station, David asked Karl, "When do you think you can get leave again? Hopefully, within a couple of weeks, or will you only find that out once you're back in Slough?"

Karl, always careful not to volunteer any information no matter how trivial it may appear, replied, "David, I never know until the last minute. Next year will come with its own problems; all I can say at this point is, Germany is fighting for survival. We will be overloaded in the BIS, so it could be quite a long time.

Thanks for driving me this morning. It's always tough on Claire when she drops me off; she always insists on staying with me until I board that damn train. At least today, you and Caroline will get her through that first day and staying here through New Year's Day will make it so much more tolerable. Mama, Freida, and Ronny will be joining you for a lunch that Claire and Mama are planning. Coming together like this gives her that extra support that is so important at times like this. So, thank you for staying; it makes it that much easier for me to leave."

David looked over at Karl, then said, "Karl, it's all of us who should be thanking you and everyone else involved with this senseless war. We knew this would be a rough one for both of you, so it's the least we can do staying over. Here we are at the station. I pray that next year will find you planning peaceful operations, not more espionage activities." David pulled the car up in front of the ticketing office and said one last goodbye. Karl watched David drive back down the hill, then, with sadness in his heart, he walked toward the entrance.

Unbeknownst to Karl as he boarded that train, any thought he may have had about returning home at the end of the week would not be happening. Three long months would pass before he could return to his family in Hitchin.

CHAPTER 15

1945 HOSTILITIES END

Karl walked out of the station in Slough. He had not called the motor pool, electing to take public transportation instead. Walking out of the entrance, there at the curb was his old friend and camp commander, Major William Lowes, leaning on the big Humber's mudguard.

"Bill, what are you doing here, and how did you know I would be on that train?" Karl's spirits lifted to see a familiar face. "Well, old man, your charming wife called me and asked me for a favor. You know I could never refuse such a charming lady, and she asked if I would mind picking you up today. My old friend, that woman worries about you constantly, so how could I refuse her?"

"Bill, this makes returning much easier. I was feeling pretty sorry for myself until I saw your ugly mug." Karl squeezed Bill's upper arm as he said that.

"Once all the chaps who took Christmas off have returned, I will dispatch the ones that covered for you so that they can enjoy their New Year's Holiday. That means Gunther and Herbert will be leaving for a quick holiday in wet, cold Cornwall after today's briefing. I don't think they really care, so long as it doesn't involve a uniform or some strenuous, tedious tasks for the BIS." Bill smiled as he drove out of the station toward the camp.

Back in his office, Karl called Claire to thank her for arranging Bill to meet him on his arrival. "Darling, you are always looking out for me. I wish I could be there right now because I would ravage you, maybe more than once. Who could argue that English ladies are far from cold fish more like human Piranhas if you ask me." That last line got them laughing, which was the right medicine for the frame of mind they both were in.

The following morning, Karl rose early. Heading down to the canteen, he met up with Gunther, Herbert, and some of his fellow officers who had returned the evening before. After breakfast, Karl walked to his department, a briefcase in one hand and coffee in the other. "Morning, Sir!" from his staff made Karl's spirits rise.

"And a very good morning to you all. I hope you had a wonderful Christmas. Sally, could you please bring in the latest schedule and files that need my review? What time is my first meeting today?" asked Karl, sitting down at his desk.

"You're expected in the main meeting room at 1030 hours. I'll remind you when it's time," replied Sally as she left his office.

Like all the times before, he looked at the picture of Claire, holding baby Nicholas in her arms. Placing his finger to his lips, then put that finger on the picture. Right, he thought, let's get down to business. I only have two and a half hours before I must leave for that meeting.

Karl left his department, his briefcase in his hand, wondering what devious operations they would be discussing today. "Morning, chaps, I hope you all had a nice Christmas," asked Clive, entering the room, followed by two shorthand secretaries. "Please, take your seats; we have much to cover over the next several days."

Here we go again, thought Karl, sitting next to Bill, Gunther, and Herbert. Clive, with his long pointer, tapped the large map of Europe several times before he spoke. "Gentlemen, our job functions will be changing entering the new year. All of you present have been selected to return to the European Continent within the next several weeks. If you believe you should be removed from this duty, see me after this meeting. You have done more than your duty during this war, so no judgments will be made against you; this I can assure you of.

Our latest intelligence indicates that many of Hitler's general staff are in favor of a ceasefire. Hitler, on the other hand, was banking on that atomic bomb to hold onto whatever power he has left, and we all know that will not happen." Clive nodded to Karl and Gunther as team members that hijacked the Gustav III.

"So, what's our new objective moving forward, you may be thinking. Well, gentlemen, our military and the armed forces of our Allies are crushing German resistance all the way to Hitler's Chancellery, although he is rarely there these days." After outlining the new role, the BIS would play in the upcoming months, Clive called for a brief adjournment to allow everyone present time to review the materials provided and weigh the option given to withdraw from participating.

"Majors Fisher and Vita, would you follow me for a private discussion at the back of the hall, please?" Clive sat down, pointing for Gunther and Karl to sit across the table from him before speaking. "After you returned from your last mission, I indicated you both would be assigned to a team that would interrogate members of the Kriegsmarine after the surrender. Well, as of this morning, your orders, if you accept them, have been changed. Karl, each passing week, the High Command is becoming more concerned about the lightning advancement of the Russian forces moving to occupy your homeland of Austria before the German military finally collapses and surrenders to them. With this looming problem, we would like you both to lead a team of BIS agents being assembled made up of Germans and Austrians.

"Your objective is to get to Vienna most expediently. Once there, you will coordinate intelligence on the forward movements of the Russian armies, feeding that information back to our own forces also racing to liberate Austria before the Russians can. It is imperative we have BIS personnel in Vienna to provide first-hand information to those forward units.

"Now, I realize that after that last mission, we promised that would be your last. However, considering current conditions, we need to act quickly. Who better to assess our position than you two, by far our best agents for a mission such as this one? I hope you will agree with me on that. Your local knowledge will be invaluable in providing this information to our forces. There can be no doubt those Russians have it in their minds to lay claim to all of Austria.

Before returning to the meeting, can I report back to command that you two will undertake this mission?"

Clive sat quietly while Karl and Gunther walked to another table to discuss this further. Returning to Clive waiting at the table, Gunther spoke for them both. "Clive, you have put us in a difficult position. You know all too well we cannot refuse.

However, it feels like making the promise of that being our last mission was no more than an empty statement to make us feel relieved at not returning to espionage operations. Promises like that are not becoming an officer of your rank, and, needleless to say, up to this point, a trusted friend that is putting us both back into harm's way. I believe the meeting is ready to resume," said Gunther as he turned his back on Clive, returning to the others.

Without any expression on his face, Karl tapped Clive's shoulder, then walked over to sit next to Gunther, sitting with anger written all over his face. Karl reached over, and taking Gunther's forearm, he whispered, "It's not like we will be going on another really dangerous mission this time, just infinitely unforgiving, I would say." Karl was trying to add humor to calm Gunther.

The meeting went on for two more days. Karl, still feeling betrayed by Clive, was steaming at having to go undercover once again. But, like Gunther, he would do his duty. Karl sat in his office, thinking how he would tell Claire she would not see him this weekend, nor could he tell her when she would see him next. Picking up the telephone, he dialed the home security number.

Then, with a heavy heart, he waited for Claire to answer. "Hitchin 4567, who's calling?"

"Claire, it's me, darling; how are you and Nick doing today?" Claire cut him off by saying, "Darling, it's so wonderful to hear your voice. I'm assuming that your call also includes that you will not be coming home this weekend, is that right? Karl, the tone in your voice is giving you away, am I correct?"

Karl should have guessed that his solicitor wife would pick up right away on his sadness. "As usual, Claire, you guessed where this call was going. So, you're correct, but darling, it may be much longer than a week. I can't tell you what's going on, but don't plan on hearing from me for quite a while. You need not worry; it's not dangerous, it will just require a lot of my time sorry, no phone contact. God, I miss you two. Clive will give you an update, maybe once a week. That's the best I can do right now." Karl waited for Claire's response.

"Darling, I am always preparing myself that each time you leave, it may be weeks or months before you return to me. The only consolation is this dreadful war is it's winding down, and that means, each time you leave, the dangers may still be around you, but less each time." Claire, trying very hard not to burden him with tears, waited for him to respond.

"Claire, I must go now. I'm already late for a meeting. Would you tell Mama I'll bring her some more paprika when I return home? I love you, Claire; kiss my little man for me, and a real wet one for you, bye." Karl cut it short, thinking, my wife is a smart solicitor. She'll figure out where I'm going. I hope I can find that paprika in Wien.

The following morning, the four-man team waited at the parade ground for the bus that would take them to Folkstone and the transport ship that would take them to Cherbourg, France.

From there, they would be flown by an American DC-3 transport to a drop zone, approximately twenty-five miles northwest of Vienna. A team of Austrian resistance fighters would meet them at the hilltop drop zone. Clive and Bill ventured out to see the team off.

Approaching them both, Bill spoke first, "Chaps, we know how you're feeling about being betrayed, and we can't fault you for thinking that way. If I could replace either of you, I would willingly do that, but we all know my bum leg would be a liability. Once in Vienna, Major Andy Anderson will be joining you. The Americans, like us, are becoming increasingly concerned. If the Russians keep up their present advancements, we could be facing another dangerous confrontation." Bill, standing in front of them, stopped talking. Turning to Clive, he waited for the mission commander to input his parting words.

"Thank you, Bill; that was well put. Chaps, I know, at this very moment, I may not be someone you have much confidence in. Sometimes, being the one who must make these difficult decisions can be a very lonely place. The High Command instructed me to move quickly, putting a team in the field posthaste. This escalating problem with the Russians now has the highest priority, and that is why I turned reluctantly to our best operatives to make this assessment as to what is happening. I will make you a promise if you can trust me; get the job done, and I'll pull strings to get you home in the most expedient manner. You have my word on that. Now, with better communications, I will be able Karl to relay an update for you to Claire and will do the same for you, Gunther." Clive ceased talking, allowing his friends to process what he had just said.

Gunther turned his head in Karl's direction, saying. "Colonel, thank you for saying that. It hasn't stopped the anger we both feel right now, but we totally understand your position. We will do our duty to the best of our ability. Do you have anything else to add to this, Major Vita?" Gunther waited for Karl's response.

"I only have one comment, and that is, you two clowns, on our return, will be buying us copious amounts of mild and bitter beer for the remainder of this war. Now, we must be off; thank you both for seeing us off." Karl stepped forward to shake hands, followed by Gunther, who did the same.

Boarding the American transport plane after a smooth crossing to Cherbourg, the four-man team put on their parachutes, then sat along the sides of the aircraft on uncomfortable canvas seats. Gunther removed his water flask. Taking a sip, he started to smile, which broke out into a muffled laugh. Karl, looking at him, was wondering what was so funny. "Gunther, what the hell is so funny?"

Gunther turned to him, then, still laughing, spoke out, "Well, old man, I was just thinking, when we are old buggers, sitting in our deck chairs, will we be asking our maker, is this the final mission?" Gunther was enjoying this warped thought.

"God, Gunther, sometimes, you confuse me with that German sense of humor." Sitting there in that noisy aircraft, Karl continued the conversation by saying, "You know how I hate parachute drops. I really think this was Clive's way of sticking it up our rear ends at giving him a hard time about this bloody mission. Remind me to heckle him about this on our return, assuming we will be returning." Karl clinked his water flask against Gunther's, their friendship growing stronger.

On April 2nd, Vienna Radio denied that the Austrian capital had been declared an open city. On that same day, Soviet troops approaching from the south, gathering on either side of the Danube, ready for the final assault. When Gunther and Karl's team arrived, they quickly found out that the German garrison had amassed 25 divisions, 270,000 men, and armaments, consisting of more than 770 tanks and assault guns. For rapid deployment, a further 434 personnel carriers were strategically positioned around the city to move those troop movements.

The commanders of those forces were General Rudolf Von Burau and Hungarian General Wilhelm Bittrich. On the face of things, this looked like a formidable defense force, but when compared to the Soviet forces, there was no way the Germans could hold off their advancement. Leading the Soviet Union, Romanian, and Bulgarian forces, General Fyodor Tolbukhin and Bulgarian General Vladimir Stoychev led a force of 77 divisions, 1,171,800 men, 1,600 tanks, and 5,425 assault guns. Vienna's fate was sealed from March 16th to April 15th. The Germans fought valiantly to hold their positions but to no avail. The German casualties were staggering, with over 30,000 troops killed and over 125,000 captured. The battle for Vienna was over.

Karl and Gunther's mission confirmed the Soviet forces were only days away from overrunning Vienna, disregarding the continued requests by Allied command to make that final offensive a combined effort.

Hiding in the hills above Vienna, Karl's team now included Major Anderson, sent daily reports to the BIS and the OSS, informing them that the Allied forces were too late. The Soviets controlled Austria and its capital. Andy had meetings with the Russian commander and, through him, arranged for the Allied investigation team to be given an armed escort as they toured the city, now in total ruins. Bands of people, both foreigners and Austrians, plundered and assaulted the helpless residents in the absence of a police force. Looting and countless cases of rape continued unchecked. Many of Vienna's finest buildings were battered wrecks of their former majestic splendor.

There was no water, electricity, or gas. On one of those inspection days, Karl directed the team to make a stop at his parents' home near the Prater amusement park. finding litter, empty boxes, and the signs of a rapid departure all around the courtyard, but the building was still intact. Inside, doors hung off their hinges, and there were broken windows and many holes in the walls. All the kitchen and bathroom fixtures were ripped out, leaving stains from ruptured pipes. The odors from human waste made breathing a challenge.

Gunther and Andy could only watch as Karl walked through his former happy home. Once a majestic building with manicured gardens, Annie Laurie's parents' house had been used as a German command center. It looked about the same; thank God, there were no signs of bomb damage, though. The building owned by his friend Paddy Grucker did not endure as well; it was destroyed, bombed and burned out with only two walls remaining. The front door, ironically, remained intact. Karl, seeing these familiar places, was becoming very agitated.

"I've seen enough; let's get out of here and head back to camp. There is no reason to remain here; this isn't Wien anymore. I pray to God that it can be rebuilt, but not this year anyway."

Returning to England, Karl remained withdrawn. It was almost like his heart had been ripped out of him. He remained quiet, staring into space. He had retreated into his mind to a bygone time when his city of music was gay with people enjoying their magnificent city. "Leave him alone, chaps; this is not easy for him right now. He'll be much better when he sees his wife and son," remarked Gunther. As the bus pulled into the parade ground, a group had gathered, silently waiting to greet the passengers as they disembarked.

Karl, still in a harmful place, followed Gunther out onto the parade ground. Gunther was holding him by the arm, protecting his friend. "Karl, look who has come to meet you! Karl, can you hear me; look up!" Gunther was starting to get concerned that Karl may have retreated too far. "Karl, look, it's Claire, Nicholas, your mother, sister, and nephew here to welcome you home."

Gunther was still supporting him until Claire wrapped her arm around his neck, kissing him, her tears wet on his cheek. "Karl, you're home whatever happened back there can't hurt you anymore. Clive called us and sent a car to get us here for your arrival today. Karl, darling, please, look at me; say something, I beg you. Nicholas, kiss your daddy; he's come home to us." Claire was also becoming concerned that Karl had cracked under the strain of this mission.

Clive and Bill approached, saying, "Karl, we need to get you to sickbay, old man, once you have greeted your family." Clive stepped back, looking at Gunther with surprise all over his face.

Karl slowly looked up, then reached out for Nicholas. Holding his son with both arms, his face pressed against him, they all waited while Karl stood silently holding his son. Finally, Karl spoke, "Nicholas, your dad's home; son, I will never allow you to be involved in any war, not as long as I'm alive anyway." Karl, crying uncontrollably, reached out for Claire, pulling her to him. Mama, Freida, and Franchot joined in the family reunion.

"Karl, my precious son, you need to let it all out. You're safe now," said his concerned mother. Karl looked around him at all his friends, standing quietly, waiting for him to come back to them.

"Mama, how did you know we would arrive back today?" Karl was slowly regaining his composure.

"That nice man, Clive, called us and asked us to be here to meet you. All your friends here have been very worried after hearing about your reaction to witnessing what has happened to Wien, having to see it the way you did. Son, I can only imagine how that affected you, and it was more than you could handle. Now, go and thank them all; give Nick to me." Mama, taking Nick, kissed her son, relieved that he would not remain in that distant place.

Karl turned to Claire, kissing her lightly on the cheek and holding her with all his might; he turned her face toward him, then in a voice laboring with turmoil, he said softly, "Claire, I will always thank my maker for the life we have yet to share. I'm alright now. Clive, as much as I value our friendship, at this very moment, you can stick this bloody BIS where the sun doesn't shine. I'm going home! Gunther, thank you, friend, for getting me back. See you all soon. Now, where is that transportation back to Hitchin?" Karl was back and heading home alive.

EPILOGUE

On October 10th, 1945, family and friends and many serving in BIS gathered on the parade ground to witness a very special ceremony. The weather was very sunny, with a slight chill in the air, setting the perfect conditions for today's presentation. A military band played cheerful, uplifting music befitting this ceremony for Majors Gunther Fisher and Karl Vita, standing at attention out in front of the Army honor guard. Now in England, Gunther's family joined with Karl's family to witness this very special occasion. From the doors leading out to the parade ground, General Arthur Jacks, followed by Lieutenant Colonel Clive Knight, Major William Lowes, and members of General Jacks' staff filed out, wearing their ceremonial dress uniforms, approaching the officers standing out in front of the honor guard.

"Parade Attention," yelled the officer.

"Major Fisher and Major Vita, step forward!" yelled Lieutenant Colonel Knight. Gunther and Karl stepped forward, coming to attention once again.

Stepping up to the public address microphone, General Jacks started speaking. "Today, all of us in the BIS and invited guests can be proud of these officers standing in front of us. When the call to go into harm's way came throughout this war, Major Fisher and Major Vita could always be counted on to put personal safety aside, going back into occupied Europe many times. On two occasions, Major Vita returned to this camp mortally wounded. More recently, both of these officers volunteered to undertake an extremely dangerous mission that had less than forty percent chance for them returning alive. But still, they went because it was their duty. That mission, if not successful, would have put this country in grave danger and under the prospect of total annihilation.

"Today, I am proud to award both these officers with the Military Star and the War Medal."

Major Lowes stepped forward, carrying two sets of medals. Alongside the general, he approached Gunther and Karl. Saluting, General Jacks pinned the medals first to Gunther's chest, saying, "On behalf of His Royal Highness King George VI, it is my honor to present you with these medals for service above and beyond the call of duty." Moving over to Karl, General Jacks repeated the award. Gunther and Karl saluted as General Jacks stepped back.

"Parade dismissed," yelled the young lieutenant, ending the ceremony.

Clive, Bill, and General Jacks came forward, followed by many from the general staff to shake hands with these heroes. The crowd was getting quite large, all trying to shake hands as well, but Karl's eyes were looking at his wife and family.

"Make way, please, for the family members so that they can join the two majors," said Ronny, proud to be Karl's brother-in-law as they made their way through the sea of well-wishers.

"Karl, I am… we are so proud of you today. I never thought I would be standing on a parade ground to witness my husband being honored like this. Gunther that applies to you as well." Claire smiled at Gunther's wife and family and said, "Gunther, she is so charming and very easy to talk to. She speaks such fluent English. I'm glad we could all come together for this special occasion." Claire stopped talking as Karl's Mother, with difficulty, squeezed her way up to her youngest son.

"Karl, today, you have honored the Vita family." With both arms out, she hugged her son; the emotion of what just happened was restricting her from saying more. Finally, the crowd dispersed. Saying his goodbyes to all his friends and loyal staff, Karl reached over to take his son from his wife, saying softly, "Let's go home, son."

With his other hand, he reached for his wife's hand. Looking into her eyes, he smiled. There really was no need to say more; they both had what they needed. The family walked to the waiting transportation. Being the last to board, Karl turned back to Gunther, still standing with his family in the parade ground. "I say, Major

Fisher, are we still on for this weekend? If so, see you Saturday morning."

Gunther waved, then put his thumb up in the air, yelling, "Count on it, you crazy Austrian. My family is really looking forward to some goulash and strudel." Karl, laughing, waved once more, then took his seat next to Claire and Nicholas, thinking, this time, I really feel safe. I am looking forward to a new career away from the BIS. Maybe the sea is still calling for me to return. Well, I guess that may or may not happen. Reaching over the seat, he reached for his mother's hand again, thinking that getting Mama out of Wien was the start of this life I have now. It's funny how things work out. A peaceful smile now took over his face as he fell asleep.

1945 would end with the unconditional surrender of all German forces in Europe on May 7th, 1945. General Alfred Jodl signed the surrender documents for all German forces, East and West, for the German High Command. The signing was held in Reims, northeastern France.

Later in 1945, the surrender of all the Imperial Japanese forces was announced by Emperor Hirohito on August 15th and formally signed on September 2nd aboard the American Battleship, the USS Missouri. General Douglas McArthur signed for the Allied forces, and foreign Minister Mamoru Shigemitsu signed the instrument of unconditional surrender for Emperor Hirohito.

THE END

The conclusion to this series will be in book four.

ABOUT THE AUTHOR

PETER A. MOSCOVITA grew up in England and had a love for exploring different countries, sparked by exciting family trips across Europe. His Dad's adventure stories from his early years as a ship's officer made him dream about discovering new lands far beyond.

In 1966, his dreams came true, when he emigrated to the United States of America as a design and development engineer. In later years he would enter medical device manufacturing.

In 1982, he met Martine, who shared his passion for travel, sailing, cruising, culinary clubs and the love of history.

In 1986, alone with two fellow engineers they founded a startup company that designed and developed a line of advanced Medical Vascular Diagnostic instruments. Once the instruments were ready for market he turned his attention to creating a National Sales and Marketing Division. As the company grew he convinced his wife Martine to join the company as its event coordinator.

When time permitted the couple continued their long distant traveling all over the world, exploring was in their blood.

In 2010, the partners agreed they would sell the company, now traveling and exploring had no boundaries.

In 2011, The couple moved to Florida in their boat, living on it in Sarasota before settling ashore in Lakewood Ranch. Since then, they've continued to explore distant lands and enjoy life to the fullest.

In 2018, the author wrote his first book, *'The Following Storm'* which readers loved, that first book turned into a series. The four thrilling books follow the life, loves and dangers of Karl Vita throughout World War II into the early 1950's. *'The Last Train Home'* wraps up Karl Vita's story.

Since then, his books continue to receive five-star reviews.

To review additional titles and updates please visit the authors website:

www.petermoscovita.net

Note: *'The Ultimate Sacrifice'* from the same period but not associated with The Following Storm series is available through various outlets like Amazon and Barnes & Noble and other online retailers. *'The Unexpected Encounter'* takes place in the 1960s during the cold war between America and Russia. This gripping story of espionage, romance and commitment will keep you guessing with its never-ending twist through numerous continents. Another book available during the first quarter of 2025 takes on a completely different story.

'My Journey To You' centers on two major characters, a high powered American advertising executive and a German superstar. Both very successful in their chosen careers but in their private lives they both lack that relationship they both crave to find. This story starts off with an online relationship you will embrace but don't get comfortable with. It will take you by surprise as you read on.

Am I considering another series? Stay tuned to find out!